Critical Praise for the Original *Los Angeles Noir*

- Winner of an Edgar Award (for "The Golden Gopher"   Straight)
- A *Los Angeles Times* Best Seller
- Winner of a Southern California Booksellers A   d
- A Book Sense Notable Pick
- Two stories selected for *Best American M*   and
  Drive" by Michael Connelly and "   Comes
  In" by Robert Ferrigno)

"These seventeen very different storie   many places L.A. has become . . . Janet Fitch, as usual, o   ary level of intensity. Her story, 'The Method,' opens with a str   ppy one-liners that out-Chandler Chandler . . . I wanted to take my eyes off the page and couldn't."
—*Los Angeles Times*

"Editor Denise Hamilton does a terrific job assembling seventeen pieces of short fiction into a darkly entertaining mosaic of the contemporary City of Angels. Echoes of Chandler's prose and Cain's plots are everywhere in these pages, but Hamilton apparently encouraged her contributors to avoid direct allusion or homage, which is smart and refreshing . . . The writers' evocative glimpses into distinct sections of the sprawling megalopolis are entertaining and insightful, unexpectedly playing off each other and weaving themselves into a satisfying tapestry."
—*San Francisco Chronicle*

"New short stories from some of the area's best writers, including Susan Straight, Michael Connelly, Gary Phillips, and Denise Hamilton, the book's editor. Evil was never so delicious. The book crisscrosses the city, with stops in Koreatown, Leimert Park, and Los Feliz."
—*Los Angeles Magazine*

"A collection of short stories set in post-Chandler Los Angeles, by some of the city's finest writers. Millennial L.A. is just as noir as the '40s L.A. that birthed the genre, but far more diverse."
—NPR's *Day to Day* Holiday Books List

"A worthy tribute to the genre. Seventeen stories by some of the best of L.A.'s current literary generation explore the dark side of sunny Southern California . . . The Los Angeles of Raymond Chandler and Dorothy Hughes lives on . . . The marvelous descriptions of the diverse settings from Rodeo Drive to Skid Row to Commerce and Belmont Shore speak volumes of the cultural and economic diversity that is the City of Angels.

This third-generation Angelino loved it; highly recommended for all crime fiction collections." —*Library Journal* (starred review)

"The movie industry, both latter-day and the present, offers a rich background for tight tales of trapped men and women whose passions or desperate circumstances lead them to violent ends, such as the book's stand-out, Janet Fitch's 'The Method.' Another highpoint is the collection's concluding story, Diana Wagman's 'What You See,' a depressing but compelling tale of a tragic obsession." —*Publishers Weekly*

"A collection of devilishly dark tales . . . Readers will revel in this eclectic collection of murder, desperation, and obsession."
—*Mystery Scene Magazine*

"A top pick for any fan of crime fiction and for libraries both located in California and beyond." —*Midwest Book Review/California Bookwatch*

"Sheds even more light on the dark side of Los Angeles . . . The book not only offers an array of enticing stories but also serves as an intriguing travelogue of L.A.'s neighborhoods and side cities." —*Pasadena Weekly*

"In Denise Hamilton's Los Angeles, Russian mobsters mingle with Korean day-spa workers, cleaning ladies share the secrets of the rich and glamorous, and menace lurks around every palm tree–studded corner."
—*San Luis Obispo Tribune*

"*Los Angeles Noir* is chock-full of terrific reads."
—*South Florida Sun Sentinel*

"Features terrific stories of liars, lovers, police, and thieves by a wildly diverse rogue's gallery . . . Picking over the bones of Phillip Marlowe would have been easy, but editor Denise Hamilton has managed to infuse the collection with a bracing mix of tales that match the dizzying diversity that has always been one of the city's hallmarks . . ." —*Bookslut*

"A top pick for SoCal book lovers this holiday season."
—*Westways Magazine*

"These stories are cinematic, violent little gems of contemporary crime fiction that are a must-read for any true fan of noir." —*Elegant Variation*

LOS ANGELES NOIR 2
THE CLASSICS

EDITED BY DENISE HAMILTON

Published by Akashic Books
©2010 Akashic Books
Series concept by Tim McLoughlin and Johnny Temple
Los Angeles map by Sohrab Habibion

ISBN-13: 978-1-936070-02-2
Library of Congress Control Number: 2009911099
All rights reserved | Second printing

Akashic Books | PO Box 1456 | New York, NY 10009
info@akashicbooks.com | www.akashicbooks.com

Grateful acknowledgment is made for permission to reprint the stories in this anthology. "Murder in Blue" by Paul Cain was originally published in *Black Mask* (June 1933) as "Murder Done in Blue," © 1933 by Pro-Distributors Publishing Co., Inc., renewed © 1961 by Popular Publications, Inc., assigned to Keith Alan Deutsch, publisher and proprietor of *Black Mask Magazine*; "I Feel Bad Killing You" by Leigh Brackett was originally published in *New Detective Magazine* (November 1944), © 1944 by Leigh Brackett, reprinted by permission of the Huntington National Bank for the Estate of Leigh Brackett, c/o Spectrum Literary Agency; "Dead Man" by James M. Cain was originally published in the *American Mercury* (March 1936), © 1936 by the American Mercury, Inc., renewed © 1963 by James M. Cain, reprinted by permission of Harold Ober Associates, Inc.; "The Night's for Cryin'" by Chester Himes was originally published in *Esquire* (January 1937), licensed here from *The Collected Stories of Chester Himes*, © 1990 by Lesley Himes, reprinted by permission of Da Capo/Thunder's Mouth, a member of Perseus Book Group; "I'll Be Waiting" by Raymond Chandler was originally published in the *Saturday Evening Post* (14 October 1939), licensed here from *The Simple Art of Murder* by Raymond Chandler, © 1934, 1935, 1936, 1938, 1939, 1944, 1950 by Raymond Chandler, © 1939 by the Curtis Publishing Company, used by permission of Vintage Books, a division of Random House, Inc.; "Find the Woman" by Ross Macdonald was originally published in *Ellery Queen Mystery Magazine* (June 1946), © 1946 by Kenneth Millar, renewed © 1973 by the Margaret Millar Charitable Remainder Unitrust u/a 12 April 1982, reprinted by permission of Harold Ober Associates, Inc.; "The Chirashi Covenant" by Naomi Hirahara was originally published in *A Hell of a Woman: An Anthology of Female Noir* (Houston: Busted Flush Press, 2007), © 2007 by Naomi Hirahara; "High Darktown" by James Ellroy was originally published in *The New Black Mask No. 5* (New York: Harcourt Brace Jovanovich, 1986), © 1986 by James Ellroy; "The People Across the Canyon" by Margaret Millar was originally published in *Ellery Queen Mystery Magazine* (October 1962), © 1962 by Margaret Millar, renewed © 1990 by the Margaret Millar Charitable Remainder Unitrust u/a 12 April 1982, reprinted by permission of Harold Ober Associates, Inc.; "Surf" by Joseph Hansen was originally published in *Playguy* (January 1976), © 1976 by Joseph Hansen, reprinted by permission of Johnson & Alcock Literary Agency; "The Kerman Kill" by William Campbell Gault was originally published in *Murder in Los Angeles* (New York: William Morrow & Co., 1987), © 1987 by William Campbell Gault, reprinted by permission of Shelley Gault; "Crimson Shadow" by Walter Mosley was originally published in *Edward Hopper and the American Imagination* (New York: Whitney Museum of American Art, 1995), © 1995 by Walter Mosley, reprinted by permission of the Watkins/Loomis Agency, Inc.; "Rika" (excerpted from the novel *Understand This*) by Jervey Tervalon was originally published by William Morrow & Co., in 1994, © 1994 by Jervey Tervalon; "Lucía" (excerpted from the novel *Locas*) by Yxta Maya Murray was originally published by Grove Press, in 1997, © 1997 by Yxta Maya Murray, reprinted by permission of Grove/Atlantic, Inc.; "Tall Tales from the Mekong Delta" by Kate Braverman was originally published in *Squandering the Blue: Stories* (New York: Fawcett, 1990), © 1990 by Kate Braverman.

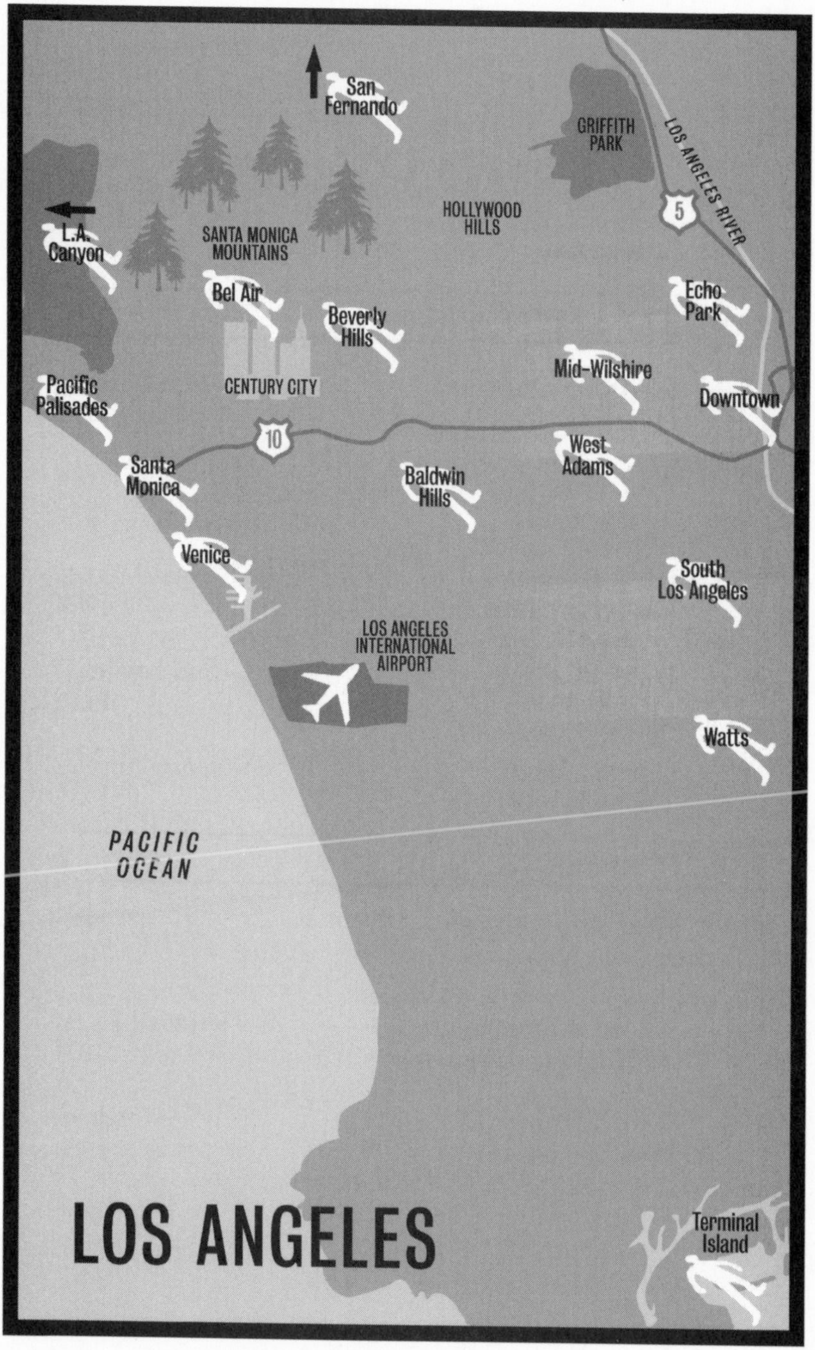

San Fernando
GRIFFITH PARK
LOS ANGELES RIVER
5
HOLLYWOOD HILLS
SANTA MONICA MOUNTAINS
L.A. Canyon
Bel Air
Beverly Hills
Echo Park
Mid-Wilshire
CENTURY CITY
Pacific Palisades
Downtown
10
West Adams
Santa Monica
Baldwin Hills
Venice
South Los Angeles
LOS ANGELES INTERNATIONAL AIRPORT
Watts
PACIFIC OCEAN
LOS ANGELES
Terminal Island

TABLE OF CONTENTS

PART III: KILLER VIEWS

PART IV: MODERN CLASSICS

INTRODUCTION
TOILING IN THE DREAM FACTORY

L os Angeles is a young city. As recently as the 1860s, it was still a dusty Spanish pueblo where the Zanjero who regulated the water flow from the L.A. River earned more than the mayor.

Unlike the eastern seaboard, whose world of arts and letters predates the American Revolution, Los Angeles literature bloomed late. But our scant history and tradition freed us up to create new myths. We made it up as we went along.

Visiting writers were both intrigued and appalled. They praised the city's golden light and stunning landscapes while damning its vulgarity, hedonism, and the surreal spectacle of Hollywood.

But love it or hate it, they came to toil in the Dream Factory.

Los Angeles was the most alluring femme fatale imaginable, dangling glittering wealth and reinvention. In return, all she wanted was a little wordsmithing. How difficult could it be?

And so they came—Cornell Woolrich, William Faulkner, F. Scott Fitzgerald, Norman Mailer, James M. Cain, Chester Himes, Horace McCoy, Paul Cain, Dorothy Parker, and Ernest Hemingway. They were miserable, of course, punching studio clocks and having their work rewritten by less talented writers.

Luckily for us, many used their sunny new digs as settings for fiction. Some of what they wrote, including Fitzgerald's nuanced Hollywood stories, aren't noir enough for this anthology. Others are too long, such as McCoy's dark masterpiece "They Shoot Horses, Don't They?" set amidst a 1930s dance marathon on the Santa Monica pier.

But many of the genre's masters—including Raymond Chandler—*have* sidled into this anthology. Perhaps the hardest-boiled of them all is Paul Cain, whose prose explodes like a bullet from a bootlegger's gun. When not scripting for Hollywood under the name Peter Ruric, Cain wrote stories for trailblazing noir showcase *Black Mask* magazine and a novel, *Fast One*, before fading into alcoholic obscurity and dying forgotten in a shabby Hollywood apartment in 1966.

It's funny how two noir writers share the ultimate biblical bad boy name—Cain. The better-known is James M. Cain, whose novels *The Postman Always Rings Twice* and *Double Indemnity* ooze with sex, murder, and betrayal. The movie adaptations are pretty twisted too—we all know Fred MacMurray's a goner as soon as Barbara Stanwyck opens that door. In this collection, James M. Cain's story about a Depression-era hobo riding the rails into town offers an even bleaker take on crime and punishment.

Then there's "The Night's for Cryin'" by Chester Himes. Set near historically African American Central Avenue, this story packs more love, brutality, and revenge into five short pages than most 500-page novels.

Throughout this anthology, characters swill bootleg liquor, take bribes, get hooked on morphine, work as grifters, taxi-dancers, and hired guns, hang out at speakeasies and soda fountains, and betray their lovers. Nobody dies naturally.

Most literary lions did their time in Hollywood, then went home. But for Raymond Chandler, whose name is indelibly linked to the city's dark glamour, L.A. was home. "I'll Be Waiting" shows the master stylist sketching out the white knight who would find his apotheosis in world-weary Philip Marlowe. The story's crisp dialogue and lyric descriptions of elegant hotels, mousy clerks, languid ladies, unsavory gangsters, and a chivalrous house dick prefigure Chandler's classic novels.

"Find the Woman," a story with a strong postwar flavor, provides an early look at another godfather of crime fiction—Ross Macdonald. Some critics argue that Macdonald, who stole his plots from Greek myth, was the best of the bunch. "Find the Woman," a twisty tale of family secrets and betrayal, introduces the tough yet compassionate private eye who'd earn acclaim in Macdonald's later novels as Lew Archer.

I've also included a tale of dark psychological suspense set in an unnamed L.A. canyon by Macdonald's equally talented but lamentably lesser known wife Margaret Millar.

The truth is that early noir was a man's world where sexism prevailed.

All the more impressive, then, that the hard-boiled writing of Leigh Brackett stands up to anything her male contemporaries ever dreamed up. Brackett's 1949 story "I Feel Bad Killing You" certainly wins the "best title" award. It also includes the most diabolical scene with a cigarette lighter ever written that contains no actual violence. Director Howard Hawks was such a fan that he ordered his secretary to get "this guy Brackett" on board to help William Faulkner write the screenplay to *The Big Sleep.*" Which Brackett did! She also wrote science fiction and ended her amazing fifty-year career cowriting *The Empire Strikes Back* for George Lucas.

I was especially interested in stories that reflected the city's historic diversity. Walter Mosley has written terrific novels about Easy Rawlins, a black, midcentury PI, but the story in this collection features another memorable Mosley character—ex-con and reformed murderer Socrates Fortlow, who lives in a two-room apartment off an alley in Watts.

Naomi Hirahara takes us back to 1949 Terminal Island with "The Chirashi Covenant," the tale of an adulterous young Japanese American woman who married her husband in a World War II internment camp. As the daughter of an L.A. Harbor fisherman, Helen Miura knows how to gut fish, a skill that finds grisly use before this story ends.

In "The Kerman Kill," William Campbell Gault introduces an Armenian-American PI with a large, boisterous family who munches lahmajoon and hangs out in his Uncle Vartan's carpet store. And in 1970, back when homosexuality was still a relatively taboo subject, Joseph Hansen published his first novel about a gay insurance investigator named Dave Brandstetter, who investigates a murder in the story "Surf."

Moving east, the ever-reliable James Ellroy pens a furious tale of murder and deception in the West Adams district of Los Angeles just after World War II. Ellroy did impeccable historic research, and indeed this entire collection bristles with the evocative slang of various eras: ixnay, coppers, chumps, saps, shivs, cinch, dames, toot sweet, swells, rumdums, rye, and girls who "gargle" champagne.

Inevitably, some of the earlier stories reflect the racism, homophobia, and religious prejudices of their times. But it's important to remember that crime fiction was the first to liberate language from the parlors of "proper" society. As Chandler told his publisher in explaining his use of barroom vernacular: "I write in a sort of broken-down patois which is something like the way a Swiss waiter talks."

Swiss waiters have gone the way of metal Venetian blinds, so what exactly makes a story "classic"? For starters, it has to have a "historic" feel. That's why I included Kate Braverman's "Tall Tales from the Mekong Delta," a hallucinogenic, paranoid tale filled with echoes of the Vietnam War.

Jervey Tervalon's story "Rika" from his novel *Understand This* is a brilliant depiction of a crack-addled city just before the L.A. riots of 1992. Yxta Maya Murray's story "Lucía," excerpted from her powerful and moving novel *Locas*, recounts a girl gang leader plotting revenge for the shooting of one of her "locas." Set in the impoverished, as yet ungentrified barrio of 1980s Echo Park, it's a gritty postcard from the recent past, just before the boho artists and yuppies took over.

With some of these stories, the challenge lay in tracking down the real-life identity of fictional neighborhoods. Is Brackett's "Surfside" supposed to be Santa Monica? What canyon was Margaret Millar thinking of when she wrote her short story? Is Hansen's fictional beach community "Surf" a stand-in for Venice?

The sleuthing through old tales, dusty copies of *Ellery Queen's Mystery Magazine*, and long defunct publications like *Black Mask* provided its own joys. I hope the stories in this volume convey the same thrilling sense of discovery and nostalgia to you, the reader.

Denise Hamilton
Los Angeles, CA
January 2010

PART I

KISS KISS BANG BANG

PART I

I'LL BE WAITING

BY RAYMOND CHANDLER

Mid-Wilshire

(Originally published in 1939)

At one o'clock in the morning, Carl, the night porter, turned down the last of three table lamps in the main lobby of the Windermere Hotel. The blue carpet darkened a shade or two and the walls drew back into remoteness. The chairs filled with shadowy loungers. In the corners were memories like cobwebs.

Tony Reseck yawned. He put his head on one side and listened to the frail, twittery music from the radio room beyond a dim arch at the far side of the lobby. He frowned. That should be his radio room after one A.M. Nobody should be in it. That red-haired girl was spoiling his nights.

The frown passed and a miniature of a smile quirked at the corners of his lips. He sat relaxed, a short, pale, paunchy, middle-aged man with long, delicate fingers clasped on the elk's tooth on his watch chain; the long delicate fingers of a sleight-of-hand artist, fingers with shiny, molded nails and tapering first joints, fingers a little spatulate at the ends. Handsome fingers. Tony Reseck rubbed them gently together and there was peace in his quiet, sea-gray eyes.

The frown came back on his face. The music annoyed him. He got up with a curious litheness, all in one piece, without moving his clasped hands from the watch chain. At one moment he was leaning back relaxed, and the next he was standing balanced on his feet, perfectly still, so that the movement of rising seemed to be a thing imperfectly perceived, an error of vision.

He walked with small, polished shoes delicately across the blue carpet and under the arch. The music was louder. It contained the hot, acid blare, the frenetic, jittering runs of a jam session. It was too loud. The red-haired girl sat there and stared silently at the fretted part of the big radio cabinet as though she could see the band with its fixed professional grin and the sweat running down its back. She was curled up with her feet under her on a davenport which seemed to contain most of the cushions in the room. She was tucked among them carefully, like a corsage in the florist's tissue paper.

She didn't turn her head. She leaned there, one hand in a small fist on her peach-colored knee. She was wearing lounging pajamas of heavy ribbed silk embroidered with black lotus buds.

"You like Goodman, Miss Cressy?" Tony Reseck asked.

The girl moved her eyes slowly. The light in there was dim, but the violet of her eyes almost hurt. They were large, deep eyes without a trace of thought in them. Her face was classical and without expression.

She said nothing.

Tony smiled and moved his fingers at his sides, one by one, feeling them move. "You like Goodman, Miss Cressy?" he repeated gently.

"Not to cry over," the girl said tonelessly.

Tony rocked back on his heels and looked at her eyes. Large, deep, empty eyes. Or were they? He reached down and muted the radio.

"Don't get me wrong," the girl said. "Goodman makes money, and a lad that makes legitimate money these days is a lad you have to respect. But this jitterbug music gives me the backdrop of a beer flat. I like something with roses in it."

"Maybe you like Mozart," Tony said.

"Go on, kid me," the girl said.

"I wasn't kidding you, Miss Cressy. I think Mozart was the greatest man that ever lived—and Toscanini is his prophet."

"I thought you were the house dick." She put her head back on a pillow and stared at him through her lashes. "Make me some of that Mozart," she added.

"It's too late," Tony sighed. "You can't get it now."

She gave him another long lucid glance. "Got the eye on me, haven't you, flatfoot?" She laughed a little, almost under her breath. "What did I do wrong?"

Tony smiled his toy smile. "Nothing, Miss Cressy. Nothing at all. But you need some fresh air. You've been five days in this hotel and you haven't been outdoors. And you have a tower room."

She laughed again. "Make me a story about it. I'm bored."

"There was a girl here once had your suite. She stayed in the hotel a whole week, like you. Without going out at all, I mean. She didn't speak to anybody hardly. What do you think she did then?"

The girl eyed him gravely. "She jumped her bill."

He put his long delicate hand out and turned it slowly, fluttering the fingers, with an effect almost like a lazy wave breaking. "Unh-uh. She sent down for her bill and paid it. Then she told the hop to be back in half an hour for her suitcases. Then she went out on her balcony."

The girl leaned forward a little, her eyes still grave, one hand capping her peach-colored knee. "What did you say your name was?"

"Tony Reseck."

"Sounds like a hunky."

"Yeah," Tony said. "Polish."

"Go on, Tony."

"All the tower suites have private balconies, Miss Cressy. The walls of them are too low, for fourteen stories above the street. It was a dark night, that night, high clouds." He dropped his hand with a final gesture, a farewell gesture. "Nobody saw her jump. But when she hit, it was like a big gun going off."

"You're making it up, Tony." Her voice was a clean dry whisper of sound.

He smiled his toy smile. His quiet sea-gray eyes seemed almost to be smoothing the long waves of her hair. "Eve Cressy," he said musingly. "A name waiting for lights to be in."

"Waiting for a tall dark guy that's no good, Tony. You wouldn't care why. I was married to him once. I might be married to him again. You can make a lot of mistakes in just one lifetime." The hand on her knee opened slowly until the fingers were strained back as far as they would go. Then they closed quickly and tightly, and even in that dim light the knuckles shone like little polished bones. "I played him a low trick once. I put him in a bad place—without meaning to. You wouldn't care about that either. It's just that I owe him something."

He leaned over softly and turned the knob on the radio. A waltz formed itself dimly on the warm air. A tinsel waltz, but a waltz. He turned the volume up. The music gushed from the loudspeaker in a swirl of shadowed melody. Since Vienna died, all waltzes are shadowed.

The girl put her head on one side and hummed three or four bars and stopped with a sudden tightening of her mouth.

"Eve Cressy," she said. "It was in lights once. At a bum nightclub. A dive. They raided it and the lights went out."

He smiled at her almost mockingly. "It was no dive while you were there, Miss Cressy. . . . That's the waltz the orchestra always played when the old porter walked up and down in front of the hotel entrance, all swelled up with his medals on his chest. *The Last Laugh.* Emil Jannings. You wouldn't remember that one, Miss Cressy."

"*Spring, Beautiful Spring,*" she said. "No, I never saw it."

He walked three steps away from her and turned. "I have to go upstairs and palm doorknobs. I hope I didn't bother you. You ought to go to bed now. It's pretty late."

The tinsel waltz stopped and a voice began to talk. The girl spoke through the voice, "You really thought something like that—about the balcony?"

He nodded. "I might have," he said softly. "I don't any more."

"No chance, Tony." Her smile was a dim lost leaf. "Come and talk to me some more. Redheads don't jump, Tony. They hang on—and wither."

He looked at her gravely for a moment and then moved away over the carpet. The porter was standing in the archway that led to the main lobby. Tony hadn't looked that way yet, but he knew somebody was there. He always knew if anybody was close to him. He could hear the grass grow, like the donkey in *The Blue Bird*.

The porter jerked his chin at him urgently. His broad face above the uniform collar looked sweaty and excited. Tony stepped up close to him and they went together through the arch and out to the middle of the dim lobby.

"Trouble?" Tony asked wearily.

"There's a guy outside to see you, Tony. He won't come in. I'm doing a wipe-off on the plate glass of the doors and he comes up beside me, a tall guy. 'Get Tony,' he says, out of the side of his mouth."

Tony said: "Uh-huh," and looked at the porter's pale blue eyes. "Who was it?"

"Al, he said to say he was."

Tony's face became as expressionless as dough. "Okey." He started to move off.

The porter caught his sleeve. "Listen, Tony. You got any enemies?"

Tony laughed politely, his face still like dough.

"Listen, Tony." The porter held his sleeve tightly. "There's a big black car down the block, the other way from the hacks. There's a guy standing beside it with his foot on the running board. This guy that spoke to me, he wears a dark-colored, wrap-around overcoat with a high collar turned up against his ears. His hat's way low. You can't hardly see his face. He says, 'Get Tony,' out of the side of his mouth. You ain't got any enemies, have you, Tony?"

"Only the finance company," Tony said. "Beat it."

He walked slowly and a little stiffly across the blue carpet, up the three shallow steps to the entrance lobby with the three elevators on one side and the desk on the other. Only one elevator was working. Beside the open doors, his arms folded, the night operator stood silent in a neat blue uniform with silver facings. A lean, dark Mexican named Gomez. A new boy, breaking in on the night shift.

The other side was the desk, rose marble, with the night clerk leaning on it delicately. A small neat man with a wispy reddish mustache and cheeks so rosy they looked rouged. He stared at Tony and poked a nail at his mustache.

Tony pointed a stiff index finger at him, folded the other three fingers tight to his palm, and flicked his thumb up and down on the stiff finger. The clerk touched the other side of his mustache and looked bored.

Tony went on past the closed and darkened newsstand and the side entrance to the drugstore, out to the brassbound plate-glass doors. He stopped just inside them and took a deep, hard breath. He squared his shoulders, pushed the doors open and stepped out into the cold, damp, night air.

The street was dark, silent. The rumble of traffic on Wilshire, two blocks away, had no body, no meaning. To the left were two taxis. Their drivers leaned against a fender, side by side, smoking. Tony walked the other way. The big dark car was a third of a block from the hotel entrance. Its lights were dimmed and it was only when he was almost up to it that he heard the gentle sound of its engine turning over.

A tall figure detached itself from the body of the car and strolled toward him, both hands in the pockets of the dark overcoat with the high collar. From the man's mouth a cigarette tip glowed faintly, a rusty pearl.

They stopped two feet from each other.

The tall man said, "Hi, Tony. Long time no see."

"Hello, Al. How's it going?"

"Can't complain." The tall man started to take his right hand out of his overcoat pocket, then stopped and laughed quietly. "I forgot. Guess you don't want to shake hands."

"That don't mean anything," Tony said. "Shaking hands. Monkeys can shake hands. What's on your mind, Al?"

"Still the funny little fat guy, eh, Tony?"

"I guess." Tony winked his eyes tight. His throat felt tight.

"You like your job back there?"

"It's a job."

Al laughed his quiet laugh again. "You take it slow, Tony. I'll take it fast. So it's a job and you want to hold it. Okey. There's a girl named Eve Cressy flopping in your quiet hotel. Get her out. Fast and right now."

"What's the trouble?"

The tall man looked up and down the street. A man behind in the car coughed lightly. "She's hooked with a wrong number. Nothing against her personal, but she'll lead trouble to you. Get her out, Tony. You got maybe an hour."

"Sure," Tony said aimlessly, without meaning.

Al took his hand out of his pocket and stretched it against Tony's chest. He gave him a light lazy push. "I wouldn't be telling you just for the hell of it, little fat brother. Get her out of there."

"Okey," Tony said, without any tone in his voice.

The tall man took back his hand and reached for the car door. He opened it and started to slip in like a lean black shadow.

Then he stopped and said something to the men in the car and got out again. He came back to where Tony stood silent, his pale eyes catching a little dim light from the street.

"Listen, Tony. You always kept your nose clean. You're a good brother, Tony."

Tony didn't speak.

Al leaned toward him, a long urgent shadow, the high collar almost touching his ears. "It's trouble business, Tony. The boys won't like it, but I'm telling you just the same. This Cressy was married to a lad named Johnny Ralls. Ralls is out of Quentin two, three days, or a week. He did a three-spot for manslaughter. The girl put him there. He ran down an old man one night when he was drunk, and she was with him. He wouldn't stop. She told him to go in and tell it, or else. He didn't go in. So the Johns come for him."

Tony said, "That's too bad."

"It's kosher, kid. It's my business to know. This Ralls flapped his mouth in stir about how the girl would be waiting for him when he got out, all set to forgive and forget, and he was going straight to her."

Tony said, "What's he to you?" His voice had a dry, stiff crackle, like thick paper.

Al laughed. "The trouble boys want to see him. He ran a table at a spot on the Strip and figured out a scheme. He and another guy took the house for fifty grand. The other lad coughed up, but we still need Johnny's twenty-five. The trouble boys don't get paid to forget."

Tony looked up and down the dark street. One of the taxi drivers flicked a cigarette stub in a long arc over the top of one of the cabs. Tony watched it fall and spark on the pavement. He listened to the quiet sound of the big car's motor.

"I don't want any part of it," he said. "I'll get her out."

Al backed away from him, nodding. "Wise kid. How's Mom these days?"

"Okey," Tony said.

"Tell her I was asking for her."

"Asking for her isn't anything," Tony said.

Al turned quickly and got into the car. The car curved lazily in the middle of the block and drifted back toward the corner. Its lights went up and sprayed on a wall. It turned a corner and was gone. The lingering smell of its exhaust drifted past Tony's nose. He turned and walked back to the hotel, and into it. He went along to the radio room.

The radio still muttered, but the girl was gone from the davenport in front of it. The pressed cushions were hollowed out by her body. Tony reached down and touched them. He thought they were still warm. He turned the radio off and stood there, turning a thumb slowly in front of his body, his hand flat against his stomach. Then he went back through the lobby toward the elevator bank and stood beside a majolica jar of white sand. The clerk fussed behind a pebbled-glass screen at one end of the desk. The air was dead.

The elevator bank was dark. Tony looked at the indicator of the middle car and saw that it was at 14.

"Gone to bed," he said under his breath.

The door of the porter's room beside the elevators opened and the little Mexican night operator came out in street clothes. He looked at Tony with a quiet sidewise look out of eyes the color of dried-out chestnuts.

"Good night, boss."

"Yeah," Tony said absently.

He took a thin dappled cigar out of his vest pocket and smelled it. He examined it slowly, turning it around in his neat fingers. There was a small tear along the side. He frowned at that and put the cigar away.

There was a distant sound and the hand on the indicator began to steal around the bronze dial. Light glittered up in the shaft and the straight line of the car floor dissolved the darkness below. The car stopped and the doors opened, and Carl came out of it.

His eyes caught Tony's with a kind of jump and he walked over to him, his head on one side, a thin shine along his pink upper lip.

"Listen, Tony."

Tony took his arm in a hard swift hand and turned him. He pushed him quickly, yet somehow casually, down the steps to the dim main lobby and steered him into a corner. He let go of the arm. His throat tightened again, for no reason he could think of.

"Well?" he said darkly. "Listen to what?"

The porter reached into a pocket and hauled out a dollar bill. "He gimme this," he said loosely. His glittering eyes looked past Tony's shoulder at nothing. They winked rapidly. "Ice and ginger ale."

"Don't stall," Tony growled.

"Guy in 14B," the porter said.

"Lemme smell your breath."

The porter leaned toward him obediently.

"Liquor," Tony said harshly.

"He gimme a drink."

Tony looked down at the dollar bill. "Nobody's in 14B. Not on my list," he said.

"Yeah. There is." The porter licked his lips and his eyes opened and shut several times. "Tall dark guy."

"All right," Tony said crossly. "All right. There's a tall dark guy in 14B and he gave you a buck and a drink. Then what?"

"Gat under his arm," Carl said, and blinked.

Tony smiled, but his eyes had taken on the lifeless glitter of thick ice. "You take Miss Cressy up to her room?"

Carl shook his head. "Gomez. I saw her go up."

"Get away from me," Tony said between his teeth. "And don't accept any more drinks from the guests."

He didn't move until Carl had gone back into his cubbyhole by the elevators and shut the door. Then he moved silently up the three steps and stood in front of the desk, looking at the veined rose marble, the onyx pen set, the fresh registration card in its leather frame. He lifted a hand and smacked it down hard on the marble. The clerk popped out from behind the glass screen like a chipmunk coming out of its hole.

Tony took a flimsy out of his breast pocket and spread it on the desk. "No 14B on this," he said in a bitter voice.

The clerk wisped politely at his mustache. "So sorry. You must have been out to supper when he checked in."

"Who?"

"Registered as James Watterson, San Diego." The clerk yawned.

"Ask for anybody?"

The clerk stopped in the middle of the yawn and looked at the top of Tony's head. "Why yes. He asked for a swing band. Why?"

"Smart, fast and funny," Tony said. "If you like 'em that way." He wrote on his flimsy and stuffed it back into his pocket. "I'm going upstairs and palm doorknobs. There's four tower rooms you ain't rented yet. Get up on your toes, son. You're slipping."

"I made out," the clerk drawled, and completed his yawn. "Hurry back, pop. I don't know how I'll get through the time."

"You could shave that pink fuzz off your lip," Tony said, and went across to the elevators.

He opened up a dark one and lit the dome light and shot the car up to 14. He darkened it again, stepped out and closed the doors. This lobby was smaller than any other, except the one immediately below it. It had a single blue-paneled door in each of the walls other than the elevator wall. On each door was a gold number and letter with a gold wreath around it. Tony walked over to 14A and put his ear to the panel. He heard nothing. Eve Cressy might be in bed asleep, or in the bathroom, or out on the balcony. Or she might be sitting there in the room, a few feet from the door, looking at the wall. Well, he wouldn't expect to be able to hear her sit and look at the wall. He went over to 14B and put his ear to that panel. This was different. There was a sound in there. A man coughed. It sounded somehow like a solitary cough. There were no voices. Tony pressed the small nacre button beside the door.

Steps came without hurry. A thickened voice spoke through the panel. Tony made no answer, no sound. The thickened voice repeated the question. Lightly, maliciously, Tony pressed the bell again.

Mr. James Watterson, of San Diego, should now open the door and give forth noise. He didn't. A silence fell beyond that door that was like the silence of a glacier. Once more Tony put his ear to the wood. Silence utterly.

He got out a master key on a chain and pushed it delicately into the lock of the door. He turned it, pushed the door inward three inches and withdrew the key. Then he waited.

"All right," the voice said harshly. "Come in and get it."

Tony pushed the door wide and stood there, framed against the light from the lobby. The man was tall, black-haired, angular and white-faced. He held a gun. He held it as though he knew about guns.

"Step right in," he drawled.

Tony went in through the door and pushed it shut with his shoulder. He kept his hands a little out from his sides, the clever fingers curled and slack. He smiled his quiet little smile.

"Mr. Watterson?"

"And after that what?"

"I'm the house detective here."

"It slays me."

The tall, white-faced, somehow handsome and somehow not handsome man backed slowly into the room. It was a large room with a low balcony around two sides of it. French doors opened out on the little private open-air balcony that each of the tower rooms had. There was a grate set for a log fire behind a paneled screen in front of a cheerful davenport. A tall misted glass stood on a hotel tray beside a deep, cozy chair. The man backed toward this and stood in front of it. The large, glistening gun drooped and pointed at the floor.

"It slays me," he said. "I'm in the dump an hour and the house copper gives me the bus. Okey, sweetheart, look in the closet and bathroom. But she just left."

"You didn't see her yet," Tony said.

The man's bleached face filled with unexpected lines. His thickened voice edged toward a snarl. "Yeah? Who didn't I see yet?"

"A girl named Eve Cressy."

The man swallowed. He put his gun down on the table beside the tray. He let himself down into the chair backwards, stiffly, like a man with a touch of lumbago. Then he leaned forward and put his hands on his kneecaps and smiled brightly between his teeth. "So she got here, huh? I didn't ask about her yet. I'm a careful guy. I didn't ask yet."

"She's been here five days," Tony said. "Waiting for you. She hasn't left the hotel a minute."

The man's mouth worked a little. His smile had a knowing tilt to it. "I got delayed a little up north," he said smoothly. "You know how it is. Visiting old friends. You seem to know a lot about my business, copper."

"That's right, Mr. Ralls."

The man lunged to his feet and his hand snapped at the gun. He stood leaning over, holding it on the table, staring. "Dames talk too much," he said with a muffled sound in his voice, as though he held something soft between his teeth and talked through it.

"Not dames, Mr. Ralls."

"Huh?" The gun slithered on the hard wood of the table. "Talk it up, copper. My mind reader just quit."

"Not dames. Guys. Guys with guns."

The glacier silence fell between them again. The man straightened his body slowly. His face was washed clean of expression, but his eyes were haunted. Tony leaned in front of him, a shortish plump man with a quiet, pale, friendly face and eyes as simple as forest water.

"They never run out of gas—those boys," Johnny Ralls said, and licked at his lip. "Early and late, they work. The old firm never sleeps."

"You know who they are?" Tony said softly.

"I could maybe give nine guesses. And twelve of them would be right."

"The trouble boys," Tony said, and smiled a brittle smile.

"Where is she?" Johnny Ralls asked harshly.

"Right next door to you."

The man walked to the wall and left his gun lying on the table. He stood in front of the wall, studying it. He reached up and gripped the grillwork of the balcony railing. When he dropped his hand and turned, his face had lost some of its lines. His eyes had a quieter glint. He moved back to Tony and stood over him.

"I've got a stake," he said. "Eve sent me some dough and I built it up with a touch I made up north. Case dough, what I mean. The trouble boys talk about twenty-five grand." He smiled crookedly. "Five C's I can count. I'd have a lot of fun making them believe that, I would."

"What did you do with it?" Tony asked indifferently.

"I never had it, copper. Leave that lay. I'm the only guy in the world that believes it. It was a little deal I got suckered on."

"I'll believe it," Tony said.

"They don't kill often. But they can be awful tough."

"Mugs," Tony said with a sudden bitter contempt. "Guys with guns. Just mugs."

Johnny Ralls reached for his glass and drained it empty. The ice cubes tinkled softly as he put it down. He picked his gun up, danced it on his palm, then tucked it, nose down, into an inner breast pocket. He stared at the carpet.

"How come you're telling me this, copper?"

"I thought maybe you'd give her a break."

"And if I wouldn't?"

"I kind of think you will," Tony said.

Johnny Ralls nodded quietly. "Can I get out of here?"

"You could take the service elevator to the garage. You could rent a car. I can give you a card to the garage-man."

"You're a funny little guy," Johnny Ralls said.

Tony took out a worn ostrich-skin billfold and scribbled on a printed card. Johnny Ralls read it, and stood holding it, tapping it against a thumbnail.

"I could take her with me," he said, his eyes narrow.

"You could take a ride in a basket too," Tony said. "She's been here five days, I told you. She's been spotted. A guy I know called me up and told me to get her out of here. Told me what it was all about. So I'm getting you out instead."

"They'll love that," Johnny Ralls said. "They'll send you violets."

"I'll weep about it on my day off."

Johnny Ralls turned his hand over and stared at the palm. "I could see her, anyway. Before I blow. Next door to here, you said?"

Tony turned on his heel and started for the door. He said over his shoulder, "Don't waste a lot of time, handsome. I might change my mind."

The man said, almost gently: "You might be spotting me right now, for all I know."

Tony didn't turn his head. "That's a chance you have to take."

He went on to the door and passed out of the room. He shut it carefully, silently, looked once at the door of 14A and got into his dark elevator. He rode it down to the linen-room floor and got out to remove the basket that held the service elevator open at that floor. The door slid quietly shut. He held it so that it made no noise. Down the corridor, light came from the open door of the housekeeper's office. Tony got back into his elevator and went on down to the lobby.

The little clerk was out of sight behind his pebbled-glass screen, auditing accounts. Tony went through the main lobby and turned into the radio room. The radio was on again, soft. She was there, curled on the davenport again. The speaker hummed to her, a vague sound so low that what it said was as wordless as the murmur of trees. She turned her head slowly and smiled at him.

"Finished palming doorknobs? I couldn't sleep worth a nickel. So I came down again. Okey?"

He smiled and nodded. He sat down in a green chair and patted the plump brocade arms of it. "Sure, Miss Cressy."

"Waiting is the hardest kind of work, isn't it? I wish you'd talk to that radio. It sounds like a pretzel being bent."

Tony fiddled with it, got nothing he liked, set it back where it had been.

"Beer-parlor drunks are all the customers now."

She smiled at him again.

"I don't bother you being here, Miss Cressy?"

"I like it. You're a sweet little guy, Tony."

He looked stiffly at the floor and a ripple touched his spine. He waited for it to go away. It went slowly. Then he sat back, relaxed again, his neat fingers clasped on his elk's tooth. He listened. Not to the radio—to far-off, uncertain things, menacing things. And perhaps to just the safe whir of wheels going away into a strange night.

"Nobody's all bad," he said out loud.

The girl looked at him lazily. "I've met two or three I was wrong on, then."

He nodded. "Yeah," he admitted judiciously. "I guess there's some that are."

The girl yawned and her deep violet eyes half closed. She nestled back into the cushions. "Sit there a while, Tony. Maybe I could nap."

"Sure. Not a thing for me to do. Don't know why they pay me."

She slept quickly and with complete stillness, like a child. Tony hardly breathed for ten minutes. He just watched her, his mouth a little open. There was a quiet fascination in his limpid eyes, as if he was looking at an altar.

Then he stood up with infinite care and padded away under the arch to the entrance lobby and the desk. He stood at the desk listening for a little while. He heard a pen rustling out of sight. He went around the corner to the row of house phones in little glass cubbyholes. He lifted one and asked the night operator for the garage.

It rang three or four times and then a boyish voice answered: "Windermere Hotel. Garage speaking."

"This is Tony Reseck. That guy Watterson I gave a card to. He leave?"

"Sure, Tony. Half an hour almost. Is it your charge?"

"Yeah," Tony said. "My party. Thanks. Be seein' you."

He hung up and scratched his neck. He went back to the desk and slapped a hand on it. The clerk wafted himself around the screen with his greeter's smile in place. It dropped when he saw Tony.

"Can't a guy catch up on his work?" he grumbled.

"What's the professional rate on 14B?"

The clerk stared morosely. "There's no professional rate in the tower."

"Make one. The fellow left already. Was there only an hour."

"Well, well," the clerk said airily. "So the personality didn't click tonight. We get a skip-out."

"Will five bucks satisfy you?"

"Friend of yours?"

"No. Just a drunk with delusions of grandeur and no dough."

"Guess we'll have to let it ride, Tony. How did he get out?"

"I took him down the service elevator. You was asleep. Will five bucks satisfy you?"

"Why?"

The worn ostrich-skin wallet came out and a weedy five slipped across the marble. "All I could shake him for," Tony said loosely.

The clerk took the five and looked puzzled. "You're the boss," he said, and shrugged. The phone shrilled on the desk and he reached for it. He listened and then pushed it toward Tony. "For you."

Tony took the phone and cuddled it close to his chest. He put his mouth close to the transmitter. The voice was strange to him. It had a metallic sound. Its syllables were meticulously anonymous.

"Tony? Tony Reseck?"

"Talking."

"A message from Al. Shoot?"

Tony looked at the clerk. "Be a pal," he said over the mouthpiece. The clerk flicked a narrow smile at him and went away. "Shoot," Tony said into the phone.

"We had a little business with a guy in your place. Picked him up scramming. Al had a hunch you'd run him out. Tailed him and took him to the curb. Not so good. Backfire."

Tony held the phone very tight and his temples chilled with the evaporation of moisture. "Go on," he said. "I guess there's more."

"A little. The guy stopped the big one. Cold. Al—Al said to tell you good-by."

Tony leaned hard against the desk. His mouth made a sound that was not speech.

"Get it?" The metallic voice sounded impatient, a little bored. "This guy had him a rod. He used it. Al won't be phoning anybody any more."

Tony lurched at the phone, and the base of it shook on the rose marble. His mouth was a hard dry knot.

The voice said: "That's as far as we go, bud. G'night." The phone clicked dryly, like a pebble hitting a wall.

Tony put the phone down in its cradle very carefully, so as not to make any sound. He looked at the clenched palm of his left hand. He took a handkerchief out and rubbed the palm softly and straightened the fingers out with his other hand. Then he wiped his forehead. The clerk came around the screen again and looked at him with glinting eyes.

"I'm off Friday. How about lending me that phone number?"

Tony nodded at the clerk and smiled a minute frail smile. He put his handkerchief away and patted the pocket he had put it in. He turned and walked away from the desk, across the entrance lobby, down the three shallow steps, along the shadowy reaches of the main lobby, and so in through the arch to the radio room once more. He walked softly, like a man moving in a room where somebody is very sick. He reached the chair he had sat in before and lowered himself into it inch by inch. The girl slept on, motionless, in that curled-up looseness achieved by some women and all cats. Her breath made no slightest sound against the vague murmur of the radio.

Tony Reseck leaned back in the chair and clasped his hands on his elk's tooth and quietly closed his eyes.

MURDER IN BLUE

BY PAUL CAIN

Downtown

(Originally published in 1933)

C oleman said: "Eight ball in the corner."

There was soft click of ball against ball and then sharper click as the black ball dropped into the pocket Coleman had called.

Coleman put his cue in the rack. He rolled down the sleeves of his vividly striped silk shirt and put on his coat and a pearl gray velour hat. He went to the pale fat man who slouched against a neighboring table and took two crisp hundred dollar notes from the fat man's outstretched hand, glanced at the slim, pimpled youth who had been his opponent, smiled thinly, said: "So long," went to the door, out into the street.

There was sudden roar from a black, curtained roadster on the other side of the street; the sudden ragged roar of four or five shots close together, a white pulsing finger of flame in the dusk, and Coleman sank to his knees. He swayed backwards once, fell forward onto his face hard; his gray hat rolled slowly across the sidewalk. The roadster was moving, had disappeared before Coleman was entirely still. It became very quiet in the street.

Mazie Decker curved her orange mouth to its best "Customer" smile. She took the little green ticket that the dark-haired boy held out to her and tore off one corner and dropped the rest into the slot. He took her tightly in his arms and as the violins melted to sound and the lights dimmed they swung out across the crowded floor.

Her head was tilted back, her bright mouth near the blue smoothness of his jaw.

She whispered: "Gee—I didn't think you was coming."

He twisted his head down a little, smiled at her.

She spoke again without looking at him: "I waited till one o'clock for you last night." She hesitated a moment then went on rapidly: "Gee—I act like I'd known you for years, an' it's only two days. What a sap I turned out to be!" She giggled mirthlessly.

He didn't answer.

The music swelled to brassy crescendo, stopped. They stood with a hundred other couples and applauded mechanically.

She said: "Gee—I love a waltz! Don't you?"

He nodded briefly and as the orchestra bellowed to a moaning foxtrot he took her again in his arms and they circled towards the far end of the floor.

"Let's get out of here, kid." He smiled a thin line against the whiteness of his skin, his large eyes half closed.

She said: "All right—only let's try to get out without the manager seeing me. I'm supposed to work till eleven."

They parted at one of the little turnstiles; he got his hat and coat from the check-room, went downstairs and got his car from a parking station across the street.

When she came down he had double-parked near the entrance. He honked his horn and held the door open for her as she trotted breathlessly out and climbed in beside him. Her eyes were very bright and she laughed a little hysterically.

"The manager saw me," she said. "But I said I was sick—an' it worked." She snuggled up close to him as he swung the car into Sixth Street. "Gee—what a swell car!"

He grunted affirmatively and they went out Sixth a block or so in silence.

As they turned north on Figueroa she said: "What've you got the side curtains on for? It's such a beautiful night."

He offered her a cigarette and lighted one for himself and leaned back comfortably in the seat.

He said: "I think it's going to rain."

It was very dark at the side of the road. A great pepper tree screened the roadster from whatever light there was in the sky.

Mazie Decker spoke softly: "Angelo. Angelo—that's a beautiful name. It sounds like angel."

The dark youth's face was hard in the narrow glow of the dashlight. He had taken off his hat and his shiny black hair looked like a metal skullcap. He stroked the heel of his hand back over one ear, over the oily blackness, and then he took his hand down and wriggled it under his coat. His other arm was around the girl.

He took his hand out of the darkness of his coat and there was brief flash of bright metal; the girl said: "My God!" slowly and put her hands up to her breast. . . .

He leaned in front of her and pressed the door open and as her body sank into itself he pushed her gently and her body slanted, toppled through the door, fell softly on the leaves beside the road. Her sharp breath and a far quavering "Ah!" were blotted out as he pressed the starter and the motor roared; he swung the door closed and put on his hat carefully, shifted gears and let the clutch in slowly.

As he came out of the darkness of the dirt road on to the highway he thrust one hand through a slit in the side-curtain, took it in and leaned forward over the wheel.

It was raining, a little.

R.F. Winfield stretched one long leg out and planted his foot on a nearby leather chair. The blonde woman got up and walked unsteadily to the phonograph. This latter looked like a grandfather clock, had cost well into four figures, would probably have collapsed at the appellation "phonograph"—but it was.

The blonde woman snapped the little tin brake; she lifted the record, stared empty-eyed at the other side.

She said: "'s Minnie th' Moocher. Wanna hear it?"

Mr. Winfield said: "Uh-huh." He tilted an ice and amber filled glass to his mouth, drained it. He stood up and gathered his very blue dressing-gown about his lean shanks. He lifted his head and walked through a short corridor to the bathroom, opened the door, entered.

Water splashed noisily in the big blue porcelain tub. He braced himself with one hand on the shower-tap, turned off the water, slipped out of the dressing-gown and into the tub.

The blonde woman's voice clanged like cold metal through the partially open door.

"Took 'er down to Chinatown; showed 'er how to kick the gong aroun'."

Mr. Winfield reached up into the pocket of the dressing-gown, fished out a cigarette, matches. He lighted the cigarette, leaned back in the water, sighed. His face was a long tan oblong of contentment. He flexed his jaw, then mechanically put up one hand and removed an upper plate, put the little semi-circle of shining teeth on the basin beside the tub, ran his tongue over thick, sharply etched lips, sighed again. The warm water was soft, caressing; he was very comfortable.

He heard the buzzer and he heard the blonde woman stagger along the corridor past the bathroom to the outer door of the apartment. He listened but could hear no word of anything said there; only the sound of the door opening and closing, and silence broken faintly by the phonograph's "Hi-de-ho-oh, Minnie."

Then the bathroom door swung slowly open and a man stood outlined against the darkness of the corridor. He was bareheaded and the electric light was reflected in a thin line across his hair, shone dully on the moist pallor of his skin. He wore a tightly belted raincoat and his hands were thrust deep into his pockets.

Winfield sat up straight in the tub, spoke tentatively "Hello!" He said "hello" with an incredulous rising inflection, blinked incredulously upward. The cigarette dangled loosely from one corner of his mouth.

The man leaned against the frame of the door and took a short thick automatic out of his coat pocket and held it steadily, waist high.

Winfield put his hands on the sides of the tub and started to get up.

The automatic barked twice.

Winfield half stood, with one hand and one leg braced against the side of the tub for perhaps five seconds. His eyes were wide, blank. Then he sank down slowly, his head fell back against the smooth blue porcelain, slid slowly under the water. The cigarette still hung in the corner of his clenched mouth and as his head went under the water it hissed briefly, was gone.

The man in the doorway turned, disappeared.

The water reddened. Faintly, the phonograph lisped: "Hi-de-ho. . . ."

Doolin grinned up at the waiter. "An' see the eggs are four minutes, an' don't put any cream in my coffee."

The waiter bobbed his head sullenly and disappeared through swinging doors.

Doolin unfolded his paper and turned to the comic page. He read it carefully, chuckling audibly, from top to bottom. Then he spread pages two and three across the counter and began at the top of page two. Halfway across he read the headline: *Winfield, Motion Picture Executive, Slain by Sweetheart: Story continued from page one.*

He turned to the front page and stared at a two-column cut of Winfield, read the accompanying account, turned back to page two and finished it. There was another cut of Winfield, and a woman. The caption under the woman's picture read: *Elma O'Shea Darmond, well-known screen actress and friend of Winfield, who was found unconscious in his apartment with the automatic in her hand.*

Doolin yawned and shoved the paper aside to make room for the eggs and toast and coffee that the sour-faced waiter carried. He devoured the eggs and had half finished his coffee before he saw something that interested him on page three. He put his cup down, leaned over the paper, read:

Man shot in Glendale Mystery. H.J. (Jake) Coleman, alleged gambler, was shot and killed as he came out of the Lyric Billiards Parlor in Glendale yesterday evening. The shots were fired from a mysterious black roadster which the police are attempting to trace.

Doolin read the rest of the story, finished his coffee. He sat several minutes staring expressionlessly at his reflection in the mirror behind the counter, got up, paid his check and went out into the bright morning.

He walked briskly down Hill Street to First, over First, to the Los Angeles Bulletin Building. He was whistling as the elevator carried him up.

In the back files of the *Bulletin* he found what he was looking for, a front-page spread in the Home Edition of December 10th:

MASSACRE IN NIGHTCLUB
Screen-Stars Duck for Cover as
Machine-Guns Belch Death

Early this morning The Hotspot, famous cabaret near Culver City, was the scene of the bloodiest battle the local gang war has afforded to date. Two men who police believe to be Frank Riccio and Edward (Whitey) Conroy of the Purple Gang in Detroit were instantly killed when a private room in the club was invaded by four men with sub-machine guns. A third man, a companion of Riccio and Conroy, was seriously wounded and is not expected to live.

Doolin skimmed down the column, read:

R.F. Winfield, prominent motion-picture executive, who was one of the party in the private room, said that he could not identify any of the killers. He said it all happened too quickly to be sure of any of them, and explained his presence in the company of the notorious gangsters as the result of his desire for first-hand information about the underworld in connection with a picture of that type which he is supervising. The names of others in the party are being withheld. . . .

Under a sub-head Doolin read:

H.J. Coleman and his companion, Miss Mazie Decker, were

*in the corridor leading to the private room when the killers
entered. Miss Decker said she could positively identify two of
them. Coleman, who is nearsighted, was equally positive that
he could not. . . .*

An hour and a half later, Doolin left the Bulletin Building. He had
gone carefully through the December file, and up to the middle of
January. He had called into service the City Directory, Telephone
Book, Dun & Bradstreet, and the telephone, and he had whee-
dled all the inside dope he could out of a police-reporter whom he
knew casually.

He stood on the wide stone steps and looked at the sheet of
paper on which he had scrawled notes. It read:

> *People in private room and corridor who might be able to iden-
> tify killers of Riccio and Conroy:*
>> *Winfield. Dead.*
>> *Coleman. Dead.*
>> *Martha Grainger. Actress. In show, in N.Y.*
>> *Betty Crane. Hustler. Died of pneumonia January 4th.*
>> *Isabel Dolly. Hustler and extra-girl. Was paralyzed drunk
>> during shooting; probably not important. Can't locate.*
>> *Mazie Decker. Taxi-dancer. Works at Dreamland on
>> Sixth and Hill. Failed to identify killers from rogues-gal-
>> lery photographs.*
>> *Nelson Halloran. Man-about-town. Money. Friend of
>> Winfield's. Lives at Fontenoy, same apartment-house as
>> Winfield.*

Doolin folded and creased the sheet of paper. He wound it
abstractedly around his forefinger and walked down the steps,
across the sidewalk to a cab. He got into the cab and sat down
and leaned back.

The driver slid the glass, asked: "Where to?"

Doolin stared at him blankly, then laughed. He said: "Wait a
minute," spread the sheet of paper across his knee. He took a stub

of pencil out of his pocket and slowly, thoughtfully, drew a line through the first five names; that left Mazie Decker and Nelson Halloran.

Doolin leaned forward and spoke to the driver: "Is that Dreamland joint at Sixth an' Hill open in the afternoon?"

The driver thought a moment, shook his head.

Doolin said: "All right, then—Fontenoy Apartment—on Whitley in Hollywood."

Nelson Halloran looked like Death. His white face was extremely long, narrow; his sharp chin tapered upward in unbroken lines to high sharp cheekbones, great deep-sunken eyes; continued to a high, almost degenerately narrow forehead. His mouth was wide, thin, dark against the whiteness of his skin. His hair was the color of water. He was six-feet-three inches tall, weighed a hundred and eighty.

He half lay in a deeply upholstered chair in the living room of his apartment and watched a round spot of sunlight move across the wall. The shades were drawn and the apartment was in semi-darkness. It was a chaos of modern furniture, books, magazines, papers, bottles; there were several good but badly hung reproductions on the pale walls.

Halloran occasionally lifted one long white hand languidly to his mouth, inhaled smoke deeply and blew it upward into the ray of sunlight.

When the phone buzzed he shuddered involuntarily, leaned sidewise and took it up from a low table.

He listened a moment, said: "Send him up." His voice was very low. There was softness in it; and there was coldness and something very far-away.

He moved slightly in the chair so that one hand was near his side, in the folds of his dressing-gown. There was a Luger there in the darkness of the chair. He was facing the door.

With the whirl of the buzzer he called: "Come in."

The door opened and Doolin came a little way into the room, closed the door behind him.

Halloran did not speak.

Doolin stood blinking in the half-light, and Halloran watched him and was silent.

Doolin was around thirty; of medium height, inclined to thickness through all the upper part of his body. His face was round and on the florid side and his eyes were wide-set, blue. His clothes didn't fit him very well.

He stood with his hat in his hand, his face expressionless, until Halloran said coldly: "I didn't get the name."

"Doolin. D—double o-l-i-n." Doolin spoke without moving his mouth very much. His voice was pleasant; his vowels colored slightly by brogue.

Halloran waited.

Doolin said: "I read a couple of things in the paper this morning that gave me an idea. I went over to the *Bulletin* an' worked on the idea, an' it pans out you're in a very bad spot."

Halloran took a drag of his cigarette, stared blankly at Doolin, waited. Doolin waited, too. They were both silent, looking at one another for more than a minute. Doolin's eyes were bright, pleased.

Halloran finally said: "This is a little embarrassing." He hesitated a moment. "Sit down."

Doolin sat on the edge of a wide steel and canvas chair against the wall. He dropped his hat on the floor and leaned forward, put his elbows on his knees. The little circle of sunlight moved slowly across the wall above him.

Halloran mashed his cigarette out, changed his position a little, said: "Go on."

"Have you read the papers?" Doolin took a cellophane-wrapped cigar out of his pocket and ripped off the wrapper, clamped the cigar between his teeth.

Halloran nodded, if moving his head the merest fraction of an inch could be called a nod.

Doolin spoke around the cigar: "Who rubbed Riccio and Conroy?"

Halloran laughed.

Doolin took the cigar out of his mouth. He said very earnestly: "Listen. Last night Winfield was murdered—an' Coleman. You're next. I don't know why the people who did it waited so long— maybe because the trial of a couple of the boys they've been holding comes up next week. . . ."

Halloran's face was a blank white mask.

Doolin leaned back and crossed his legs. "Anyway—they got Winfield an' Coleman. That leaves the Decker broad—the one who was with Coleman—an' you. The rest of them don't count— one's in New York an' one died of pneumonia an' one was cock-eyed. . . ."

He paused to chew his cigar, Halloran rubbed his left hand down over one side of his face, slowly.

Doolin went on: "I used to be a stunt-man in pictures. For the last year all the breaks have been bad. I haven't worked for five months." He leaned forward, emphasized his words with the cigar held like a pencil: "I want to work for you."

There was thin amusement in Halloran's voice: "What are your qualifications?"

"I can shoot straight, an' fast, an' I ain't afraid to take a chance— any kind of a chance! I'd make a hell of a swell bodyguard."

Doolin stood up in the excitement of his sales-talk, took two steps towards Halloran.

Halloran said: "Sit down." His voice was icy. The Luger glistened in his hand.

Doolin looked at the gun and smiled a little, stuck the cigar in his mouth and backed up and sat down.

Halloran said: "How am I supposed to know you're on the level?"

Doolin slid his lower lip up over the upper. He scratched his nose with the nail of his thumb and shook his head slowly, grinning.

"Anyway—it sounds like a pipe dream to me," Halloran went on. "The paper says Miss Darmond killed Winfield." He smiled. "And Coleman was a gambler—any one of a half dozen suckers is liable to have shot him."

Doolin shrugged elaborately. He leaned forward and picked up his hat and put it on, stood up.

Halloran laughed again. His laugh was not a particularly pleasing one.

"Don't be in a hurry," he said.

They were silent a while and then Halloran lighted a cigarette and stood up. He was so tall and spare that Doolin stared involuntarily as he crossed, holding the Luger loosely at his side, patted Doolin's pockets, felt under his arms with his free hand. Then Halloran went to a table across a corner of the room and dropped the Luger into a drawer.

He turned and smiled warmly at Doolin, said: "What will you drink?"

"Gin."

"No gin."

Doolin grinned.

Halloran went on: "Scotch, rye, bourbon, brandy, rum, Kirsch, champagne. No gin."

Doolin said: "Rye."

Halloran took two bottles from a tall cabinet, poured two drinks. "Why don't you go to the Decker girl? She's the one who said she could identify the men who killed Riccio and Conroy. She's the one who needs a bodyguard."

Doolin went over to the table and picked up his drink. "I ain't had a chance," he said. "She works at Dreamland downtown, an' it ain't open in the afternoon." They drank.

Halloran's mouth was curved to a small smile. He picked up a folded newspaper, pointed to a headline, handed it to Doolin.

Doolin took the paper, a late edition of the *Morning Bulletin*, read:

MURDERED GIRL IDENTIFIED AS TAXI-DANCER
The body of the girl who was found stabbed to death on the road near Lankershim early this morning has been identified as Mazie Decker of 305 S. Lake Street, an employee of the Dreamland Dancing Studio.

The identification was made by Peggy Galbraith, the murdered girl's room-mate. Miss Decker did not return home last night, and upon reading an account of the tragedy in the early editions, Miss Galbraith went to the morgue and positively identified Miss Decker. The police are. . . .

Doolin put the paper down, said: "Well, well. . . . Like I said. . . ." There was a knock at the door, rather a curious rhythmic tapping of fingernails.

Halloran called: "Come in."

The door opened and a woman came in slowly, closed the door. She went to Halloran and put her arms around him and tilted her head back.

Halloran kissed her lightly. He smiled at Doolin, said: "This is Mrs. Sare." He turned his smile to the woman. "Lola, meet Mr. Doolin—my bodyguard."

Lola Sare had no single feature, except her hair, that was beautiful; yet she was very beautiful.

Her hair was red, so dark that it was black in certain lights. Her eyes slanted; were so dark a green they were usually black. Her nose was straight but the nostrils flared the least bit too much; her mouth red and full; too wide and curved. Her skin was smooth, very dark. Her figure was good, on the slender side. She was ageless; perhaps twenty-six, perhaps thirty-six.

She wore a dark green robe of heavy silk, black mules; her hair was gathered in a large roll at the nape of her neck.

She inclined her head sharply towards Doolin, without expression.

Doolin said: "Very happy to know you, Mrs. Sare."

She went to one of the wide windows and jerked the drape aside a little; a broad flat beam of sunshine yellowed the darkness.

She said: "Sorry to desecrate the tomb." Her voice was deep, husky.

Halloran poured three drinks and went back to his chair and sat down. Mrs. Sare leaned against the table, and Doolin, after a hesitant glance at her, sat down on the chair against the wall.

Halloran sipped his drink. "The strange part of it all," he said, "is that I couldn't identify any of the four men who came in that night if my life depended upon it—and I'm almost sure Winfield couldn't. We'd been on a bender together for three days—and my memory for faces is bad, at best. . . ."

He put his glass on the floor beside the chair, lighted a cigarette. "Who else did you mention, besides the Decker girl and Coleman and Winfield and myself, who might . . . ?"

Doolin took the folded sheet of paper out of his pocket, got up and handed it to Halloran.

Halloran studied it a while, said: "You missed one."

Mrs. Sare picked up the two bottles and went to Doolin, refilled his glass.

Doolin stared questioningly at Halloran, his eyebrows raised to a wide inverted V.

"The man who was with Riccio and Conroy," Halloran went on. "The third man, who was shot. . . ."

Doolin said: "I didn't see any more about him in the files—the paper said he wasn't expected to live. . . ."

Halloran clicked the nail of his forefinger against his teeth, said: "I wonder."

Mrs. Sare had paused to listen. She went to Halloran and refilled his glass and put the bottles on the floor, sat down on the arm of Halloran's chair.

"Winfield and I went to The Hotspot alone," Halloran went on. "We had some business to talk over with a couple girls in the show." He grinned faintly, crookedly at Mrs. Sare. "Riccio and Conroy and this third man—I think his name was Martini or something dry like that—and the three girls on your list, passed our table on their way to the private room. . . ."

Doolin was leaning forward, chewing his cigar, his eyes bright with interest.

Halloran blew smoke up into the wedge of sun. "Winfield knew Conroy casually—had met him in the East. They fell on one another's necks, and Conroy invited us to join their party. Winfield went for that—he was doing a gangster picture and Conroy was a big shot in the East—Winfield figured he could get a lot of angles. . . ."

Doolin said: "That was on the level, then?"

"Yes," Halloran nodded emphatically. "Winfield even talked of making Conroy technical expert on the picture—before the fireworks started."

"What did this third man—this Martini—look like?"

Halloran looked a little annoyed. He said: "I'll get to that. There were eight of us in the private room—the three men and the three girls and Winfield and I. Riccio was pretty drunk, and one of the girls was practically under the table. We were all pretty high."

Halloran picked up his glass, leaned forward. "Riccio and Martini were all tangled up in some kind of drunken argument and I got the idea it had something to do with drugs—morphine. Riccio was pretty loud. Winfield and I were talking to Conroy, and the girls were amusing themselves gargling champagne, when the four men—I guess there were four—crashed in and opened up on Riccio and Conroy. . . ."

"What about Martini?" Doolin's unlighted cigar was growing rapidly shorter.

Halloran looked annoyed again. "That's the point," he said. "They didn't pay any attention to Martini—they wanted Riccio and Conroy. And it wasn't machine-guns—that was newspaper color. It was automatics. . . ."

Doolin said: "What about Martini?"

"For Christ's sake—shut up!" Halloran grinned cheerlessly, finished his drink. "Riccio shot Martini."

Doolin stood up slowly, said: "Can I use the phone?"

Halloran smiled at Mrs. Sare, nodded.

Doolin called several numbers, asked questions, said "Yes" and "No" monotonously.

Halloran and Mrs. Sare talked quietly. Between two calls, Halloran spoke to Doolin: "You've connections—haven't you." It was an observation, not a question.

Doolin said: "If I had as much money as I have connections, I'd retire."

He finished after a while, hung up and put the phone back on the low round table.

"Martinelli," he said, "not Martini. Supposed to have been Riccio and Conroy's partner in the East. They had the drug business pretty well cornered. He showed up out here around the last of November, and Riccio and Conroy came in December 10th, were killed the night they got in. . . ."

Halloran said: "I remember that—they were talking about the trip."

Doolin took the cigar out of his mouth long enough to take a drink. "Martinelli was discharged from St. Vincent's Hospital January 16th—day before yesterday. He's plenty bad—beat four or five murder raps in the East and was figured for a half dozen others. They called him The Executioner. Angelo Martinelli—The Executioner."

Mrs. Sare said: "Come and get it."

Doolin and Halloran got up and went into the little dining room. They sat down at the table and Mrs. Sare brought in a steaming platter of bacon and scrambled eggs, a huge double-globe of bubbling coffee.

Doolin said: "Here's the way it looks to me: If Martinelli figured you an' Winfield an' whoever else was in the private room had seen Riccio shoot him, he'd want to shut you up; it was a cinch he'd double-crossed Riccio and if it came out at the trial, the Detroit boys would be on his tail."

Halloran nodded, poured a large rosette of chili-sauce on the plate beside his scrambled eggs.

"But what did he want to rub Coleman an' Decker for?"

Halloran started to speak with his mouth full, but Doolin interrupted him: "The answer to that is that Martinelli had hooked up with the outfit out here, the outfit that Riccio and Conroy figured on moving in on. . . ."

Halloran said: "Martinelli probably came out to organize

things for a narcotic combination between here and Detroit, in opposition to our local talent. He liked the combination here the way it was and threw in with them—and when Riccio and Conroy arrived Martinelli put the finger on them, for the local boys. . . ."

Doolin swallowed a huge mouthful of bacon and eggs, said: "Swell," out of the corner of his mouth to Mrs. Sare.

He picked up his cigar and pointed it at Halloran. "That's the reason he wanted all of you—you an' Winfield because you'd get the Detroit outfit on his neck if you testified; Decker an' Coleman because they could spot the L.A. boys. He didn't try to proposition any of you—he's the kind of guy who would figure killing was simpler."

Halloran said: "He's got to protect himself against the two men who are in jail too. They're liable to spill their guts. If everybody who was in on it was bumped there wouldn't be a chance of those two guys being identified—everything would be rosy."

They finished their bacon and eggs in silence.

With the coffee, Doolin said: "Funny he didn't make a pass at you last night—before or after he got Winfield. The same building an' all. . . ."

"Maybe he did." Halloran put his arm around Mrs. Sare who was standing beside his chair. "I didn't get home till around three—he was probably here, missed me."

Doolin said: "We better go downtown an' talk to the DA. That poor gal of Winfield's is probably on the grill. We can clear that up an' have Martinelli picked up. . . ."

Halloran said: "No." He said it very emphatically.

Doolin opened his eyes wide, slowly. He finished his coffee, waited.

Halloran smiled faintly, said: "In the first place, I hate coppers." He tightened his arm around Mrs. Sare. "In the second place, I don't particularly care for Miss Darmond—she can goddamned well fry on the griddle from now on, so far as I'm concerned. In the third place—I like it. . . ."

Doolin glanced at Mrs. Sare, turned his head slowly back towards Halloran.

"I've got three months to live," Halloran went on—"at the outside." His voice was cold, entirely unemotional. "I was shell-shocked and gassed and kicked around pretty generally in France in 'eighteen. They stuck me together and sent me back and I've lasted rather well. But my heart is shot, and my lungs are bad, and so on—the doctors are getting pretty sore because I'm still on my feet. . . ."

He grinned widely. "I'm going to have all the fun I can in whatever time is left. We're not going to call copper, and we're going to play this for everything we can get out of it. You're my bodyguard and your salary is five hundred a week, but your job isn't to guard me—it's to see that there's plenty of excitement. And instead of waiting for Martinelli to come to us, we're going to Martinelli."

Doolin looked blankly at Mrs. Sare. She was smiling in a very curious way.

Halloran said: "Are you working?"

Doolin smiled slowly with all his face. He said: "Sure."

Doolin dried his hands and smoothed his hair, whistling tunelessly, went through the small cheaply furnished living room of his apartment to the door of the kitchenette. He picked up a newspaper from a table near the door, unfolded it and glanced at the headlines, said: "They're calling the Winfield kill 'Murder in Blue' because it happened in a blue bathtub. Is that a laugh!"

A rather pretty fresh-faced girl was stirring something in a white sauce-pan on the little gas stove. She looked up and smiled and said: "Dinner'll be ready in a minute," wiped her hands on her apron and began setting the table.

Doolin leaned against the wall and skimmed through the rest of the paper. The Coleman case was limited to a quarter column—the police had been unable to trace the car. There was even less about Mazie Decker. The police were "working on a theory. . . ."

The police were working on a theory, too, on the Winfield killing. Miss Darmond had been found near the door of Winfield's apartment with a great bruise on her head, the night of the murder; she said the last she remembered was opening the door and struggling with someone. The "best minds" of the Force believed her story up to that point; they were working on the angle that she had an accomplice.

Doolin rolled up the paper and threw it on a chair. He said: "Five hundred a week—an' expenses! Gee—is that swell!" He was grinning broadly.

The girl said: "I'm awfully glad about the money, darling— if you're *sure* you'll be safe. God knows it's about time we had a break." She hesitated a moment. "I hope it's all right. . . ."

She was twenty-three or -four, a honey-blonde pink-cheeked girl with wide gray eyes, a slender well-curved figure.

Doolin went to her and kissed the back of her neck.

"Sure, it's all right, Mollie," he said. "Anything is all right when you get paid enough for it. The point is to make it last—five hundred is a lot of money, but a thousand will buy twice as many lamb chops."

She became very interested in a tiny speck on one of the cheap white plates, rubbed it industriously with a towel. She spoke without looking up: "I keep thinking about that Darmond girl—in jail. What do you suppose Halloran has against her?"

"I don't know." Doolin sat down at the table. "Anyway—she's okay. We can spring her any time, only we can't do it now because we'd have to let the Law in on the Martinelli angle an' they'd pick him up—an' Halloran couldn't have his fun."

"It's a funny kind of fun." The girl smiled with her mouth.

Doolin said: "He's a funny guy. Used to be a police reporter in Chi—maybe that has something to do with it. Anyway, the poor bastard's only got a little while to go—let him have any kind of fun he wants. He can afford it. . . ."

They were silent while the girl cut bread and got the butter out of the Frigidaire and finished setting the table.

Doolin was leaning forward with his elbows on the table, his chin in his hands. "As far as the Darmond gal is concerned, a little of that beef stew they dish up at the County will be good for her. These broads need a little of that—to give them perspective."

The girl was heaping mashed potatoes into a big bowl. She did not speak.

"The way I figure it," Doolin went on—"Halloran hasn't got the guts to bump himself off. He's all washed up, an' he knows it—an' the idea has made him a little batty. Then along comes Martinelli—a chance for him to go out dramatically—the way he's lived—an' he goes for it. Jesus! so would I if I was as near the edge as he is. He doesn't give a goddamn about anything—he doesn't have to. . . ."

The girl finished putting food on the table, sat down. Doolin heaped their plates with chops and potatoes and cauliflower while she served salad. They began to eat.

Doolin got up and filled two glasses with water and put them on the table.

The girl said: "I'm sorry I forgot the water. . . ."

Doolin bent over and kissed her, sat down.

"As far as Halloran is concerned," he went on—"I'm just another actor in his show. Instead of sitting and waiting for Martinelli to come to get him—we go after Martinelli. That's Halloran's idea of fun—that's the kind of sense of humor he's got. What the hell!—he's got nothing to lose. . . ."

The girl said: "Eat your dinner before it gets cold."

They were silent a while.

Finally she said: "What if Martinelli shoots first?"

Doolin laughed. "Martinelli isn't going to shoot at all. Neither am I—an' neither is Mr. Halloran."

The girl lighted a cigarette, sipped her coffee. She stared expressionlessly at Doolin, waited.

"Halloran is having dinner with Mrs. Sare," Doolin went on. "Then they're going to a show an' I'm picking them up afterwards—at the theatre. Then Halloran an' I are going to have a look around for Martinelli."

He finished his coffee, refilled both their cups. "In the meantime I'm supposed to be finding out where we're most likely to find him—Halloran is a great believer in my 'connections.'"

Doolin grinned, went on with a softly satisfied expression,

as if he were taking a rabbit out of a hat: "I've already found Martinelli—not only where he hangs out, but where he lives. It was a cinch. He hasn't any reason to think he's pegged for anything—he's not hiding out."

The girl said: "So what?"

He stood up, stretched luxuriously. "So I'm going to Martinelli right now." He paused dramatically. "An' I'm going to tell him what kind of a spot he's in—with half a dozen murder raps hanging over his head, and all. I'm going to tell him that plenty people besides myself know about it an' that the stuff's on the way to the DA's office an' that he'd better scram toot sweet. . . ."

The girl said: "You're crazy."

Doolin laughed extravagantly. "Like a fox," he said. "Like a fox. I'm doing Martinelli a big favor—so I'm set with him. I'm keeping Halloran from running a chance of being killed—an' he'll think he's still running the chance, an' get his throb out of it. I'm keeping five hundred smackers coming into the cash register every week as long as Halloran lives, or as long as I can give him a good show. An' everybody's happy. What more do you want?"

"Sense." The girl mashed her cigarette out, stood up. "I never heard such a crazy idea in all my life! . . ."

Doolin looked disgusted. He walked into the living room, came back to the doorway. "Sure, it's crazy," he said. "Sure, it's crazy. So is Halloran—an' you—an' me. So is Martinelli—probably. It's the crazy ideas that work—an' this one is going to work like a charm."

The girl said: "What about Darmond? If Martinelli gets away she'll be holding the bag for Winfield's murder."

"Oh, no, she won't! As soon as the Halloran angle washes up I'll turn my evidence over to the DA an' tell him it took a few weeks to get it together—an' be sure about it. It's as plain as the nose on your face that Martinelli killed all three of them. Those chumps downtown are too sappy to see it now but they won't be when I point it out to them. It's a setup case against Martinelli!"

The girl smiled coldly. She said: "You're the most conceited, bull-headed Mick that ever lived. You've been in one jam after another ever since we were married. This is one time I'm not going to let you make a fool of yourself—an' probably get killed. . . ."

Doolin's expression was stubborn, annoyed. He turned and strode across the living room, squirmed into his coat, put on his hat and jerked it down over his eyes.

She stood in the doorway. Her face was very white and her eyes were wide, round.

She said: "Please. Johnny. . . ."

He didn't look at her. He went to the desk against one wall and opened a drawer, took a nickel-plated revolver out of the drawer and dropped it into his coat pocket.

She said: "If you do this insane thing—I'm leaving." Her voice was cold, brittle.

Doolin went to the outer-door, went out, slammed the door.

She stood there a little while looking at the door.

Angelo Martinelli stuck two fingers of his left hand into the little jar, took them out pale, green, sticky with Smoothcomb Hair Dressing. He dabbed it on his head, held his hands stiff with the fingers bent backwards and rubbed it vigorously into his hair. Then he wiped his hands and picked up a comb, bent towards the mirror.

Martinelli was very young—perhaps twenty-four or -five. His face was pale, unlined; pallor shading to blue towards his long angular jaw; his eyes red-brown, his nose straight and delicately cut. He was of medium height but the high padded shoulders of his coat made him appear taller.

The room was small, garishly furnished. A low bed and two or three chairs in the worst modern manner were made a little more objectionable by orange and pink batik throws; there was an elaborately wrought iron floor lamp, its shade made of whiskey labels pasted on imitation parchment.

Martinelli finished combing his hair, spoke over his shoulder to a woman who lounged across the foot of the bed: "Tonight does it. . . ."

Lola Sare said: "Tonight does it—if you're careful. . . ."

Martinelli glanced at his wrist-watch. "I better get going—it's nearly eight. He said he'd be there at eight."

Lola Sare leaned forward and dropped her cigarette into a half-full glass on the floor.

"I'll be home from about eight-thirty on," she said. "Call as soon as you can."

Martinelli nodded. He put on a lightweight black felt hat, tilted it to the required angle in front of the mirror. He helped her into her coat, and then he put his arms around her, kissed her mouth lingeringly.

She clung to him, whispered: "Make it as fast as you can, darling."

They went to the door and Martinelli snapped off the light and they went out.

Martinelli said: "Turn right at the next corner."

The cab driver nodded; they turned off North Broadway into a dimly lighted street, went several blocks over bad pavement.

Martinelli pounded on the glass, said: "Oke."

The cab slid to an abrupt stop and Martinelli got out and paid the driver, stood at the curb until the cab had turned around in the narrow street, disappeared.

He went to a door above which one pale electric globe glittered, felt in the darkness for the button, pressed it. The door clicked open; Martinelli went in and slammed it shut behind him.

There were a half dozen or so men strung out along the bar in the long dim room. A few more sat at tables against the wall.

Martinelli walked to the far end of the bar, leaned across it to speak quietly to a chunky bald-headed man who sat on a high stool near the cash register: "Chief here?"

The bald man bobbed his head, jerked it towards a door behind Martinelli.

Martinelli looked surprised, said mildly: "He's on time for once in his life!"

The man bobbed his head. His face was blank.

Martinelli went through the door, up two short flights of stairs to a narrow hallway. At the end of the hallway he knocked at a heavy steel-sheathed fire-door.

After a little while the door opened and a voice said: "Come in."

Doolin stood on his toes and tried to make out the number above the door but the figures were too faded by weather, time; the electric light was too dim.

He walked down the dark street a half block and then walked back and pressed the button beside the door; the door clicked open and he went through the short passageway into the long barroom.

A bartender wiped off the stained wood in front of him, questioned with his eyes.

Doolin said: "Rye."

He glanced idly at the men at the bar, at the tables, at the heavily built bald man who sat on a stool at the far end of the bar. The little bald man was stooped over a wide-spread newspaper.

The bartender put a glass on the bar in front of Doolin, put a flat brightly labeled flask beside it.

Doolin said: "Seen Martinelli tonight?"

The bartender watched Doolin pour his drink, picked up the bottle and put it under the bar, said: "Yeah. He came in a little while ago. He's upstairs."

Doolin nodded, tasted the rye. It wasn't too bad. He finished it and put a quarter on the bar, sauntered towards the door at the back of the room.

The little bald man looked up from his paper.

Doolin said: "Martinelli's expecting me. He's upstairs—ain't he?"

The little man looked at Doolin. He began at his face and went down to his feet and then back up, slowly. "He didn't say anything about you." He spat with the admirable precision of age and confidence into a cuspidor in the corner.

Doolin said: "He forgot." He put his hand on the doorknob.

The little man looked at him, through him, blankly.

Doolin turned the knob and opened the door, went through, closed the door behind him.

The stairs were dimly lighted by a sputtering gas-jet. He went up slowly. There was one door at the top of the first flight; it was dark; there was no light under it, no sound beyond it. Doolin went up another flight very quietly. He put his ear against the steel-sheathed door; he could hear no sound, but a little light filtered through under the door. He doubled up his fist, knocked with the heel of his hand.

Martinelli opened the door. He stood a moment staring questioningly at Doolin and then he glanced over his shoulder, smiled, said: "Come in."

Doolin put his hands in his overcoat pockets, his right hand holding the revolver tightly, went forward into the room.

Martinelli closed the door behind him, slid the heavy bolt.

The room was large, bare; somewhere around thirty-five by forty. It was lighted by a single green-shaded droplight over a very large round table in the center; there were other tables and chairs stacked in the dusk of the corner. There were no windows, no other doors.

Halloran sat in one of the four chairs at the table. He was leaning slightly forward with his elbows on the table, his long waxen hands framing his face. His face was entirely cold, white, expressionless.

Martinelli stood with his back against the door, his hands behind him.

Doolin glanced over his shoulder at Martinelli, looked back at Halloran. His eyebrows were lifted to the wide V, his mouth hung a little open.

Halloran said: "Well, well—this is a surprise."

He moved his eyes to Martinelli, said: "Angelo. Meet Mr. Doolin—my bodyguard. . . ." For an instant his wide thin mouth flickered a fraction of an inch upward; then his face became a blank, white mask again. "Mr. Doolin—Mr. Martinelli. . . ."

Martinelli had silently come up behind Doolin, suddenly thrust his hands into Doolin's pockets, hard, grabbed Doolin's hands. Doolin bent sharply forward. They struggled for possibly half a minute, silently except for the tearing sound of their breath;

then Martinelli brought his knee up suddenly, savagely; Doolin groaned, sank to his knees, the nickel-plated revolver clattered to the floor, slid halfway across the room.

Martinelli darted after it.

Halloran had not appeared to move. He said: "Wait a minute, baby. . . ." The blunt Luger that Doolin had experienced in the afternoon glittered on the table between his two hands.

Martinelli made an impatient gesture, stooped to pick up Doolin's gun.

"Wait a minute, baby." Halloran's voice was like a cold swift scythe.

Martinelli stood up very straight.

Doolin got to his feet slowly. He bent over and held the middle of his body, rolled his head towards Martinelli, his eyes narrow, malevolent. He said very quietly, as if to himself: "Dirty son of a bitch—dirty, dirty son of a bitch!"

Martinelli grinned, stood very straight. His hands, cupped close to his thighs, trembled rigidly.

Halloran said slowly: "Don't do it, baby. I'll shoot both your eyes out before you get that shiv of yours into the air—and never touch your nose."

Martinelli looked like a clothing store dummy. He was balanced on the balls of his feet, his hands trembling at his sides; his grin artificial, empty.

Doolin laughed suddenly. He stood up straight and looked at Martinelli and laughed.

Halloran moved his eyes to Doolin, smiled faintly. He said: "Gentlemen—sit down."

Martinelli tottered forward, sank into one of the chairs.

Halloran said: "Put your hands on the table, please."

Martinelli obediently put his hands on the table. The empty grin seemed to have congealed on his face.

Halloran turned his eyes towards Doolin. Doolin smiled, walked gingerly to the other chair and sat down.

Halloran said: "Now. . . ." He put one hand up to his face; the other held the Luger loosely on the table.

Doolin cleared his throat, said: "What's it all about, Mr. Halloran?"

Martinelli laughed suddenly. The empty grin exploded into loud high-pitched mirth. "What's it all about! Dear God—what's it all about! . . ."

Halloran was watching Doolin, his shadowed sunken eyes half-closed.

Martinelli leaned forward, lifted his hands and pointed two fingers at Doolin. "Listen—wise guy. . . . You've got minutes to live—if you're lucky. That's what it's all about!"

Doolin regarded Martinelli with faint amusement.

Martinelli laughed again. He moved his hand slowly until the two fingers pointed at Halloran. "He killed Coleman," he said. "He shot Coleman an' I drove the car. An' he killed Winfield himself. An' his outfit killed Riccio an' Conroy. . . ."

Doolin glanced at Halloran, turned back to smile dimly, dumbly at Martinelli.

"He propositioned me into killing the dance-hall dame," Martinelli went on—"an' now he's going to kill you an' me. . . ."

Doolin grinned broadly but it was all done with his mouth. He didn't look like he felt it very much. He looked at Halloran. Halloran's face was white and immovable as plaster.

"Listen—wise guy!" Martinelli leaned forward, moved his hand back to point at Doolin. He was suddenly very intense; his dark eyes burned into Doolin's. "I came out here for Riccio to make connections to peddle M——a lot of it—an' I met Mr. Halloran." Martinelli moved his head an eighth of an inch towards Halloran. "Mr. Halloran runs the drug racket out here—did you know that?"

Doolin glanced swiftly at Halloran, looked back at Martinelli's tense face.

"Mr. Halloran aced me into double-crossing Frankie Riccio an' Conroy," Martinelli went on. "Mr. Halloran's men rubbed Riccio an' Conroy, an' would've taken care of me if Riccio hadn't almost beat 'em to it. . . ."

Halloran said coldly, amusedly: "Oh—come, come, Angelo. . . ."

Martinelli did not look at Halloran. He said: "I met Riccio an' Conroy at the train that night an' took them to that joint in Culver City to talk business to Mr. Halloran—only I didn't know the kind of business Mr. Halloran was going to talk. . . ."

"Is it quite necessary to go into all this?" Halloran spoke sidewise to Martinelli, smiled at Doolin. It was his first definite change of expression since Doolin had come into the room.

Martinelli said: "Yes," emphatically. He scowled at Halloran, his eyes thin black slits. "Bright-boy here" he indicated Doolin with his hand—"wants to know what it's all about. I'd like to have somebody know—besides me. One of us might leave here alive—if I get this all out of my system it's a cinch it won't be Bright-boy."

Halloran's smile was very cheerful. He said: "Go on."

"One of the men the Law picked up for the Hotspot shooting was a good guess—he's on Mr. Halloran's payroll," Martinelli went on. He was accenting the "Mr." a little unnecessarily, a little too much. "When I got out of the hospital Mr. Halloran suggested we clean things up—move Coleman an' Decker an' Winfield—anybody who might identify his man or testify that Riccio shot me—out of the way. He hated Winfield anyway, for beating his time with the Darmond gal—an' he hated her. . . ."

Halloran was beaming at Doolin, his hand tight and steady on the Luger. Doolin thought about the distance across the big table to Halloran, the distance to the light.

Martinelli was leaning forward, talking swiftly, eagerly: "I brought eighty-five grand worth of morphine out with me, an' I turned it over to his nibs here when we threw in together. I ain't had a nickel out of it. That's the reason I went for all this finagling—I wanted my dough. I was supposed to get it tonight, but I found out about ten minutes ago I ain't going to get it at all. . . ."

Martinelli smiled at Halloran, finished: "Mr. Halloran says it was hijacked." He stood up slowly.

Halloran asked: "All through, baby?"

Martinelli was standing very stiff and straight, his hands cupped at his sides.

Doolin ducked suddenly, exerted all his strength to upset the table. For a moment he was protected by the edge, could see neither Martinelli nor Halloran; then the big round table-top slid off its metal base, crashed to the floor.

Halloran was holding Martinelli very much in the way a great ape would hold a smaller animal. One long arm was out stiff, the long white hand at Martinelli's throat, almost encircling it. Halloran's other hand held Martinelli's wrist, waved it back and forth slowly. The blade of a short curved knife glistened in Martinelli's hand. Except for the slow waving of their two hands they were as if frozen, entirely still. There was nothing human in their position, nothing human in their faces.

Doolin felt in that instant that Halloran was not human. He was mad, insane; but it was not the madness of a man, it was the cold murderous lust of an animal.

The Luger and Doolin's revolver were on the floor near their feet. Doolin circled until he was behind Halloran, moved slowly towards them.

As he dived for one of the guns Halloran swung Martinelli around swiftly, kicked viciously at Doolin's head. He missed once, but the second caught Doolin's hand as it closed over the Luger, sent the Luger spinning to a corner.

As Doolin half rose, Halloran's long leg lashed out again, his heavy shoe struck the side of Doolin's head. Doolin grunted, fell sidewise to the floor.

Doolin lay on his back and the room went around him. Later, in remembering what followed, it was like short strips of motion-picture film, separated by strips of darkness.

Halloran backed Martinelli slowly to the wall. It was as if they were performing some strange ritualistic dance; their steps were measured; Halloran's face was composed, his expression almost tender. Martinelli's face was darkening from the pressure on his throat. Halloran waved the hand holding the knife slowly back and forth.

The next time the darkness in Doolin's head cleared, they were against the wall, his head high, at a curious twisted angle above Halloran's white relentless hand, his face purpling. Halloran's other hand had slipped down over Martinelli's chest.

Martinelli's eyes bulged. His face was the face of a man who saw death coming, and was afraid. Doolin could no longer see Halloran's face. He watched the knife near Martinelli's chest, slowly.

Martinelli, some way, made a high piercing sound in his throat as the knife went into him. And again as Halloran withdrew the knife, pressed it in again slowly. Halloran did not stab mercifully on the left side, but on the right puncturing the lung again and again, slowly.

Doolin rolled over on his side. The revolver lay on the floor midway between him and Halloran. He shook his head sharply, crawled towards it.

Halloran suddenly released Martinelli, stepped back a pace. Martinelli's knees buckled, he sank slowly down, sat on the floor with his back against the wall, his legs out straight. He sucked in air in great rattling gasps, held both hands tightly against his chest, tightly against the shaft of the knife.

He lifted his head and there was blood on his mouth. He laughed; and Doolin forgot the gun, stopped, stared fascinated at Martinelli.

Martinelli laughed and the sound was as if everything inside him was breaking. His head rolled back and he grinned upward with glazing eyes at Halloran, held his hands tightly against his chest, spoke: "Tell Lola we can't go away now. . . ." He paused, sucked in air. "She's waiting for me. . . . Tell her Angelo sends his regrets. . . ." His voice was thick, high-pitched, but his words were telling, deadly, took deadly effect.

Halloran seemed to grow taller, his great shoulders seemed to widen as Doolin watched.

Martinelli laughed again. He said: "So long—sucker. . . ."

Halloran kicked him savagely in the chest. He drew his long leg back and as Martinelli slumped sidewise he kicked his face, hard, repeatedly.

Doolin scrambled swiftly forward, picked up the revolver, raised it.

Halloran turned slowly.

Doolin held the revolver unsteadily in his right hand, aimed at Halloran's chest while the muzzle described little circles, pulled the trigger twice.

Halloran came towards him. Doolin made a harsh sound in his throat, scuttled backwards a few feet, held the revolver out limply and fired again.

Halloran's face was cold, impassive; his eyes were great black holes in his skull. He came towards Doolin slowly.

Doolin tried to say something but the words stuck in his throat, and then Halloran was above him and there was a terribly crushing weight against Doolin's forehead and it was suddenly dark.

Slowly, Doolin came to, lay a little while with his eyes closed. There were sharp twisting wires of pain in his head; he put his hand up, took it away wet, sticky.

He opened his eyes. It was entirely dark, a cold penetrating darkness; entirely still.

Suddenly he laughed, a curious hysterical sound in the quiet room; and as suddenly, panic seized him. He struggled to his knees, almost fell down again as the pain in his head throbbed to the swift movement. He got to his feet slowly, fumbled in his pockets and found a match, lighted it.

Martinelli's body was slumped in the angle of floor and wall at one side of the room. There was no one else. Doolin's revolver shone dimly on the floor in the flare of the match. The door was ajar.

Doolin lighted another match and picked up his revolver, his hat. He took out a handkerchief and wiped his face and the handkerchief was wet, dark. He walked, unsteadily, to the door, down the dark stairs.

One faint globe burned above the deserted bar. Doolin felt his way along the wall, lifted the heavy bar across the outside door and went out, closed the door behind him. It was raining lightly a thin cold drizzle.

He took air into his lungs in great gulps, soaked the handkerchief in a little puddle of rainwater and tried to clean his face. Then he went down the dark street swiftly towards Broadway.

The druggist looked at him through thick spectacles, gestured towards the back of the store.

Doolin said: "Fix me up some peroxide an' bandages an' stuff—I had an accident." He went back to the telephone booth, found the number of the Fontenoy, called it, asked for Mrs. Sare.

The operator said Mrs. Sare didn't answer.

Doolin hung up and went out and cleaned the blood from his face in front of a mirror. A little girl stared at him wide-eyed from the soda fountain; the druggist said: "Automobile . . . ?"

Doolin nodded.

The druggist asked: "How much bandage do you want?"

Doolin said: "Let it go—it's not as bad as I thought it was."

He put his hat on the back of his head and went out and got into a cab, said: "Fontenoy Apartments—Hollywood. An' make it snappy."

Lola Sare's voice said: "Yes," with rising inflection.

Doolin opened the door, went in.

She was sitting in a long low chair beneath a crimson-shaded bridge lamp. It was the only light in the room. Her arms were bare, straight on the arms of the chair, her hands hanging limply downward. Her dark head was against the back of the chair and her face was taut, her eyes wide, vacant.

Doolin took off his hat, said: "Why the hell don't you answer your phone?"

She did not speak, nor move.

"You'd better get out of here—quick." Doolin went towards her. "Halloran killed Martinelli—an' Martinelli opened up about you before he died. Halloran will be coming to see you. . . ."

Her blank eyes moved slowly from his face to some place in the dusk behind him. He followed her gaze, turned slowly.

Halloran was standing against the wall near the door. The door had covered him when Doolin entered; he put out one hand and pushed it gently, it swung closed with a sharp click.

As Doolin's eyes became used to the dimness of the room he saw Halloran clearly. He was leaning against the wall and the right shoulder and breast of his light gray suit was dark, sodden. He held the short blunt Luger in his left hand.

He said: "You're a little late. . . ."

The Luger roared.

Lola Sare put her hands up to the middle of her breast, low; her head came forward slowly. She started to get up and the Luger leaped in Halloran's hand, roared again.

At the same instant Doolin shot, holding the revolver low. The two explosions were simultaneous, thundered in the dark and narrow room.

Halloran fell as a tree falls; slowly, stiffly, his arms stiff at his sides; crashed to the floor.

Doolin dropped the revolver, walked unsteadily towards Lola Sare. His knees buckled suddenly and he sank forward, down.

There was someone pounding at the door.

Doolin finished dabbing iodine on his head, washed his hands and went into the little living room of his apartment. A first dull streak of morning grayed the windows. He pulled down the shades and went into the kitchenette, lighted the gas under the percolator.

When the coffee was hot he poured a cup, dropped four lumps of sugar into it absently, carried it into the living room. He sat down on the davenport and put the coffee on an endtable, picked up the phone and dialed a number.

He said: "Hello, Grace? Is Mollie there? . . ." He listened a moment, went on: "Oh—I thought she might be there. Sorry I woke you up. . . ." He hung up, sipped his steaming coffee.

After a few minutes he picked up the phone, dialed again, said: "Listen, Grace—please put Mollie on. . . . Aw nuts! I know she's there—please make her talk to me. . . ."

Then he smiled, waited a moment, said: Hello darling. . . . Listen—please come on home—will you? . . . Aw listen, Honey—I did what you said—everything's all right. . . . Uh-huh. . . . Halloran's dead—an' Martinelli. . . . Uh-huh. . . . The Sare dame is shot up pretty bad, but not too much to give evidence an' clean it all up. . . . Uh-huh. . . ."

He reached over and picked up the cup and took a long drink of coffee, smiled into the phone, said: "Sure—I'm all right—I got a little scratch on my head but I'm all right. . . . Sure. . . . Sure—we were right. . . . All right, Honey—I'll be waiting for you. Hurry up. . . . G'bye. . . ."

He hung up, curved his mouth to a wide grin, finished his coffee, lit a cigarette and waited.

I FEEL BAD KILLING YOU
BY LEIGH BRACKETT

Santa Monica

(Originally published in 1944)

1
Dead End Town

Los Angeles, Apr. 21.—The death of Henry Channing, 24, policeman attached to the Surfside Division and brother of the once-prominent detective Paul Channing, central figure in the Padway gang-torture case, has been termed a suicide following investigation by local authorities. Young Channing's battered body was found in the surf under Sunset Pier in the beach community three days ago. It was first thought that Channing might have fallen or been thrown from the end of the pier, where his cap was found, but there is no evidence of violence and a high guard rail precludes the accident theory. Sunset Pier was part of his regular beat.

Police Captain Max Gandara made the following statement: "We have reliable testimony that Channing had been nervous and despondent following a beating by pachucos two months ago." He then cited the case of the brother, Paul Channing, who quit the force and vanished into obscurity following his mistreatment at the hands of the once-powerful Padway gang in 1934. "They were both good cops," Gandara said, "but they lost their nerve."

Paul Channing stood for a moment at the corner. The crossing-light, half a block along the highway, showed him only as a gaunt shadow among shadows. He looked down the short street in somber hesitation. Small tired houses crouched patiently under the wind. Somewhere a rusted screen door slammed with the protesting futility of a dying bird beating its wing. At the end of the deserted pavement was the gray pallor of sand and, beyond it, the sea.

He stood listening to the boom and hiss of the waves, thinking of them rushing black and foam-streaked through the pilings of Sunset Pier, the long weeds streaming out and the barnacles pink and fluted and razor sharp behind it. He hoped that Hank had struck his head at once against a timber.

He lifted his head, his body shaken briefly by a tremor. *This is it*, he thought. *This is the deadline.*

He began to walk, neither slowly nor fast, scraping sand under his feet. The rhythm of the scraping was uneven, a slight dragging, off-beat. He went to the last house on the right, mounted three sagging steps to a wooden porch, and rapped with his knuckles on a door blistered and greasy with the salt sweat of the sea. There was a light behind drawn blinds, and a sound of voices. The voices stopped, sliced cleanly by the knocking.

Someone walked heavily through the silence. The door opened, spilling yellow light around the shadow of a thick-set, powerful man in shirtsleeves. He let his breath out in what was not quite a laugh and relaxed against the jamb.

"So you did turn up," he said. He was well into middle age, hard-eyed, obstinate. His name was Max Gandara, Police Captain, Surfside Division, L.A.P.D. He studied the man on the porch with slow, deliberate insolence.

The man on the porch seemed not to mind. He seemed not to be in any hurry. His dark eyes looked, unmoved, at the big man, at him and through him. His face was a mask of thin sinewy flesh, laid close over ruthless bone, expressionless. And yet, in spite of his face and his lean erect body, there was a shadow on him. He was like a man who has drawn away, beyond the edge of life.

"Did you think I wouldn't come?" he asked.

Gandara shrugged. "They're all here. Come on in and get it over with."

Channing nodded and stepped inside. He removed his hat. His dark hair was shot with gray. He turned to lay the hat on a table and the movement brought into focus a scar that ran up from his shirt collar on the right side of his neck, back of the ear. Then he followed Gandara into the living room.

There were three people there, and the silence. Three people watching the door. A red-haired, green-eyed girl with a smoldering, angry glow deep inside her. A red-haired, green-eyed boy with a sullen, guarded face. And a man, a neat, lean, swarthy man with aggressive features that seemed always to be on the edge of laughter and eyes that kept all their emotion on the surface.

"Folks," said Gandara, "this is Paul Channing." He indicated them, in order: "Marge Krist, Rudy Krist, Jack Flavin."

Hate crawled into the green eyes of Rudy Krist, brilliant and poisonous, fixed on Channing.

Out in the kitchen a woman screamed. The swing door burst open. A chubby pink man came through in a tottering rush, followed by a large, bleached blonde with an ice pick. Her dress was torn slightly at the shoulder and her mouth was smeared. Her incongruously black eyes were owlish and mad.

Gandara yelled. The sound of his voice got through to the blonde. She slowed down and said sulkily, to no one in particular, "He better keep his fat paws off or I'll fix him." She went back to the kitchen.

The chubby pink man staggered to a halt, swayed, caught hold of Channing's arm and looked up at him, smiling foolishly. The smile faded, leaving his mouth open like a baby's. His eyes, magnified behind rimless lenses, widened and fixed.

"Chan," he said. "My God. Chan."

He sat down on the floor and began to cry, the tears running quietly down his cheeks.

"Hello, Budge." Channing stooped and touched his shoulder.

"Take it easy." Gandara pulled Channing's arms. "Let the little lush alone. Him and—that." He made a jerky gesture at the girl, flung himself heavily into a chair and glowered at Channing. "All right, we're all curious—tell us why we're here."

Channing sat down. He seemed in no hurry to begin. A thin film of sweat made the tight pattern of muscles very plain under his skin.

"We're here to talk about a lot of things," he said. "Who murdered Henry?" No one seemed particularly moved except Budge Hanna, who stopped crying and stared at Channing. Rudy Krist made a small derisive noise in his throat. Gandara laughed.

"That ain't such a bombshell, Chan. I guess we all had an idea of what you was driving at, from the letters you wrote us. What we want to know is what makes you think you got a right to holler murder."

Channing drew a thick envelope from his inside pocket, laying it on his knee to conceal the fact that his hands trembled. He said, not looking at anybody, "I haven't seen my brother for several years, but we've been in fairly close touch through letters. I've kept most of his. Hank was good at writing letters, good at saying things. He's had a lot to say since he was transferred to Surfside—and not one word of it points to suicide."

Max Gandara's face had grown rocky. "Oh, he had a lot to say, did he?"

Channing nodded. Marge Krist was leaning forward, watching him intently. Jack Flavin's terrier face was interested, but unreadable. He had been smoking nervously when Channing entered. The nervousness seemed to be habitual, part of his wiry personality. Now he lighted another cigarette, his hands moving with a swiftness that seemed jerky but was not. The match flared and spat. Paul Channing started involuntarily. The flame seemed to have a terrible fascination for him. He dropped his gaze. Beads of sweat came out along his hairline. Once again, harshly, Gandara laughed.

"Go on," he said. "Go on."

"Hank told me about that brush with the *pachucos*. They didn't hurt him much. They sure as hell didn't break him."

"Flavin, here, says different. Rudy says different. Marge says different."

"That's why I wanted to talk to them—and you, Max. Hank

mentioned you all in his letters." He was talking to the whole room now. "Max I knew from the old days. You, Miss Krist, I know because Hank went with you—not seriously, I guess, but you liked each other. He liked your brother, too."

The kid stared at him, his eyes blank and bright. Channing said, "Hank talked a lot about you, Rudy. He said you were a smart kid, a good kid but headed for trouble. He said some ways you were so smart you were downright stupid."

Rudy and Marge both started to speak, but Channing was going on. "I guess he was right, Rudy. You've got it on you already—a sort of grayness that comes from prison walls, or the shadow of them. You've got that look on your face, like a closed door."

Rudy got halfway to his feet, looking nasty. Flavin said quietly, "Shut up." Rudy sat down again. Flavin seemed relaxed. His brown eyes held only a hard glitter from the light. "Hank seems to have been a great talker. What did he say about me?"

"He said you smell of stripes."

Flavin laid his cigarette carefully in a tray. He got up, very light and easy. He went over to Channing and took a handful of his shirt, drawing him up slightly, and said with gentle kindness, "I don't think I like that remark."

Marge Krist cried, "Stop it! Jack, don't you dare start trouble."

"Maybe you didn't understand what he meant, Marge." Flavin still did not sound angry. "He's accusing me of having a record, a prison record. He didn't pick a very nice way of saying it."

"Take it easy, Jack," Gandara said. "Don't you get what he's doing? He's trying to wangle himself a little publicity and stir up a little trouble, so that maybe the public will think maybe Hank didn't do the Dutch after all." He pointed at Budge Hanna. "Even the press is here." He rose and took hold of Flavin's shoulder. "He's just making a noise with his mouth, because a long time ago people used to listen when he did it and he hasn't forgotten how good that felt."

Flavin shrugged and returned to his chair. Gandara lighted a cigarette, holding the match deliberately close to Channing's sweaty face. "Listen, Chan. Jack Flavin is a good citizen of Surfside. He owns a store, legitimate, and Rudy works for him, legitimate. I don't like people coming into my town and making cracks about the citizens. If they step out of line, I'll take care of them. If they don't, I'll see they're let alone."

He sat down again, comfortably. "All right, Chan. Let's get this all out of your system. What did little brother have to say about me?"

Channing's dark eyes flickered with what might have been malice. "What everybody's always said about you, Max. That you were too goddam dumb even to be crooked."

Gandara turned purple. He moved and Jack Flavin laughed. "No fair, Max. You wouldn't let me."

Budge Hanna giggled with startling shrillness. The blonde had come in and sat down beside him. Her eyes were half closed but she seemed somehow less drunk than she had been. Gandara settled back. He said ominously, "Go on."

"All right. Hank said that Surfside was a dirty town, dirty from the gutters up. He said any man with the brains of a sick flea would know that most of the liquor places were run illegally, and most of the hotels, too, and that two-thirds of the police force was paid to have bad eyesight. He said it wasn't any use trying to do a good job as a decent cop. He said every report he turned in was thrown away for lack of evidence, and he was sick of it."

Marge Krist said, "Then maybe that's what he was worried about."

"He wasn't afraid," said Channing. "All his letters were angry, and an angry man doesn't commit suicide."

Budge Hanna said shrilly, "Look out."

Max Gandara was on his feet. He was standing over Channing. His lips had a white line around them.

"Listen," he said. "I been pretty patient with you. Now I'll tell you something. Your brother committed suicide. All these three people testified at the inquest. You can read the transcript. They all said Hank was worried; he wasn't happy about things. There was no sign of violence on Hank, or the pier."

"How could there be?" said Channing. "Hard asphalt paving doesn't show much. And Hank's body wouldn't show much, either."

"Shut up. I'm telling you. There's no evidence of murder, no reason to think it's murder. Hank was like you, Channing. He couldn't take punishment. He got chicken walking a dark beat down here, and he jumped, and that's all."

Channing said slowly, "Only two kinds of people come to Surfside—the ones that are starting at the bottom, going up, and the ones that are finished, coming down. It's either a beginning or an end, and I guess we all know where we stand on that scale."

He got up, tossing the packet of letters into Budge Hanna's lap. "Those are photostats. The originals are already with police headquarters in L.A. I don't think you have to worry much, Max. There's nothing definite in them. Just a green young harness cop griping at the system, making a few personal remarks. He hasn't even accused you of being dishonest, Max. Only dumb—and the powers-that-be already know that. That's why you're here in Surfside, waiting for the age of retirement."

Gandara struck him in the mouth. Channing took three steps backward, caught himself, swayed, and was steady again. Blood ran from the corner of his mouth down his chin. Marge Krist was on her feet, her eyes blazing, but something about Channing kept her from speaking. He seemed not to care about the blood, about Gandara, or about anything but what he was saying.

"You used to be a good reporter, Budge, before you drank yourself onto the scrapheap. I thought maybe you'd like to be in at the beginning on this story. Because there's going to be a story, if it's only the story of my death.

"I knew Hank. There was no yellow in him. Whether there's yellow in me or not, doesn't matter. Hank didn't jump off that pier. Somebody threw him off, and I'm going to find out who, and why. I used to be a pretty good dick once. I've got a reason now for remembering all I learned."

Max Gandara said, "Oh, God," in a disgusted voice. "Take that somewhere else, Chan. It smells." He pushed him roughly toward the door, and Rudy Krist laughed.

"Yellow," he said. "Yellower than four Japs. Both of 'em, all talk and no guts. Get him out, Max. He stinks up the room."

Flavin said, "Shut up, Rudy." He grinned at Marge. "You're getting your sister sore."

"You bet I'm sore!" she flared. "I think Mr. Channing is right. I knew Hank pretty well, and I think you ought to be ashamed to push him around like this."

Flavin said, "Who? Hank or Mr. Channing?"

Marge snapped, "Oh, go to hell." She turned and went out. Gandara shoved Channing into the hall after her. "You know where the door is, Chan. Stay away from me, and if I was you I'd stay away from Surfside." He turned around, reached down and got a handful of Budge Hanna's coat collar and slung him out bodily. "You, too, rumdum. *And* you." He made a grab for the blonde, but she was already out. He followed the four of them down the hall and closed the door hard behind them.

Paul Channing said, "Miss Krist—and you too, Budge." The wind felt ice cold on his skin. His shirt stuck to his back. It turned clammy and he began to shiver. "I want to talk to you."

The blonde said, "Is this private?"

"I don't think so. Maybe you can help." Channing walked slowly toward the beach front and the boardwalk. "Miss Krist, if you didn't think Hank committed suicide, why did you testify as you did at the inquest?"

"Because I didn't know." She sounded rather angry, with him and possibly herself. "They asked me how he acted, and I had to say he'd been worried and depressed, because he had been. I told them I didn't think he was the type for suicide, but they didn't care."

"Did Hank ever hint that he knew something—anything that might have been dangerous to him?" Channing's eyes were alert, watchful in the darkness.

"No. Hank pounded a beat. He wasn't a detective."

"He was pretty friendly with your brother, wasn't he?"

"I thought for a while it might bring Rudy back to his senses.

He took a liking to Hank, they weren't so far apart in years, and Hank was doing him good. Now, of course—"

"What's wrong with Rudy? What's he doing?"

"That's just it, I don't know. He's 4-F in the draft, and that hurts him, and he's always been restless, never could hold a job. Then he met Jack Flavin, and since then he's been working steady, but he—he's changed. I can't put my finger on it, I don't know of anything wrong he's done, but he's hardened and drawn into himself, as though he had secrets and didn't trust anybody. You saw how he acted. He's turned mean. I've done my best to bring him up right."

Channing said, "Kids go that way sometimes. Know anything about him, Budge?"

The reporter said, "Nuh-uh. He's never been picked up for anything, and as far as anybody knows even Flavin is straight. He owns a haberdashery and pays his taxes."

"Well," said Channing, "I guess that's all for now."

"No." Marge Krist stopped and faced him. He could see her eyes in the pale reflection of the water, dark and intense. The wind blew her hair, pressed her light coat against the long lifting planes of her body. "I want to warn you. Maybe you're a brilliant, nervy man and you know what you're doing, and if you do it's all right. But if you really are what you acted like in there, you'd better go home and forget about it. Surfside is a bad town. You can't insult people and get away with it." She paused. "For Hank's sake, I hope you know what you're doing. I'm in the phone book if you want me. Good night."

"Good night." Channing watched her go. She had a lovely way of moving. Absently, he began to wipe the blood off his face. His lip had begun to swell.

Budge Hanna said, "Chan."

"Yeah."

"I want to say thanks, and I'm with you. I'll give you the biggest break I can in the paper."

"We used to work pretty well together, before I got mine and you found yours, in a bottle."

"Yeah. And now I'm in Surfside with the rest of the scrap. If this turns out a big enough story, I might—oh, well." He paused, rubbing a pudgy cheek with his forefinger.

Channing said, "Go ahead, Budge. Say it."

"All right. Every crook in the western states knows that the Padway mob took you to the wall. They know what was done to you, with fire. They know you broke. The minute they find out you're back, even unofficially, you know what'll happen. You sent up a lot of guys in your time. You sent a lot of 'em down, too—down to the morgue. You were a tough dick, Chan, and a square one, and you know how they love you."

"I guess I know all that, Budge."

"Chan—" he looked up, squinting earnestly through the gloom, his spectacles shining—"how is it? I mean, can you—"

Channing put a hand on his shoulder, pushing him around slightly. "You watch your step, kid, and try to stay sober. I don't know what I may be getting into. If you want out—"

"Hell, no. Just—well, good luck, Chan."

"Thanks."

The blonde said, "Ain't you going to ask me something?"

"Sure," said Channing. "What do you know?"

"I know who killed your brother."

2
Badge of Carnage

The blood swelled and thickened in Channing's veins. It made a hard pain over his eyes and pressed against the stiff scar tissue on his neck. No one spoke. No one moved.

The wind blew sand in riffles across the empty beach. The waves rushed and broke their backs in thunder and slipped out again, sighing. Up ahead Sunset Pier thrust its black bulk against the night. Beyond it was the huge amusement pier. Here and there a single light was burning, swaying with the wind, and the reaching skeletons of the roller coaster and the giant slide were desolate in the pre-season quiet. Vacant lots and a single unlighted house were as deserted as the moon.

Paul Channing looked at the woman with eyes as dark and lonely as the night. "We're not playing a game," he said. "This is murder."

The blonde's teeth glittered white between moist lips.

Budge Hanna whispered, "She's crazy. She couldn't know."

"Oh, couldn't I!" The blonde's whisper was throatily venomous. "Young Channing was thrown off the pier about midnight, wasn't he? Okay. Well, you stood me up on a date that evening, remember, Budgie dear? And my room is on the same floor as yours, remember? And I can hear every pair of hoofs clumping up and down those damn stairs right outside, remember?"

"Listen," Budge said, "I told you I got stewed and—"

"And got in a fight. I know. Sure, you told me. But how can you prove it? I heard your fairy footsteps. They didn't sound very stewed to me. So I looked out, and you were hitting it for your room like your pants were on fire. Your shirt was torn, and so was your coat, and you didn't look so good other ways. I could hear you heaving clear out in the hall. And it was just nineteen minutes after twelve."

Budge Hanna's voice had risen to a squeak. "Damn you, Millie, I—Chan, she's crazy! She's just trying—"

"Sure," said Millie. She thrust her face close to his. "I been shoved around enough. I been called enough funny names. I been stood up enough times. I loaned you enough money I'll never get back. And I ain't so dumb I don't know you got dirt on your hands from somewhere. Me, I'm quitting you right now and—"

"Shut up. Shut up!"

"And I got a few things to say that'll interest some people!" Millie was screeching now. "You killed that Channing kid, or you know who did!"

Budge Hanna slapped her hard across the mouth.

Millie reeled back. Then she screamed like a cat. Her hands flashed up, curved and wicked, long red nails gleaming. She went for Budge Hanna.

Channing stepped between them. He was instantly involved

in a whirlwind of angry flailing hands. While he was trying to quiet them the men came up behind him.

There were four of them. They had come quietly from the shadows beside the vacant house. They worked quickly, with deadly efficiency. Channing got his hand inside his coat, and after that he didn't know anything for a long time.

Things came back to Channing in disconnected pieces. His head hurt. He was in something that moved. He was hot. He was covered with something, lying flat on his back, and he could hardly breathe. There was another person jammed against him. There were somebody's feet on his chest, and somebody else's feet on his thighs. Presently he found that his mouth was covered with adhesive, that his eyes were taped shut, and that his hands and feet were bound, probably also with tape. The moving thing was an automobile, taking its time.

The stale, stifling air under the blanket covering him was heavy with the scent of powder and cheap perfume. He guessed that the woman was Millie. From time to time she stirred and whimpered.

A man's voice said, "Here is okay."

The car stopped. Doors were opened. The blanket was pulled away. Cold salt air rushed over Channing, mixed with the heavy sulphurous reek of sewage. He knew they were somewhere on the road above Hyperion, where there was nothing but miles of empty dunes.

Hands grabbed him, hauled him bodily out of the car. Somebody said, "Got the Thompson ready?"

"Yeah." The speaker laughed gleefully, like a child with a bass voice. "Just like old times, ain't it? Good ole Dolly. She ain't had a chansta sing in a long time. Come on, honey. Loosen up the pipes."

A rattling staccato burst out, and was silent.

"For cripesake, Joe! That stuff ain't so plentiful. Doncha know there's a war on? We gotta conserve. C'mon, help me with this guy." He kicked Channing. "On your feet, you."

He was hauled erect and leaned against a post. Joe said, "What about the dame?"

The other man laughed. "Her turn comes later. Much later."

A fourth voice, one that had not spoken before, said, "Okay, boys. Get away from him now." It was a slow, inflectionless and yet strangely forceful voice, with a hint of a lisp. The lisp was not in the least effeminate or funny. It had the effect of a knife blade whetted on oilstone. The man who owned it put his hands on Channing's shoulders.

"You know me," he said.

Channing nodded. The uncovered parts of his face were greasy with sweat. It had soaked loose the corners of the adhesive. The man said, "You knew I'd catch up with you some day."

The man struck him, deliberately and with force, twice across the face with his open palms.

"I'm sorry you lost your guts, Channing. This makes me feel like I'm shooting a kitten. Why didn't you do the Dutch years ago, like your brother?"

Channing brought his bound fists up, slammed them into the man's face, striking at the sound of his voice. The man grunted and fell, making a heavy soft thump in the sand. Somebody yelled, "Hey!" and the man with the quiet lisping voice said, "Shut up. Let him alone."

Channing heard him scramble up and the voice came near again. "Do that again."

Channing did.

The man avoided his blow this time. He laughed softly. "So you still have insides, Chan. That makes it better. Much better."

Joe said, "Look, somebody may come along—"

"Shut up." The man brought something from his pocket, held his hand close to Channing's ear, and shook it. "You know what that is?"

Channing stiffened. He nodded.

There was a light thin rattling sound, and then a scratching of emery and the quick spitting of a match-head rubbed to flame.

The man said softly, "How are your guts now?"

The little sharp tongue of heat touched Channing's chin. He drew his head back. His mouth worked under the adhesive. Cords stood out in his throat. The flame followed. Channing began to shake. His knees gave. He braced them, braced his body against the post. Sweat ran down his face and the scar on his neck turned dark and livid.

The man laughed. He threw the match down and stepped away. He said, "Okay, Joe."

Somebody said, sharply, "There's a car coming. Two cars."

The man swore. "Bunch of sailors up from Long Beach. Okay, we'll get out of here. Back in the car, Joe. Can't use the chopper, they'd hear it." Joe cursed unhappily. Feet scruffed hurriedly in the sand. Leather squeaked, the small familiar sound of metal clearing a shoulder clip. The safety snicked open.

The man said, "So long, Channing."

Channing was already falling sideways when the shot came. There was a second one close behind it. Channing dropped into the ditch and lay perfectly still, hidden from the road. The car roared off. Presently the two other cars shot by, loaded with sailors. They were singing and shouting and not worrying about what somebody might have left at the side of the road.

Sometime later Channing began to move, at first in uncoordinated jerks and then with reasonable steadiness. He was conscious that he had been hit in two places. The right side of his head was stiff and numb clear down to his neck. Somebody had shoved a red-hot spike through the flesh over his heart-ribs and forgotten to take it out. He could feel blood oozing, sticky with sand.

He rolled over slowly and started to peel the adhesive from his face, fumbling awkwardly with his bound hands. When that was done he used his teeth on his wrist bonds. It took a long time. After that the ankles were easy.

It was no use trying to see how much damage had been done. He decided it couldn't be as bad as it felt. He smiled, a crooked and humorless grimace, and swore and laughed shortly. He wad-ded the clean handkerchief from his hip pocket into the gash under his arm and tightened the holster strap to hold it there. The display handkerchief in his breast pocket went around his head. He found that after he got started he could walk quite well. His gun had not been removed. Channing laughed again, quietly. He did not touch nor in any way notice the burn on his chin.

It took him nearly three hours to get back to Surfside, crouching in the ditch twice to let cars go by.

He passed Gandara's street, and the one beyond where Marge and Rudy Krist lived. He came to the ocean front and the dark loom of the pier and the vacant house from behind which the men had come. He found Budge Hanna doubled up under a clump of Monterey cypress. The cold spring wind blew sand into Hanna's wide-open eyes, but he didn't seem to mind it. He had bled from the nose and ears—not much.

Channing went through Hanna's pockets, examining things swiftly by the light of a tiny pocket flash shielded in his hand. There was just the usual clutter of articles. Channing took the key ring. Then, tucked into the watch pocket, he found a receipt from Flavin's Men's Shop for three pairs of socks. The date was April 22. Channing frowned. April 21 was the day on which Hank Channing's death had been declared a suicide. April 21 was a Saturday.

Channing rose slowly and walked on down the front to Surfside Avenue. It was hours past midnight. The bars were closed. The only lights on the street were those of the police station and the lobby of the Surfside Hotel, which was locked and deserted. Channing let himself in with Budge Hanna's key and walked up dirty marble steps to the second floor and found Budge Hanna's number. He leaned against the jamb, his knees sagging, managed to force the key around and get inside. He switched on the lights, locked the door again, and braced his back against it. The first thing he saw was a bottle on the bedside table.

He drank straight from the neck. It was scotch, good scotch. In a few minutes he felt much better. He stared at the label, turning the bottle around in his hands, frowning at it. Then, very quietly, he began to search the room.

He found nothing until, in the bottom drawer of the dresser, he discovered a brand new shirt wrapped in cheap green paper. The receipt was from Flavin's Men's Shop. Channing looked at the date. It was for the day which had just begun, Monday.

Channing studied the shirt, poking his fingers into the folds. Between the tail and the cardboard he found an envelope. It was unaddressed, unsealed, and contained six one hundred–dollar bills.

Channing's mouth twisted. He replaced the money and the shirt and sat down on the bed. He scowled at the wall, not seeing it, and drank some more of Budge Hanna's scotch. He thought Budge wouldn't mind. It would take more even than good scotch to warm him now.

A picture on the wall impressed itself gradually upon Channing's mind.

He looked at it more closely. It was a professional photograph of a beautiful woman in a white evening gown. She had a magnificent figure and a strong, provocative, heart-shaped face. Her gown and hairdress were of the late twenties. The picture was autographed in faded ink, *Lots of Luck, Skinny, from your pal Dorothy Balf.*

Skinny had been crossed out and *Budge* written above.

Channing took the frame down and slid the picture out. It had been wiped off, but both frame and picture showed the ravages of time, dust and stains and faded places, as though they had hung a long time with only each other for company. On the back of the picture was stamped:

SKINNY CRAIL'S
Surfside at Culver
"Between the Devil and the Deep"

Memories came back to Channing. Skinny Crail, that badluck boy of Hollywood, plunging his last dime on a nightclub that flurried into success and then faded gradually to a pathetically mediocre doom, a white elephant rotting hugely in the empty flats between Culver City and the beach. Dorothy Balf had been the leading feminine star of that day, and Budge Hanna's idol. Channing glanced again at the scrawled *Budge*. He sighed and replaced the picture carefully. Then he turned out the lights and sat a long while in the dark, thinking.

Presently he sighed again and ran his hand over his face, wincing. He rose and went out, locking the door carefully behind him. He moved slowly, his limp accentuated by weakness and a slight unsteadiness from the scotch. His expression was that of a man who hopes for nothing and is therefore immune to blows.

There was a phone booth in the lobby. Channing called Max Gandara. He talked for a long time. When he came out his face was chalk-colored and damp, utterly without expression. He left the hotel and walked slowly down the beach.

The shapeless, colorless little house was dark and silent, with two empty lots to seaward and a cheap brick apartment house on its right. No lights showed anywhere. Channing set his finger on the rusted bell.

He could hear it buzzing somewhere inside. After a long time lights went on behind heavy crash draperies, drawn close. Channing turned suddenly sick. Sweat came out on his wrists and his ears rang. Through the ringing he heard Marge Krist's clear voice asking who was there.

He told her. "I'm hurt," he said. "Let me in."

The door opened. Channing walked through it. He seemed to be walking through dark water that swirled around him, very cold, very heavy. He decided not to fight it.

When he opened his eyes again he was stretched out on a studio couch. Apparently he had been out only a moment or two. Marge and Rudy Krist were arguing fiercely.

"I tell you he's got to have a doctor!"

"All right, tell him to go get one. You don't want to get in trouble."

"Trouble? Why would I get in trouble?"

"The guy's been shot. That means cops. They'll be trampling all over, asking you why he should have come here. How do you know what the little rat's been doing? If he's square, why didn't he go to the cops himself? Maybe it's a frame, or maybe he shot himself."

"Maybe," said Marge slowly, "you're afraid to be questioned."

Rudy swore. He looked almost as white and hollow as Channing felt. Channing laughed. It was not a pleasant sound.

He said, "Sure he's scared. Start an investigation now and that messes up everything for tonight."

Marge and Rudy both started at the sound of his voice. Rudy's face went hard and blank as a pine slab. He walked over toward the couch.

"What does that crack mean?"

"It means you better call Flavin quick and tell him to get his new shirt out of Budge Hanna's room. Budge Hanna won't be needing it now, and the cops are going to be very interested in the accessories."

Rudy's lips had a curious stiffness. "What's wrong with Hanna?"

"Nothing much. Only one of Dave's boys hit him a little too hard. He's dead."

"Dead?" Rudy shaped the word carefully and studied it as though he had never heard it before. Then he said, "Who's Dave? What are you talking about?"

Channing studied him. "Flavin's still keeping you in the nursery, is he?"

"That kind of talk don't go with me, Channing."

"That's tough, because it'll go with the cops. You'll sound kind of silly, won't you, bleating how you didn't know what was going on because Papa never told you."

Rudy moved toward Channing. Marge yelled and caught him. Channing grinned and drew his gun. His head was propped fairly high on pillows, so he could see what he was doing without making any disastrous attempt to sit up.

"Fine hood you are, Rudy. Didn't even frisk me. Listen, punk. Budge Hanna's dead, murdered. His Millie is dead, too, by now. I'm supposed to be dead, in a ditch above Hyperion, but Dave

Padway always was a lousy shot. Where do you think you come in on this?"

Rudy's skin had a sickly greenish tinge, but his jaw was hard. "You're a liar, Channing. I never heard of Dave Padway. I don't know anything about Budge Hanna or that dame. I don't know anything about you. Now get the hell out."

"You make a good Charlie McCarthy, Rudy. Maybe Flavin will hold you on his knee in the death-chair at San Quentin."

Marge stopped Rudy again. She said quietly, "What happened, Mr. Channing?"

Channing told her, keeping his eyes on Rudy. "Flavin's heading a racket," he said finally. "His store is just a front, useful for background and a way to make pay-offs and pass on information. He doesn't keep the store open on Sunday, does he, Rudy?"

Rudy didn't answer. Marge said, "No."

"Okay. Budge Hanna worked for Flavin. I'll make a guess. I'll say Flavin is engineering liquor robberies, hijacking, and so forth. Budge Hanna was a well-known lush. He could go into any bar and make a deal for bootleg whiskey, and nobody would suspect him. Trouble with Budge was, he couldn't handle his women. Millie got sore, and suspicious, and began to yell out loud. I guess Dave Padway's boys overheard her. Dave never did trust women and drunks."

Channing stared narrow-eyed at Rudy. His blood-caked face was twisted into a cruel grin. "Dave never liked punks, either. There's going to be trouble between Dave and your pal Flavin, and I don't see where you're going to come in, except maybe on a morgue slab, like the others. Like Hank."

"Oh, cripes," said Rudy, "we're back to Hank again."

"Yeah. Always back to Hank. You know what happened, Rudy. You kind of liked Hank. You're a smart kid, Rudy. You've probably got a better brain than Flavin, and if you're going to be a successful crook these days you need brains. So Flavin pushed Hank off the pier and called it suicide, so you'd think he was yellow."

Rudy laughed. "That's good. That's very good. Marge was out with Jack Flavin that night." His green eyes were dangerous.

Marge nodded, dropping her gaze. "I was."

Channing shrugged. "So what? He hired it done. Just like he hired this tonight. Only Dave Padway isn't a boy you can hire for long. He used to be big time, and ten years in clink won't slow him up too much. You better call Flavin, Rudy. They're liable to find Budge Hanna any time and start searching his room." He laughed. "Flavin wasn't so smart to pay off on Saturday, too late for the banks."

Marge said, "Why haven't you called the police?"

"With what I have to tell them I'd only scare off the birds. Let 'em find out for themselves."

She looked at him with level, calculating eyes. "Then you're planning to do it all by yourself?"

"I've got the whip hand right now. Only you two know I'm alive. But I know about Budge Hanna's shirt, and the cops will too, pretty soon. Somebody's got to get busy, and the minute he does I'll know for sure who's who in this little tinpot crime combine."

Marge rose. "That's ridiculous. You're in no condition to handle anyone. And even if you were—" She left that hanging and crossed to the telephone.

Channing said, "Even if I were, I'm still yellow, is that it? Sure. Stand still, Rudy. I'm not too yellow or too weak to shoot your ankle off." His face was gray, gaunt, infinitely tired. He touched the burn on his chin. His cheek muscles tightened.

He lay still and listened to Marge Krist talking to Max Gandara.

When she was through she went out into the kitchen. Rudy sat down, glowering sullenly at Channing. He began to tremble, a shallow nervous vibration. Channing laughed.

"How do you like crime now, kiddie? Fun, isn't it?"

Rudy gave him a lurid and prophetic direction.

Marge came back with hot water and a clean cloth. She wiped Channing's face, not touching the handkerchief. The wound had stopped bleeding, but the gash in his side was still oozing. The pad had slipped. Marge took his coat off, waiting while he changed hands with the gun, and then his shoulder clip and shirt. When she saw his body she let the shirt drop and put her hand to her mouth. Channing, sitting up now on the couch, glanced from her to Rudy's slack pale face, and said quietly, "You see why I don't like fire."

Marge was working gently on his side when the bell rang. "That's the police," she said, and went to the front door. Channing held Rudy with the gun.

He heard nothing behind him, but quite suddenly there was a cold object pressing the back of his neck and a voice said quietly, "Drop it, bud."

It was Joe's voice. He had come in through the kitchen. Channing dropped his gun. The men coming in the front door were not policemen. They were Dave Padway and Jack Flavin.

Flavin closed the door and locked it. Channing nodded, smiling faintly. Dave Padway nodded back. He was a tall, shambling man with white eyes and a long face, like a pinto horse.

"I see I'm still a bum shot," he said.

"Ten years in the can doesn't help your eye, Dave." Channing seemed relaxed and unemotional. "Well, now we're all here we can talk. We can talk about murder."

Marge and Ruby were both staring at Padway. Flavin grinned. "My new business partner, Dave Padway. Dave, meet Marge Krist and Rudy."

Padway glanced at them briefly. His pale eyes were empty of expression. He said, in his soft way, "It's Channing that interests me right now. How much has he told, and who has he told it to?"

Channing laughed, with insolent mockery.

"Fine time to worry about that," Flavin grunted. "Who was it messed up the kill in the first place?"

Padway's eyelids drooped. "Everyone makes mistakes, Jack," he said mildly. Flavin struck a match. The flame trembled slightly.

Rudy said, "Jack. Listen, Jack, this guy says Budge Hanna and his girl were killed. Did you—"

"No. That was Dave's idea."

Padway said, "Any objections to it?"

"Hanna was a good man. He was my contact with all the bars."

"He was a bum. Him and that floozie between them were laying the whole thing in Channing's lap. I heard 'em."

"Okay, okay! I'm just sorry, that's all."

Rudy said, "Jack, honest to God, I don't want to be messed up in killing. I don't mind slugging a watchman, that's okay, and if you had to shoot it out with the cops, well, that's okay too, I guess. But murder, Jack!" He glanced at Channing's scarred body. "Murder, and things like that—" He shook.

Padway muttered, "My God, he's still in diapers."

"Take it easy, kid," Flavin said. "You're in big time now. It's worth getting sick at your stomach a couple times." He looked at Channing, grinning his hard white grin. "You were right when you said Surfside was either an end or a beginning. Dave and I both needed a place to begin again. Start small and grow, like any other business."

Channing nodded. He looked at Rudy. "Hank told you it would be like this, didn't he? You believe him now?"

Rudy repeated his suggestion. His skin was greenish. He sat down and lighted a cigarette. Marge leaned against the wall, watching with bright, narrow-lidded eyes. She was pale. She had said nothing.

Channing said, "Flavin, you were out with Marge the night Hank was killed."

"So what?"

"Did you leave her at all?"

"A couple of times. Not long enough to get out on the pier to kill your brother."

Marge said quietly, "He's right, Mr. Channing."

Channing said, "Where did you go?"

"Ship Cafe, a bunch of bars, dancing. So what?" Flavin gestured impatiently.

Channing said, "How about you, Dave? Did you kill Hank to pay for your brother, and then wait for me to come?"

"If I had," Padway said, "I'd have told you. I'd have made sure you'd come." He stepped closer, looking down. "You don't seem very surprised to see us."

"I'm not surprised at anything anymore."

"Yeah." Padway's gun came smoothly into his hand. "At this range I ought to be able to hit you, Chan." Marge Krist caught her breath sharply. Padway said, "No, not here, unless he makes me. Go ahead, Joe."

Joe got busy with the adhesive tape again. This time he did a better job. They wrapped his trussed body in a blanket. Joe picked up the feet. Flavin motioned Rudy to take hold. Rudy hesitated. Padway flicked the muzzle of his gun. Rudy picked up Channing's shoulders. They turned out the lights and carried Channing out to a waiting car. Marge and Rudy Krist walked ahead of Padway, who had forgotten to put away his gun.

3
"I Feel Bad Killin' You . . ."

The room was enormous in the flashlight beams. There were still recognizable signs of its former occupation—dust-blackened, tawdry bunting dangling ragged from the ceiling, a floor worn by the scraping of many feet, a few forgotten tables and chairs, the curling fly-specked photographs of bygone celebrities autographed to *Dear Skinny*, an empty, dusty band platform.

One of Padway's men lighted a coal-oil lamp. The boarded windows were carefully reinforced with tarpaper. In one end of the ballroom were stacks of liquor cases built into a huge square mountain. Doors opened into other rooms, black and disused. The place was utterly silent, odorous with the dust and rot of years.

Padway said, "Put him over there." He indicated a camp cot beside a table and a group of chairs. The men carrying Channing dropped him there. The rest straggled in and sat down, lighting cigarettes. Padway said, "Joe, take the Thompson and go upstairs. Yell if anybody looks this way."

Jack Flavin swore briefly. "I told you we weren't tailed, Dave. Cripes, we've driven all over this goddam town to make sure. Can't you relax?"

"Sure, when I'm ready to. You may have hair on your chest, Jack, but it's no bulletproof vest." He went over to the cot and pulled the blanket off Channing. Channing looked up at him, his eyes sunk deep under hooded lids. He was naked to the waist. Padway inspected the two gashes.

"I didn't miss you by much, Chan," he said slowly.

"Enough."

"Yeah." Padway pulled a cigarette slowly out of the pack. "Who did you talk to, Chan, besides Marge Krist? What did you say?"

Channing bared his teeth. It might have been meant for a smile. It was undoubtedly malicious.

Padway put the cigarette in his mouth and got a match out. It was a large kitchen match with a blue head. "You got me puzzled, Chan. You sure have. And it worries me. I can smell copper, but I can't see any. I don't like that, Channing."

"That's tough," Channing said.

"Yeah. It may be." Padway struck the match.

Rudy Krist rose abruptly and went off into the shadows. No one else moved. Marge Krist was hunched up on a blanket near Flavin. Her eyes were brilliant green under her tumbled red hair.

Dave Padway held the match low over Channing's eyes. There was no draft, no tremor in his hand. The flame was a perfect triangle, gold and blue. Padway said somberly, "I don't trust you, Chan. You were a good cop. You were good enough to take me once, and you were good enough to take my brother, and he was a better man than me. I don't trust this setup, Chan. I don't trust you."

Flavin said impatiently, "Why didn't you for godsake kill him the first time? You're to blame for this mess, Dave. If you hadn't loused it up—okay, okay! The guy's crazy afraid of fire. Look at him now. Put it to him, Dave. He'll talk."

"Will he?" said Padway. "Will he?" He lowered the match. Channing screamed. Padway lighted his cigarette and blew out the match. "Will you talk, Chan?"

Channing said hoarsely, "Offer me the right coin, Dave. Give me the man who killed my brother, and I'll tell you where you stand."

Padway stared at him with blank light eyes, and then he began to laugh, quietly, with a terrible humor.

"Tie him down, Mack," he said, "and bring the matches over here."

The room was quiet, except for Channing's breathing. Rudy Krist sat apart from the others, smoking steadily, his hands never still. The three gunsels bent with scowling concentration over a game of blackjack. Marge Krist had not moved since she sat down. Perhaps twenty minutes had passed. Channing's corded body was spotted with small vicious marks.

Dave Padway dropped the empty matchbox. He sighed and leaned over, slapping Channing lightly on the cheek. Channing opened his eyes.

"You going to talk, Chan?"

Channing's head moved, not much, from right to left.

Jack Flavin swore. "Dave, the guy's crazy afraid of fire. If he'd had anything to tell he'd have told it." His shirt was open, the space around his feet littered with cigarette ends. His harsh terrier face had no laughter in it now. He watched Padway obliquely, his lids hooded.

"Maybe," said Padway. "Maybe not. We got a big deal on tonight, Jack. It's our first step toward the top. Channing read your receipt, remember. He knows about that. He knows a lot of people out here. Maybe he has a deal on, and maybe it isn't with the cops. Maybe it isn't supposed to break until tonight. Maybe it'll break us when it does."

Channing laughed, a dry husky mockery.

Flavin got up, scraping his chair angrily. "Listen, Dave, you getting chicken or something? Looks to me like you've got a fixation on this bird."

"Look to me, Jack, like nobody ever taught you manners."

The room became perfectly still. The men at the table put their cards down slowly, like men playing cards in a dream. Marge Krist rose silently and moved toward the cot.

Channing whispered, "Take it easy, boys. There's no percentage in a shroud." He watched them, his eyes holding a deep, cruel glint. It was something new, something born within the last quarter of an hour. It changed, subtly, his whole face, the lines of it, the shape of it. "You've got a business here, a going concern. Or maybe you haven't. Maybe you're bait for the meat wagon. I talked, boys, oh yes, I talked. Give me Hank's killer, and I'll tell you who."

Flavin said, "Can't you forget that? The guy jumped."

Channing shook his head.

Padway said softly, "Suppose you're right, Chan. Suppose you get the killer. What good does that do you?"

"I'm not a cop anymore. I don't care how much booze you run. All I want is the guy that killed Hank."

Jack Flavin laughed. It was not a nice sound.

"Dave knows I keep a promise. Besides, you can always shoot me in the back."

Flavin said, "This is crazy. You haven't really hurt the guy, Dave. Put it to him. He'll talk."

"His heart would quit first." Padway smiled almost fondly at Channing. "He's got his guts back in. That's good to know, huh, Chan?"

"Yeah."

"But bad, too. For both of us."

"Go ahead and kill me, Dave, if you think it would help any."

Flavin said, with elaborate patience, "Dave, the man is crazy. Maybe he wants publicity. Maybe he's trying to chisel himself back on the force. Maybe he's a masochist. But he's nuts. I don't believe he talked to anybody. Either make him talk, or shoot him. Or I will."

"Will you, now?" Padway asked.

Channing said, "What are you so scared of, Flavin?"

Flavin snarled and swung his hand. Padway caught it, pulling Flavin around. He said, "Seems to me whoever killed Hank has made us all a lot of trouble. He's maybe busted us wide open. I'd kind of like to know who did it, and why. We were working together then, Jack, remember? And nobody told me about any cop named Channing."

Flavin shook him off. "The kid committed suicide. And don't try manhandling me, Dave. It was my racket, remember. I let you in."

"Why," said Padway mildly, "that's so, ain't it?" He hit Flavin in the mouth so quickly that his fist made a blur in the air. Flavin fell, clawing automatically at his armpit. Padway's men rose from the table and covered him. Flavin dropped his hand. He lay still, his eyes slitted and deadly.

Marge Krist slid down silently beside Channing's cot. She might have been fainting, leaning forward against it, her hands out of sight. She was not fainting. Channing felt her working at his wrists.

Flavin said, "Rudy. Come here."

Rudy Krist came into the circle of lamplight. He looked like a small boy dreaming a nightmare and knowing he can't wake up.

Flavin said, "All right, Dave. You're boss. Go ahead and give Channing his killer." He looked at Rudy, and everybody else looked, too, except the men covering Flavin.

Rudy Krist's eyes widened, until white showed all around the green. He stopped, staring at the hard, impassive faces turned toward him.

Flavin said contemptuously, "He turned you soft, Rudy. You spilled over and then you didn't have the nerve to go through with it. You knew what would happen to you. So you shoved Hank off the pier to save your own hide."

Rudy made a stifled, catlike noise. He leaped suddenly down onto Flavin. Padway motioned to his boys to hold it. Channing cried out desperately, "Don't do anything. Wait! Dave, drag him off."

Rudy had Flavin by the throat. He was frothing slightly. Flavin writhed, jerking his heels against the floor. Suddenly there was a sharp slamming noise from underneath Rudy's body. Rudy bent his back, as though he were trying to double over backwards. He let go of Flavin. He relaxed, his head falling sleepily against Flavin's shoulder.

Channing rolled off the cot, scrambling toward Flavin.

Flavin fired again, twice, so rapidly the shots sounded like one. One of Padway's boys knelt down and bowed forward over his knees like a praying Jap. Another of Padway's men fell. The second shot clipped Padway, tearing the shoulder pad of his suit.

Channing grabbed Flavin's wrist from behind.

"Okay," said Padway grimly. "Hold it, everybody."

Before he got the words out a small sharp crack came from behind the cot. Flavin relaxed. He lay looking up into Channing's face with an expression of great surprise, as though the third eye just opened in his forehead gave him a completely new perspective.

Marge Krist stood green-eyed and deadly with a little pearl-handled revolver smoking in her hand.

Padway turned toward her slowly. Channing's mouth twitched dourly. He hardly glanced at the girl, but rolled the boy's body over carefully.

Channing said, "Did you kill Hank?"

Rudy whispered, "Honest to God, no."

"Did Flavin kill him?"

"I don't know . . ." Tears came in Rudy's eyes. "Hank," he whispered, "I wish . . ." The tears kept running out of his eyes for several seconds after he was dead.

By that time the police had come into the room, from the dark disused doorways, from behind the stacked liquor. Max Gandara said, "Everybody hold still."

Dave Padway put his hands up slowly, his eyes at first wide with surprise and then narrow and ice-hard. His gunboy did the same, first dropping his rod with a heavy clatter on the bare floor.

Padway said, "They've been here all the time."

Channing sat up stiffly. "I hope they were. I didn't know whether Max would play with me or not."

"You dirty double-crossing louse."

"I feel bad, crossing up an ape like you, Dave. You treated me so square, up there by Hyperion." Channing raised his voice. "Max, look out for the boy with the chopper."

Gandara said, "I had three men up there. They took him when he went up, real quiet."

Marge Krist had come like a sleepwalker around the cot. She was close to Padway. Quite suddenly she fainted. Padway caught her, so that she shielded his body, and his gun snapped into his hand.

Max Gandara said, "Don't shoot. Don't anybody shoot."

"That's sensible," said Padway softly.

Channing's hand, on the floor, slid over the gun Flavin wasn't using anymore. Then, very quickly, he threw himself forward into the table with the lamp on it.

A bullet slammed into the wood, through it, and past his ear, and then Channing fired twice, deliberately, through the flames.

Channing rose and walked past the fire. He moved stiffly, limping, but there was a difference in him. Padway was down on one knee, eyes shut and teeth clenched against the pain of a shattered wrist. Marge Krist was still standing. She was staring with stricken eyes at the hole in her white forearm and the pattern of brilliant red threads spreading from it.

Max Gandara caught Channing. "You crazy—"

Channing hit him, hard and square. His face didn't change expression. "I owe you that one, Max. And before you start preaching the sanctity of womanhood, you better pry out a couple of those slugs that just missed me. You'll find they came from Miss Krist's pretty little popgun—the same one that killed her boyfriend, Jack Flavin." He went over and tilted Marge Krist's face to his, quite gently. "You came out of your faint in a hurry, didn't you, sweetheart?"

She brought up her good hand and tried to claw his eye out.

Channing laughed. He pushed her into the arms of a policeman. "It'll all come out in the wash. Meantime, there are the bullets from Marge's gun. The fact that she had a gun at all proves she was in on the gang. They'd have searched her, if all that pious stuff about poor Rudy's evil ways had been on the level. She was a little surprised about Padway and sore because Flavin had kept it from her. But she knew which was the better man, all right. She was going along with Padway, and she shot Flavin to keep his mouth shut about Hank, and to make sure he didn't get Padway by accident. Flavin was a gutty little guy, and he came close to doing just that. Marge untied me because she hoped I'd get shot in the confusion, or start trouble on my own account. If you hadn't come in, Max, she'd probably have shot me herself. She didn't want any more fussing about Hank Channing, and with me and Flavin dead she was in the clear."

Gandara said with ugly stubbornness, "Sounded to me like Flavin made a pretty good case against Rudy."

"Sure, sure. He was down on the ground with half his teeth out and three guys holding guns on him."

Marge Krist was sitting now on the cot, while somebody worked over her with a first aid kit. Channing stood in front of her.

"You've done a good night's work, Marge. You killed Rudy just as much as you did Flavin, or Hank. Rudy had decent stuff in him. You forced him into the game, but Hank was turning him soft. You killed Hank."

Channing moved closer to her. She looked up at him, her green eyes meeting his dark ones, both of them passionate and cruel.

"You're a smart girl, Marge. You and your mealy-mouthed hypocrisy. I know now what you meant when you accused Rudy of being afraid to be questioned. Flavin couldn't kill Hank by himself. He wasn't big enough, and Hank wasn't that dumb. He didn't trust Flavin. But you, Marge, sure, he trusted you. He'd stand on a dark pier at midnight and talk to you, and never notice who was sneaking up behind with a blackjack." He bent over her. "A smart girl, Marge, and a pretty one. I don't think I'll want to stand outside the window while you die."

"I wish I'd killed you too," she whispered. "By God, I wish I'd killed you too!"

Channing nodded. He went over and sat down wearily. He looked exhausted and weak, but his eyes were alive.

"Somebody give me a cigarette," he said. He struck the match himself. The smoke tasted good.

It was his first smoke in ten years.

DEAD MAN

BY JAMES M. CAIN

San Fernando

(Originally published in 1936)

1

He felt the train check, knew what it meant. In a moment, from up toward the engine, came the chant of the railroad detective: "Rise and shine, boys, rise and shine." The hoboes began dropping off. He could hear them out there in the dark, cursing as the train went by. That was what they always did on these freights: let the hoboes climb on in the yards, making no effort to dislodge them there; for that would have meant a foolish game of hide-and-seek between two or three detectives and two or three hundred hoboes, with the hoboes swarming on as fast as the detectives put them off. What they did was let the hoboes alone until the train was several miles under way; then they pulled down to a speed slow enough for men to drop off, but too fast for them to climb back on. Then the detective went down the line, brushing them off, like caterpillars from a twig. In two minutes they would all be ditched, a crowd of bitter men in a lonely spot, but they always cursed, always seemed surprised.

He crouched in the coal gondola and waited. He hadn't boarded a flat or a refrigerator with the others, back in the Los Angeles yards, tempting though this comfort was. He wasn't long on the road, and he still didn't like to mix with the other hoboes, admit he was one of them. Also, he couldn't shake off a notion that he was sharper than they were, that playing a lone hand he might think of some magnificent trick that would defeat the detective, and thus, even at this ignoble trade, give him a sense of accomplishment, of being good at it. He had slipped into the gond not in spite of its harshness, but because of it; it was black, and would give him a chance to hide, and the detective, not expecting him there, might pass him by. He was nineteen years old, and was proud of the nickname they had given him in the poolroom back home. They called him Lucky.

"Rise and shine, boys, rise and shine."

Three dropped off the tank car ahead, and the detective climbed into the gond. The flashlight shot around, and Lucky held his breath. He had curled into one of the three chutes for unloading coal. The trick worked. These chutes were dangerous, for if you stepped into one and the bottom dropped, it would dump you under the train. The detective took no chances. He first shot the flash, then held on to the side while he climbed over the chutes. When he came to the last one, where Lucky lay, he shot the flash, but carelessly, and not squarely into the hole, so that he saw nothing. Stepping over, he went on, climbed to the boxcar behind, and resumed his chant: there were more curses, more feet sliding on ballast on the roadbed outside. Soon the train picked up speed. That meant the detective had reached the caboose, that all the hoboes were cleared.

Lucky stood up, looked around. There was nothing to see, except hot-dog stands along the highway, but it was pleasant to poke your head up, let the wind whip your hair, and reflect how you had outwitted the detective. When the click of the rails slowed and station lights showed ahead, he squatted down again, dropped his feet into the chute. As soon as lights flashed alongside, he braced against the opposite side of the chute: that was one thing he had learned, the crazy way they shot the brakes on these freights. When the train jerked to a shrieking stop, he was ready, and didn't get slammed. The bell tolled, the engine pulled away, there was an interval of silence. That meant they had cut the train, and would be picking up more cars. Soon they would be going on.

"Ah-ha! Hiding out on me, hey?"

The flashlight shot down from the boxcar. Lucky jumped, seized the side of the gond, scrambled up, vaulted. When he hit the roadbed, his ankles stung from the impact, and he staggered for footing. The detective was on him, grappling. He broke away, ran down the track, past the caboose, into the dark. The detective followed, but he was a big man and began to lose ground. Lucky was clear, when all of a sudden his foot drove against a switch bar and he went flat on his face, panting from the hysteria of shock.

The detective didn't grapple this time. He let go with a barrage of kicks.

"Hide out on me, will you? Treat you right, give you a break, and you hide out on me. I'll learn you to hide out on me."

Lucky tried to get up, couldn't. He was jerked to his feet, rushed up the track on the run. He pulled back, but couldn't get set. He sat down, dug in with his sliding heels. The detective kicked and jerked, in fury. Lucky clawed for something to hold on to, his hand caught the rail. The detective stamped on it. He pulled it back in pain, clawed again. This time his fingers closed on a spike, sticking an inch or two out of the tie. The detective jerked, the spike pulled out of the hole, and Lucky resumed his unwilling run.

"Lemme go! Why don't you lemme go?"

"Come on! Hide out on me, will you? I'll learn you to hide out on Larry Nott!"

"Lemme go! Lemme—"

Lucky pulled back, braced with his heels, got himself stopped. Then his whole body coiled like a spring and let go in one convulsive, passionate lunge. The spike, still in his hand, came down on the detective's head, and he felt it crush. He stood there, looking down at something dark and formless, lying across the rails.

2

Hurrying down the track, he became aware of the spike, gave it a toss, heard it splash in the ditch. Soon he realized that his steps on the ties were being telegraphed by the listening rail, and he plunged across the ditch to the highway. There he resumed his rapid walk, trying not to run. But every time a car overtook him his heels lifted queerly, and his breath first stopped, then came in gasps as he listened for the car to stop. He came to a crossroads, turned quickly to his right. He let himself run here, for the road wasn't lighted as the main highway was, and there weren't many cars. The running tired him, but it eased the sick feeling in his stomach. He came to a sign that told him Los Angeles was seventeen miles, and to his left. He turned, walked, ran, stooped down sometimes, panting, to rest. After a while it came to him why he had to get to Los Angeles, and so soon. The soup kitchen opened at seven o'clock. He had to be there, in that same soup kitchen where he had had supper, so it would look as though he had never been away.

When the lights went off, and it came broad daylight with the suddenness of Southern California, he was in the city, and a clock told him it was ten minutes after five. He thought he had time. He pressed on, exhausted, but never relaxing his rapid, half-shuffling walk.

It was ten minutes to seven when he got to the soup kitchen, and he quickly walked past it. He wanted to be clear at the end of the line, so he could have a word with Shorty, the man who dished out the soup, without impatient shoves from behind, and growls to keep moving.

Shorty remembered him. "Still here, hey?"

"Still here."

"Three in a row for you. Holy smoke, they ought to be collecting for you by the month."

"Thought you'd be off."

"Who, me?"

"Sunday, ain't it?"

"Sunday? Wake up. This is Saturday."

"Saturday? You're kidding."

"Kidding my eye, this is Saturday, and a big day in this town, too."

"One day looks like another to me."

"Not this one. Parade."

"Yeah?"

"Shriners. You get that free."

"Well, that's my name, Lucky."

"My name's Shorty, but I'm over six feet."

"Nothing like that with me. I really got luck."

"You sure?"

"Like, for instance, getting a hunk of meat."

"I didn't give you no meat."

"Ain't you going to?"

"Shove your plate over quick. Don't let nobody see you."

"Thanks."

"Okay, Lucky. Don't miss the parade."

"I won't."

He sat at the rough table with the others, dipped his bread in the soup, tried to eat, but his throat kept contracting from excitement and he made slow work of it. He had what he wanted from Shorty. He had fixed the day, and not only the day but the date, for it would be the same date as the big Shriners' parade. He had fixed his name, with a little gag. Shorty wouldn't forget him. His throat relaxed, and he wolfed the piece of meat.

Near the soup kitchen he saw signs: *Lincoln Park Pharmacy, Lincoln Park Cafeteria.*

"Which way is the park, buddy?" If it was a big park, he might find a thicket where he could lie down, rest his aching legs.

"Straight down, you'll see it."

There was a fence around it, but he found a gate, opened it, slipped in. Ahead of him was a thicket, but the ground was wet from a stream that ran through it. He crossed a small bridge, followed a path. He came to a stable, peeped in. It was empty, but the floor was thickly covered with new hay. He went in, made for a dark corner, burrowed under the hay, closed his eyes. For a few moments everything slipped away, except warmth, relaxation, ease. But then something began to drill into the back of his mind: Where did he spend last night? Where would he tell them he spent last night? He tried to think, but nothing would come to him. He would have said that he spent it where he spent the night before, but he hadn't spent it in Los Angeles. He had spent it in Santa Barbara, and come down in the morning on a truck. He had never spent a night in Los Angeles. He didn't know the places. He had no answers to the questions that were now pounding at him like sledge hammers:

"What's that? Where you say you was?"

"In a flophouse."

"Which flophouse?"

"I didn't pay no attention which flophouse. It was just a flop-house."

"Where was this flophouse at?"

"I don't know where it was at. I never been to Los Angeles before. I don't know the names of no streets."

"What this flophouse look like?"

"Looked like a flophouse."

"Come on, don't give us no gags. What this flophouse look like? Ain't you got eyes, can't you say what this here place looked like? What's the matter, can't you talk?"

Something gripped his arm, and he felt himself being lifted. Something of terrible strength had hold of him, and he was going straight up in the air. He squirmed to get loose, then was plopped on his feet and released. He turned, terrified.

An elephant was standing there, exploring his clothes with its trunk. He knew then that he had been asleep. But when he backed away, he bumped into another elephant. He slipped be-tween the two elephants, slithered past a third to the door, which was open about a foot. Out in the sunlight, he made his way back across the little bridge, saw what he hadn't noticed before: pens with deer in them, and ostriches, and mountain sheep, that told him he had stumbled into a zoo. It was after four o'clock, so he must have slept a long time in the hay. Back on the street, he felt a sobbing laugh rise in his throat. That was where he had spent the night. "In the elephant house at Lincoln Park."

"*What?*"

"That's right. In the elephant house."

"What you giving us? A stall?"

"It ain't no stall. I was in the elephant house."

"With them elephants?"

"That's right."

"How you get in there?"

"Just went in. The door was open."

"Just went in there, seen the elephants, and bedded down with them?"

"I thought they was horses."

"You thought them elephants was horses?"

"It was dark. I dug in under the hay. I never knowed they was elephants till morning."

"How come you went in this place?"

"I left the soup kitchen, and in a couple of minutes I came to the park. I went in there, looking for some grass to lie down on. Then I come to this here place, looked to me like a stable. I peeped in, seen the hay, and hit it."

"And you wasn't scared of them elephants?"

"It was dark, I tell you, and I could hear them eating the hay, but I thought they was horses. I was tired, and I wanted someplace to sleep."

"Then what?"

"Then when it got light, and I seen they was elephants, I run out of there, and beat it."

"Couldn't you tell them elephants by the smell?"

"I never noticed no smell."

"How many elephants was there?"

"Three."

3

He brushed wisps of hay off his denims. They had been fairly new, but now they were black with the grime of the coal gond. Suddenly his heart stopped, a suffocating feeling swept over him. The questions started again, hammered at him, beat into his brain.

"Where that coal dust come from?"

"I don't know. The freights, I guess."

"Don't you know it ain't no coal ever shipped into this part of the state? Don't you know that here all they burn is gas? Don't you know it ain't only been but one coal car shipped in here in six months, and that come in by a misread train order? Don't you know that car was part of that train this here detective was rid-

ing that got killed? *Don't you know that?* Come on, out with it.
WHERE THAT COAL DUST COME FROM?"

Getting rid of the denims instantly became an obsession. He
felt that people were looking at him on the street, spying the coal
dust, waiting till he got by, then running into drugstores to phone
the police that he had just passed by. It was like those dreams he
sometimes had, where he was walking through crowds naked, except that this was no dream, and he wasn't naked, he was wearing
these denims, these telltale denims with coal dust all over them.
He clenched his hands, had a moment of terrible concentration,
headed into a filling station.

"Hello."

"Hello."

"What's the chances on a job?"

"No chances."

"Why not?"

"Don't need anybody."

"That's not the only reason."

"There's about forty-two other reasons, one of them is I can't
even make a living myself, but it's all the reason that concerns you.
Here's a dime, kid. Better luck somewhere else."

"I don't want your dime. I want a job. If the clothes were better, that might help, mightn't it?"

"If the clothes were good enough for Clark Gable in the swell
gambling-house scene, that wouldn't help a bit. Not a bit. I just
don't need anybody, that's all."

"Suppose I got better clothes. Would you talk to me?"

"Talk to you any time, but I don't need anybody."

"I'll be back when I get the clothes."

"Just taking a walk for nothing."

"What's your name?"

"Hook's my name. Oscar Hook."

"Thanks, Mr. Hook. But I'm coming back. I just got a idea I
can talk myself into a job. I'm some talker."

"You're all that, kid. But don't waste your time. I don't need
anybody."

"Okay. Just the same, I'll be back."

He headed for the center of town, asked the way to the cheap clothing stores. At Los Angeles and Temple, after an hour's trudge, he came to a succession of small stores in a Mexican quarter that were what he wanted. He went into one. The storekeeper was a Mexican, and two or three other Mexicans were standing around smoking.

"Mister, will you trust me for a pair of white pants and a shirt?"

"No trust. Hey, scram."

"Look. I can have a job Monday morning if I can show up in that outfit. White pants and a white shirt. That's all."

"No trust. What you think this is, anyway?"

"Well, I got to get that outfit somewhere. If I get that, they'll let me go to work Monday. I'll pay you soon as I get paid off Saturday night."

"No trust. Sell for cash."

He stood there. The Mexicans stood there, smoked, looked out at the street. Presently one of them looked at him. "What kind of job, hey? What you mean, got to have white pants a white shirt a hold a job?"

"Filling station. They got a rule you got to have white clothes before you can work there."

"Oh. Sure. Filling station."

After a while the storekeeper spoke. "Ha! Is a joke. Job in filling station, must have a white pants, white shirt. Ha! Is a joke."

"What else would I want them for? Holy smoke, these are better for the road, ain't they? Say, a guy don't want white pants to ride freights, does he?"

"What filling station? Tell me that."

"Guy name of Hook, Oscar Hook, got a Acme station. Main near Twentieth. You don't believe me, call him up."

"You go to work there, hey?"

"I'm *supposed* to go to work. I *told* him I'd get the white pants and white shirt, somehow. Well—if I don't get them, I don't go to work."

"Why you come to me, hey?"

"Where else would I go? If it's not you, it's another guy down the street. No place else I can dig up the stuff over Sunday, is there?"

"Oh."

He stood around. They all stood around. Then once again the storekeeper looked up. "What size you wear, hey?"

He had a wash at a tap in the backyard, then changed there, between piled-up boxes and crates. The storekeeper gave him a white shirt, white pants, necktie, a suit of thick underwear, and a pair of shoes to replace his badly worn brogans. "Is pretty cold, nighttime, now. A thick underwear feel better."

"Okay. Much obliged."

"Can roll this other stuff up."

"I don't want it. Can you throw it away for me?"

"Is pretty dirty."

"Plenty dirty."

"You no want?"

"No."

His heart leaped as the storekeeper dropped the whole pile into a rubbish brazier and touched a match to some papers at the bottom of it. In a few minutes, the denims and everything else he had worn were ashes.

He followed the storekeeper inside. "Okay, here is a bill, I put all a stuff on a bill, no charge you more than anybody else. Is six dollar ninety-eight cents, then is a service charge one dollar."

All of them laughed. He took the "service charge" to be a gyp overcharge to cover the trust. He nodded. "Okay on the service charge."

The storekeeper hesitated. "Well, six ninety-eight. We no make a service charge."

"Thanks."

"See you keep a white pants clean till Monday morning."

"I'll do that. See you Saturday night."

"*Adios.*"

Out in the street, he stuck his hand in his pocket, felt something, pulled it out. It was a $1 bill. Then he understood about the "service charge," and why the Mexicans had laughed. He went back, kissed the $1 bill, waved a cheery salute into the store. They all waved back.

He rode a streetcar down to Mr. Hook's, got turned down for the job, rode a streetcar back. In his mind, he tried to check over everything. He had an alibi, fantastic and plausible. So far as he could recall, nobody on the train had seen him, not even the other hoboes, for he had stood apart from them in the yards, and had done nothing to attract the attention of any of them. The denims were burned, and he had a story to account for the whites. It even looked pretty good, this thing with Mr. Hook, for anybody who had committed a murder would be most unlikely to make a serious effort to land a job.

But the questions lurked there, ready to spring at him, check and recheck as he would. He saw a sign, *5-Course Dinner, 35 Cents.* He still had ninety cents, and went in, ordered steak and fried potatoes, the hungry man's dream of heaven. He ate, put a ten-cent tip under the plate. He ordered cigarettes, lit one, inhaled. He got up to go. A newspaper was lying on the table.

He froze as he saw the headline:

L.R. NOTT, R.R. MAN, KILLED.

4

On the street, he bought a paper, tried to open it under a street light, couldn't, tucked it under his arm. He found Highway 101, caught a hay truck bound for San Francisco. Going out Sunset Boulevard, it unexpectedly pulled over to the curb and stopped. He looked warily around. Down a side street, about a block away, were the two red lights of a police station. He was tightening to jump and run, but the driver wasn't looking at the lights. "I told them bums that air hose was leaking. They set you nuts. Supposed to keep the stuff in shape and all they ever do is sit around and play blackjack."

The driver fished a roll of black tape from his pocket and got out. Lucky sat where he was a few minutes, then climbed down, walked to the glare of the headlights, opened his paper. There it was:

L.R. NOTT, R.R. MAN, KILLED

The decapitated body of L.R. Nott, 1327 De Soto Street, a detective assigned to a northbound freight, was found early this morning on the track near San Fernando station. It is believed he lost his balance while the train was shunting cars at the San Fernando siding and fell beneath the wheels. Funeral services will be held tomorrow from the De Soto Street Methodist Church.

Mr. Nott is survived by a widow, formerly Miss Elsie Snowden of Mannerheim, and a son, L.R. Nott, Jr., 5.

He stared at it, refolded the paper, tucked it under his arm, walked back to where the driver was taping the air hose. He was clear, and he knew it. "Boy, do they call you Lucky? Is your name Lucky? I'll say it is."

He leaned against the trailer, let his eye wander down the street. He saw the two red lights of the police station glowing. He looked away quickly. A queer feeling began to stir inside him. He wished the driver would hurry up.

Presently he went back to the headlights again, found the notice, re-read it. He recognized that feeling now; it was the old Sunday-night feeling that he used to have back home, when the bells would ring and he would have to stop playing hide in the twilight, go to church, and hear about the necessity for being saved. It shot through his mind, the time he had played hookey from church, and hid in the livery stable; and how lonely he had felt, because there was nobody to play hide with; and how he had sneaked into church, and stood in the rear to listen to the necessity for being saved.

His eyes twitched back to the red lights, and slowly, shakily, but unswervingly he found himself walking toward them.

"I want to give myself up."

"Yeah, I know, you're wanted for grand larceny in Hackensack, New Jersey."

"No, I—"

"We quit giving them rides when the New Deal come in. Beat it."

"I killed a man."

"You—? . . . When was it you done this?"

"Last night."

"Where?"

"Near here. San Fernando. It was like this—"

"Hey, wait till I get a card. . . . Okay, what's your name?"

"Ben Fuller."

"No middle name?"

"They call me Lucky."

"Lucky like in good luck?"

"Yes, sir. . . . Lucky like in good luck."

THE NIGHT'S FOR CRYIN'

BY CHESTER HIMES

South Los Angeles

(Originally published in 1937)

B lack boy slammed his Tom Collins down on the bar with an irritated bang, turned a slack scowl toward Gigilo. Gigilo, yellow and fat like a well-fed hog, was saying in a fat, whiskey-thickened voice: "Then she pulled out a knife and cut me 'cross the back. I just looked at 'er. Then she threw 'way the knife and hit me in the mouth with her pocketbook. I still looked at her. Then she raised her foot and stomped my corns. I pushed her down then."

Black Boy said: "Niggah, ef'n yo is talkin' tuh me, Ah ain' liss'nin'." Black Boy didn't like yellow niggers, he didn't want no yellow nigger talking to him now, for he was waiting for Marie, his high yellow heart, to take her to her good-doing job.

Gigilo took another sip of rye, but he didn't say anymore.

Sound bubbled about them, a bubble bursting here in a strident laugh, there in accented profanity. A woman's coarse, heavy voice said: "Cal, Ah wish you'd stop Fo'-Fo' frum drinkin' so much" . . . A man's flat, unmusical drone said: "Ah had uh ruff on 632 and 642 come out." He had repeated the same words a hundred solid times . . . "Aw, she ain' gibin' dat chump nuttin," a young, loud voice clamored for attention . . . A nickel victrola in the rear blared a husky, negroid bellow: "*Anybody heah wanna buy* . . ."

The mirror behind the bar reflected the lingering scowl on Black Boy's face, the blackest blot in the ragged jam of black and yellow faces lining the bar.

Wall lights behind him spilled soft stain on the elite at the tables. Cigarette smoke cut thin blue streamers ceilingward through the muted light, mingled with whiskey fumes and perfume scents and Negro smell. Bodies squirmed, inching riotous-colored dresses up from yellow, shapely legs. Red-lacquered nails gleamed like bright blood drops on the stems of whiskey glasses, and the women's yellow faces looked like powdered masks beneath sleek hair, bruised with red mouths.

Four white people pushed through the front door, split a hurried, half apologetic path through the turn of displeased faces toward the cabaret entrance at the rear. Black Boy's muddy, negroid eyes followed them, slightly resentful.

A stoop-shouldered, consumptive-looking Negro leaned over Black Boy's shoulder and whispered something in his ear.

Black Boy's sudden strangle blew a spray of Tom Collins over the bar. He put the tall glass quickly down, sloshing the remaining liquid over his hand. His red tongue slid twice across his thick, red lips, and his slack, plate-shaped face took on a popeyed expression, as startlingly unreal beneath the white of his precariously perched Panama as an eight ball with suddenly sprouted features. The puffed, bluish scar on his left cheek, memento of a pick-axe duel on a chain gang, seemed to swell into an embossed reproduction of a shell explosion, ridges pronging off from it in spokes.

He slid back from his stool, his elbow digging into a powdered, brownskin back to his right, caught on his feet with a flat-footed clump. Standing, his body was big, his six foot height losing impressiveness in slanting shoulders and long arms like an ape's.

He paused for a moment, undecided, a unique specimen of sartorial splendor—white Panama stuck on the back of his shiny shaved skull, yellow silk polo shirt dirtied slightly by the black of his bulging muscles, draped trousers of a brilliant pea green, tight waisted and slack hanging above size eleven shoes of freshly shined tan.

The woman with the back turned a ruffled countenance, spat a stream of lurid profanity at him through twisted red lips. But he wedged through the jam toward the door, away from her, smashed out of the Log Cabin bar into a crowd of idling avenue pimps.

The traffic lights at the corner turned from green to red. Four shiny, new automobiles full of laughing black folks, purred casually through the red. A passing brownskin answered to the call of "Babe," paused before her "nigger" in saddle-backed stance, arms akimbo, tight dress tightened on the curve of her hips.

Black Boy's popped eyes filled with yellow specks, slithered across the front of the weather-stained Majestic Hotel across the street, lingering a searching instant on every woman whose face was light. Around the corner, down on Central Avenue, he caught a fleeting glimpse of a yellow gal climbing into a green sedan, then a streetcar clanged across his vision.

He pulled in his red lips, wet them with his tongue. Then he broke into a shuffling, flat-footed run—through the squawk of a horn, across suddenly squealing brakes, never looked around. A taxi-driver's curse lashed him across the street. His teeth bared slightly, but the bloated unreality of his face never changed.

He turned right in front of the Majestic, roughed over a brown dandy with two painted crones, drew up at the corner, panting. The green sedan burnt rubber, pulled right through the red light in a whining, driving first.

But too late to keep Black Boy from catching a flash of the pretty, frightened face of Marie and the nervous profile of the driver bent low over the wheel. A yellow nigger. He turned and watched the red tail-light sink into the distant darkness, his body twisting on flatly planted feet. His lower lip went slack, hung down like a red smear on his black face. His bulging eyes turned a vein-laced red. Sweat popped out on his face, putting a sheen on its lumpy blackness, grew in beads on his shiny head, trickled in streams down his body.

He turned and ran for a cab, but his actions were dogged now instead of apprehensive. He'd already seen Marie with that yellow hotel nigger. He caught a cab pointing the right way, said: "Goose it, Speed," before he swung through the open door.

Speed goosed it. The cab took sudden life, jumped ahead from the shove of eight protesting cylinders. Black Boy leaned tensely forward, let the speedometer needle hit fifty before he spoke.

"Dar's uh green sedan up front, uh fo' do' job. Latch on it 'n earn dis dime, big dime."

The lank, loose-bodied brown boy driving threw him a careless, toothy grin, coiled around the wheel. He headed into the red light at Cedar Avenue doing a crisp seventy, didn't slacken. He pulled inside the line of waiting cars, smashed into the green while the red still lingered in his eyes. The green turned to red at Carnegie, and the car in front stopped, but he burst the red wide open doing a sheer eighty-five, leaning on the horn.

"Ri' at Euclid," Black Boy directed through lips that hung so slack they seemed to be turned wrong side out. He was gambling on those yellow folk seeking the protection of their white folk where they worked, for they had lost the green sedan.

The driver braked for the turn, eyes roving for traffic cops. He didn't see any and he turned at a slow fifty, not knowing whether the light was red, white or blue. The needle walked right up the street numbers, fifty-seven at 57th Street, seventy-one at 71st. It was hovering on eighty again when Black Boy said: "Turn 'round."

Marie was just getting out of the green sedan in front of the Regis where she worked as a maid. When she heard that shrill cry of rubber on asphalt she broke into a craven run.

Black Boy hit the pavement in a flat-footed lope, caught her just as she was about to climb the lobby stairs. He never said a word, he just reached around from behind and smacked her in the face with the open palm of his right hand. She drew up short against the blow. Then he hit her under her right breast with a short left jab and chopped three rights into her face when she turned around with the edge of his fist like he was driving nails.

She wilted to her knees and he bumped her in the mouth with his knee, knocking her sprawling on her side. He kicked her in the body three rapid, vicious times, slobber drooling from his slack, red lips. His bloated face was a tar ball in the spill of sign light, his eyes too dull to notice. Somehow his Panama still clung on his eight ball head, whiter than ever, and his red lips were a split, bleeding incision in his black face.

Marie screamed for help. Then she whimpered. Then she begged. "Doan kill me, Black Boy, daddy deah, honey darlin', daddy-daddy deah. Marie luvs yuh, daddy darlin'. Doan kill me, please, daddy. Doan kill yo' lil' honeybunch, Marie . . ."

The yellow boy, slowly following from the car, paused a moment in indecision as if he would get back in and drive away. But he couldn't bear seeing Black Boy kick Marie. The growth of emotion was visible in his face before it pushed him forward.

After an instant he realized that that was where he worked as a bellhop, that those white folk would back him up against a strange nigger. He stepped quickly over to Black Boy, spoke in a cultural preëmptory voice: "Stop kicking that woman, you dirty black nigger."

Black Boy turned his bloated face toward him. His dull eyes explored him, dogged. His voice was flatly telling him: "You keep outta dis, yellow niggah. Dis heah is mah woman an' Ah doan lak you no way."

The yellow boy was emboldened by the appearance of two white men in the hotel doorway. He stepped over and slung a weighted blow to Black Boy's mouth. Black Boy shifted in quick rage, drew a spring-blade barlow chiv and slashed the yellow boy to death before the two white men could run down the stairs. He broke away from their restraining hands, made his way to the alley beside the theater in his shambling, flat-footed run before the police cruiser got there.

He heard Marie's loud, fear-shrill voice crying: "He pulled a gun on Black Boy, he pulled a gun on Black Boy. Ah saw 'im do it—"

He broke into a laugh, satisfied. She was still his . . .

Three rapid shots behind him stopped his laugh, shattered his face into black fragments. The cops had begun shooting without calling halt. He knew that they knew he was a "dinge," and he knew they wanted to kill him, so he stepped into the light behind a Clark's Restaurant, stopped dead still with upraised hands, not turning around.

The cops took him down to the station and beat his head

into an open, bloody wound from his bulging eyes clear around to the base of his skull—"You'd bring your nigger cuttings down on Euclid Avenue, would you, you black—"

They gave him the electric chair for that.

But if it is worrying him, he doesn't show it during the slow drag of days in death row's grilled enclosure. He knows that that high yellow gal with the ball-bearing hips is still his, heart, soul and body. All day long, you can hear his loud, crowing voice, kidding the other condemned men, jibing the guards, telling lies. He can tell some tall lies, too—"You know, me 'n Marie wuz in Noo Yawk dat wintah. Ah won leben grands in uh dice game 'n brought her uh sealskin—"

All day long, you can hear his noisy laugh.

Marie comes to see him as often as they let her, brings him fried chicken and hot, red lips; brings him a wide smile and tiny yellow specs in her big, brown, ever-loving eyes. You can hear his assured love-making all over the range, his casual "honeybunch," his chuckling, contented laugh.

All day long . . .

It's at night, when she's gone and the cells are dark and death row is silent, that you'll find Black Boy huddled in the corner of his cell, thinking of her, perhaps in some other nigger's loving arms. Crying softly. Salty tears making glistening streaks down the blending blackness of his face.

PART II

AFTER THE WAR

PART II

FIND THE WOMAN

BY ROSS MACDONALD
Beverly Hills
(Originally published in 1946)

I sat in my brand-new office with the odor of paint in my nostrils and waited for something to happen. I had been back on the Boulevard for one day. This was the beginning of the second day. Below the window, flashing in the morning sun, the traffic raced and roared with a noise like battle. It made me nervous. It made me want to move. I was all dressed up in civilian clothes with no place to go and nobody to go with.

Till Millicent Dreen came in.

I had seen her before, on the Strip with various escorts, and knew who she was: publicity director for Tele-Pictures. Mrs. Dreen was over forty and looked it, but there was electricity in her, plugged in to a secret source that time could never wear out. Look how high and tight I carry my body, her movements said. My hair is hennaed but comely, said her coiffure, inviting not to conviction but to suspension of disbelief. Her eyes were green and inconstant like the sea. They said what the hell.

She sat down by my desk and told me that her daughter had disappeared the day before, which was September the seventh.

"I was in Hollywood all day. We keep an apartment here, and there was some work I had to get out fast. Una isn't working, so I left her at the beach house by herself."

"Where is it?"

"A few miles above Santa Barbara."

"That's a long way to commute."

"It's worth it to me. When I can maneuver a weekend away from this town, I like to get *really* away."

"Maybe your daughter feels the same, only more so. When did she leave?"

"Sometime yesterday. When I drove home to the beach house last night she was gone."

"Did you call the police?"

"Hardly. She's twenty-two and knows what she's doing. I hope. Anyway, apron strings don't become me." She smiled like a cat and moved her scarlet-taloned fingers in her narrow lap. "It was very late and I was—tired. I went to bed. But when I woke up this morning it occurred to me that she might have drowned. I objected to it because she wasn't a strong swimmer, but she went in for solitary swimming. I think of the most dreadful things when I wake up in the morning."

"*Went* in for solitary swimming, Mrs. Dreen?"

"'Went' slipped out, didn't it? I told you I think of dreadful things when I wake up in the morning."

"If she drowned you should be talking to the police. They can arrange for dragging and such things. All I can give you is my sympathy."

As if to estimate the value of that commodity, her eyes flickered from my shoulders to my waist and up again to my face. "Frankly, I don't know about the police. I do know about you, Mr. Archer. You just got out of the army, didn't you?"

"Last week." I failed to add that she was my first postwar client.

"And you don't belong to anybody, I've heard. You've never been bought. Is that right?"

"Not outright. You can take an option on a piece of me, though. A hundred dollars would do for a starter."

She nodded briskly. From a bright black bag she gave me five twenties. "Naturally, I'm conscious of publicity angles. My daughter retired a year ago when she married—"

"Twenty-one is a good age to retire."

"From pictures, maybe you're right. But she could want to go back if her marriage breaks up. And I have to look out for myself. It isn't true that there's no such thing as bad publicity. *I* don't know why Una went away."

"Is your daughter Una Sand?"

"Of course. I assumed you knew." My ignorance of the details of her life seemed to cause her pain. She didn't have to tell me that she had a feeling for publicity angles.

Though Una Sand meant less to me than Hecuba, I remembered the name and with it a glazed blonde who had had a year or two in the sun, but who'd made a better pin-up than an actress.

"Wasn't her marriage happy? I mean, isn't it?"

"You see how easy it is to slip into the past tense?" Mrs. Dreen smiled another fierce and purring smile, and her fingers fluttered in glee before her immobile body. "I suppose her marriage is happy enough. Her Ensign's quite a personable young man—handsome in a masculine way, and passionate she tells me, and naive enough."

"Naive enough for what?"

"To marry Una. Jack Rossiter was quite a catch in this woman's town. He was runner-up at Forest Hills the last year he played tennis. And now of course he's a flier. Una did right well by herself, even if it doesn't last."

What do you expect of a war marriage? she seemed to be saying. Permanence? Fidelity? The works?

"As a matter of fact," she went on, "it was thinking about Jack, more than anything else, that brought me here to you. He's due back this week, and naturally"—like many unnatural people, she overused that adverb—"he'll expect her to be waiting for him. It'll be rather embarrassing for me if he comes home and I can't tell him where she's gone, or why, or with whom. You'd really think she'd leave a note."

"I can't keep up with you," I said. "A minute ago Una was in the clutches of the cruel crawling foam. Now she's taken off with a romantic stranger."

"I consider possibilities, is all. When I was Una's age, married to Dreen, I had quite a time settling down. I still do."

Our gazes, mine as impassive as hers I hoped, met, struck no spark, and disengaged. The female spider who eats her mate held no attraction for me.

"I'm getting to know you pretty well," I said with the necessary smile, "but not the missing girl. Who's she been knocking around with?"

"I don't think we need to go into that. She doesn't confide in me, in any case."

"Whatever you say. Shall we look at the scene of the crime?"

"There isn't any *crime*."

"The scene of the accident, then, or the departure. Maybe the beach house will give me something to go on."

She glanced at the wafer-thin watch on her brown wrist. Its diamonds glittered coldly. "Do I have to drive all the way back?"

"If you can spare the time, it might help. We'll take my car."

She rose decisively but gracefully, as though she had practiced the movement in front of a mirror. An expert bitch, I thought as I followed her high slim shoulders and tight-sheathed hips down the stairs to the bright street. I felt a little sorry for the army of men who had warmed themselves, or been burned, at that secret electricity. And I wondered if her daughter Una was like her.

When I did get to see Una, the current had been cut off; I learned about it only by the marks it left. It left marks.

We drove down Sunset to the sea and north on 101 Alternate. All the way to Santa Barbara, she read a typescript whose manila cover was marked: *Temporary—This script is not final and is given to you for advance information only.* It occurred to me that the warning might apply to Mrs. Dreen's own story.

As we left the Santa Barbara city limits, she tossed the script over her shoulder into the backseat. "It *really* smells. It's going to be a smash."

A few miles north of the city, a dirt road branched off to the left beside a filling station. It wound for a mile or more through broken country to her private beach. The beach house was set well back from the sea at the convergence of brown bluffs which huddled over it like scarred shoulders. To reach it we had to drive along the beach for a quarter of a mile, detouring to the very edge of the sea around the southern bluff.

The blue-white dazzle of sun, sand, and surf was like an arc-furnace. But I felt some breeze from the water when we got out of the car. A few languid clouds moved inland over our heads. A little high plane was gamboling among them like a terrier in a henyard.

"You have privacy," I said to Mrs. Dreen.

She stretched, and touched her varnished hair with her fingers. "One tires of the goldfish role. When I lie out there in the afternoons I—forget I have a name." She pointed to the middle of the cove beyond the breakers, where a white raft moved gently in the swells. "I simply take off my clothes and revert to protoplasm. All my clothes."

I looked up at the plane whose pilot was doodling in the sky. It dropped, turning like an early falling leaf, swooped like a hawk, climbed like an aspiration.

She said with a laugh: "If they come too low I cover my face, of course."

We had been moving away from the house towards the water. Nothing could have looked more innocent than the quiet cove held in the curve of the white beach like a benign blue eye in a tranquil brow. Then its colors shifted as a cloud passed over the sun. Cruel green and violent purple ran in the blue. I felt the old primitive terror and fascination. Mrs. Dreen shared the feeling and put it into words:

"It's got queer moods. I hate it sometimes as much as I love it." For an instant she looked old and uncertain. "I hope she isn't in there."

The tide had turned and was coming in, all the way from Hawaii and beyond, all the way from the shattered islands where bodies lay unburied in the burnt-out caves. The waves came up towards us, fumbling and gnawing at the beach like an immense soft mouth.

"Are there bad currents here, or anything like that?"

"No. It's deep, though. It must be twenty feet under the raft. I could never bottom it."

"I'd like to look at her room," I said. "It might tell us where she went, and even with whom. You'd know what clothes were missing?"

She laughed a little apologetically as she opened the door. "I used to dress my daughter, naturally. Not any more. Besides, more than half her things must be in the Hollywood apartment. I'll try to help you, though."

It was good to step out of the vibrating brightness of the beach into shadowy stillness behind Venetian blinds. "I noticed that you unlocked the door," I said. "It's a big house with a lot of furniture in it. No servants?"

"I occasionally have to knuckle under to producers. But I won't to my employees. They'll be easier to get along with soon, now that the plane plants are shutting down."

We went to Una's room, which was light and airy in both atmosphere and furnishings. But it showed the lack of servants. Stockings, shoes, underwear, dresses, bathing suits, lipstick-smeared tissue littered the chairs and the floor. The bed was unmade. The framed photograph on the night table was obscured by two empty glasses which smelt of highball, and flanked by overflowing ashtrays.

I moved the glasses and looked at the young man with the wings on his chest. Naive, handsome, passionate were words which suited the strong, blunt nose, the full lips and square jaw, the wide proud eyes. For Mrs. Dreen he would have made a single healthy meal, and I wondered again if her daughter was a carnivore. At least the photograph of Jack Rossiter was the only sign of a man in her room. The two glasses could easily have been from separate nights. Or separate weeks, to judge by the condition of the room. Not that it wasn't an attractive room. It was like a pretty girl in disarray. But disarray.

We examined the room, the closets, the bathroom, and found nothing of importance, either positive or negative. When we had waded through the brilliant and muddled wardrobe which Una had shed, I turned to Mrs. Dreen.

"I guess I'll have to go back to Hollywood. It would help me if you'd come along. It would help me more if you'd tell me who your daughter knew. Or rather who she liked—I suppose she knew everybody. Remember you suggested yourself that there's a man in this."

"I take it you haven't found anything?"

"One thing I'm pretty sure of. She didn't intentionally go away for long. Her toilet articles and pills are still in her bathroom. She's got quite a collection of pills."

"Yes, Una's always been a hypochondriac. Also she left Jack's picture. She only had the one, because she liked it best."

"That isn't so conclusive," I said. "I don't suppose you'd know whether there's a bathing suit missing?"

"I really couldn't say, she had so many. She was at her best in them."

"Still *was?*"

"I guess so, as a working hypothesis. Unless you can find me evidence to the contrary."

"You didn't like your daughter much, did you?"

"No. I didn't like her father. And she was prettier than I."

"But not so intelligent?"

"Not as bitchy, you mean? She was bitchy enough. But I'm still worried about Jack. He loved her. Even if I didn't."

The telephone in the hall took the cue and began to ring. "This is Millicent Dreen," she said into it. "Yes, you may read it to me." A pause. "'Kill the fatted calf, ice the champagne, turn down the sheets and break out the black silk nightie. Am coming home tomorrow.' Is that right?"

Then she said, "Hold it a minute. I wish to send an answer. To Ensign Jack Rossiter, USS *Guam*, CVE 173, Naval Air Station, Alameda—is that Ensign Rossiter's correct address? The text is: 'Dear Jack join me at the Hollywood apartment there is no one at the beach house. Millicent.' Repeat it, please. . . . Right. Thank you."

She turned from the phone and collapsed in the nearest chair, not forgetting to arrange her legs symmetrically.

"So Jack is coming home tomorrow?" I said. "All I had before was no evidence. Now I have no evidence and until tomorrow."

She leaned forward to look at me. "I've been wondering how far I can trust you."

"Not so far. But I'm not a blackmailer. I'm not a mind reader, either, and it's sort of hard to play tennis with the invisible man."

"The invisible man has nothing to do with this. I called him when Una didn't come home. Just before I came to your office."

"All right," I said. "You're the one that wants to find Una. You'll get around to telling me. In the meantime, who else did you call?"

"Hilda Karp, Una's best friend—her *only* female friend."

"Where can I get hold of her?"

"She married Gray Karp, the agent. They live in Beverly Hills."

Their house, set high on a plateau of rolling lawn, was huge and fashionably grotesque: Spanish Mission with a dash of Paranoia. The room where I waited for Mrs. Karp was as big as a small barn and full of blue furniture. The bar had a brass rail.

Hilda Karp was a Dresden blonde with an athletic body and brains. By appearing in it, she made the room seem more real. "Mr. Archer, I believe?" She had my card in her hand, the one with *Private Investigator* on it.

"Una Sand disappeared yesterday. Her mother said you were her best friend."

"Millicent—Mrs. Dreen—called me early this morning. But, as I said then, I haven't seen Una for several days."

"Why would she go away?"

Hilda Karp sat down on the arm of a chair, and looked thoughtful. "I can't understand why her mother should be worried. She can take care of herself, and she's gone away before. I don't know why this time. I know her well enough to know that she's unpredictable."

"Why did she go away before?"

"Why do girls leave home, Mr. Archer?"

"She picked a queer time to leave home. Her husband's coming home tomorrow."

"That's right, she told me he sent her a cable from Pearl. He's a nice boy."

"Did Una think so?"

She looked at me frigidly as only a pale blonde can look, and said nothing.

"Look," I said. "I'm trying to do a job for Mrs. Dreen. My job is laying skeletons to rest, not teaching them the choreography of the *Danse Macabre*."

"Nicely put," she said. "Actually there's no skeleton. Una has played around, in a perfectly casual way I mean, with two or three men in the last year."

"Simultaneously, or one at a time?"

"One at a time. She's monandrous to that extent. The latest is Terry Neville."

"I thought he was married."

"In an interlocutory way only. For God's sake don't bring my name into it. My husband's in business in this town."

"He seems to be prosperous," I said, looking more at her than at the house. "Thank you very much, Mrs. Karp. Your name will never pass my lips."

"Hideous, isn't it? The name, I mean. But I couldn't help falling in love with the guy. I hope you find her. Jack will be terribly disappointed if you don't."

I had begun to turn towards the door, but turned back. "It couldn't be anything like this, could it? She heard he was coming home, she felt unworthy of him, unable to face him, so she decided to lam out?"

"Millicent said she didn't leave a letter. Women don't go in for all such drama and pathos without leaving a letter. Or at least a marked copy of Tolstoi's *Resurrection*."

"I'll take your word for it." Her blue eyes were very bright in the great dim room. "How about this? She didn't like Jack at all. She went away for the sole purpose of letting him know that. A little sadism, maybe?"

"But she did like Jack. It's just that he was away for over a year. Whenever the subject came up in a mixed gathering, she always insisted that he was a wonderful lover."

"Like that, eh? Did Mrs. Dreen say you were Una's best friend?"

Her eyes were brighter and her thin, pretty mouth twisted in amusement. "Certainly. You should have heard her talk about me."

"Maybe I will. Thanks. Good-bye."

A telephone call to a screenwriter I knew, the suit for which I had paid a hundred and fifty dollars of separation money in a moment of euphoria, and a false air of assurance got me past the studio guards and as far as the door of Terry Neville's dressing room. He had a bungalow to himself, which meant that he was as important as the publicity claimed. I didn't know what I was going to say to him, but I knocked on the door and, when someone said, "Who is it?" showed him.

Only the blind had not seen Terry Neville. He was over six feet, colorful, shapely, and fragrant like a distant garden of flowers. For a minute he went on reading and smoking in his brocaded armchair, carefully refraining from raising his eyes to look at me. He even turned a page of his book.

"Who are you?" he said finally. "I don't know you."

"Una Sand—"

"I don't know her, either." Grammatical solecisms had been weeded out of his speech, but nothing had been put in their place. His voice was impersonal and lifeless.

"Millicent Dreen's daughter," I said, humoring him. "Una Rossiter."

"Naturally I know Millicent Dreen. But you haven't said anything. Good day."

"Una disappeared yesterday. I thought you might be willing to help me find out why."

"You still haven't said anything." He got up and took a step towards me, very tall and wide. "What I said was *good day.*"

But not tall and wide enough. I've always had an idea, probably incorrect, that I could handle any man who wears a scarlet silk bath-robe. He saw that idea on my face and changed his tune: "If you don't get out of here, my man, I'll call a guard."

"In the meantime I'd straighten out that marcel of yours. I might even be able to make a little trouble for you." I said that on the assumption that any man with his face and sexual opportunities would be on the brink of trouble most of the time.

It worked. "What do you mean by saying that?" he said. A

sudden pallor made his carefully plucked black eyebrows stand out starkly. "You could get into a very great deal of hot water by standing there talking like that."

"What happened to Una?"

"I don't know. Get out of here."

"You're a liar."

Like one of the clean-cut young men in one of his own movies, he threw a punch at me. I let it go over my shoulder and while he was off balance placed the heel of my hand against his very flat solar plexus and pushed him down into his chair. Then I shut the door and walked fast to the front gate. I'd just as soon have gone on playing tennis with the invisible man.

"No luck, I take it?" Mrs. Dreen said when she opened the door of her apartment to me.

"I've got nothing to go on. If you really want to find your daughter you'd better go to Missing Persons. They've got the organization and the connections."

"I suppose Jack will be going to them. He's home already."

"I thought he was coming tomorrow."

"That telegram was sent yesterday. It was delayed somehow. His ship got in yesterday afternoon."

"Where is he now?"

"At the beach house by now, I guess. He flew down from Alameda in a Navy plane and called me from Santa Barbara."

"What did you tell him?"

"What could I tell him? That Una was gone. He's frantic. He thinks she may have drowned." It was late afternoon, and in spite of the whiskey which she was absorbing steadily, like an alcohol lamp, Mrs. Dreen's fires were burning low. Her hands and eyes were limp, and her voice was weary.

"Well," I said, "I might as well go back to Santa Barbara. I talked to Hilda Karp but she couldn't help me. Are you coming along?"

"Not again. I have to go to the studio tomorrow. Anyway, I don't want to see Jack just now. I'll stay here."

The sun was low over the sea, gold-leafing the water and

bloodying the sky, when I got through Santa Barbara and back onto the coast highway. Not thinking it would do any good but by way of doing something or other to earn my keep, I stopped at the filling station where the road turned off to Mrs. Dreen's beach house.

"Fill her up," I said to the woman attendant. I needed gas anyway.

"I've got some friends who live around here," I said when she held out her hand for her money. "Do you know where Mrs. Dreen lives?"

She looked at me from behind disapproving spectacles. "You should know. You were down there with her today, weren't you?"

I covered my confusion by handing her a five and telling her: "Keep the change."

"No, thank you."

"Don't misunderstand me. All I want you to do is tell me who was there yesterday. You see all. Tell a little."

"Who are you?"

I showed her my card.

"Oh." Her lips moved unconsciously, computing the size of the tip. "There was a guy in a green convert, I think it was a Chrysler. He went down around noon and drove out again around four, I guess it was, like a bat out of hell."

"That's what I wanted to hear. You're wonderful. What did he look like?"

"Sort of dark and pretty good-looking. It's kind of hard to describe. Like the guy that took the part of the pilot in that picture last week—*you* know—only not so good-looking."

"Terry Neville."

"That's right, only not so good-looking. I've seen him go down there plenty of times."

"I don't know who that would be," I said, "but thanks anyway. There wasn't anybody with him, was there?"

"Not that I could see."

I went down the road to the beach house like a bat into hell. The sun, huge and angry red, was horizontal now, half-eclipsed by the sea and almost perceptibly sinking. It spread a red glow over the shore like a soft and creeping fire. After a long time, I thought, the cliffs would crumble, the sea would dry up, the whole earth would burn out. There'd be nothing left but bone-white cratered ashes like the moon.

When I rounded the bluff and came within sight of the beach I saw a man coming out of the sea. In the creeping fire which the sun shed he, too, seemed to be burning. The diving mask over his face made him look strange and inhuman. He walked out of the water as if he had never set foot on land before.

I walked towards him. "Mr. Rossiter?"

"Yes." He raised the glass mask from his face and with it the illusion of strangeness lifted. He was just a handsome young man, well-set-up, tanned, and worried-looking.

"My name is Archer."

He held out his hand, which was wet, after wiping it on his bathing trunks, which were also wet. "Oh, yes, Mr. Archer. My mother-in-law mentioned you over the phone."

"Are you enjoying your swim?"

"I am looking for the body of my wife." It sounded as if he meant it. I looked at him more closely. He was big and husky, but he was just a kid, twenty-two or -three at most. Out of school into the air, I thought. Probably met Una Sand at a party, fell hard for all that glamour, married her the week before he shipped out, and had dreamed bright dreams ever since. I remembered the brash telegram he had sent, as if life was like the people in slick magazine advertisements.

"What makes you think she drowned?"

"She wouldn't go away like this. She knew I was coming home this week. I cabled her from Pearl."

"Maybe she never got the cable."

After a pause he said: "Excuse me." He turned towards the waves which were breaking almost at his feet. The sun had disappeared, and the sea was turning gray and cold-looking, an anti-human element.

"Wait a minute. If she's in there, which I doubt, you should call the police. This is no way to look for her."

"If I don't find her before dark, I'll call them then," he said. "But if she's here, I want to find her myself." I could never have guessed his reason for that, but when I found it out it made sense. So far as anything in the situation made sense.

He walked a few steps into the surf, which was heavier now that the tide was coming in, plunged forward, and swam slowly towards the raft with his masked face under the water. His arms and legs beat the rhythm of the crawl as if his muscles took pleasure in it, but his face was downcast, searching the darkening sea floor. He swam in widening circles about the raft, raising his head about twice a minute for air.

He had completed several circles and I was beginning to feel that he wasn't really looking for anything, but expressing his sorrow, dancing a futile ritualistic water dance, when suddenly he took air and dived. For what seemed a long time but was probably about twenty seconds, the surface of the sea was empty except for the white raft. Then the masked head broke water, and Rossiter began to swim towards shore. He swam a laborious side stroke, with both arms submerged. It was twilight now, and I couldn't see him very well, but I could see that he was swimming very slowly. When he came nearer I saw a swirl of yellow hair.

He stood up, tore off his mask, and threw it away into the sea. He looked at me angrily, one arm holding the body of his wife against him. The white body half-floating in the shifting water was nude, a strange bright glistening catch from the sea floor.

"Go away," he said in a choked voice.

I went to get a blanket out of the car, and brought it to him where he laid her out on the beach. He huddled over her as if to protect her body from my gaze. He covered her and stroked her wet hair back from her face. Her face was not pretty. He covered that, too.

I said: "You'll have to call the police now."

After a time he answered: "I guess you're right. Will you help me carry her into the house?"

I helped him. Then I called the police in Santa Barbara, and told them that a woman had been drowned and where to find her.

I left Jack Rossiter shivering in his wet trunks beside her blanketed body, and drove back to Hollywood for the second time.

Millicent Dreen was in her apartment in the Park-Wilshire. In the afternoon there had been a nearly full decanter of scotch on her buffet. At ten o'clock it was on the coffee table beside her chair, and nearly empty. Her face and body had sagged. I wondered if every day she aged so many years, and every morning recreated herself through the power of her will.

She said: "I thought you were going back to Santa Barbara. I was just going to go to bed."

"I did go. Didn't Jack phone you?"

"No." She looked at me, and her green eyes were suddenly very much alive, almost fluorescent. "You found her?" she said.

"Jack found her in the sea. She was drowned."

"I was afraid of that." But there was something like relief in her voice. As if worse things might have happened. As if at least she had lost no weapons and gained no foes in the daily battle to hold position in the world's most competitive city.

"You hired me to find her," I said. "She's found, though I had nothing to do with finding her—and that's that. Unless you want me to find out who drowned her."

"What do you mean?"

"What I said. Perhaps it wasn't an accident. Or perhaps somebody stood by and watched her drown."

I had given her plenty of reason to be angry with me before, but for the first time that day she was angry. "I gave you a hundred dollars for doing nothing. Isn't that enough for you? Are you trying to drum up extra business?"

"I did one thing. I found out that Una wasn't by herself yesterday."

"Who was with her?" She stood up and walked quickly back and forth across the rug. As she walked her body was remolding itself into the forms of youth and vigor. She recreated herself before my eyes.

"The invisible man," I said. "My tennis partner."

Still she wouldn't speak the name. She was like the priestess of a cult whose tongue was forbidden to pronounce a secret word. But she said quickly and harshly: "If my daughter was killed I want to know who did it. I don't care who it was. But if you're giving me a line and if you make trouble for me and nothing comes of it, I'll have you kicked out of Southern California. I could do that."

Her eyes flashed, her breath came fast, and her sharp breast rose and fell with many of the appearances of genuine feeling. I liked her very much at that moment. So I went away, and instead of making trouble for her I made trouble for myself.

I found a booth in a drugstore on Wilshire and confirmed what I knew, that Terry Neville would have an unlisted number. I called a girl I knew who fed gossip to a movie columnist, and found out that Neville lived in Beverly Hills but spent most of his evenings around town. At this time of night he was usually at Ronald's or Chasen's, a little later at Ciro's. I went to Ronald's because it was nearer, and Terry Neville was there.

He was sitting in a booth for two in the long, low, smoke-filled room, eating smoked salmon and drinking stout. Across from him there was a sharp-faced terrier-like man who looked like his business manager and was drinking milk. Some Hollywood actors spend a lot of time with their managers, because they have a common interest.

I avoided the headwaiter and stepped up to Neville's table. He saw me and stood up, saying: "I warned you this afternoon. If you don't get out of here I'll call the police."

I said quietly: "I sort of am the police. Una is dead." He didn't answer and I went on: "This isn't a good place to talk. If you'll step outside for a minute I'd like to mention a couple of facts to you."

"You say you're a policeman," the sharp-faced man snapped, but quietly. "Where's your identification? Don't pay any attention to him, Terry."

Terry didn't say anything. I said: "I'm a private detective. I'm investigating the death of Una Rossiter. Shall we step outside, gentlemen?"

"We'll go out to the car," Terry Neville said tonelessly. "Come on, Ed," he added to the terrier-like man.

The car was not a green Chrysler convertible, but a black Packard limousine equipped with a uniformed chauffeur. When we entered the parking lot he got out of the car and opened the door. He was big and battered-looking.

I said: "I don't think I'll get in. I listen better standing up. I always stand up at concerts and confessions."

"You're not going to listen to anything," Ed said.

The parking lot was deserted and far back from the street, and I forgot to keep my eye on the chauffeur. He rabbit-punched me and a gush of pain surged into my head. He rabbit-punched me again and my eyes rattled in their sockets and my body became invertebrate. Two men moving in a maze of lights took hold of my upper arms and lifted me into the car. Unconsciousness was a big black limousine with a swiftly purring motor and the blinds down.

Though it leaves the neck sore for days, the effect of a rabbit punch on the centers of consciousness is sudden and brief. In two or three minutes I came out of it, to the sound of Ed's voice saying:

"We don't like hurting people and we aren't going to hurt you. But you've got to learn to understand, whatever your name is—"

"Sacher-Masoch," I said.

"A bright boy," said Ed. "But a bright boy can be too bright for his own good. You've got to learn to understand that you can't go around annoying people, especially very important people like Mr. Neville here."

Terry Neville was sitting in the far corner of the backseat, looking worried. Ed was between us. The car was in motion, and I could see lights moving beyond the chauffeur's shoulders hunched over the wheel. The blinds were down over the back windows.

"Mr. Neville should keep out of my cases," I said. "At the moment you'd better let me out of this car or I'll have you arrested for kidnaping."

Ed laughed, but not cheerfully. "You don't seem to realize what's happening to you. You're on your way to the police station, where Mr. Neville and I are going to charge you with attempted blackmail."

"Mr. Neville is a very brave little man," I said. "Inasmuch as he was seen leaving Una Sand's house shortly after she was killed. He was seen leaving in a great hurry and a green convertible."

"My God, Ed," Terry Neville said, "you're getting me in a frightful mess. You don't know what a frightful mess you're getting me in." His voice was high, with a ragged edge of hysteria.

"For God's sake, you're not afraid of this bum, are you?" Ed said in a terrier yap.

"You get out of here, Ed. This is a terrible thing, and you don't know how to handle it. I've got to talk to this man. Get out of this car."

He leaned forward to take the speaking tube, but Ed put a hand on his shoulder. "Play it your way, then, Terry. I still think I had the right play, but you spoiled it."

"Where are we going?" I said. I suspected that we were headed for Beverly Hills, where the police know who pays them their wages.

Neville said into the speaking tube: "Turn down a side street and park. Then take a walk around the block."

"That's better," I said when we had parked. Terry Neville looked frightened. Ed looked sulky and worried. For no good reason, I felt complacent.

"Spill it," I said to Terry Neville. "Did you kill the girl? Or did she accidentally drown—and you ran away so you wouldn't get mixed up in it? Or have you thought of a better one than that?"

"I'll tell you the truth," he said. "I didn't kill her. I didn't even know she was dead. But I was there yesterday afternoon. We were sunning ourselves on the raft, when a plane came over flying very low. I went away, because I didn't want to be seen there with her—"

"You mean you weren't exactly sunning yourselves?"

"Yes. That's right. This plane came over high at first, then he circled back and came down very low. I thought maybe he recognized me, and might be trying to take pictures or something."

"What kind of a plane was it?"

"I don't know. A military plane, I guess. A fighter plane. It was a single-seater painted blue. I don't know military planes."

"What did Una Sand do when you went away?"

"I don't know. I swam to shore, put on some clothes, and drove away. She stayed on the raft, I guess. But she was certainly all right when I left her. It would be a terrible thing for me if I was dragged into this thing. Mr.—"

"Archer."

"Mr. Archer. I'm terribly sorry if we hurt you. If I could make it right with you—" He pulled out a wallet.

His steady pallid whine bored me. Even his sheaf of bills bored me. The situation bored me.

I said: "I have no interest in messing up your brilliant career, Mr. Neville. I'd like to mess up your brilliant pan sometime, but that can wait. Until I have some reason to believe that you haven't told me the truth, I'll keep what you said under my hat. In the meantime, I want to hear what the coroner has to say."

They took me back to Ronald's, where my car was, and left me with many protestations of good fellowship. I said good night to them, rubbing the back of my neck with an exaggerated gesture. Certain other gestures occurred to me.

When I got back to Santa Barbara the coroner was working over Una. He said that there were no marks of violence on her body, and very little water in her lungs and stomach, but this condition was characteristic of about one drowning in ten.

I hadn't known that before, so I asked him to put it into sixty-four-dollar words. He was glad to.

"Sudden inhalation of water may result in a severe reflex spasm of the larynx, followed swiftly by asphyxia. Such a laryngeal spasm is more likely to occur if the victim's face is upward, allowing water to rush into the nostrils, and would be likely to be facilitated by emotional or nervous shock. It may have happened like that or it may not."

"Hell," I said, "she may not even be dead."

He gave me a sour look. "Thirty-six hours ago she wasn't."

I figured it out as I got in my car. Una couldn't have drowned much later than four o'clock in the afternoon on September the seventh.

It was three in the morning when I checked in at the Barbara Hotel. I got up at seven, had breakfast in a restaurant, and went to the beach house to talk to Jack Rossiter. It was only about eight o'clock when I got there, but Rossiter was sitting on the beach in a canvas chair watching the sea.

"You again?" he said when he saw me.

"I'd think you'd have had enough of the sea for a while. How long were you out?"

"A year." He seemed unwilling to talk.

"I hate bothering people," I said, "but my business is always making a nuisance out of me."

"Evidently. What exactly is your business?"

"I'm currently working for your mother-in-law. I'm still trying to find out what happened to her daughter."

"Are you trying to needle me?" He put his hands on the arms of the chair as if to get up. For a moment his knuckles were white. Then he relaxed. "You saw what happened, didn't you?"

"Yes. But do you mind my asking what time your ship got into San Francisco on September the seventh?"

"No. Four o'clock. Four o'clock in the afternoon."

"I suppose that could be checked?"

He didn't answer. There was a newspaper on the sand beside his chair and he leaned over and handed it to me. It was the Late Night Final of a San Francisco newspaper for the seventh.

"Turn to page four," he said.

I turned to page four and found an article describing the arrival of the USS *Guam* at the Golden Gate, at four o'clock in the afternoon. A contingent of Waves had greeted the returning heroes, and a band had played "California, Here I Come."

"If you want to see Mrs. Dreen, she's in the house," Jack Rossiter said. "But it looks to me as if your job is finished."

"Thanks," I said.

"And if I don't see you again, good-bye."

"Are you leaving?"

"A friend is coming out from Santa Barbara to pick me up in a few minutes. I'm flying up to Alameda with him to see about getting leave. I just had a forty-eight, and I've got to be here for the inquest tomorrow. And the funeral." His voice was hard. His whole personality had hardened overnight. The evening before his nature had been wide open. Now it was closed and invulnerable.

"Good-bye," I said, and plodded through the soft sand to the house. On the way I thought of something, and walked faster.

When I knocked, Mrs. Dreen came to the door holding a cup of coffee, not very steadily. She was wearing a heavy wool dressing robe with a silk rope around the waist, and a silk cap on her head. Her eyes were bleary.

"Hello," she said. "I came back last night after all. I couldn't work today anyway. And I didn't think Jack should be by himself."

"He seems to be doing all right."

"I'm glad you think so. Will you come in?"

I stepped inside. "You said last night that you wanted to know who killed Una no matter who it was."

"Well?"

"Does that still go?"

"Yes. Why? Did you find out something?"

"Not exactly. I thought of something, that's all."

"The coroner believes it was an accident. I talked to him on the phone this morning." She sipped her black coffee. Her hand vibrated steadily, like a leaf in the wind.

"He may be right," I said. "He may be wrong."

There was the sound of a car outside, and I moved to the window and looked out. A station wagon stopped on the beach, and a Navy officer got out and walked towards Jack Rossiter. Rossiter got up and they shook hands.

"Will you call Jack, Mrs. Dreen, and tell him to come into the house for a minute?"

"If you wish." She went to the door and called him.

Rossiter came to the door and said a little impatiently: "What is it?"

"Come in," I said. "And tell me what time you left the ship the day before yesterday."

"Let's see. We got in at four—"

"No, you didn't. The ship did, but not you. Am I right?"

"I don't know what you mean."

"You know what I mean. It's so simple that it couldn't fool anybody for a minute, not if he knew anything about carriers. You flew your plane off the ship a couple of hours before she got into port. My guess is that you gave that telegram to a buddy to send for you before you left the ship. You flew down here, caught your wife being made love to by another man, landed on the beach—and drowned her."

"You're insane!" After a moment he said less violently: "I admit I flew off the ship. You could easily find that out anyway. I flew around for a couple of hours, getting in some flying time—"

"Where did you fly?"

"Along the coast. I didn't get down this far. I landed at Alameda at five-thirty, and I can prove it."

"Who's your friend?" I pointed through the open door to the other officer, who was standing on the beach looking out to sea.

"Lieutenant Harris. I'm going to fly up to Alameda with him. I warn you, don't make any ridiculous accusations in his presence, or you'll suffer for it."

"I want to ask him a question," I said. "What sort of plane were you flying?"

"FM-3."

I went out of the house and down the slope to Lieutenant Harris. He turned towards me and I saw the wings on his blouse.

"Good morning, lieutenant," I said. "You've done a good deal of flying, I suppose?"

"Thirty-two months. Why?"

"I want to settle a bet. Could a plane land on this beach and take off again?"

"I think maybe a Piper Cub could. I'd try it anyway. Does that settle the bet?"

"It was a fighter I had in mind. An FM-3."

"Not an FM-3," he said. "Not possibly. It might just conceivably be able to land but it'd never get off again. Not enough room, and very poor surface. Ask Jack, he'll tell you the same."

I went back to the house and said to Jack: "I was wrong. I'm sorry. As you said, I guess I'm all washed up with this case."

"Good-bye, Millicent," Jack said, and kissed her cheek. "If I'm not back tonight I'll be back first thing in the morning. Keep a stiff upper lip."

"You do, too, Jack."

He went away without looking at me again. So the case was ending as it had begun, with me and Mrs. Dreen alone in a room wondering what had happened to her daughter.

"You shouldn't have said what you did to him," she said. "He's had enough to bear."

My mind was working very fast. I wondered whether it was producing anything. "I suppose Lieutenant Harris knows what he's talking about. He says a fighter couldn't land and take off from this beach. There's no other place around here he could have landed without being seen. So he didn't land.

"But I still don't believe that he wasn't here. No young husband flying along the coast within range of the house where his wife was—well, he'd fly low and dip his wings to her, wouldn't he? Terry Neville saw the plane come down."

"Terry Neville?"

"I talked to him last night. He was with Una before she died. The two of them were out on the raft together when Jack's plane came down. Jack saw them, and saw what they were doing. They saw him. Terry Neville went away. Then what?"

"You're making this up," Mrs. Dreen said, but her green eyes were intent on my face.

"I'm making it up, of course. I wasn't here. After Terry Neville ran away, there was no one here but Una, and Jack in a plane circling over her head. I'm trying to figure out why Una died. I *have* to make it up. But I think she died of fright. I think Jack dived at her and forced her into the water. I think he kept on diving at her until she was gone. Then he flew back to Alameda and chalked up his flying time."

"Fantasy," she said. "And very ugly. I don't believe it."

"You should. You've got that cable, haven't you?"

"I don't know what you're talking about."

"Jack sent Una a cable from Pearl, telling her what day he was arriving. Una mentioned it to Hilda Karp. Hilda Karp mentioned it to me. It's funny you didn't say anything about it."

"I didn't know about it," Millicent Dreen said. Her eyes were blank.

I went on, paying no attention to her denial: "My guess is that the cable said not only that Jack's ship was coming in on the seventh, but that he'd fly over the beach house that afternoon. Fortunately, I don't have to depend on guesswork. The cable will be on file at Western Union, and the police will be able to look at it. I'm going into town now."

"Wait," she said. "Don't go to the police about it. You'll only get Jack in trouble. I destroyed the cable to protect him, but I'll tell you what was in it. Your guess was right. He said he'd fly over on the seventh."

"When did you destroy it?"

"Yesterday, before I came to you. I was afraid it would implicate Jack."

"Why did you come to me at all, if you wanted to protect Jack? It seems that you knew what happened."

"I wasn't sure. I didn't know what had happened to her, and until I found out I didn't know what to do."

"You're still not sure," I said. "But I'm beginning to be. For one thing, it's certain that Una never got her cable, at least not as it was sent. Otherwise she wouldn't have been doing what she was doing on the afternoon that her husband was going to fly over and say hello. You changed the date on it, perhaps? So that Una expected Jack a day later? Then you arranged to be in Hollywood on the seventh, so that Una could spend a final afternoon with Terry Neville."

"Perhaps." Her face was completely alive, controlled but full of dangerous energy, like a cobra listening to music.

"Perhaps you wanted Jack for yourself," I said. "Perhaps you had another reason, I don't know. I think even a psychoanalyst would have a hard time working through your motivations, Mrs. Dreen, and I'm not one. All I know is that you precipitated a murder. Your plan worked even better than you expected."

"It was accidental death," she said hoarsely. "If you go to the police you'll only make a fool of yourself, and cause trouble for Jack."

"You care about Jack, don't you?"

"Why shouldn't I?" she said. "He was mine before he ever saw Una. She took him away from me."

"And now you think you've got him back." I got up to go. "I hope for your sake he doesn't figure out for himself what I've just figured out."

"Do you think he will?" Sudden terror had jerked her face apart. I didn't answer her.

THE CHIRASHI COVENANT

BY NAOMI HIRAHARA

Terminal Island

(Originally published in 2007)

There were Alice Watanabe's deviled eggs, lined up in diagonal lines on her white ceramic serving plate, Betty Shoda's potato salad mixed in with a smidge of her secret ingredient, *wasabi*, and Dorothy Takeyama's ambrosia, peeled orange slices with coconut flakes.

Next to the hostess's ham was a wedge of iceberg lettuce with Green Goddess dressing dripping from the sides. Not a surprise—Sets Kamimura hated to cook and always took the lazy way out. The rest of the women knew this but would never say anything to Sets, even in jest.

And finally, in a huge round lacquerware container was Helen Miura's *chirashi*. The women were amazed by Helen's handiwork. Each piece of vegetable—carrot, *shiitake* mushroom, burdock root—was uniformly cut and mixed in with the rice like scattered tiny leaves and twigs blown by the Santa Ana winds. Others may have used a grater or a Japanese *daikon suri*, but Helen was a master with the knife. Her father had been a fisherman in Terminal Island before the war and Helen, being the oldest, was in charge of cleaning the catch he brought home for dinner. Her mother worked in the tuna cannery, so Helen was destined to get things done.

In the ice box was a vanilla cake, which had been purchased at a Japanese American bakery on Jefferson Boulevard in the Crenshaw area. Written in thick pastel icing were the words *Japanese American Court Reunion* and, below, *10-Year Anniversary*.

In 1941, these seven women had ridden on a float in a parade down the streets of Little Tokyo. Yoshiko Kumai, who was hosting the reunion, had been the queen, but everyone knew that Helen was the most beautiful one of them all. Even today, with her thin frame despite having a baby girl two years ago and her long legs, she captured second looks from men of every color and income bracket.

But what Helen lacked was charm. She didn't smile easily; even in all the photos with the rest of the court she never showed her teeth. Helen and Yoshiko, both twenty-year-olds at the time, stood together at the Yamato Hall in Little Tokyo, waiting for the winner's name to be called. Yoshiko groped for Helen's hand, her own hand moist and warm. Helen's hand remained limp and cool, and when Yoshiko squeezed, Helen did not reciprocate.

Even though Helen hadn't won the 1941 beauty contest, she had won life's competition so far. She had married Frank, probably the most eligible Nisei man in the Manzanar War Relocation Center. By all counts, the insurance company he had started for the resettled Japanese Americans was headed for success.

"I just don't know how you do it, Helen," said Alice. "I'm always embarrassed to make *chirashi*, because I know how beautiful yours comes out."

"It's nothing, really. Just a lot of chopping and cutting. You need to start off with a good knife."

The conversation then quickly turned to children and the Japanese American women's club that three of them belonged to. While the women giggled and laughed, Helen grew more distant.

"I'll be right back," she excused herself, taking her clutch purse with her.

When Helen was nearly out the back door, Sets pressed two fingers to her mouth and then mimed blowing smoke from her lips. "Ta-ba-co," she commented to the others, with a wink.

Helen took a package of cigarettes from her purse. She had started smoking just recently. Frank didn't approve, of course, and his mother had been aghast to find her smoking in the backyard of their rented Boyle Heights wood-framed house. No matter how much Frank and his mother commented on her smoking, Helen refused to give it up. She needed something of her own.

"Hello." On the other side of the low fence stood a *hakujin* man in a suit. He was clean-cut and handsome with a large open forehead. A William Holden type.

Helen lit a cigarette with a lighter she had purchased in a department store in Little Tokyo.

A young white couple emerged from the back of the next door neighbor's house. The woman was visibly pregnant. "We love it, Bob. It's perfect," she said. They then noticed Helen on the other side of the fence. Helen could feel their enthusiasm wane immediately.

"You'll love the neighbors," the man who had greeted Helen said enthusiastically. Almost like he meant it. "Ken was in the U.S. Army, fought over in both Italy and France, I think. Works for the city as a draftsman. He and Yoshiko have two children. They're good people. Go to a congregational church not far from here."

"That's nice," the pregnant woman said weakly. She was disappointed, Helen could tell. Her picture-perfect world was shattered. Helen knew what that felt like.

"Don't worry," Helen spoke up. "There's not too many of us living on this block. Give us ten years, it might be a different story. But you will have moved out by then."

The couple exchanged glances and looked down at the lawn. "Well," the pregnant woman said a little too brightly, "let's take another look at the laundry room." The couple surveyed the backyard wistfully, as if saying a final goodbye before returning to the inside of the house. The man in the suit remained outside.

"I think that I might have cost you a sale," Helen said without any regret.

"Well, good riddance, then. Ken and Yoshiko are good people. Anyone would be lucky to have them or any of their friends as neighbors."

Helen was surprised. She had expected to be met with anger.

"Bob Burkard." The man walked to the low fence and stuck

out his hand. Helen hesitated. She moved her lit cigarette from her right hand to her left to better shake hands. She murmured back her name.

"Are you in the market for a new home?"

"What do you mean?"

"You look hungry for a new house." The agent then laughed. "I can tell these things. In my job, you need to be observant." Frank had said the same thing in his line of work. He was constantly selling, but in a comfortable, non-threatening way. Usually by the end of his sales pitch, his customers thought it was they who had approached him for insurance.

"Not here," Helen said. Not Montebello, a few cities east from where they lived now. Montebello was a growing suburb, but it was inland. Helen hated to be landlocked.

"Where, then?"

"The ocean."

"Ocean? Do you mean Sawtelle?"

Helen almost burst out laughing. Alice Watanabe had represented the Sawtelle area in their beauty pageant. Unincorporated, it drew a cluster of Japanese American nurseries and small shops just a stone's throw away from the Veteran's Administration Hospital.

"Not Sawtelle. Pacific Palisades. Malibu. Right by the ocean."

The agent didn't even blink. Helen was impressed.

"I grew up near the water," she offered up more.

"Where?"

"Terminal Island."

"The military base?"

"It wasn't always the military's."

Helen snuffed out her cigarette on the Kumais' cement patio floor and turned to go back inside.

"Wait," Bob called out.

Helen took a few steps into the soft grass again, restaining the pointy heels of her pumps.

Bob handed Helen his business card. "Call me at my office. We'll see what we can do."

* * *

Helen had told Frank her dream to live in Pacific Palisades months ago.

"Dear," he said, refolding the Japanese American newspaper that was delivered to their rented house every afternoon. "That's impossible."

"They can't keep us away. Not anymore, right?" Helen re-adjusted the embroidered doily on the middle of their dining room table.

"It doesn't matter what the Supreme Court says. Remember what happened to the Uchidas in South Pasadena—they had to be interviewed by all the neighbors. Do you want to go through that? Get their seal of approval? I don't want to be where I'm not wanted."

"Who cares what they want? How about what *we* want?"

"It's too far. I need to be around Japanese people. They are my customer base, our livelihood. Someplace like Gardena is a better bet for us. And what would Mama do in Pacific Palisades? She needs to be close to Japanese people too."

Helen said nothing. She went outside and smoked two ciga-rettes right below her mother-in-law's bedroom window.

Helen had absolutely not wanted to get married in camp. She hated the idea of being imprisoned with other Japanese Americans on her wedding day. Frank's bachelor friends had agreed to move out of their barracks so that the newlyweds could have a proper honeymoon night, but Helen refused to go along with it. If Frank insisted that they get married in Manzanar's mess hall with tissue paper flowers, Helen would force him to spend their first night together on a bumpy mattress next to his widowed mother's, only separated by some hanging wool blankets.

"We need to get out of here," she told Frank. "Let's apply for special clearance." She brought back bulletins about work in De-troit and Chicago.

But the answer was always the same. "What about Mama? At least in camp she has her friends nearby."

Helen thought everything would have changed when Japanese Americans were allowed to move back to the West Coast in early 1945. But Mama would live with them and they had to be close to Little Tokyo.

Then came the birth of Diana. When Helen looked down at her perfectly formed daughter, this mini–human being that both she and Frank had created, she knew that she had a renewed purpose in life.

"I won't let anything happen to you," she had whispered in her daughter's ear. "You will have everything life has to offer."

Despite their earlier conversations, Helen told Frank that she was going to be looking for a new house. Frank was busy with work after all. "You should use Jun. I have his office phone number somewhere." He rifled through the layers of paper on his desk in the corner of the living room.

"There's an agent I met through Yoshiko," Helen said. "I think I'd rather use him."

Frank shrugged his shoulders. "Just don't sign anything."

The next day Helen kissed Diana's forehead and left for Bob Burkard's office in Montebello. Bob's hair seemed freshly combed and the scent of his cologne was so strong that it tickled her nose.

They drove in his new Studebaker towards the beach.

"Who's watching your daughter?" he asked.

"My mother-in-law."

He showed Helen two homes and then drove her back to his office. This routine continued for four days straight.

On the fifth day, Bob parked his car in a dirt lot overlooking the ocean. "I brought us lunch," he said, taking out a blanket and picnic basket from his trunk.

Helen thought it was strange for a bachelor to own a picnic basket. "You've never married?" she couldn't help but to ask him after eating one of his egg salad sandwiches.

"Came close," he said. "It's just taken me some time to meet the right woman."

"So you're picky."

"And what's wrong with that? It's the rest of your life, right? You want to get that right."

Tears came to Helen's eyes. She knew that she was being silly.

"What did I say?" Bob became flustered and fished a hand-kerchief from the breast pocket of his suit. "I'm so sorry. I didn't mean anything by it." Before Helen could stop him, he was wiping her tears with his handkerchief. He then rested his hand on her cheek. "You are a remarkably beautiful woman. Do you know that, Helen?" With that, he kissed her. Helen had never been kissed by a white man before.

On their silent drive home, all Helen could think was, *What have I done?*

The picnics continued the next day and then the next. Bob's kisses quickly moved from her mouth to her neck, down to her breasts and beyond. Helen knew that what she was doing was wrong. That she would be punished someday.

"*Hausu sagashi?* Mama asked when she returned from one of her expeditions with Bob.

"Yes, house hunting," said Helen, feeling grains of sand in her panties.

"Really," Mama said in Japanese, not looking convinced of it at all.

Helen wasn't sure if Mama had spoken to Frank about her long hours away from the house and their daughter. Frank, for all his earnestness, wasn't the type to deal with a problem directly. Instead he usually found a solution through a side door.

"I found it," Frank reported one evening upon returning home. "A beautiful house. It's in Gardena, but southern Gardena. Not that far from the ocean, and when you breathe hard, you can smell salt air, really."

Frank even had a photo of the property. A single-story wood-framed house, which didn't look that different from the property they were renting.

"What are those?"

"Oil derricks. But you can pretend they're towers. The Eiffel Tower."

In the past, Helen would have been amused by her husband's fancifulness.

"So, what do you think?"

Gardena was at least thirty miles away from Bob's office, even further from their spot in Malibu. Helen said nothing.

"You'll love it, dear. Really. It'll grow on you."

"I'm moving to Gardena. Frank's bought a house," Helen told Bob over the phone while Mama was bathing Diana.

"Gardena?"

Helen nodded. "I won't be able to see you anymore."

"Why?"

"I can't be driving all the way to Montebello. Diana will be ready to go to school soon. I need to spend more time with her."

"Well, then, I'll find us a meeting place down there."

"In Gardena?" Both Helen and Bob knew very few secrets could be hidden there.

"Listen, I've found the perfect house for you in Malibu. It's just come out on the market."

"It's too late, Bob."

"It's never too late. I'll show it to him. He can always sell the Gardena house. He'll fall in love with it, really."

"But why? It's not like I'll be able to see you in Malibu much."

"I want you to be happy."

Bob was being ridiculous, and Helen was angry that he couldn't accept the inevitable. Their affair couldn't last. Diana was getting fussy from her long hours away from her mother. Helen had to bury her feelings. She had practice, but obviously *gaman*, perseverance, was a new concept for Bob.

That Thursday evening, Frank didn't come home for dinner. He hadn't called and Helen was becoming worried. She called Frank's secretary at home and was told that he was meeting a real estate agent on the west side of town.

At nine o'clock, the phone rang. "Is this Mrs. Frank Miura?" A male voice that Helen didn't recognize.

"Yes."

"This is the sherriff's department. There's been an accident."

Helen was surprised that Frank's mother wanted to come with her to the coroner's office. Helen told her to take care of Diana. "Mama, it will be better if you stay behind."

"This is your fault," Mama said in Japanese.

Helen's legs had been shaky to begin with, but now she felt like her knees would buckle underneath her.

"You told him that you wanted to move near the water. He only wanted to make you happy."

The coroner had warned Helen that she might not recognize her husband. His body had been severely battered from the rocks. It had been a fifty-foot drop, after all.

His neck was twisted; his beautiful face now raw and torn. Helen thought that his nose was missing, but she saw that it was instead flattened into a pulpy mass.

His ears were still intact, and Helen checked behind his left earlobe, and sure enough, his mole was there. She studied his hands. His fingers were stiff but his nails were still well manicured, a little squarish at the top.

It was definitely Frank.

Later a police officer sat down with her and asked Helen what her husband was doing on a cliff in Malibu.

"I'm not sure. His secretary told me that he was there to look at a house. A new house that we were thinking of buying." Helen's voice shook. Should she mention Bob? She wasn't sure it had been Bob. But it had to be him.

"Yes, we found the address in his pocket. The real estate agent, in fact, was the one who discovered your husband's body. Do you know a man named Bob Burkard?"

The police car parked in front of their rented house and Helen got out, her hands still trembling.

She thanked the officer, and the car slowly disappeared down the street. Before she got to the stairs, someone pulled at her arm.

"How dare you come here?" Helen said to Bob.

He pulled her into some pine trees framing the side of the house.

"You killed him," she declared.

Bob shook his head. "I didn't even make it on time for our appointment. He had fallen by the time I arrived. I was the one who called the police."

"I'm going to tell the police about us." Helen was ashamed that she had not been more revealing during the police interview. All she mentioned was that Bob had been their agent. Purely business.

"That we were having an affair? What do you think that will do to your daughter? People will talk. You'll be implicated, you know."

Bob was right. Tongues would wag. Helen Miura was having an adulterous affair with a white man. Diana would be shunned by the parents of her peers. Her family shamed. And if something happened to Helen, who would take care of Diana? Mama couldn't do it on her own. Helen's parents were too old, and her siblings had their own children to raise. Helen knew what it was like to be one of many. She didn't want that to happen to her Diana.

"I'll wait for you. Even a year. In respect of your husband's death."

Respect? Helen felt like screaming, tearing Bob's hair out. *I know what you have done.* She wanted to spit in his face, but she used all her rage to manage a slight smile on her lips.

That night Helen lay in their double bed by herself. The doctor at the Japanese hospital had dropped off some sleeping medicine for her. Something to stir into hot water. But Helen didn't want to sleep. She didn't deserve to sleep.

Helen reached out for the crumpled sheets Frank had slept

in the night before. She planned to never wash them. Instead she would save them in a box so that she could periodically go and smell her late husband.

She wrapped the sheets around her legs and stared at Frank's pillow. There were a few loose hairs coated with oil.

She felt now that Frank, in his death, could see everything. He could see her deception, the romantic trysts in Bob's car and on the beach.

"I'm so sorry, Frank," she whispered. And then she knew what she had to do.

Helen's parents had an old family friend, Kaji-*san*. A Japanese immigrant like Helen's father, Kaji-*san* had been a fisherman as well. He was *rambo*, rough. A lot of Terminal Islanders had been that way, cured in the sun and salt water. But Kaji-*san* had a callused face in addition to his callused hands.; a face with dried-up crevices like earthquake faults.

After the war, Helen's relatives had taken in the old bachelor for a while before he got back on his feet and opened a Japanese restaurant in Little Tokyo. To everyone's surprise, Kaji-*san* succeeded, and before long he had even purchased a boat that was docked at Pierpoint Landing in Long Beach.

Kaji-*san* felt indebted to Helen's family, so much so that they eventually stopped going to his restaurant because he never took their money. But Helen needed a favor now, and Kaji-*san* was, of course, more than willing to comply. Besides, he already had questions and concerns. Helen had lost some weight—she was thin to begin with, but now her high cheekbones were even more prominent and defined. Frank's death had definitely taken a toll on her, but Kaji-*san* knew that Helen would never do anything rash. She wasn't that type of woman.

Helen arrived at the empty restaurant three hours before her appointment and let herself in the back with Kaji-*san*'s key. She needed the extra time to get ready.

Bob came early too, fifteen minutes early. Helen could tell from the flush in his cheeks that he was excited. She even let him give her a peck on her cheek. That much she could tolerate.

Helen had him sit at the wooden counter and served him a piping-hot cup of green tea.

"I've never had green tea before." He sipped carefully and then grimaced. "Bitter."

"You'll get used to it. This tea is expensive; you'll insult me if you don't finish it."

By the time the teacup was empty, Bob's head rested on the wooden counter. Helen went to the kitchen and put on her rubber gloves. And then rolled out the wheelbarrow.

One time she had been out on the fishing boat when her father had caught a bluefin tuna. It had been a magnificent fish, almost six feet tall, almost three hundred pounds. It took three men to handle it. The fish first needed to be stunned. Helen's father used one of her brother's baseball bats. This time Helen used Frank's.

The fishermen found the soft spot in the fish's head and pushed a spike in its brain. Helen was amazed how easy it was to kill a huge fish like that. It shuddered as if it was hoping for another chance at life, then went limp.

There was a method to cutting a bluefin tuna. You first needed time to bleed the fish so that its sheen would still be maintained. And then go right to the internal organs in the gilling and gutting. Later you would cut the meat into chunks and sell them by the pound.

Helen could skip many of the steps she had learned as a child. The most important tools here were the knife and the mallet. She was thankful some family friends had watched over her father's tools while they had been in Manzanar.

After Helen was done, she carefully packed different parts of Bob in three different suitcases and cleaned the cement floor of Kaji-*san*'s kitchen. She had brought extra bottles of bleach for the task. She then drove to Pierpoint Landing and took Kaji-*san*'s motorized fishing boat as far as she could, and dropped each suitcase into different parts of the ocean. The water was black as the ink of an octopus, and for a moment Helen imagined a huge sea monster emerging from the darkness and tearing her, too, into shreds. But her mind was only playing tricks on her. After closing her eyes hard and reopening them, she found that her fear had disappeared.

Shortly thereafter, Helen, Diana, and Mama moved into the wood-framed house in southern Gardena. Next door was a flower farm and packing shed.

"That Miura widow is a cold one," the grower's wife said to her husband as they were bunching up flowers at night to get ready for the early-morning drive to the Flower Market in Los Angeles.

The flower grower, Tad, simply nodded, so that his wife would be under the impression that he was listening.

"Never says hello. She was on one of those beauty queen courts back in 1941. But she wasn't the queen. Too stuck-up for the judges, I think."

Tad grunted. He wasn't one to spread stories. But he knew who she was. One day when he was driving back from the Flower Market in the morning after the children left for school, he saw her in the middle of his snapdragon blooms, next to one of the oil derricks. She was screaming and crying; at first he thought she had been injured. When he slowed his panel truck, she straightened her hair and rubbed the smeared makeup from below her eyes.

"You okay?" he asked from his open car window.

She stared back at him, her eyes shiny like wet black stones. She then spoke, her voice barely audible above the rhythmic squeak of the derricks. "Are any of us?"

Tad's panel truck remained idling as the widow slowly walked back into her house and closed the door.

HIGH DARKTOWN

BY JAMES ELLROY

West Adams

(Originally published in 1986)

From my office windows I watched L.A. celebrate the end of World War II. Central Division Warrants took up the entire north side of City Hall's eleventh floor, so my vantage point was high and wide. I saw clerks drinking straight from the bottle in the Hall of Records parking lot across the street and harness bulls forming a riot squad and heading for Little Tokyo a few blocks away, bent on holding back a conga line of youths with 2 by 4s who looked bent on going the atom bomb one better. Craning my neck, I glimpsed tall black plumes of smoke on Bunker Hill—a sure sign that patriotic Belmont High students were stripping cars and setting the tires on fire. Over on Sunset and Figueroa, knots of zooters were assembling in violation of the Zoot Suit Ordinance, no doubt figuring that today it was anything goes.

The tiny window above my desk had an eastern exposure, and it offered up nothing but smog and a giant traffic jam inching toward Boyle Heights. I stared into the brown haze, imagining shitloads of code 2s and 3s thwarted by noxious fumes and bumper-to-bumper revelry. My daydreams got more and more vivid, and when I had a whole skyful of A-bombs descending on the offices of the L.A.P.D. Detective Bureau, I slammed my desk and picked up the two pieces of paper I had been avoiding all morning.

The first sheet was a scrawled memo from the Daywatch Robbery boss down the hall: *Lee—Wallace Simpkins paroled from Quentin last week—to our jurisdiction. Thought you should know. Be careful. G.C.*

Cheery V-J Day tidings.

The second page was an interdepartmental teletype issued from University Division, and, when combined with Georgie Caulkins's warning, it spelled out the beginning of a new one-front war.

Over the past five days there had been four heavy-muscle stickups in the West Adams district, perpetrated by a two-man heist team, one white, one negro. The MO was identical in all four cases: liquor stores catering to upper-crust negroes were hit at night, half an hour before closing, when the cash registers were full. A well-dressed male Caucasian would walk in and beat the clerk to the floor with the barrel of a .45 automatic, while the negro heister stuffed the till cash into a paper bag. Twice customers had been present when the robberies occurred; they had also been beaten senseless—one elderly woman was still in critical condition at Queen of Angels.

It was as simple and straightforward as a neon sign. I picked up the phone and called Al Van Patten's personal number at the County Parole Bureau.

"Speak, it's your nickel."

"Lee Blanchard, Al."

"Big Lee! You working today? The war's over!"

"No, it's not. Listen, I need the disposition on a parolee. Came out of Quentin last week. If he reported in, I need an address; if he hasn't, just tell me."

"Name? Charge?"

"Wallace Simpkins, 655 PC. I sent him up myself in '39."

Al whistled. "Light jolt. He got juice?"

"Probably kept his nose clean and worked a war industries job inside; his partner got released to the army after Pearl Harbor. Hurry it up, will you?"

"Off and running."

Al dropped the receiver to his desk, and I suffered through long minutes of static-filtered party noise—male and female giggles, bottles clinking together, happy county flunkies turning radio dials trying to find dance music but getting only jubilant accounts of the big news. Through Edward R. Murrow's uncharacteristically cheerful drone I pictured Wild Wally Simpkins, flush with cash and armed for bear, looking for *me*. I was shivering when Al came back on the line and said, "He's hot, Lee."

"Bench warrant issued?"

"Not yet."

"Then don't waste your time."

"What are you talking about?"

"Small potatoes. Call Lieutenant Holland at University dicks and tell him Simpkins is half of the heist team he's looking for. Tell him to put out an APB and add, 'armed and extremely dangerous' and 'apprehend with all force deemed necessary.'"

Al whistled again. "That bad?"

I said, "Yeah," and hung up. "Apprehend with all force deemed necessary" was the L.A.P.D. euphemism for "shoot on sight." I felt my fear decelerate just a notch. Finding fugitive felons was my job. Slipping an extra piece into my back waistband, I set out to find the man who had vowed to kill me.

After picking up standing mugs of Simpkins and a carbon of the robbery report from Georgie Caulkins, I drove toward the West Adams district. The day was hot and humid, and sidewalk mobs spilled into the street, passing victory bottles to horn-honking motorists. Traffic was bottlenecked at every stoplight, and paper debris floated down from office windows—a makeshift ticker-tape parade. The scene made me itchy, so I attached the roof light and hit my siren, weaving around stalled cars until downtown was a blur in my rearview mirror. When I slowed, I was all the way to Alvarado and the city I had sworn to protect looked normal again. Slowing to a crawl in the right-hand lane, I thought of Wallace Simpkins and knew the itch wouldn't stop until the bastard was bought and paid for.

We went back six years, to the fall of '39, when I was a vice officer in University Division and a regular light-heavyweight attraction at the Hollywood-Legion Stadium. A black-white stickup gang had been clouting markets and juke joints on West Adams, the white guy passing himself off as a member of Mickey Cohen's mob, coercing the proprietor into opening up the safe for the monthly protection payment while the negro guy looked around

innocently, then hit the cash registers. When the white guy got to
the safe, he took all the money, then pistol-whipped the proprietor
senseless. The heisters would then drive slowly north into the respectable Wilshire district, the white guy at the wheel, the negro
guy huddled down in the backseat.

I got involved in the investigation on a fluke.

After the fifth job, the gang stopped cold. A stoolie of mine
told me that Mickey Cohen found out that the white muscle was
an ex-enforcer of his and had him snuffed. Rumor had it that the
colored guy—a cowboy known only as Wild Wallace—was looking for a new partner and a new territory. I passed the information
along to the dicks and thought nothing more of it. Then, a week
later, it all hit the fan.

As a reward for my tip, I got a choice moonlight assignment:
bodyguarding a high-stakes poker game frequented by L.A.P.D.
brass and navy bigwigs up from San Diego. The game was held in
the back room at Minnie Roberts's Casbah, the swankiest police-
sanctioned whorehouse on the south side. All I had to do was look
big, mean, and servile and be willing to share boxing anecdotes.
It was a major step toward sergeant's stripes and a transfer to the
Detective Division.

It went well—all smiles and backslaps and recountings of my
split-decision loss to Jimmy Bivins—until a negro guy in a chauffeur's outfit and an olive-skinned youth in a navy officer's uniform
walked in the door. I saw a gun bulge under the chauffeur's left
arm, and chandelier light fluttering over the navy man's face re-
vealed pale negro skin and processed hair.

And I knew.

I walked up to Wallace Simpkins, my right hand extended.
When he grasped it, I sent a knee into his balls and a hard left
hook at his neck. When he hit the floor, I pinned him there with
a foot on his gun bulge, drew my own piece, and leveled it at his
partner. "Bon voyage, admiral," I said.

The admiral was named William Boyle, an apprentice armed
robber from a black bourgeois family fallen on hard times. He
turned state's evidence on Wild Wallace, drew a reduced three-

to-five jolt at Chino as part of the deal, and was paroled to the war effort early in '42. Simpkins was convicted of five counts of robbery one with aggravated assault, got five-to-life at Big Q, and voodoo-hexed Billy Boyle and me at his trial, vowing on the soul of Baron Samedi to kill both of us, chop us into stew meat, and feed it to his dog. I more than half believed his vow, and for the first few years he was away, every time I got an unexplainable ache or pain I thought of him in his cell, sticking pins into a blue-suited Lee Blanchard voodoo doll.

I checked the robbery report lying on the seat beside me. The addresses of the four new black-white stickups covered 26th and Gramercy to La Brea and Adams. Hitting the racial demarcation line, I watched the topography change from negligent middle-class white to proud colored. East of St. Andrews, the houses were unkempt, with peeling paint and ratty front lawns. On the west the homes took on an air of elegance: small dwellings were encircled by stone fencing and well-tended greenery; the mansions that had earned West Adams the sobriquet High Darktown put Beverly Hills pads to shame—they were older, larger, and less architecturally pretentious, as if the owners knew that the only way to be rich and black was to downplay the performance with the quiet noblesse oblige of old white money.

I knew High Darktown only from the scores of conflicting legends about it. When I worked University Division, it was never on my beat. It was the lowest per capita crime area in L.A. The University brass followed an implicit edict of letting rich black police rich black, as if they figured blue suits couldn't speak the language there at all. And the High Darktown citizens did a good job. Burglars foolish enough to trek across giant front lawns and punch in Tiffany windows were dispatched by volleys from thousand-dollar skeet guns held by negro financiers with an aristocratic panache to rival that of *anyone* white and big-moneyed. High Darktown did a damn good job of being inviolate.

But the legends were something else, and when I worked University, I wondered if they had been started and repeatedly embellished only because square-john white cops couldn't take the fact that there were "niggers," "shines," "spooks," and "jigs" who were capable of buying their low-rent lives outright. The stories ran from the relatively prosaic: negro boot-leggers with mob connections taking their loot and buying liquor stores in Watts and wetback-staffed garment mills in San Pedro, to exotic: the same thugs flooding low darktowns with cut-rate heroin and pimping out their most beautiful high-yellow sweethearts to L.A.'s powers-that-be in order to circumvent licensing and real estate statutes enforcing racial exclusivity. There was only one common denominator to all the legends: it was agreed that although High Darktown money started out dirty, it was now squeaky clean and snow white.

Pulling up in front of the liquor store on Gramercy, I quickly scanned the dick's report on the robbery there, learning that the clerk was alone when it went down and saw both robbers up close before the white man pistol-whipped him unconscious. Wanting an eyeball witness to back up Lieutenant Holland's APB, I entered the immaculate little shop and walked up to the counter.

A negro man with his head swathed in bandages walked in from the back. Eyeing me top to bottom, he said, "Yes, officer?"

I liked his brevity and reciprocated it. Holding up the mug shot of Wallace Simpkins, I said, "Is this one of the guys?"

Flinching backward, he said, "Yes. Get him."

"Bought and paid for," I said.

An hour later I had three more eyeball confirmations and turned my mind to strategy. With the all-points out on Simpkins, he'd probably get juked by the first blue suit who crossed his path, a thought only partly comforting. Artie Holland probably had stake-out teams stationed in the back rooms of other liquor stores in the area, and a prowl of Simpkins's known haunts was a ridiculous play for a solo white man. Parking on an elm-lined street, I watched Japanese gardeners tend football field–sized lawns and started to sense that Wild Wallace's affinity for High Darktown and white partners was the lever I needed. I set out to trawl for pale-skinned intruders like myself.

South on La Brea to Jefferson, then up to Western and back over to Adams. Runs down 1st Avenue, 2nd Avenue, 3rd, 4th, and 5th. The only white men I saw were other cops, mailmen, store owners, and poontang prowlers. A circuit of the bars on Washington yielded no white faces and no known criminal types I could shake down for information.

Dusk found me hungry, angry, and still itchy, imagining Simpkins poking pins in a brand-new, plainclothes Blanchard doll. I stopped at a barbecue joint and wolfed down a beef sandwich, slaw, and fries. I was on my second cup of coffee when the mixed couple came in.

The girl was a pretty high yellow—soft angularity in a pink summer dress that tried to downplay her curves, and failed. The man was squat and muscular, wearing a rumpled Hawaiian shirt and pressed khaki trousers that looked like army issue. From my table I heard them place their order: jumbo chicken dinners for six with extra gravy and biscuits. "Lots of big appetites," the guy said to the counterman. When the line got him a deadpan, he goosed the girl with his knee. She moved away, clenching her fists and twisting her head as if trying to avoid an unwanted kiss. Catching her face full view, I saw loathing etched into every feature.

They registered as trouble, and I walked out to my car in order to tail them when they left the restaurant. Five minutes later they appeared, the girl walking ahead, the man a few paces behind her, tracing hourglass figures in the air and flicking his tongue like a lizard. They got into a prewar Packard sedan parked in front of me, Lizard Man taking the wheel. When they accelerated, I counted to ten and pursued.

The Packard was an easy surveillance. It had a long radio antenna topped with a foxtail, so I was able to remain several car lengths in back and use the tail as a sighting device. We moved out of High Darktown on Western, and within minutes mansions and proudly tended homes were replaced by tenements and tar-paper shacks encircled by chicken wire. The farther south we drove the worse it got; when the Packard hung a left on 94th and headed east, past auto graveyards, storefront voodoo mosques, and hair-straightening parlors, it felt like entering White Man's Hell.

At 94th and Normandie, the Packard pulled to the curb and parked; I continued on to the corner. From my rearview I watched Lizard Man and the girl cross the street and enter the only decent-looking house on the block, a whitewashed adobe job shaped like a miniature Alamo. Parking myself, I grabbed a flashlight from under the seat and walked over.

Right away I could tell the scene was way off. The block was nothing but welfare cribs, vacant lots, and gutted jalopies, but six beautiful '40–'41 vintage cars were stationed at curbside. Hunkering down, I flashed my light at their license plates, memorized the numbers, and ran back to my unmarked cruiser. Whispering hoarsely into the two-way, I gave R&I the figures and settled back to await the readout.

I got the kickback ten minutes later, and the scene went from way off to way, *way* off.

Cupping the radio mike to my ear and clamping my spare hand over it to hold the noise down, I took in the clerk's spiel. The Packard was registered to Leotis McCarver, male negro, age 41, of 1348 West 94th Street, L.A.—which had to be the cut-rate Alamo. His occupation was on file as union officer in the Brotherhood of Sleeping Car Porters. The other vehicles were registered to negro and white thugs with strong-arm convictions dating back to 1922. When the clerk read off the last name—Ralph "Big Tuna" De Santis, a known Mickey Cohen trigger—I decided to give the Alamo a thorough crawling.

Armed with my flashlight and two pieces, I cut diagonally across vacant lots toward my target's backyard. In the far distance I could see fireworks lighting up the sky, but down here no one seemed to be celebrating—their war of just plain living was still dragging on. When I got to the Alamo's yard wall, I took it at a run and kneed and elbowed my way over the top, coming down onto soft grass.

The back of the house was dark and quiet, so I risked flashing my light. Seeing a service porch fronted by a flimsy wooden door, I tiptoed over and tried it—and found it unlocked.

I walked in flashlight first, my beam picking up dusty walls and floors, discarded lounge chairs, and a broom-closet door standing half open. Opening it all the way, I saw army officers' uniforms on hangers, replete with campaign ribbons and embroidered insignias.

Shouted voices jerked my attention toward the house proper. Straining my ears, I discerned both white- and negro-accented insults being hurled. There was a connecting door in front of me, with darkness beyond it. The shouting had to be issuing from a front room, so I nudged the door open a crack, then squatted down to listen as best I could.

". . . and I'm just tellin' you we gots to find a place and get us off the streets," a negro voice was yelling, "'cause even if we splits up, colored with colored and the whites with the whites, there is still gonna be roadblocks!"

A babble rose in response, then a shrill whistle silenced it, and a white voice dominated: "We'll be stopping the train way out in the country. Farmland. We'll destroy the signaling gear, and if the passengers take off looking for help, the nearest farmhouse is ten fucking miles away—and those dogfaces are gonna be on foot."

A black voice tittered, "They gonna be mad, them soldiers."

Another black voice: "They gonna fought the whole fucking war for free."

Laughter, then a powerful negro baritone took over: "Enough clowning around, this is money we're talking about and nothing else!"

"'Cepting revenge, mister union big shot. Don't you forget I got me other business on that train."

I knew that voice by heart—it had voodoo-cursed my soul in court. I was on my way out the back for reinforcements when my legs went out from under me and I fell head first into darkness.

The darkness was soft and rippling, and I felt like I was swimming in a velvet ocean. Angry shouts reverberated far away, but I knew they were harmless; they were coming from another planet. Every so often I felt little stabs in my arms and saw pinpoints of light that made the voices louder, but then everything would go even softer, the velvet waves caressing me, smothering all my hurt.

Until the velvet turned to ice and the friendly little stabs became wrenching thuds up and down my back. I tried to draw myself into a ball, but an angry voice from this planet wouldn't let me. "Wake up, shitbird! We ain't wastin' no more pharmacy morph on you! Wake up! Wake up, goddamnit!"

Dimly I remembered that I was a police officer and went for the .38 on my hip. My arms and hands wouldn't move, and when I tried to lurch my whole body, I knew they were tied to my sides and that the thuds were kicks to my legs and rib cage. Trying to move away, I felt head-to-toe muscle cramps and opened my eyes. Walls and a ceiling came into hazy focus, and it all came back. I screamed something that was drowned out by laughter, and the Lizard Man's face hovered only inches above mine. "Lee Blanchard," he said, waving my badge and ID holder in front of my eyes. "You got sucker-punched again, shitbird. I saw Jimmy Bivins put you down at the Legion. Left hook outta nowhere, and you hit your knees, then worthless-shine muscle puts you down on your face. I got no respect for a man who gets sucker-punched by niggers."

At "niggers" I heard a gasp and twisted around to see the negro girl in the pink dress sitting in a chair a few feet away. Listening for background noises and hearing nothing, I knew the three of us were alone in the house. My eyes cleared a little more, and I saw that the velvet ocean was a plushly furnished living room. Feeling started to return to my limbs, sharp pain that cleared my fuzzy head. When I felt a grinding in my lower back, I winced; the extra .38 snub I had tucked into my waistband at City Hall was still there, slipped down into my skivvies. Reassured by it, I looked up at Lizard Face and said, "Robbed any liquor stores lately?"

He laughed. "A few. Chump change compared to the big one this after—"

The girl shrieked, "Don't tell him nothin'!"

Lizard Man flicked his tongue. "He's dead meat, so who cares? It's a train hijack, canvasback. Some army brass chartered the Super Chief, L.A. to Frisco. Poker games, hookers in the sleeping cars, smut movies in the lounge. Ain't you heard? The war's over, time to celebrate. We got hardware on board—shines playing porters, white guys in army suits. They all got scatter-guns, and sweetie pie's boyfriend Voodoo, he's got himself a tommy. They're gonna take the train down tonight, around Salinas, when the brass is smashed to the gills, just achin' to throw away all that good separation pay. Then Voodoo's gonna come back here and perform some religious rites on you. He told me about it, said he's got this mean old pit bull named Revenge. A friend kept him while he was in Quentin. The buddy was white, and he tormented the dog so he hates white men worse than poison. The dog only gets fed about twice a week, and you can just bet he'd love a nice big bowl of canvasback stew. Which is you, white boy. Voodoo's gonna cut you up alive, turn you into dog food out of the can. Wanna take a bet on what he cuts off first?"

"That's not true! That's not what—"

"Shut up, Cora!"

Twisting on my side to see the girl better, I played a wild hunch. "Are you Cora Downey?"

Cora's jaw dropped, but Lizard spoke first. "Smart boy. Billy Boyle's ex, Voodoo's current. These high-yellow coozes get around. You know canvasback here, don't you, sweet? He sent both your boyfriends up, and if you're real nice, maybe Voodoo'll let you do some cutting on him."

Cora walked over and spat in my face. She hissed "Mother" and kicked me with a spiked toe. I tried to roll away, and she sent another kick at my back.

Then my ace in the hole hit me right between the eyes, harder than any of the blows I had absorbed so far. Last night I had heard Wallace Simpkins's voice through the door: "'Cepting revenge, mister union big shot. I got me other business on that train." In my mind that "business" buzzed as snuffing Lieutenant Billy Boyle, and I was laying five-to-one that Cora wouldn't like the idea.

Lizard took Cora by the arm and led her to the couch, then squatted next to me. "You're a sucker for a spitball," he said.

I smiled up at him. "Your mother bats cleanup at a two-dollar whorehouse."

He slapped my face. I spat blood at him and said, "And you're ugly."

He slapped me again; when his arm followed through I saw the handle of an automatic sticking out of his right pants pocket. I made my voice drip with contempt: "You hit like a girl. Cora could take you easy."

His next shot was full force. I sneered through bloody lips and said, "You queer? Only nancy boys slap like that."

A one-two set hit me in the jaw and neck, and I knew it was now or never. Slurring my words like a punch-drunk pug, I said, "Let me up. Let me up and I'll fight you man-to-man. Let me up."

Lizard took a penknife from his pocket and cut the rope that bound my arms to my sides. I tried to move my hands, but they were jelly. My battered legs had some feeling in them, so I rolled over and up onto my knees. Lizard had backed off into a chump's idea of a boxing stance and was firing roundhouse lefts and rights at the living room air. Cora was sitting on the couch, wiping angry tears from her cheeks. Deep breathing and lolling my torso like a hophead, I stalled for time, waiting for feeling to return to my hands.

"Get up, shitbird!"

My fingers still wouldn't move.

"I said get up!"

Still no movement.

Lizard came forward on the balls of his feet, feinting and shadowboxing. My wrists started to buzz with blood, and I began to get unprofessionally angry, like I was a rookie heavy, not a thirty-one-year-old cop. Lizard hit me twice, left, right, open-handed.

In a split second he became Jimmy Bivins, and I zoomed back to the ninth round at the Legion in '37. Dropping my left shoulder, I sent out a right lead, then pulled it and left-hooked him to the breadbasket. Bivins gasped and bent forward; I stepped backward for swinging room. Then Bivins was Lizard going for his piece, and I snapped to where I really was.

We drew at the same time. Lizard's first shot went above my head, shattering a window behind me; mine, slowed by my awkward rear pull, slammed into the far wall. Recoil spun us both around, and before Lizard had time to aim I threw myself to the floor and rolled to the side like a carpet-eating dervish. Three shots cut the air where I had been standing a second before, and I extended my gun arm upward, braced my wrist, and emptied my snub-nose at Lizard's chest. He was blasted backward, and through the shots' echoes I heard Cora scream long and shrill.

I stumbled over to Lizard. He was on his way out, bleeding from three holes, unable to work the trigger of the .45. He got up the juice to give me a feeble middle-finger farewell, and when the bird was in midair I stepped on his heart and pushed down, squeezing the rest of his life out in a big arterial burst. When he finished twitching, I turned my attention to Cora, who was standing by the couch, putting out another shriek.

I stifled the noise by pinning her neck to the wall and hissing, "Questions and answers. Tell me what I want to know and you walk, fuck with me and I find dope in your purse and tell the DA you've been selling it to white nursery-school kids." I let up on my grip. "First question. Where's my car?"

Cora rubbed her neck. I could feel the obscenities stacking up on her tongue, itching to be hurled. All her rage went into her eyes as she said, "Out back. The garage."

"Have Simpkins and the stiff been clouting the liquor stores in West Adams?"

Cora stared at the floor and nodded, "Yes." Looking up, her eyes were filled with the self-disgust of the freshly turned stoolie. I said, "McCarver the union guy thought up the train heist?"

Another affirmative nod.

Deciding not to mention Billy Boyle's probable presence on the train, I said, "Who's bankrolling? Buying the guns and uniforms?"

"The liquor store money was for that, and there was this rich guy fronting money."

Now the big question. "When does the train leave Union Station?"

Cora looked at her watch. "In half an hour."

I found a phone in the hallway and called the Central Division squadroom, telling Georgie Caulkins to send all his available plainclothes and uniformed officers to Union Station, that an army-chartered Super Chief about to leave for 'Frisco was going to be hit by a white-negro gang in army and porter outfits. Lowering my voice so Cora wouldn't hear, I told him to detain a negro quartermaster lieutenant named William Boyle as a material witness, then hung up before he could say anything but "Jesus Christ."

Cora was smoking a cigarette when I reentered the living room. I picked my badge holder up off the floor and heard sirens approaching. "Come on," I said. "You don't want to get stuck here when the bulls show up."

Cora flipped her cigarette at the stiff, then kicked him one for good measure. We took off.

I ran code three all the way downtown. Adrenaline smothered the dregs of the morph still in my system, and anger held down the lid on the aches all over my body. Cora sat as far away from me as she could without hanging out the window and never blinked at the siren noise. I started to like her and decided to doctor my arresting officer's report to keep her out of the shithouse.

Nearing Union Station, I said, "Want to sulk or want to survive?"

Cora spat out the window and balled her fists.

"Want to get skin searched by some dyke matrons over at city jail or you want to go home?"

Cora's fist balls tightened up; the knuckles were as white as my skin.

"Want Voodoo to snuff Billy Boyle?"

That got her attention. "What!"

I looked sidelong at Cora's face gone pale. "He's on the train. You think about that when we get to the station and a lot of cops start asking you to snitch off your pals."

Pulling herself in from the window, Cora asked me the question that hoods have been asking cops since they patrolled on dinosaurs: "Why you do this shitty kind of work?"

I ignored it and said, "Snitch. It's in your best interest."

"That's for me to decide. Tell me."

"Tell you what?"

"Why you do—"

I interrupted, "You've got it all figured out, you tell me."

Cora started ticking off points on her fingers, leaning toward me so I could hear her over the siren. "One, you yourself figured your boxin' days would be over when you was thirty, so you got yourself a nice civil service pension job; two, the bigwig cops loves to have ball players and fighters around to suck up to them—so's you gets the first crack at the cushy 'signments. Three, you likes to hit people, and *po*-lice work be full of that; four, your ID card said Warrants Division, and I knows that warrants cops all serves process and does repos on the side, so I knows you pickin' up lots of extra change. Five—"

I held up my hands in mock surrender, feeling like I had just taken four hard jabs from Billy Conn and didn't want to go for sloppy fifths. "Smart girl, but you forgot to mention that I work goon squad for Firestone Tire and get a kickback for fingering wetbacks to the Border Patrol."

Cora straightened the knot in my disreputable necktie. "Hey, baby, a gig's a gig, you gots to take it where you finds it. I done things I ain't particularly proud of, and I—"

I shouted, "That's not it!"

Cora moved back to the window and smiled. "It certainly is, Mr. *Po*-liceman."

Angry now, angry at losing, I did what I always did when I smelled defeat: attack. "Shitcan it. Shitcan it now, before I forget I was starting to like you."

Cora gripped the dashboard with two white-knuckled hands and stared through the windshield. Union Station came into view, and pulling into the parking lot I saw a dozen black-and-whites and unmarked cruisers near the front entrance. Bullhorn-barked commands echoed unintelligibly as I killed my siren, and behind the police cars I glimpsed plainclothesmen aiming riot guns at the ground.

I pinned my badge to my jacket front and said, "Out." Cora stumbled from the car and stood rubber-kneed on the pavement. I got out, grabbed her arm, and shoved-pulled her all the way over to the pandemonium. As we approached, a harness bull leveled his .38 at us, then hesitated and said, "Sergeant Blanchard?"

I said "Yeah" and handed Cora over to him, adding, "She's a material witness, be nice to her." The youth nodded, and I walked past two bumper-to-bumper black-and-whites into the most incredible shakedown scene I had ever witnessed:

Negro men in porter uniforms and white men in army khakis were lying facedown on the pavement, their jackets and shirts pulled up to their shoulders, their trousers and undershorts pulled down to their knees. Uniformed cops were spread searching them while plainclothesmen held the muzzles of .12 gauge pumps to their heads. A pile of confiscated pistols and sawed-off shotguns lay a safe distance away. The men on the ground were all babbling their innocence or shouting epithets, and every cop trigger finger looked itchy.

Voodoo Simpkins and Billy Boyle were not among the six suspects. I looked around for familiar cop faces and saw Georgie Caulkins by the station's front entrance, standing over a sheet-covered stretcher. I ran up to him and said, "What have you got, Skipper?"

Caulkins toed the sheet aside, revealing the remains of a fortyish negro man. "The shine's Leotis McCarver," Georgie said. "Upstanding colored citizen, Brotherhood of Sleeping Car Porters big shot, a credit to his race. Put a .38 to his head and blew his brains out when the black-and-whites showed up."

Catching a twinkle in the old lieutenant's eyes, I said, "Really?"

Georgie smiled. "I can't shit a shitter. McCarver came out waving a white handkerchief, and some punk kid rookie cancelled his ticket. Deserves a commendation, don't you think?"

I looked down at the stiff and saw that the entry wound was right between the eyes. "Give him a sharpshooter's medal and a desk job before he plugs some innocent civilian. What about Simpkins and Boyle?"

"Gone," Georgie said. "When we first got here, we didn't know the real soldiers and porters from the heisters, so we threw a net over the whole place and shook everybody down. We held every legit shine lieutenant, which was two guys, then cut them loose when they weren't your boy. Simpkins and Boyle probably got away in the shuffle. A car got stolen from the other end of the lot—citizen said she saw a nigger in a porter's suit breaking the window. That was probably Simpkins. The license number's on the air along with an all points. That shine is dead meat."

I thought of Simpkins invoking protective voodoo gods and said, "I'm going after him myself."

"You owe me a report on this thing!"

"Later."

"*Now!*"

I said, "Later, *sir*," and ran back to Cora, Georgie's "now" echoing behind me. When I got to where I had left her, she was gone. Looking around, I saw her a few yards away on her knees, handcuffed to the bumper of a black-and-white. A cluster of blue suits were hooting at her, and I got very angry.

I walked over. A particularly callow-looking rookie was regaling the others with his account of Leotis McCarver's demise. All four snapped to when they saw me coming. I grabbed the story-teller by his necktie and yanked him toward the back of the car. "Uncuff her," I said.

The rookie tried to pull away. I yanked at his tie until we were face-to-face and I could smell Sen-Sen on his breath. "And apologize."

The kid flushed, and I walked back to my unmarked cruiser. I heard muttering behind me, and then I felt a tap on my shoulder. Cora was there, smiling. "I owe you one," she said.

I pointed to the passenger seat. "Get in. I'm collecting."

The ride back to West Adams was fueled by equal parts of my nervous energy and Cora's nonstop spiel on her loves and criminal escapades. I had seen it dozens of times before. A cop stands up for a prisoner against another cop, on general principles or because the other cop is a turd, and the prisoner takes it as a sign of affection and respect and proceeds to lay out a road map of his life, justifying every wrong turn because he wants to be the cop's moral equal. Cora's tale of her love for Billy Boyle back in his heister days, her slide into call-house service when he went to prison, and her lingering crush on Wallace Simpkins was predictable and mawkishly rendered. I got more and more embarrassed by her "you dig?" punctuations and taps on the arm, and if I didn't need her as a High Darktown tour guide I would have kicked her out of the car and back to her old life. But then the monologue got interesting.

When Billy Boyle was cut loose from Chino, he had a free week in L.A. before his army induction and went looking for Cora. He found her hooked on ether at Minnie Roberts's Casbah, seeing voodoo visions, servicing customers as Coroloa, the African Slave Queen. He got her out of there, eased her off the dope with steambaths and vitamin B-12 shots, then ditched her to fight for Uncle Sam. Something snapped in her brain when Billy left, and, still vamped on Wallace Simpkins, she started writing him at Quentin. Knowing his affinity for voodoo, she smuggled in some slave-queen smut pictures taken of her at the Casbah, and they got a juicy correspondence going. Meanwhile, Cora went to work at Mickey Cohen's southside numbers mill, and everything looked peachy. Then Simpkins came out of Big Q, the voodoo sex fantasy stuff became tepid reality, and the Voodoo Man himself went back to stickups, exploiting her connections to the white criminal world.

When Cora finished her story, we were skirting the edge of High Darktown. It was dusk; the temperature was easing off; the neon signs of the Western Avenue juke joints had just started flashing. Cora lit a cigarette and said, "All Billy's people is from around here. If he's lookin' for a hideout or a travelin' stake, he'd hit the clubs on West Jeff. Wallace wouldn't show his evil face around here, 'less he's lookin' for Billy, which I figure he undoubtedly is. I—"

I interrupted, "I thought Billy came from a square-john family. Wouldn't he go to them?"

Cora's look said I was a lily-white fool. "Ain't no square-john families around here, 'ceptin those who work domestic. West Adams was built on bootleggin', sweetie. Black sellin' white lightnin' to black, gettin' fat, then investin' white. Billy's folks was runnin' shine when I was in pigtails. They're respectable now, and they hates him for takin' a jolt. He'll be callin' in favors at the clubs, don't you worry."

I hung a left on Western, heading for Jefferson Boulevard.

"How do you know all this?"

"I am from High, *High* Darktown, sweet."

"Then why do you hold on to that Aunt Jemima accent?"

Cora laughed. "And I thought I sounded like Lena Horne. Here's why, sweetcakes. Black woman with a law degree they call 'nigger.' Black girl with three-inch heels and a shiv in her purse they call 'baby.' You dig?"

"I dig."

"No, you don't. Stop the car, Tommy Tucker's club is on the next block."

I said, "Yes, ma'am," and pulled to the curb. Cora got out ahead of me and swayed around the corner on her three-inch heels, calling, "I'll go in," over her shoulder. I waited underneath a purple neon sign heralding *Tommy Tucker's Playroom*. Cora come out five minutes later, saying, "Billy was in here 'bout half an hour ago. Touched the barman for a double saw."

"Simpkins?"

Cora shook her head. "Ain't been seen."

I hooked a finger in the direction of the car. "Let's catch him."

For the next two hours we followed Billy Boyle's trail through High Darktown's nightspots. Cora went in and got the information, while I stood outside like a white wallflower, my gun unholstered and pressed to my leg, waiting for a voodoo killer with a tommy gun to aim and fire. Her info was always the same: Boyle had been in, had made a quick impression with his army threads, had gotten a quick touch based on his rep, and had practically run out the door. And no one had seen Wallace Simpkins.

11 p.m. found me standing under the awning of Hanks' Swank Spot, feeling pinpricks all over my exhausted body. Square-john

negro kids cruised by waving little American flags out of backseat windows, still hopped up that the war was over. Male and female, they all had mug-shot faces that kept my trigger finger at half-pull even though I knew damn well they couldn't be *him*. Cora's sojourn inside was running three times as long as her previous ones, and when a car backfired and I aimed at the old lady behind the wheel, I figured High Darktown was safer with me off the street and went in to see what was keeping Cora.

The Swank Spot's interior was Egyptian: silk wallpaper embossed with pharaohs and mummies, papier-mâché pyramids surrounding the dance floor, and a long bar shaped like a crypt lying sideways. The patrons were more contemporary: negro men in double-breasted suits and women in evening gowns who looked disapprovingly at my rumpled clothes and two-and-a-half-day beard.

Ignoring them, I eyeballed in vain for Cora. Her soiled pink dress would have stood out like a beacon amid the surrounding hauteur, but all the women were dressed in pale white and sequined black. Panic was rising inside me when I heard her voice, distorted by bebop, pleading behind the dance floor.

I pushed my way through minglers, dancers, and three pyramids to get to her. She was standing next to a phonograph setup, gesturing at a black man in slacks and a camel-hair jacket. The man was sitting in a folding chair, alternately admiring his manicure and looking at Cora like she was dirt.

The music was reaching a crescendo; the man smiled at me; Cora's pleas were engulfed by saxes, horns, and drums going wild. I flashed back to my Legion days—rabbit punches and elbows and scrubbing my laces into cuts during clinches. The past two days went topsy-turvy, and I kicked over the phonograph. The Benny Goodman sextet exploded into silence, and I aimed my piece at the man and said, "*Tell me now.*"

Shouts rose from the dance floor, and Cora pressed herself into a toppled pyramid. The man smoothed the pleats in his trousers and said, "Cora's old flame was in about half an hour ago, begging. I turned him down, because I respect my origins and hate snitches. But I told him about an old mutual friend—a soft touch.

Another Cora flame was in about ten minutes ago, asking after flame number one. Seems he has a grudge against him. I sent him the same place."

I croaked, "Where?" and my voice sounded disembodied to my own ears.

The man said, "No. You can apologize now, officer. Do it, and I won't tell my good friends Mickey Cohen and Inspector Waters about your behavior."

I stuck my gun in my waistband and pulled out an old Zippo I used to light suspects' cigarettes. Sparking a flame, I held it inches from a stack of brocade curtains. "Remember the Coconut Grove?"

The man said, "You wouldn't," and I touched the flame to the fabric. It ignited immediately, and smoke rose to the ceiling. Patrons were screaming "Fire!" in the club proper. The brocade was fried to a crisp when the man shrieked, "John Downey," ripped off his camel-hair, and flung it at the flames. I grabbed Cora and pulled her through the club, elbowing and rabbit-punching panicky revelers to clear a path. When we hit the sidewalk, I saw that Cora was sobbing. Smoothing her hair, I whispered hoarsely, "What, babe, what?"

It took a moment for Cora to find a voice, but when she spoke, she sounded like a college professor. "John Downey's my father. He's very big around here, and he hates Billy because he thinks Billy made me a whore."

"Where does he li—"

"Arlington and Country Club."

We were there within five minutes. This was High, *High* Darktown—Tudor estates, French chateaus, and Moorish villas with terraced front lawns. Cora pointed out a plantation-style mansion and said, "Go to the side door. Thursday's the maid's night off, and nobody'll hear you if you knock at the front."

I stopped the car across the street and looked for other out-of-place vehicles. Seeing nothing but Packards, Caddys, and Lincolns nestled in driveways, I said, "Stay put. Don't move, no matter what you see or hear."

Cora nodded mutely. I got out and ran over to the plantation, hurdling a low iron fence guarded by a white iron jockey, then treading down a long driveway. Laughter and applause issued from the adjoining mansion, separated from the Downey place by a high hedgerow. The happy sounds covered my approach, and I started looking in windows.

Standing on my toes and moving slowly toward the back of the house, I saw rooms festooned with crewelwork wall hangings and hunting prints. Holding my face up to within a few inches of the glass, I looked for shadow movement and listened for voices, wondering why all the lights were on at close to midnight.

Then faceless voices assailed me from the next window down. Pressing my back to the wall, I saw that the window was cracked for air. Cocking an ear toward the open space, I listened.

". . . and after all the setup money I put in, you still had to knock down those liquor stores?"

The tone reminded me of a mildly outraged negro minister rebuking his flock, and I braced myself for the voice that I knew would reply.

"I gots cowboy blood, Mister Downey, like you musta had when you was a young man runnin' shine. That cop musta got loose, got Cora and Whitey to snitch. Blew a sweet piece of work, but we can still get off clean. McCarver was the only one 'sides me knew you was bankrollin', and he be dead. Billy be the one *you* wants dead, and he be showin' up soon. Then I cuts him and dumps him somewhere, and nobody knows he was even here."

"You want money, don't you?"

"Five big get me lost somewheres nice, then maybe when he starts feelin' safe again, I comes back and cuts that cop. That sound about—"

Applause from the big house next door cut Simpkins off. I pulled out my piece and got up some guts, knowing my only safe bet was to backshoot the son of a bitch right where he was. I heard more clapping and joyous shouts that Mayor Bowron's reign was over, and then John Downey's preacher baritone was back in force: "I want him dead. My daughter is a white-trash consort and a whore, and he's—"

A scream went off behind me, and I hit the ground just as machine-gun fire blew the window to bits. Another burst took out the hedgerow and the next-door window. I pinned myself back first to the wall and drew myself upright as the snout of a tommy gun was rested against the ledge a few inches away. When muzzle flame and another volley exploded from it, I stuck my .38 in blind and fired six times at stomach level. The tommy strafed a reflex burst upward, and when I hit the ground again, the only sound was chaotic shrieks from the other house.

I reloaded from a crouch, then stood up and surveyed the carnage through both mansion windows. Wallace Simpkins lay dead on John Downey's Persian carpet, and across the way I saw a banner for the West Adams Democratic Club streaked with blood. When I saw a dead woman spread-eagled on top of an antique table, I screamed myself, elbowed my way into Downey's den, and picked up the machine gun. The grips burned my hands, but I didn't care; I saw the faces of every boxer who had ever defeated me and didn't care; I heard grenades going off in my brain and was glad they were there to kill all the innocent screaming. With the tommy's muzzle as my directional device, I walked through the house.

All my senses went into my eyes and trigger finger. Wind ruffled a window curtain, and I blew the wall apart; I caught my own image in a gilt-edged mirror and blasted myself into glass shrapnel. Then I heard a woman moaning, "Daddy, Daddy, Daddy," dropped the tommy, and ran to her.

Cora was on her knees on the entry hall floor, plunging a shiv into a man who had to be her father. The man moaned baritone low and tried to reach up, almost as if to embrace her. Cora's "Daddy's" got lower and lower, until the two seemed to be working toward harmony. When she let the dying man hold her, I gave them a moment together, then pulled Cora off of him and dragged her outside. She went limp in my arms, and with lights going on everywhere and sirens converging from all directions, I carried her to my car.

PART III

KILLER VIEWS

PART III

THE PEOPLE ACROSS THE CANYON

BY MARGARET MILLAR

L.A. Canyon

(Originally published in 1962)

The first time the Bortons realized that someone had moved into the new house across the canyon was one night in May when they saw the rectangular light of a television set shining in the picture window. Marion Borton knew it had to happen eventually, but that didn't make it any easier to accept the idea of neighbors in a part of the country she and Paul had come to consider exclusively their own.

They had discovered the site, had bought six acres, and built the house over the objections of the bank, which didn't like to lend money on unimproved property, and of their friends, who thought the Bortons were foolish to move so far out of town. Now other people were discovering the spot, and here and there through the eucalyptus trees and the live oaks, Marion could see half-finished houses.

But it was the house directly across the canyon that bothered her most; she had been dreading this moment ever since the site had been bulldozed the previous summer.

"There goes our privacy." Marion went over and snapped off the television set, a sign to Paul that she had something on her mind which she wanted to transfer to his. The transference, intended to halve the problem, often merely doubled it.

"Well, let's have it," Paul said, trying to conceal his annoyance.

"Have what?"

"Stop kidding around. You don't usually cut off Perry Mason in the middle of a sentence."

"All I said was, there goes our privacy."

"We have plenty left," Paul said.

"You know how sounds carry across the canyon."

"I don't hear any sounds."

"You will. They probably have ten or twelve children and a howling dog and a sports car."

"A couple of children wouldn't be so bad—at least Cathy would have someone to play with."

Cathy was eight, in bed now, and ostensibly asleep, with the night light on and her bedroom door open just a crack.

"She has plenty of playmates at school," Marion said, pulling the drapes across the window so that she wouldn't have to look at the exasperating rectangle of light across the canyon. "Her teacher tells me Cathy gets along with everyone and never causes any trouble. You talk as if she's deprived or something."

"It would be nice if she had more interests, more children of her own age around."

"A lot of things would be nice *if*. I've done my best."

Paul knew it was true. He'd heard her issue dozens of weekend invitations to Cathy's schoolmates. Few of them came to anything. The mothers offered various excuses: poison oak, snakes, mosquitoes in the creek at the bottom of the canyon, the distance of the house from town in case something happened and a doctor was needed in a hurry . . . these excuses, sincere and valid as they were, embittered Marion. *"For heaven's sake, you'd think we lived on the moon or in the middle of a jungle."*

"I guess a couple of children would be all right," Marion said. "But please, no sports car."

"I'm afraid that's out of our hands."

"Actually, they might even be quite *nice* people."

"Why not? Most people are."

Both Marion and Paul had the comfortable feeling that something had been settled, though neither was quite sure what. Paul went over and turned the television set back on. As he had suspected, it was the doorman who'd killed the nightclub owner with a baseball bat, not the blonde dancer or her young husband or the jealous singer.

It was the following Monday that Cathy started to run away.

Marion, ironing in the kitchen and watching a quiz program on the portable set Paul had given her for Christmas, heard the school bus groan to a stop at the top of the driveway. She waited for the front door to open and Cathy to announce in her high thin voice, "I'm home, Mommy."

The door didn't open.

From the kitchen window Marion saw the yellow bus round the sharp curve of the hill like a circus cage full of wild captive children screaming for release.

Marion waited until the end of the program, trying to convince herself that another bus had been added to the route and would come along shortly, or that Cathy had decided to stop off at a friend's house and would telephone any minute. But no other bus appeared, and the telephone remained silent.

Marion changed into her hiking boots and started off down the canyon, avoiding the scratchy clumps of chapparal and the creepers of poison oak that looked like loganberry vines.

She found Cathy sitting in the middle of the little bridge that Paul had made across the creek out of two fallen eucalyptus trees. Cathy's short plump legs hung over the logs until they almost touched the water. She was absolutely motionless, her face hidden by a straw curtain of hair. Then a single frog croaked a warning of Marion's presence and Cathy responded to the sound as if she was more intimate with nature than adults were, and more alert to its subtle communications of danger.

She stood up quickly, brushing off the back of her dress and drawing aside the curtain of hair to reveal eyes as blue as the periwinkles that hugged the banks of the creek.

"Cathy."

"I was only counting waterbugs while I was waiting. Forty-one."

"Waiting for what?"

"The ten or twelve children, and the dog."

"What ten or twelve chil—" Marion stopped. "I see. You were listening the other night when we thought you were asleep."

"I wasn't listening," Cathy said righteously. "My ears were hearing."

Marion restrained a smile. "Then I wish you'd tell those ears of yours to hear properly. I didn't say the new neighbors had ten or twelve children, I said they *might* have. Actually, it's very unlikely. Not many families are that big these days."

"Do you have to be old to have a big family?"

"Well, you certainly can't be very young."

"I bet people with big families have station wagons so they have room for all the children."

"The lucky ones do."

Cathy stared down at the thin flow of water carrying fat little minnows down to the sea. Finally she said, "They're too young, and their car is too small."

In spite of her aversion to having new neighbors, Marion felt a quickening of interest. "Have you seen them?"

But the little girl seemed deaf, lost in a water world of minnows and dragonflies and tadpoles.

"I asked you a question, Cathy. Did you see the people who just moved in?"

"Yes."

"When?"

"Before you came. Their name is Smith."

"How do you know that?"

"I went up to the house to look at things and they said, Hello, little girl, what's your name? And I said, Cathy, what's yours? And they said Smith. Then they drove off in the little car."

"You're not supposed to go poking around other people's houses," Marion said brusquely. "And while we're at it, you're not supposed to go anywhere after school without first telling me where you're going and when you'll be back. You know that perfectly well. Now why didn't you come in and report to me after you got off the school bus?"

"I didn't want to."

"That's not a satisfactory answer."

Satisfactory or not, it was the only answer Cathy had. She

looked at her mother in silence, then she turned and darted back up the hill to her own house.

After a time Marion followed her, exasperated and a little confused. She hated to punish the child, but she knew she couldn't ignore the matter entirely—it was much too serious. While she gave Cathy her graham crackers and orange juice, she told her, reasonably and kindly, that she would have to stay in her room the following day after school by way of learning a lesson.

That night, after Cathy had been tucked in bed, Marion related the incident to Paul. He seemed to take a less serious view of it than Marion, a fact of which the listening child became well aware.

"I'm glad she's getting acquainted with the new people," Paul said. "It shows a certain degree of poise I didn't think she had. She's always been so shy."

"You're surely not condoning her running off without telling me?"

"She didn't run far. All kids do things like that once in a while."

"We don't want to spoil her."

"Cathy's always been so obedient I think she has *us* spoiled. Who knows, she might even teach us a thing or two about going out and making new friends." He realized, from past experience, that this was a very touchy subject. Marion had her house, her garden, her television sets; she didn't seem to want any more of the world than these, and she resented any implication that they were not enough. To ward off an argument he added, "You've done a good job with Cathy. Stop worrying . . . Smith, their name is?"

"Yes."

"Actually, I think it's an excellent sign that Cathy's getting acquainted."

At three the next afternoon the yellow circus cage arrived, released one captive, and rumbled on its way.

"I'm home, Mommy."

"Good girl."

Marion felt guilty at the sight of her: the child had been

cooped up in school all day, the weather was so warm and lovely, and besides, Paul hadn't thought the incident of the previous afternoon too important.

"I know what," Marion suggested, "let's you and I go down to the creek and count waterbugs."

The offer was a sacrifice for Marion because her favorite quiz program was on and she liked to answer the questions along with the contestants. "How about that?"

Cathy knew all about the quiz program; she'd seen it a hundred times, had watched the moving mouths claim her mother's eyes and ears and mind. "I counted the waterbugs yesterday."

"Well, minnows, then."

"You'll scare them away."

"Oh, will I?" Marion laughed self-consciously, rather relieved that Cathy had refused her offer and was clearly and definitely a little guilty about the relief. "Don't you scare them?"

"No. They think I'm another minnow because they're used to me."

"Maybe they could get used to me, too."

"I don't think so."

When Cathy went off down the canyon by herself, Marion realized, in a vaguely disturbing way, that the child had politely but firmly rejected her mother's company. It wasn't until dinnertime that she found out the reason why.

"The Smiths," Cathy said, "have an Austin-Healey."

Cathy, like most girls, had never shown any interest in cars, and her glib use of the name moved her parents to laughter.

The laughter encouraged Cathy to elaborate. "An Austin-Healey makes a lot of noise—like Daddy's lawn mower."

"I don't think the company would appreciate a commercial from you, young lady," Paul said. "Are the Smiths all moved in?"

"Oh, yes. I helped them."

"Is that a fact? And how did you help them?"

"I sang two songs. And then we danced and danced."

Paul looked half pleased, half puzzled. It wasn't like Cathy to perform willingly in front of people. During the last Christmas concert at the school she'd left the stage in tears and hidden in the cloak room . . . Well, maybe her shyness was only a phase and she was finally getting over it.

"They must be very nice people," he said, "to take time out from getting settled in a new house to play games with a little girl."

Cathy shook her head. "It wasn't games. It was real dancing—like on *Ed Sullivan*."

"As good as that, eh?" Paul said, smiling. "Tell me about it."

"Mrs. Smith is a nightclub dancer."

Paul's smile faded, and a pulse began to beat in his left temple like a small misplaced heart. "Oh? You're sure about that, Cathy?"

"Yes."

"And what does Mr. Smith do?"

"He's a baseball player."

"You mean that's what he does for a living?" Marion asked. "He doesn't work in an office like Daddy?"

"No, he just plays baseball. He always wears a baseball cap."

"I see. What position does he play on the team?" Paul's voice was low.

Cathy looked blank.

"Everybody on a ball team has a special thing to do. What does Mr. Smith do?"

"He's a batter."

"A batter, eh? Well, that's nice. Did he tell you this?"

"Yes."

"Cathy," Paul said, "I know you wouldn't deliberately lie to me, but sometimes you get your facts a little mixed up."

He went on in this vein for some time but Cathy's story remained unshaken: Mrs. Smith was a nightclub dancer, Mr. Smith a professional baseball player, they loved children, and they never watched television.

"That, at least, must be a lie," Marion said to Paul later when she saw the rectangular light of the television set shining in the Smiths' picture window. "As for the rest of it, there isn't a nightclub within fifty miles, or a professional ball club within two hundred."

"She probably misunderstood. It's quite possible that at one time Mrs. Smith was a dancer of sorts and that he played a little baseball."

Cathy, in bed and teetering dizzily on the brink of sleep, wondered if she should tell her parents about the Smiths' child—the one who didn't go to school.

She didn't tell them; Marion found out for herself the next morning after Paul and Cathy had gone. When she pulled back the drapes in the living room and opened the windows, she heard the sharp slam of a screen door from across the canyon and saw a small child come out on the patio of the new house. At that distance she couldn't tell whether it was a boy or a girl. Whichever it was, the child was quiet and well behaved; only the occasional slam of the door shook the warm, windless day.

The presence of the child, and the fact that Cathy hadn't mentioned it, gnawed at Marion's mind all day. She questioned Cathy about it as soon as she came home.

"You didn't tell me the Smiths have a child."

"No."

"Why not?"

"I don't know why not."

"Is it a boy or a girl?"

"Girl."

"How old?"

Cathy thought it over carefully, frowning up at the ceiling. "About ten."

"Doesn't she go to school?"

"No."

"Why not?"

"She doesn't want to."

"That's not a very good reason."

"It's her reason," Cathy said flatly. "Can I go out to play now?"

"I'm not sure you should. You look a little feverish. Come here and let me feel your forehead."

Cathy's forehead was cool and moist, but her cheeks and the bridge of her nose were very pink, almost as if she'd been sun-burned.

"You'd better stay inside," Marion said, "and watch some cartoons."

"I don't like cartoons."

"You used to."

"I like real people."

She means the Smiths, of course, Marion thought as her mouth tightened. "People who dance and play baseball all the time?"

If the sarcasm had any effect on Cathy she didn't show it. After waiting until Marion had become engrossed in her quiz program, Cathy lined up all her dolls in her room and gave a concert for them, to thunderous applause.

"Where are your old Navy binoculars?" Marion asked Paul when she was getting ready for bed.

"Oh, somewhere in the sea chest, I imagine. Why?"

"I want them."

"Not thinking of spying on the neighbors, are you?"

"I'm thinking of just that," Marion said grimly.

The next morning, as soon as she saw the Smith child come out on the patio, Marion went downstairs to the storage room to search through the sea chest. She located the binoculars and was in the act of dusting them off when the telephone started to ring in the living room. She hurried upstairs and said breathlessly, "Hello?"

"Mrs. Borton?"

"Yes."

"This is Miss Park speaking, Cathy's teacher."

Marion had met Miss Park several times at P.T.A. meetings and report-card conferences. She was a large, ruddy-faced, and unfailingly cheerful young woman—the kind, as Paul said, you wouldn't want to live with but who'd be nice to have around in an emergency. "How are you, Miss Park?"

"Oh, fine, thank you, Mrs. Borton. I meant to call you yesterday but things were a bit out of hand around here, and I knew there was no great hurry to check on Cathy; she's such a well-behaved little girl."

Even Miss Park's loud, jovial voice couldn't cover up the ominous sound of the word *check*. "I don't think I quite understand. Why should you check on Cathy?"

"Purely routine. The school doctor and the health department like to keep records of how many cases of measles or flu or chicken pox are going the rounds. Right now it looks like the season for mumps. Is Cathy all right?"

"She seemed a little feverish yesterday afternoon when she got home from school, but she acted perfectly normal when she left this morning."

Miss Park's silence was so protracted that Marion became painfully conscious of things she wouldn't otherwise have noticed—the weight of the binoculars in her lap, the thud of her own heartbeat in her ears. Across the canyon the Smith child was playing quietly and alone on the patio. *There is definitely something the matter with that girl*, Marion thought. *Perhaps I'd better not let Cathy go over there anymore, she's so imitative.* "Miss Park, are you still on the line? Hello? Hello—"

"I'm here," Miss Park's voice seemed fainter than usual, and less positive. "What time did Cathy leave the house this morning?"

"Eight, as usual."

"Did she take the school bus?"

"Of course. She always does."

"Did you see her get on?"

"I kissed her goodbye at the front door," Marion said. "What's this all about, Miss Park?"

"Cathy hasn't been at school for two days, Mrs. Borton."

"Why, that's absurd, impossible! You must be mistaken." But even as she was speaking the words, Marion was raising the binoculars to her eyes: the little girl on the Smiths' patio had a straw curtain of hair and eyes as blue as the periwinkles along the creek banks.

"Mrs. Borton, I'm not likely to be mistaken about which of my children are in class or not."

"No. No, you're—you're not mistaken, Miss Park. I can see Cathy from here—she's over at the neighbor's house."

"Good. That's a load off my mind."

"Off yours, yes," Marion said. "Not mine."

"Now we mustn't become excited, Mrs. Borton. Don't make too much of this incident before we've had a chance to confer. Suppose you come and talk to me during my lunch hour and bring Cathy along. We'll all have a friendly chat."

But it soon became apparent, even to the optimistic Miss Park, that Cathy didn't intend to take part in any friendly chat. She stood by the window in the classroom, blank-eyed, mute, unresponsive to the simplest questions, refusing to be drawn into any conversation even about her favorite topic, the Smiths. Miss Park finally decided to send Cathy out to play in the schoolyard while she talked to Marion alone.

"Obviously," Miss Park said, enunciating the word very distinctly because it was one of her favorites, "obviously, Cathy's got a crush on this young couple and has concocted a fantasy about belonging to them."

"It's not so obvious what my husband and I are going to do about it."

"Live through it, the same as other parents. Crushes like this are common at Cathy's age. Sometimes the object is a person, a whole family, even a horse. And, of course, to Cathy a nightclub dancer and a baseball player must seem very glamorous indeed. Tell me, Mrs. Borton, does she watch television a great deal?"

Marion stiffened. "No more than any other child."

Oh dear, Miss Park thought sadly, *they all do it; the most confirmed addicts are always the most defensive.* "I just wondered," she said. "Cathy likes to sing to herself and I've never heard such a repertoire of television commercials."

"She picks things up very fast."

"Yes. Yes, she does indeed." Miss Park studied her hands, which were always a little pale from chalk dust and were even paler now because she was angry—at the child for deceiving her, at Mrs. Borton for brushing aside the television issue, at herself for not preventing, or at least anticipating, the current situation, and perhaps most of all at the Smiths who ought to have known better than to allow a child to hang around their house when she should obviously be in school.

"Don't put too much pressure on Cathy about this," she said finally, "until I talk the matter over with the school psychologist. By the way, have you met the Smiths, Mrs. Borton?"

"Not yet," Marion said grimly. "But believe me, I intend to."

"Yes, I think it would be a good idea for you to talk to them and make it clear that they're not to encourage Cathy in this fantasy."

The meeting came sooner than Marion expected.

She waited at the school until classes were dismissed, then she took Cathy into town to do some shopping. She had parked the car and she and Cathy were standing hand in hand at a corner waiting for a traffic light to change; Marion was worried and impatient, Cathy still silent, unresisting, inert, as she had been ever since Marion had called her home from the Smiths' patio.

Suddenly, Marion felt the child's hand tighten in a spasm of excitement. Cathy's face had turned so pink it looked ready to explode and with her free hand she was waving violently at two people in a small cream-colored sports car—a very pretty young woman with blonde hair in the driver's seat, and beside her a young man wearing a wide friendly grin and a baseball cap. They both waved back at Cathy just before the lights changed and then the car roared through the intersection.

"The Smiths!" Cathy shouted, jumping up and down in a frenzy. "That was the Smiths."

"Sssh, not so loud. People will—"

"But it was the *Smiths*!"

"Hurry up before the light changes."

The child didn't hear. She stood as if rooted to the curb, staring after the cream-colored car.

With a little grunt of impatience Marion picked her up, carried her across the road, and let her down quite roughly on the other side. "There. If you're going to act like a baby, I'll carry you like a baby."

"I saw the Smiths!"

"All right. What are you so excited about? It's not very un-usual to meet someone in town whom you know."

"It's unusual to meet *them*."

"Why?"

"Because it is." The color was fading from Cathy's cheeks, but her eyes still looked bedazzled, quite as if they'd seen a miracle.

"I'm sure they're very unique people," Marion said coldly. "Nevertheless, they must stop for groceries like everyone else."

Cathy's answer was a slight shake of her head and a whisper heard only by herself: "No, they don't, never."

When Paul came home from work, Cathy was sent to play in the front yard while Marion explained matters to him. He listened with increasing irritation—not so much at Cathy's actions but at the manner in which Marion and Miss Park had handled things. There was too much talking, he said, and too little acting.

"The way you women beat around the bush instead of tackling the situation directly, meeting it head-on—fantasy life. Fantasy life, my foot! Now, we're going over to the Smiths' right this min-ute to talk to them and that will be that. End of fantasy. Period."

"We'd better wait until after dinner. Cathy missed her lunch."

Throughout the meal Cathy was pale and quiet. She ate noth-ing and spoke only when asked a direct question; but inside herself the conversation was very lively, the dinner a banquet with danc-ing, and afterward a wild, windy ride in the roofless car . . .

Although the footpath through the canyon provided a shorter route to the Smiths' house, the Bortons decided to go more for-mally, by car, and to take Cathy with them. Cathy, told to comb her hair and wash her face, protested: "I don't want to go over there."

"Why not?" Paul said. "You were so anxious to spend time with them that you played hooky for two days. Why don't you want to see them now?"

"Because they're not there."

"How do you know?"

"Mrs. Smith told me this morning that they wouldn't be home tonight because she's putting on a show."

"Indeed?" Paul said grim-faced. "Just where does she put on these shows of hers?"

"And Mr. Smith has to play baseball. And after that they're going to see a friend in the hospital who has leukemia."

"Leukemia, eh?" He didn't have to ask how Cathy had found out about such a thing; he'd watched a semidocumentary dealing with it a couple of nights ago. Cathy was supposed to have been sleeping.

"I wonder," he said to Marion when Cathy went to comb her hair, "just how many 'facts' about the Smiths have been borrowed from television."

"Well, I know for myself that they drive a sports car, and Mr. Smith was wearing a baseball cap. And they're both young and good-looking. Young and good-looking enough," she added wryly, "to make me feel—well, a little jealous."

"Jealous?"

"Cathy would rather belong to them than to us. It makes me wonder if it's something the Smiths have or something the Bortons don't have."

"Ask her."

"I can't very well—"

"Then I will, dammit," Paul said. And he did.

Cathy merely looked at him innocently. "I don't know. I don't know what you mean."

"Then listen again. Why did you pretend that you were the Smiths' little girl?"

"They asked me to be. They asked me to go with them."

"They actually said, Cathy, will you be our little girl?"

"Yes."

"Well, by heaven, I'll put an end to this nonsense," Paul said, and strode out to the car.

It was twilight when they reached the Smiths' house by way of the narrow, hilly road. The moon, just appearing above the horizon, was on the wane, a chunk bitten out of its side by some giant jaw. A warm dry wind, blowing down the mountain from the desert beyond, carried the sweet scent of pittosporum.

The Smiths' house was dark, and both the front door and the garage were locked. Out of defiance or desperation, Paul pressed the door chime anyway, several times. All three of them could hear it ringing inside, and it seemed to Marion to echo very curiously—as if the carpets and drapes were too thin to muffle the sound vibrations. She would have liked to peer in through the windows and see for herself, but the Venetian blinds were closed.

"What's their furniture like?" she asked Cathy.

"Like everybody's."

"I mean, is it new? Does Mrs. Smith tell you not to put your feet on it?"

"No, she never tells me that," Cathy said truthfully. "I want to go home now. I'm tired."

It was while she was putting Cathy to bed that Marion heard Paul call to her from the living room in an urgent voice, "Marion, come here a minute."

She found him standing motionless in the middle of the room, staring across the canyon at the Smiths' place. The rectangular light of the Smiths' television set was shining in the picture window of the room that opened onto the patio at the back of the Smiths' house.

"Either they've come home within the past few minutes," he said, "or they were there all the time. My guess is that they were home when we went over, but they didn't want to see us, so they just doused the lights and pretended to be out. Well, it won't work! Come on, we're going back."

"I can't leave Cathy alone. She's already got her pajamas on."

"Put a bathrobe on her and bring her along. This has gone beyond the point of observing such niceties as correct attire."

"Don't you think we should wait until tomorrow?"

"Hurry up and stop arguing with me."

Cathy, protesting that she was tired and that the Smiths weren't home anyway, was bundled into a bathrobe and carried to the car.

"They're home all right," Paul said. "And by heaven they'd better answer the door this time or I'll break it down."

"That's an absurd way to talk in front of a child," Marion said coldly. "She has enough ideas without hearing—"

"Absurd is it? Wait and see."

Cathy, listening from the backseat, smiled sleepily. She knew how to get in without breaking anything: ever since the house had been built, the real estate man who'd been trying to sell it always hid the key on a nail underneath the window box.

The second trip seemed a nightmarish imitation of the first: the same moon hung in the sky but it looked smaller now, and paler. The scent of pittosporum was funereally sweet, and the hollow sound of the chimes from inside the house was like the echo in an empty tomb.

"They must be crazy to think they can get away with a trick like this twice in one night!" Paul shouted. "Come on, we're going around to the back."

Marion looked a little frightened. "I don't like trespassing on someone else's property."

"They trespassed on our property first."

He glanced down at Cathy. Her eyes were half closed and her face was pearly in the moonlight. He pressed her hand to reassure her that everything was going to be all right and that his anger wasn't directed at her, but she drew away from him and started down the path that led to the back of the house.

Paul clicked on his flashlight and followed her, moving slowly along the unfamiliar terrain. By the time he turned the corner of the house and reached the patio, Cathy was out of sight.

"Cathy," he called. "Where are you? Come back here!"

Marion was looking at him accusingly. "You upset her with that silly threat about breaking down the door. She's probably on her way home through the canyon."

"I'd better go after her."

"She's less likely to get hurt than you are. She knows every inch of the way. Besides, you came here to break down the doors. All right, start breaking."

But there was no need to break down anything. The back door opened as soon as Paul rapped on it with his knuckles, and he almost fell into the room.

It was empty except for a small girl wearing a blue bathrobe that matched her eyes.

Paul said, "Cathy. Cathy, what are you doing here?"

Marion stood with her hand pressed to her mouth to stifle the scream that was rising in her throat. There were no Smiths. The people in the sports car whom Cathy had waved at were just strangers responding to the friendly greeting of a child—had Cathy seen them before, on a previous trip to town? The television set was no more than a contraption rigged up by Cathy herself—an orange crate and an old mirror that caught and reflected the rays of the moon.

In front of it Cathy was standing, facing her own image. "Hello, Mrs. Smith. Here I am, all ready to go."

"Cathy," Marion said in a voice that sounded torn by claws, "what do you see in that mirror?"

"It's not a mirror. It's a television set."

"What—what program are you watching?"

"It's not a program, silly. It's real. It's the Smiths. I'm going away with them to dance and play baseball."

"There are no Smiths," Paul bellowed. "Will you get that through your head? *There are no Smiths!*"

"Yes, there are. I see them."

Marion knelt on the floor beside the child. "Listen to me, Cathy. This is a mirror—only a mirror. It came from Daddy's old bureau and I had it put away in the storage room. That's where you found it, isn't it? And you brought it here and decided to pretend it was a television set, isn't that right? But it's really just a mirror, and the people in it are us—you and Mommy and Daddy."

But even as she looked at her own reflection, Marion saw it beginning to change. She was growing younger, prettier; her hair was becoming lighter and her cotton suit was changing into a dancing dress. And beside her in the mirror, Paul was turning into a stranger, a laughing-eyed young man wearing a baseball cap.

"I'm ready to go now, Mr. Smith," Cathy said, and suddenly all three of them, the Smiths and their little girl, began walking away in the mirror. In a few moments they were no bigger than matchsticks—and then the three of them disappeared, and there was only the moonlight in the glass.

"Cathy," Marion cried. "Come back, Cathy! Please come back!"

Propped up against the door like a dummy, Paul imagined he could hear above his wife's cries the mocking muted roar of a sports car.

SURF

BY JOSEPH HANSEN

Venice

(Originally published in 1976)

L ieutenant Ken Barker of the L.A.P.D. shared a gray-green office with too many other men, too many gray-green metal desks and file cabinets, too many phones that kept crying for attention like new life in a sad maternity ward. He had a broken nose. Under his eyes were bruises. He wore beard stubble. His teeth were smoky. He scowled across a sprawl of papers and spent styrofoam cups.

He said: "Yes, Robinson was murdered. On the deck of his apartment. In that slum by the sea called Surf. Shot clean through the head. He went over the rail, was dead when he hit the sand. There's nothing wrong with the case. The DA is happy. What do you want to mess it up for?"

"I don't." Dave shed a wet trench coat, hung it over a chairback, sat on another chair. "I just want to know why Robinson made Bruce K. Shevel the beneficiary of his life insurance policy. Didn't he have a wife, a mother, a girlfriend?"

"He had a boyfriend, and the boyfriend killed him. Edward Earl Lily, by name. With a deer rifle, a thirty-thirty. Probably Robinson's. He owned one." Barker blinked. "It's weird, Dave. I mean, what have you got—an instinct for this kind of case?"

"Coincidence," Dave said. "What does probably mean—Robinson was 'probably' killed with his own gun."

Barker found a bent cigarette. "Haven't located it."

"Where does Lily say it is?"

"Claims he never saw it." Barker shuffled papers, hunting a match. "But it'll be in the surf someplace along there. Or buried in the sand. We're raking for it." Dave leaned forward and snapped a thin steel gas lighter. Barker said thanks and asked through smoke, "You don't like it? Why not? What's wrong with it?"

Dave put the lighter away. "Ten years ago, Bruce K. Shevel jacked up his car on one of those trails in Topanga Canyon to change a tire, and the car rolled over on him and cost him the use of his legs. He was insured with us. We paid. We still pay. Total disability. I'd forgotten him. But I remembered him today when I checked Robinson's policy. Shevel looked to me like someone who'd tried self-mutilation to collect on his accident policy."

"Happens, doesn't it?" Barker said.

"People won't do anything for money." Dave's smile was thin. "But they will hack off a foot or a hand for it. I sized Shevel up for one of those. His business was in trouble. The policy was a fat one. I don't think paralysis was in his plans. But it paid better. The son of a bitch grinned at me from that hospital bed. He knew I knew and there was no way to prove it."

"And there still isn't," Barker said. "Otherwise you could stop paying and put him in the slams. And it pisses you off that he took you. And now you see a chance to get him." Barker looked into one of the empty plastic cups, made a face, stood up. "You'd like him to have killed Robinson."

He edged between desks to a coffee urn at the window end of the room, the glass wall end. Dave followed. Through vertical metal sun slats outside, gray rain showed itself like movie grief. "I'd like Robinson to have died peacefully in bed of advanced old age." Dave pulled a cup from a chrome tube bolted to a window strut and held the cup while Barker filled it. "And since he didn't, I'd sure as hell like him to have left his money to someone else."

"We interviewed Shevel." Next to the hot plate that held the coffee urn was cream substitute in a widemouth brown bottle and sugar in little cellophane packets. Barker used a yellow plastic spoon to stir some of each into his coffee. "We interviewed everybody in Robinson's little black book." He led the way back to his desk, sat down, twisted out his cigarette in a big glass ashtray glutted with butts. "And Shevel is a wheelchair case."

Dave tasted his coffee. Weak and tepid. "A wheelchair case can shoot a gun."

Barker snorted. "Have you seen where Robinson lived?"

"I'll go look. But first tell me about Lily." Dave sat down, then eyed the desk. "Or do I need to take your time? Shall I just read the file?"

"My time? I'd only waste it sleeping. And I'm out of practice. I wouldn't do it well." Barker glanced sourly at the folders, forms, photographs on his desk, then hung another cigarette from his mouth and leaned forward so Dave could light it. "Lily is a trick Robinson picked up at the Billy Budd. You know the place?"

Dave nodded. "Ocean Front Walk."

"Robinson tended bar there. The kid's a hustler but way out of Robinson's league. A hundred bucks a night and/or a part in your next TV segment, sir. But somehow Robinson managed to keep him. Eight, ten weeks, anyway—" The phone on Barker's desk jangled. He lifted the receiver, listened, grunted, cradled the receiver. "—till he was dead. Lily ran, but not far and not clever. He was better at crying. You know the type. Muscles, but a real girl. Kept sobbing that he loved Robinson and why would he kill him?"

"And why would he?" Dave lit a cigarette.

Barker shrugged. "Probably hysteria. Toward the end they were fighting a lot. About money. Robinson had bought him fancy clothes, an Omega watch, a custom surfboard. They'd been pricing Porsches and Aston-Martins on the lots. But Robinson was broke. He'd hocked his stereo, camera, projector. He was borrowing from friends."

"What friends?" Dave asked. "Shevel?"

"Among others," Barker said. "Which kind of louses up your theory, doesn't it? Shevel didn't need to shoot anybody for their insurance money. He's loaded."

The boy who opened the door had dressed fast. He still hadn't buttoned his white coverall with *L.A. Marina* stitched on the pocket. Under the coverall his jockeys were on inside out and backward.

Below the nick of navel in his flat brown belly a label read *Pilgrim*. He was Chicano and wore his hair long. He looked confused. "He thought it would be the layouts."

"It isn't," Dave said. "Brandstetter is my name. Death claims investigator, Medallion Life. I'm looking for Bruce K. Shevel. Is he here?"

"Brand—what?" the boy said.

At his back a dense jungle of philodendrons climbed a trellis to the ceiling. From beyond it a voice said, "Wait a minute, Manuel." A pair of chrome-spoked wheels glittered into view, a pair of wasted legs under a lap robe, a pair of no color eyes that had never forgiven anyone anything. "I remember you. What do you want?"

"Arthur Thomas Robinson is dead," Dave said.

"I've already told the police what I know."

"Not all of it." Wind blew cold rain across the back of Dave's neck. He turned up the trench coat collar. "You left out the part that interests me—that you're the beneficiary of his life insurance."

Shevel stared. There was no way for his face to grow any paler. It was parchment. But his jaw dropped. When he shut it, his dentures clicked. "You must be joking. There's got to be some mistake."

"There's not." Dave glanced at the rain. "Can I come in and talk about it?"

Shevel's mouth twitched. "Did you bring the check?"

Dave shook his head. "Murder has a way of slowing down the routine."

"Then there's nothing to talk about." The wheelchair was motorized. It started to turn away.

"Why would he name you?" Dave asked.

Shrug. "We were old friends."

Dave studied the Chicano boy who was watching them with something frantic in his eyes. "Friends?"

"Oh, come in, come in," Shevel snarled, and wheeled out of sight. Dave stepped onto deep beige carpeting and the door closed behind him. But when he turned to hand the trench coat over, there was no one to take it. Manuel had buttoned up and left. Dave laid the coat over his arm and went around the leafy screen. A long, handsome room stretched to sliding glass doors at its far end that looked down on a marina where little white boats waited row on row like children's coffins in the rain. Shevel rattled ice and glasses at a low bar. "I met Robbie in the hospital," he said, "ten years ago." He came wheeling at Dave, holding out a squat studded glass in which dark whiskey islanded an ice cube. "Just as I met you." His smile was crooked. "He worked there. An orderly."

"And you brought him along to look after you when the hospital let you go." Dave took the drink. "Thanks."

"Robbie had good hands." Shevel aimed the chair at the planter. From under it somewhere he took a small green plastic watering can. He tilted it carefully into the mulch under the climbing vines. "And patience."

"Who took his place?"

"No one. No one could. This apartment is arranged so that I don't need day-to-day help." Shevel set the watering can back. "The market sends in food and liquor." He drank from his glass. "I can cook my own meals. I'm able to bathe myself and so on. A cleaning woman comes in twice a week. I have a masseur on call."

"Manuel?" Dave wondered.

"Not Manuel," Shevel said shortly and drank again.

"You publish a lot of magazines," Dave said. "How do you get to your office? Specially equipped car?"

"No car," Shevel said. "Cars are the enemy." He purred past Dave and touched a wall switch. A panel slid back. Beyond gleamed white wet-look furniture, a highgloss white desk stacked with papers, a white electric typewriter, a photocopy machine. Blow up color photos of naked girls muraled the walls. "I don't go to the office. My work comes to me. And there's the telephone." He swallowed more whiskey. "You remember the telephone?" He touched the switch and the panel slid closed.

"Dave asked, "When did Robinson quit you?"

"Eight months, two weeks, and six days ago," Shevel said. He said it grimly with a kind of inverse satisfaction, like counting notches in a gun butt.

"Did he give a reason?"

"Reason?" Shevel snorted and worked on his drink again. "He felt old age creeping up on him. He was all of thirty-two. He decided he wanted to be the one who was looked after, for a change."

"No quarrels? No hard feelings?"

"Just boredom." Shevel looked at his glass but it was empty. Except for the ice cube. It still looked new. He wheeled abruptly back to the bar and worked the bottle again. Watching him, Dave tried his drink for the first time. Shevel bought good Bourbon with Medallion's money. Shevel asked, "If there'd been hard feelings, would he have come back to borrow money?"

"That might depend on how much he needed it," Dave said. "Or thought he did. I hear he was desperate."

Shevel's eyes narrowed. "What does that mean?"

"Trying to keep a champagne boy on a beer income."

"Exactly." Shevel's mouth tightened like a drawstring purse. "He never had any common sense."

"So you didn't lend him anything," Dave said.

"I told him not to be a fool. Forty-nine percent of the world's population is male." Shevel's chair buzzed. He steered it back, stopped it, tilted his glass, swallowed half the new drink. He looked toward the windows where the rain was gray. His voice was suddenly bleak. "I'm sorry he's dead. He was life to me for a long time."

"I'll go." Dave walked to the bar, set down his glass, began shrugging into the trench coat. "Just two more questions. Manuel. Does he take you deer hunting?"

Shevel looked blank.

Dave said, "Your thirty-thirty. When did you use it last?"

Shevel squinted. "What are you talking about?"

"A deer rifle. Winchester. Remington."

"Sorry." His bony fingers teased his white wig. He simpered like a skid row barroom floozy. "I've always preferred indoor sports."

He was suddenly drunk. He looked Dave up and down hungrily. "Next question."

"Those magazines of yours," Dave said. "The new Supreme Court decision on obscenity. You're going to have to do some retooling—right?"

Shevel's eyes got their old hardness back. "It's been on the drawing boards for months. A whole new line. Home crafts. Dune buggies. Crossword puzzles. And if you're suggesting I shot Robbie with his rifle in order to get the money to finance the changeover, then you don't know much about publishing costs. Ten thousand dollars wouldn't buy the staples."

"But you do know how much the policy paid."

The crooked smile came back. "Naturally. I bought it for him. Years ago." The smile went away. "How typical of him to have forgotten to take my name off it."

"And the thirty-thirty. Did you buy that too?"

"I paid for it, of course. He had no money."

"I'll just bet he didn't," Dave said.

The development may have looked sharp to start with but it had gone shabby fast. It was on the coast road at the north end of Surf, which had gone shabby a long time ago. You couldn't see the development from the coast road. You had to park between angled white lines on the tarmacked shoulder and walk to a cliff where an iron pipe railing was slipping, its cement footings too near the crumbling edge.

Below, along a narrow rock and sand curve of shore, stood apartment buildings. The tinwork vents on the roofs were rusting. Varnish peeled from rafter ends and wooden decks. The stucco had been laid on thin. It was webbed with cracks. Chunks had broken out at corners showing tarpaper and chickenwire underneath.

Dave saw what Ken Barker had meant. The only access to the place was down cement steps, three long flights against the cliff face. There'd been too much sand in the cement. Edges had crumbled. Today rain washed dirt and pebbles across the treads and made them treacherous. No—no wheelchair case could get down there. He was about to turn back when, the way it will sometimes for a second, the surf stopped booming. It charged and fell heavily, like a big, tired army under one of those generals that never gives up. But it breathed.

And in the sudden silence he heard from below a voice, raised in argument, protest, complaint. He went on down. The iron rail was scabby with corrosion. His hand came away rusty. He left cement for a boardwalk over parts of which sand had drifted, sand now dark and sodden with rain. He passed the backs of buildings, slope-top metal trash modules, the half-open doors of laundry rooms. The voice kept on. He turned between two buildings to walk for the beach front.

The voice came from halfway up wooden steps to a second-story deck. A small man stood there under a clear plastic umbrella. He was arguing up at the legs of a young black police officer above him on the deck. The officer wore a clear plastic slicker.

The little man shouted, "But I'm the goddamn owner of the goddamn place! A taxpayer. It's not Chief Gates that pays you—it's me. You know what the taxes are here? No—well, I'm not going to tell you because I hate to see a strong man cry. But they got to be paid, friend, if I rent it or don't rent it. And have you looked at it? I was screwed by the contractor. It's falling apart. Nineteen months old and falling apart. I'm suing the son of a bitch but the lawyers are breaking me. Not to mention the mortgage. A storm like this, carpets get soaked, plaster falls down. Could be happening in there right now. Why do you want to make things worse for me?"

Dave climbed the steps. When he'd come up to the little man, the officer said, "Mr. Brandstetter. That make three. This one. Robinson's ex-boss. Now you." His grin was very white. "This a real popular spot this morning."

"Turning people away, right?" Dave said. "Because the apartment's sealed, waiting for the DA?" He looked past the little man. Up the beach, a clutch of slickered cops was using a drag with deep teeth on the sand. Plastic wrapped their caps, their shoes.

Nothing about them looked happy. It was work for tractors. But there was no way to get tractors down here.

The black officer said, "DA been and gone."

"Yeah." The little man goggled at Dave through big horn-rims. "They talk about human rights. What happened to property rights? I own the place but I get treated like a thief. I can't get in till Robinson's brother comes and collects his stuff." His nose was red. And not from sunburn. There hadn't been any sun this month. "You're not his brother, are you?"

"Not the way you mean," Dave said. And to the officer, "Flag me when he comes, will you?" He went down the stairs and down the rain-runnelled beach. The sergeant he talked to wore plain-clothes and no hat. His name was Slocum. Rain plastered strands of pale red hair to his freckled scalp. Dave said, "What about the surf?"

"Running too high. You can't work a launch on it. Not close in where we have to look. Keep washing you up all the time." He glanced bitterly at the muddy sky. "Storm doesn't quit, we'll never find it."

"The storm could be your friend," Dave said. "Ought to wash anything ashore—all that power." And fifty yards off a cop yelled in the rain, bent, picked something out of the muddy surf, came with it at a trot, waving it above his head like a movie Apache who'd got the wrong room at Western Costume. "See?" Dave said.

"No wonder you're rich," Slocum said. It was a rifle. The cop offered it. Slocum shook his head. "You've got gloves, I don't. You hold it. Let me just look at it." He stared at it while the cop turned it over and it dripped. "Thirty-thirty Remington," Slocum said. "Eight years old but like new. Won't act like new—not unless they get the seawater out of it right away."

"Seawater doesn't erase prints," Dave said, and turned back toward the apartments because he heard his name called above the slam of surf, the hiss of rain. The black officer was waving an arm from the deck. A bulky man was with him. Dave jogged back. The landlord was yammering to a girl with ragged short hair in a

Kobe coat at the foot of the stairs, but there wasn't any hope in his voice now. Dave went up the stairs.

"Reverend Merwin Robinson," the black officer said. "Mr. Brandstetter. Insurance."

"Something wrong with the insurance?" The reverend had a hoarse voice. The kind you get from shouting—at baseball games or congregations. A thick man, red-faced. A big crooked vein bulged at one temple.

"What's wrong with it is the beneficiary," Dave said.

Robinson stiffened, glared. "I don't understand."

"Not you," Dave said. "Bruce K. Shevel."

Robinson blinked. "You must be mistaken."

"That's what Shevel said."

"But I'm Arthur's only living relative. Neither of us has anyone else. And he'd left Shevel. Said he never wanted to see him again."

"He saw him again," Dave said. "Tried to borrow money from him. I gather he saw you too."

The minister's mouth twitched. "Never at my invitation. And years would go by. He knew my stand. On how he lived. The same saintly mother raised us. He knew what the Bible says about him and his kind."

"But lately he tried to borrow money," Dave said.

"He did."

The black officer had opened the glass wall panel that was the apartment door. Robinson saw, grunted, went in. Dave followed. The room was white shag carpet, long low fake-fur couches, swag lamps in red and blue pebbled glass.

"Of course I refused. My living comes from collection plates. For the glory of God and His beloved Son. Not to buy fast automobiles for descendents of the brothels of Sodom."

"I don't think they had descendents," Dave said. "Anyway, did you have that kind of money?"

"My church is seventy years old. We've had half a dozen fires from faulty wiring. The neighborhood the church serves is just as old and just as poor." Robinson glanced at a shiny kitchenette where a plaster Michaelangelo David stood on a counter with plastic ferns. He went on to an alcove at the room's end, opened and quickly closed again a door to a bathroom papered with color photos of naked men from *Playgirl*, and went into a room where the ceiling was squares of gold-veined mirror above a round, tufted bed.

Dave watched him open drawers, scoop out the contents, dump them on the bed. Not a lot of clothes. A few papers. He slid back closet doors. Little hung inside. He took down what there was, spilling coat hangers, clumsily stooped, pushed the papers into a pocket, then bundled all the clothes into his arms and turned to face Dave. "That ten thousand dollars would have meant a lot to my church—new wiring, shingles, paint, new flooring to replace what's rotted—" He broke off, a man used to having dreams cancelled. He came at the door with his bundle of dead man's clothes and Dave made way for him. "Well, at least these will keep a few needy souls warm for the winter." He lumbered off down the length of the apartment, onto the deck and out of sight.

Dave looked after him. The view was clear from this room to the deck—maybe forty feet. Lily could have stood here with the thirty-thirty. At that distance the bullet hole wouldn't be too messy. Dave went for the door where cold, damp air came in. Also the little man who owned the place. He collided with Dave.

"Your turn," Dave said.

"It rents furnished," the little man said. "A preacher, for God sake! Crookeder than a politician. Did you see? Did he take kitchen stuff? I saw that bundle. Anything could have been in it. All the kitchen stuff stays with the place. Sheets, towels? All that's mine." He rattled open kitchen drawers, cupboards, slammed them shut again, dodged into the bathroom, banged around in there—"Jesus, look what that fag did to the walls!"—shot out of the bathroom and into the bedroom. Merwin Robinson had left the chest drawers hanging. From the doorway Dave could see their total emptiness. The little man stopped in front of them. His shoulders sagged. In relief or disappointment?

"All okay?" Dave asked.

"What? Oh, yeah. Looks like it." He didn't sound convinced.

Downstairs, Dave pressed a buzzer next to a glass panel like the one directly above that had opened into Arthur Thomas Robinson's apartment. While he'd talked to the dead man's brother and the black officer, he'd looked past their wet shoes through the slats in the deck and seen the short-haired girl go into this apartment. She came toward him now with *Daily Variety* in her hand, looking as if she didn't want to be bothered. She still wore the Kobe coat but her hair wasn't short anymore. She had on a blonde wig out of an Arthur Rackham illustration—big and fuzzy. She slid the door. A smell of fresh coffee came out.

"Were you at home when Robinson was killed?"

She studied him. Without makeup she looked like a ten-year-old boy dressed up as the dandelion fairy. "You a cop?"

He told her who he was, gave her a card. "The police like to think Lily killed him because it's easy, it will save the taxpayers money. I'm not so sure."

She tilted her head. "Whose money will that save?"

"Not Medallion's," he said. "I'd just like to see it go to somebody else."

"Than?" She shivered. "Look—come in." He did that and she slid the door to and put the weather outside where it belonged. "Coffee?" Dropping *Variety* on a couch like the ones upstairs, she led him to the kitchenette, talking. "Who did Robbie leave his money to?" She filled pottery mugs from a glass urn. "It's funny, thinking of him having money to leave when he was hitting on me and everybody else for twenty here, twenty there." She came around the counter, pushed a tall, flower-cushioned bar stool at Dave and perched on one herself. "He was really sick."

"Sick?" Dave tried the coffee. Rich and good.

"Over that Eddie. Nothing—beautiful junk. Like this pad. Robbie was nice, a really nice, gentle, sweet, warm human being. Of all things to happen to him!" She took a mouthful of coffee, froze with the cup halfway to the countertop, stared, swallowed. "You don't mean Robbie left Ed Lily that money?"

"That would be too easy," Dave said. "No—he left it to Bruce K. Shevel."

"You're kidding," she said.

Dave twitched an eyebrow, sighed, got out cigarettes. "That's what everybody thinks. Including Shevel." He held the pack for her to take one, took one himself, lit both. He dropped the lighter into his pocket. "Was Shevel ever down here?"

"How? He was a wheelchair case. Robbie told me about him. It was one of the reasons he chose this place. So Shevel couldn't get to him. The stairs. Why would he leave Shevel his money?"

"An oversight, I expect. After all, what was he—thirty-two? At that age, glimmerings of mortality are still dim. Plenty of time to make changes. Or maybe because Shevel had bought him the policy, he thought he owed him something."

"Robbie owed him? That's a laugh. He used him like a slave for ten years. If anything, it was the other way around. Shevel owed Robbie. But he wouldn't shell out a dime when Robbie asked for it."

"So I hear," Dave said. "Tell me about Lily."

She shrugged. "You know the type. Dime a dozen in this town. They drift in on their thumbs, all body, no brains. If they even get as far as a producer, they end up with their face in his pillow. Then it's back to Texas or Tennessee to pump gas for the rest of their lives. Only Eddie was just a little different. Show business he could live without. Hustling was surer and steadier. He always asked for parts in pictures but he settled for cash. A born whore. Loved it.

"I tried to tell Robbie. He wouldn't listen. Couldn't hear. Gone on the little shit, really gone. You want to know something? Eddie hadn't been here a week when he tried to get me into the sack." Her mouth twitched a half grin. "I told him, 'I don't go to bed with fags.' 'I'm not a fag,' was all he said. As if I and every other woman in the place didn't know that. Woman. Man. Everybody—except Robbie." She turned her head to look down the room at the glass front wall, the gray rain beyond it, the deserted beach, the muddy slop of surf. "Poor Robbie! What happens to people?" She turned back for an answer.

"In his case," Dave said, "murder."

"Yeah." She rolled her cigarette morosely against a little black ashtray. "And he never said a wrong word to Eddie. Never. Eddie was all over him all the time—I want this, I want that. You promised to introduce me to so-and-so. Take me here, take me there."

Dave looked at the ceiling. "Soundproofing another thing they cheated the owner on?"

"I got pretty familiar with Robbie's record collection. Sure, I could hear damn near every word. And a lot that wasn't words. The bedroom's right over mine too."

"Was that where the shot came from?" Dave asked.

"I wasn't here. Didn't I tell you? I was on location in Montana. Up to my elbows in flour in a tumble-down ranch house with little kids tugging at my skirts and my hair hanging over one eye. Twenty seconds on film. All that way on Airwest for twenty seconds."

"Too bad," Dave said. "Were you ever up there?"

"Robbie's? Yeah, for drinks. Now and then."

"Ever see a rifle?"

"They found it, didn't they?" She jerked the big fuzzy wig toward the beach. "Talking to Dieterle, I saw the cop fish it out of the kelp and run to you with it. You brought them luck. They were raking for it all day yesterday too."

"But did you ever see it in the apartment?"

She shrugged. "It was probably in a closet." She drank some coffee and frowned. "Wait a minute. I helped Robbie move in. No, I didn't know him. I parked up at the cliff edge and there he was with all this stuff to carry. I just naturally offered to help. And I hung around helping him settle in and we had a drink."

"Easy to know."

"A bartender," she said. "Had been since he was a kid, except for that period with Shevel. Easy friendliness is part of a bartender's stock in trade—right? Only he didn't fake it. He honestly liked people. Those old aunties Lauder and White fell all over themselves to get him back. Business has doubled since he took over. If he owned his own place he'd make a bundle." She remembered he was dead and sadness happened in her face. "Except for one thing."

Dave worked on his coffee. "Which was?"

"He also trusted people. And that's for losers."

"About the rifle?" he prompted her.

"He didn't own one," she said flatly. "I'd have seen it while we were putting away his stuff. No rifle. But I can tell you one thing. If there'd been one, Eddie could have used it. He used to talk about hunting rabbits when he was a kid back in Oklahoma."

"Thanks." Dave tilted up the mug, drained it, set it on the counter, got off the stool. "And for the coffee." He checked his watch. "But now it's out into the cold rain and the mean streets again."

"Aw," she said.

Climbing the gritty stairs up the cliff face, he still heard the surf. But as he neared the top there was the wet tire sibilance of traffic on the the coast road and the whine of a car engine that didn't want to start. At the railing, the little landlord, Dieterle, sat in a faded old Triumph, swearing. Dave walked over and wondered in a shout if he could help. Dieterle, with a sour twist of his mouth, gave up.

"Ah, it'll catch, it'll catch. Son of a bitch knows I'm in a hurry. Always acts like this." Rain had misted the big round lenses of his glasses. He peered up at Dave through them. "You're some kind of cop, no? I saw you with them on the beach. I heard you tell Bambi O'Mara you didn't think Lily killed Robinson." Dieterle cocked his head. "You think Bambi did it?"

"Why would I think that?"

"Hell, she was in love with Robinson. And I mean, off the deep end. Weird, a smart chick like that. Not to mention her looks. You know she was a *Playboy* centerfold?"

"It's raining and I'm getting wet," Dave said. "Tell me why she'd kill Robinson so I can go get Slocum to put cuffs on her."

Dieterle's mouth fell open. "Ah, now, wait. I didn't mean to get her in trouble. I figured you knew." He blinked anxious through the glasses. "Anybody around here could have told you. She made a spectacle of herself." Maybe the word reminded him. He took off the horn-rims, poked in the dash for a Kleenex, wiped the rain off the lenses. "I mean, what chance did she have?" He dropped the tissues on the floor and put the glasses back on. "Robinson was a fag, worked in a fag bar. It didn't faze her. So many chicks like that—figure one good lay with them and a flit will forget all about boys. Except Bambi never got the lay. And Robinson got Ed Lily. And did she hate Lily! Hoo!"

"And so she shot Robinson dead." Dave straightened, looked away to where rain-glazed cars hissed past against the rain-curtained background of another cliff. "Hell hath no fury, etcetera?"

"And framed Lily for it. You follow?"

"Thanks," Dave said. "I'll check her out."

"Any time." Dieterle reached and turned the key and the engine started with a snarl. "What'd I tell you?" he yelled. The car backed, scattering wet gravel, swung in a bucking U, and headed down the highway toward Surf. Fast. Dave watched. Being in a chronic hurry must be rough on a man who couldn't stop talking.

Nobody ate at The Big Cup because it was an openfront place and rain was lashing its white Formica. It faced a broad belt of cement that marked off the seedy shops and scabby apartment buildings of Venice from the beach where red dune fences leaned. Dave got coffee in an outsize cup and took it into a phone booth. After his first swallow, he lit a cigarette and dialled people he knew in the television business. He didn't learn anything but they'd be able to tell him later.

He returned the empty mug to the empty counter and hiked a block among puddles to the Billy Budd, whose neon sign buzzed and sputtered as if rain had leaked into it. He checked his watch. Twenty minutes ago it had been noon. A yellowed card tacked to the black door said in faded felt pen that the hours were 12 noon to 2 a.m. But the door was padlocked.

He put on reading glasses and bent to look for an emergency number on the card and a voice back of him said: "Excuse me."

The voice belonged to a bony man, a boy of fifty, in an expensive raincoat and expensive cologne. He was out of breath, pale, and when he used a key on the padlock, his hands shook. He pushed open the door and bad air came out—stale cigarette smoke, last night's spilled whiskey. He kicked a rubber wedge under the door to hold it open and went inside.

Dave followed. The place was dark but he found the bar that had a padded leather bevel for the elbows and padded leather stools that sighed. Somewhere at the back, a door opened and fell shut. Fluorescent tubing winked on behind the bar, slicking mirrors, glinting on rows of bottles, stacks of glasses. A motor whined, fan blades clattered, air began to blow along the room. The man came out without his raincoat, without his suit coat. The shirt was expensive too. But he'd sweated it.

"Weather, right? What can I get you?"

"Just the answer to a question," Dave said. "What did you want at Arthur Thomas Robinson's apartment in Surf this morning?"

The man narrowed his lovely eyes. "Who are you?"

Dave told him. "There are details the police haven't time for. I've got time. Can I have your answer?"

"Will you leave without it? No—I didn't think so." The man turned away to drop ice into glasses. He tilted in whiskey, edged in water. He set a glass in front of Dave, held one himself. The shaking of his hand made the ice tinkle. The sound wasn't Christmasy. "All right," he said. "Let's see if I can shock you. Ten years ago, Arthur Thomas Robinson and I were lovers."

"You don't shock me," Dave said. "But it's not responsive to my question."

"I wrote him letters. I wanted those letters back before his oh-so-righteous brother got his hands on them. I didn't know how to go about it. I simply drove over to Robbie's. I mean—I never see television. What do I know about police procedure?"

"Ten years ago," Dave said. "Does that mean Robinson left you for Bruce K. Shevel?"

"That evil mummy," the man said.

"Clear up something for me." Dave tried the whiskey. Rich

and smooth. They didn't serve this out of the well. "Shevel said he'd met Robinson in the hospital. Robinson was an orderly. A neighbor named Bambi O'Mara says Robinson was a barkeep all his life."

The man nodded. "I taught him all he knew. He was eighteen when he drifted in here." The man's eyes grew wet. He turned away and lit a cigarette. "He'd never had another job in his life. Orderly? Be serious! He fainted at the sight of blood. No, one sinister night Bruce Shevel walked in here, slumming. And that was the beginning of the end. An *old* man. He was, even then. He must be all glamour by now."

"You know that Robinson kept your letters?"

"Yes. He was always promising to return them but he didn't get around to it. Now he never will." The man's voice broke and he took a long swallow from his drink. "That damn brother will probably have apoplexy when he reads them. And of course he'll read them. His type are always snooping after sin. Claim it revolts them but they can't get enough. And of course he hated me. Always claimed I'd perverted his baby brother. We had some pretty ugly dialogues when he found out Robbie and I were sleeping together. I wouldn't put it past him to go to the liquor board with those letters. You've got to have unimpeachable morals to run a bar, you know. It could be the end of me."

"I don't think he's that kind of hater," Dave said. "Are you Lauder?"

"I'm White, Wilbur White. Bob Lauder and I have been partners since we got out of the Army—World War II. We've had bars all over L.A. County. Fifteen years here in Venice."

"Where is he now?"

"Bob? He'll be in at six. Today's my long day. His was yesterday. It's getting exhausting. We haven't replaced Robbie yet." He tried for a wan smile. "Of course we never will. But we'll hire somebody."

"You live in Venice?" Dave asked.

"Oh, heavens, no. Malibu."

* * *

It was a handsome new place on the beach. Raw cedar planking. An Alfa Romeo stood in the carport. Dave pulled the company car into the empty space beside it. The house door was a slab at the far end of a walk under a flat roof overhang. He worked a bell push. Bob Lauder was a time getting to the door. When he opened it he was in a bathrobe and a bad mood. He was as squat and pudgy as his partner was the opposite. His scant hair was tousled, his eyes were pouchy. He winced at the daylight, what there was of it.

"Sorry to bother you," Dave said, "but I'm death claims investigator for Medallion Life. Arthur Robinson was insured with us. He worked for you. Can I ask you a few questions?"

"The police asked questions yesterday," Lauder said.

"The police don't care about my company's ten thousand dollars," Dave said. "I do."

"Come in, stay out, I don't give a damn." Lauder flopped a hand and turned away. "All I want is sleep."

It was Dave's day for living rooms facing the Pacific. Lauder dropped onto a couch and leaned forward, head in hands, moaning quietly to himself.

"I've heard," Dave said, "that Robinson was good for business, that you were happy to get him back."

"He was good for business," Lauder droned.

"But you weren't happy to get him back?"

"Wilbur was happy." Lauder looked up, red-eyed. "Wilbur was overjoyed. Wilbur came un-goddam-glued."

"To the extent of letting Robinson take what he wanted from the till?"

"How did you know? We didn't tell the police."

Dave shrugged. "He was hurting for money."

"Yeah. Wilbur tried to cover for him. I let him think it worked. But I knew." He rose and tottered off. "I need some coffee."

Dave went after him, leaned in a kitchen doorway and watched him heat a pottery urn of leftover coffee on a bricked-in burner deck. "How long have you and Wilbur been together?"

"Thirty years"—Lauder reached down a mug from a hook—"since you ask."

"Because you didn't let the Arthur Thomas Robinsons of this world break it up, right? There were others, weren't there?"

"You don't look it, you don't sound it, but you have got to be gay. Nobody straight could guess that." Lauder peered into the mouth of the pot, hoping for steam. "Yes. It wasn't easy but it was worth it. To me. If you met Wilbur, you'd see why."

Dave didn't. "Do you own a hunting rifle? Say a thirty-thirty?"

Lauder turned and squinted. "What does that mean? Look, I was working in the bar when Robbie got it. I did not get jealous and kill him, if that's what you're thinking. Or did I do it to stop him skimming fifty bucks an evening off the take?"

"I'm trying to find out what to think," Dave said.

"Try someplace else." Lauder forgot to wait for the steam. He set the mug down hard and sloshed coffee into it. "Try now. Get out of here."

"If you bought a rifle in the past five-six years," Dave said, "there'll be a federal registration record."

"We own a little pistol," Lauder said. "We keep it at the bar. Unloaded. To scare unruly trade."

Where Los Santos Canyon did a crooked fall out of tree-green hills at the coast road, there was a cluster of Tudor-style buildings whose 1930 stucco fronts looked mushy in the rain. Between a shop that sold snorkles and swim-fins and a hamburger place Dave remembered from his childhood, lurked three telephone booths. Two were occupied by women in flowered plastic raincoats and hair curlers, trying to let somebody useful know their cars had stalled. He took the third booth and dialled the television people again.

While he learned that Bambi O'Mara had definitely been in Bear Paw, Montana at the time a bullet made a clean hole through the skull of the man she loved, Dave noticed a scabby sign across the street above a door with long black iron hinges. *L. DIETERLE REAL ESTATE.* He glanced along the street for the battered Triumph. It wasn't in sight but it could be back of the building. He'd see later. Now he phoned Lieutenant Ken Barker.

He was at his desk. Still. Or again. "Dave?"

"Shevel is lying. He wouldn't lie for no reason."

"Your grammar shocks me," Barker said.

"He claims he met Robinson when he was in the hospital. *After* his so-called accident. Says Robinson was an orderly. But at the Sea Shanty they say Shevel *walked* in one night and met Robinson. According to a girlfriend, Robinson was never anything but a bartender. You want to check Junipero Hospital's employment records?"

"For two reasons," Barker said. "First, that rifle didn't have any prints on it and it was bought long before Congress ordered hunting guns registered. Second, an hour ago the Coast Guard rescued a kid in a power boat getting battered on the rocks off Point Placentia. It wasn't his power boat. It's registered to one Bruce K. Shevel. The kid works at the Marina. My bet is he was heading for Mexico."

"Even money," Dave said. "His name is Manuel—right? Five foot six, a hundred twenty pounds, long hair? Somewhere around twenty?"

"You left out something," Barker said. "He's scared to death. He won't say why, but it's not just about what happened to the boat. I'll call Junipero."

"Thanks," Dave said. "I'll get back to you."

He left the booth and dodged rain-bright bumpers to the opposite curb. He took a worn step up and pushed the real estate office door. Glossy eight-by-tens of used Los Santos and Surf side-street bungalows curled on the walls. A scarred desk was piled with phone directories. They slumped against a finger-smeared telephone. A nameplate by the telephone said, *L. Dieterle*. But the little man wasn't in the chair back of the desk.

The room wasn't big to start with but a Masonite partition halved it and behind this a typewriter rattled. A lumberyard bargain door was shut at the end of the partition. Tacked to the door was a pasteboard dimestore sign, *NOTARY*, and under it a business card. *Verna Marie Casper, Public Stenographer*. He rapped the door and a tin voice told him to come in.

She'd used henna on her hair for a lot of years. Her makeup too was like Raggedy Ann's. Including the yarn eyelashes. She was sixty but the dress was off the Young Misses rack at Grant's. Glass diamonds sparked at her ears, her scrawny throat, her wrists, the bony hands that worked a Selectric with a finish like a Negev tank. She wasn't going to, but he said anyway: "Don't let me interrupt you. I just want to know when Mr. Dieterle will be back."

"Can't say," she said above the fast clatter of the type ball. "He's in and out. A nervous man, very nervous. You didn't miss him by long. He was shaking today. That's a new one."

"He thinks the storm is going to knock down his apartments in Surf," Dave said. "Will you take a message for him?"

"What I write down I get paid for," she said. "He was going through phone books. So frantic he tore pages. Really. Look"—suddenly she stopped typing and stared at Dave—"I just sublet this space. We're not in business together. He looks after his business. I look after mine. I'm self-sufficient."

"Get a lot of work, do you?"

"I'm part of this community," she said and began typing again. "A valued part. They gave me a testimonial dinner at the Chamber of Commerce last fall. Forty years of loyal public service."

"I believe it," Dave said. "Ever do anything for a man named Robinson? Recently, say—the last two weeks or so? Arthur Thomas Robinson?"

She broke off typing again and eyed him fiercely. "Are you a police officer? Are you authorized to have such information?"

"He wanted you to write out an affidavit for him, didn't he? And to notarize it?"

"Now, see here! You know I can't—"

"I'm not asking what was in it. I think I know. I also think it's what got him killed."

"Killed!" She went white under the circles of rouge. "But he only did it to clear his conscience! He said—" She clapped a hand to her mouth and glared at Dave. "You! You're trying to trick me. Well, it won't work. What I'm told is strictly confidential."

Dave swung away. His knuckles rapped the Masonite as he

went out of her cubbyhole. "Not with this partition," he said. "With Dieterle on the other side."

Past batting windshield wipers, he saw the steeple down the block above the dark greenery of old acacia trees. Merwin Robinson had told the truth about the neighborhood. Old one-story frame houses with weedy front yards where broken-down autos turned to rust. Stray dogs ran cracked sidewalks in the rain. An old woman in man's shoes and hat dragged a coaster wagon through puddles.

CHURCH OF GOD'S ABUNDANCE was what the weathered signboard said. God's neglect was what showed. Dave tried the front doors from which the yellow varnish was peeling. They were loose in their frame but locked. A hollow echo came back from the rattling he gave them. He followed a narrow strip of cement that led along the shingled side of the church to a shingle-sided bungalow at the rear. The paint flaking off it was the same as what flaked off the church, white turning yellow. There was even a cloverleaf of stained glass in the door. Rev. Merwin Robinson in time-dimmed ink was in a little brass frame above a bell push.

But the buzz pushing it made at the back of the house brought nobody. A dented gray and blue sedan with fifties tail fins stood at the end of the porch. Its trunk was open. Some of Arthur Thomas Robinson's clothes were getting rained on. Dave tried the tongue latch of the house door and it opened. He put his head inside, called for the preacher. It was dusky in the house. No lights anywhere. Dave stepped inside onto a threadbare carpet held down by overstuffed chairs covered in faded chintz.

"Reverend Robinson?"

No answer. He moved past a room divider of built-in bookcases with diamond-pane glass doors. There was a round golden oak dining room table under a chain-suspended stained-glass light fixture. Robinson evidently used the table as a desk. Books were stacked on it. A loose-leaf binder lay open, a page half filled with writing in ballpoint. Am I my brother's keeper? Sermon topic. But not for this week. Not for any week now.

Because on the far side of the table, by a kitchen swing door his head had pushed ajar when he fell, Merwin Robinson lay on his back and stared at Dave with the amazed eyes of the dead. One of his hands clutched something white. Dave knelt. It was an envelope, torn open, empty. But the stamp hadn't been cancelled. He put on his glasses, flicked his lighter to read the the address. *City Attorney, 200 Spring St., Los Angeles, CA.* Neatly typed on an electric machine with carbon ribbon. Probably the battered IBM in Verna Casper's office.

Which meant there wasn't time to hunt up the rectory phone in the gloom, to report, to explain. It didn't matter. Merwin Robinson wouldn't be any deader an hour from now. But somebody else might be, unless Dave got back to the beach. Fast.

Wind lashed rain across the expensive decks of the apartments facing the Marina. It made the wet trench coat clumsy, flapping around his legs. Then he quit running because he saw the door. He took the last yards in careful, soundless steps. The door was shut. That would be reflex even for a man in a chronic hurry—to shut out the storm. And that man had to be here. The Triumph was in the lot.

Dave put a hand to the cold, wet brass knob. It turned. He leaned gently against the door. It opened. He edged in and softly shut it. The same yammering voice he'd heard earlier today in Surf above the wash of rain and tide, yammered now someplace beyond the climbing vines.

"—that you got him to help you try to rip off an insurance company—accident and injury. By knocking your car off the jack while one wheel was stripped and your foot was under it. And he told you he was going to spill the whole story unless you paid out."

"I'm supposed to believe it's on that paper?" Shevel's voice came from just the other side of the philodendrons. "That Robbie actually—"

"Yeah, right—he dictated it to the old hag that's a notary public, splits my office space with me. I heard it all. He told her he'd give you twenty-four hours to cop out too, then he'd mail it. But

I didn't think it was a clear conscience he was after. He was after money—for a sports car for that hustler he was keeping."

"I'm surprised at Robbie," Shevel said. "He often threatened to do things. He rarely did them."

"He did this. And you knew he would. Only how did you waste him? You can't get out of that chair."

"I had two plans. The other was complicated—a bomb in his car. Happily, the simpler plan worked out. It was a lovely evening. The storm building up off the coast made for a handsome sunset. The sea was calm—long, slow swells. I decided to take an hour's cruise in my launch. I have a young friend who skippers it for me."

"You shot him from out there?"

"The draft is shallow. Manuel was able to steer quite close in. It can't have been a hundred fifty yards. Robbie was on the deck as I'd expected. It was warm, and he adored sunsets with his martinis. Manuel's a fine marksman. Twenty-four months in Vietnam sharpened his natural skills. And the gun was serviceable." Shevel's voice went hard. "This gun is not, but you're too close to miss. Hand over that paper. No, don't try anything. I warn you—"

Dave stepped around the screen of vines and chopped at Shevel's wrist. The gun went off with a slapping sound. The rug furrowed at Dieterle's feet. Shevel screamed rage, struggled in the wheelchair, clawed at Dave's eyes. Dieterle tried to run past. Dave put a foot in his way. He sprawled. Dave wrenched the twenty-two out of Shevel's grip, leveled it at them, backed to a white telephone, cranked zero, and asked an operator to get him the police. Ken Barker had managed a shower and a shave. He still looked wearier than this morning. But he worked up a kind of smile. "Neat," he said. "You think like a machine—a machine that gets the company's money back."

"Shevel's solvent but not that solvent," Dave said. "Hell, we paid out a hundred thousand initially. I don't remember what the monthly payments were. We'll be lucky to get half. And we'll have to sue for that." He frowned at a paper in his hands, typing on a police form, signed in shaky ballpoint—*Manuel Sanchez*. It said

Shevel had done the shooting. He, Manuel, had only run the boat. "Be sure this kid gets a good lawyer."

"The best in the public defender's office."

"No." Dave rose, flapped into the trench coat. "Not good enough. Medallion will foot the bill. I'll send Abe Greenglass. Tomorrow morning."

"Jesus." Barker blinked. "Remind me never to cross you."

Dave grinned, worked the coat's wet leather buttons, quit grinning. "I'm sorry about Robinson's brother. If I'd just been a little quicker—"

"It was natural causes," Barker said. "Don't blame yourself. Can't even blame Dieterle—or Wilbur White."

"The bar owner? You mean he was there?"

"Slocum checked him out. He had the letters."

"Yup." Dave fastened the coat belt. "Twenty minutes late to work. White, sweaty, shaking. It figures. Hell, he even talked about apoplexy, how the reverend hated him for perverting his brother."

"The man had horrible blood pressure," Barker said. "We talked to his doctor. He'd warned him. The least excitement and"—Barker snapped his fingers—"cerebral hemorrhage. Told him to retire. Robinson refused. They needed him—the people at that run-down church."

"It figures," Dave said. "He didn't make it easy, but he was the only one in this mess I could like. A little."

"Not Bambi O'Mara?" Barker went and snagged a topcoat from a rack. "She looked great in those magazine spreads." He took Dave's arm, steered him between gray-green desks toward a gray-green door. "I want to hear all about her. I'll buy you a drink."

But the phone rang and called him back. And Dave walked alone out of the beautiful, bright glass building into the rain that looked as if it would never stop falling.

THE KERMAN KILL

BY WILLIAM CAMPBELL GAULT

Pacific Palisades

(Originally published in 1987)

Pierre?" my Uncle Vartan asked. "Why Pierre? You were Pistol Pete Apoyan when you fought."

Sixteen amateur fights I'd had and won them all. Two professional fights I'd had and painfully decided it would not be my trade. I had followed that career with three years as an employee of the Arden Guard and Investigative Service in Santa Monica before deciding to branch out on my own.

We were in my uncle's rug store in Beverly Hills, a small store and not in the highest rent district, but a fine store. No machine-made imitation Orientals for him, and *absolutely* no carpeting.

"You didn't change your name," I pointed out.

"Why would I?" he asked. "It is an honorable name and suited to my trade."

"And Pierre is not an honorable name?"

He sighed. "Please do not misunderstand me. I adore your mother. But Pierre is a name for hairdressers and perfume manufacturers and those pirate merchants on Rodeo Drive. Don't your friends call you Pete?"

"My odar friends," I admitted. "Odar" means (roughly) non-Armenian. My mother is French, my father Armenian.

"Think!" he said. "Sam Spade. Mike Hammer. But Pierre?"

"Hercule Poirot," I said.

"What does that mean? Who is this Hercule Poirot? A friend?" He was frowning.

It was my turn to sigh. I said nothing. My Uncle Vartan is a stubborn man. He had four nephews, but I was his favorite. He had never married. He had come to this country as an infant with my father and their older brother. My father had sired one son and one daughter, my Uncle Sarkis three sons.

"You're so stubborn!" Uncle Vartan said.

The pot had just described the kettle. I shrugged.

He took a deep breath. "I suppose I am, too."

I nodded.

"Whatever," he said, "the decision is yours, no matter what name you decide to use."

The decision would be mine but the suggestion had been his. Tough private eye stories, fine rugs, and any attractive woman under sixty were what he cherished. His store had originally been a two-story duplex with a separate door and stairway to the second floor. That, he had suggested, would be a lucrative location for my office when I left Arden.

His reasoning was sound enough. He got the carriage trade; why wouldn't I? And he would finance the remodeling.

Why was I so stubborn?

"Don't sulk," he said.

"It's because of my mother," I explained. "She didn't like it when I was called Pistol Pete."

His smile was sad. "I know. But wouldn't Pistol Pierre have sounded worse?" He shook his head. "Lucky Pierre, always in the middle. I talked with the contractor last night. The remodeling should be finished by next Tuesday."

The second floor was large enough to include living quarters for me. Tonight I would tell my two roomies in our Pacific Palisades apartment that I would be deserting them at the end of the month. I drove out to Westwood, where my mother and sister had a French pastry shop.

My sister, Adele, was behind the counter. My mother was in the back, smoking a cigarette. She is a chain smoker, my mother, the only nicotine addict in the family. She is a slim, trim, and testy forty-seven-year-old tiger.

"Well—?" she asked.

"We won," I told her. "It will be the Pierre Apoyan Investigative Service."

"*You* won," she corrected me. "You and Vartan. It wasn't *my* idea."

"Are there any croissants left?" I asked.

"On the shelf next to the oven." She shook her head. "That horny old bastard! All the nice women I found for him—"

"Who needs a cow when milk is cheap?" I asked.

"Don't be vulgar," she said. "And if you do, get some new jokes."

I buttered two croissants, poured myself a cup of coffee, and sat down across from her. I said, "The rumor I heard years ago is that Vartan came on to you before you met Dad."

"The rumor is true," she admitted. "But if I wanted to marry an adulterer I would have stayed in France."

"And then you never would have met Dad. You did okay, Ma."

"I sure as hell did. He's *all* man."

The thought came to me that if he were all man, the macho type, my first name would not be Pierre. I didn't voice the thought; I preferred to drink my coffee, not wear it.

She said, "I suppose that you'll be carrying a gun again in this new profession you and Vartan dreamed up?"

"Ma, at Arden I carried a gun only when I worked guard duty. I *never* carried one when I did investigative work. This will not be guard duty."

She put out her cigarette and stood up. "That's something, I suppose. You're coming for dinner on Sunday, of course?"

"Of course," I said.

She went out to take over the counter. Adele came in to have a cup of coffee. She was born eight years after I was; she is twenty and romantically inclined. She has our mother's slim, dark beauty and our father's love of the theater. She was currently sharing quarters with an aspiring actor. My father was a still cameraman at Elysian Films.

"Mom looks angry," she said. "What did you two argue about this time?"

"My new office. Uncle Vartan is going to back me."

She shook her head. "What a waste! With your looks you'd be a cinch in films."

"Even prettier than your Ronnie?"

"Call it a tie," she said. "You don't like him, do you?"

Her Ronnie was an aspiring actor who called himself Ronnie Egan. His real name was Salvatore Martino. I shrugged.

"He's got another commercial coming up next week. And his agent thinks he might be able to work me into it."

"Great!" I said.

That gave him a three-year career total of four commercials. If he worked her in, it would be her second.

"Why don't you like him?"

"Honey, I only met him twice and I don't dislike him. Could we drop the subject?"

"Aagh!" she said. "You and Vartan, you two deserve each other. Bull-heads!"

"People who live in glass houses," I pointed out, "should undress in the cellar."

She shook her head again. "You and Papa, you know all the corny old ones, don't you?"

"Guilty," I admitted. "Are you bringing Ronnie to dinner on Sunday?"

"Not this Sunday. We're going to a party at his agent's house. Ronnie wants me to meet him."

"I hope it works out. I'll hold my thumbs. I love you, sis."

"It's mutual," she said.

I kissed the top of her head and went out to my ancient Camaro. On the way to the apartment I stopped in Santa Monica and talked with my former boss at Arden.

I had served him well; he promised that if they ever had any commercial reason to invade my new bailiwick, and were shorthanded, I would be their first choice for associate action.

The apartment I shared with two others in Pacific Palisades was on the crest of the road just before Sunset Boulevard curves and dips down to the sea.

My parents had bought a tract house here in the fifties for an exorbitant twenty-one thousand dollars. It was now worth enough to permit both of them to retire. But they enjoyed their work too much to consider that.

I will not immortalize my roomies' names in print. One of them was addicted to prime-time soap operas, the other changed his underwear and socks once a week, on Saturday, after his weekly shower.

When I told them, over our oven-warmed frozen TV dinners, that I would be leaving at the end of the month, they took it graciously. Dirty Underwear was currently courting a lunch-counter waitress who had been hoping to share an apartment. She would inherit my rollout bed—when she wasn't in his.

On Thursday morning my former boss phoned to tell me he had several credit investigations that needed immediate action and two operatives home with the flu. Was I available? I was.

Uncle Sarkis and I went shopping on Saturday for office and apartment furniture. Wholesale, of course. "Retail" is an obscene word to my Uncle Sarkis.

The clan was gathered on Sunday at my parents' house, all but Adele. Uncle Vartan and my father played tavlu (backgammon to you). My mother, Uncle Sarkis, his three sons, and I played twenty-five-cent-limit poker out on the patio. My mother won, as usual. I broke even; the others lost. I have often suspected that the Sunday gatherings my mother hosts are more financially motivated than familial.

My roommates told me Monday morning that I didn't have to wait until the end of the month; I could move anytime my place was ready. The waitress was aching to move in.

The remodeling was finished at noon on Tuesday, the furniture delivered in the afternoon. I moved in the next morning. All who passed on the street below would now be informed by the gilt letters on the new wide front window that the Pierre Apoyan Investigative Service was now open and ready to serve them.

There were many who passed on the street below in the next three hours, but not one came up the steps. There was no reason to expect that anyone would. Referrals and advertising were what brought the clients in. Arden was my only doubtful source for the first; my decision to open this office had come too late to make the deadline for an ad in the phone book yellow pages.

I consoled myself with the knowledge that there was no odor of sour socks in the room and I would not be subjected to the idiocies of prime-time soap opera. I read the *L.A. Times* all the way through to the classified pages.

It had been a tiring two days; I went into my small bedroom to nap around ten o'clock. It was noon when I came back to the here and now. I turned on my answering machine and went down to ask Vartan if I could take him to lunch.

He shook his head. "Not today. After your first case, you may buy. Today, lunch is on me."

He had not spent enough time in the old country to develop a taste for Armenian food. He had spent his formative years in New York and become addicted to Italian cuisine. We ate at La Famiglia on North Canon Drive.

He had whitefish poached in white wine, topped with capers and small bay shrimp. I had a Caesar salad.

Over our coffee, he asked, "Dull morning?"

I nodded. "There are bound to be a lot of them for a one-man office. I got in two days at Arden last week. I might get more when they're short-handed."

He studied me for a few seconds. Then, "I wasn't going to mention this. I don't want to get your hopes up. But I have a—a customer who might drop in this afternoon. It's about a rug I sold her. It has been stolen. For some reason, which she wouldn't tell me, she doesn't want to go to the police. I gave her your name."

He had hesitated before he called her a customer. With his history, she could have been more than that. "Was it an expensive rug?" I asked.

"I got three thousand for it eight years ago. Only God knows what it's worth now. That was a sad day for me. It's an antique Kerman."

"Wasn't it insured?"

"Probably. But if she reported the loss to her insurance company they would insist she go to the police."

"Was anything else stolen?"

"Apparently not. The rug was all she mentioned."

That didn't make sense. A woman who could afford my uncle's antique Oriental rugs must have some jewelry. That would be easier and safer to haul out of a house than a rug.

"I'd better get back to the office," I said.

"Don't get your hopes up," he warned me again. "I probably shouldn't have told you."

I checked my answering machine when I got back to the office. Nothing. I took out my contract forms and laid them on top of my desk and sat where I could watch the street below.

I decided, an hour later, that was sophomoric. The ghost of Sam Spade must have been sneering down at me.

She opened the door about twenty minutes later, a fairly tall, slim woman with jet-black hair, wearing black slacks and a white cashmere sweater. She could have been sixty or thirty; she had those high cheekbones which keep a face taut.

"Mr. Apoyan?" she asked.

I nodded.

"Your uncle recommended you to me."

"He told me. But he didn't tell me your name."

"I asked him not to." She came over to sit in my client's chair. "It's Bishop, Mrs. Whitney Bishop. Did he tell you that I prefer not to have the police involved?"

"Yes. Was anything else stolen?"

She shook her head.

"That seems strange to me," I said. "Burglars don't usually carry out anything big, anything suspicious enough to alert the neighbors."

"Our neighbors are well screened from view," she told me, "and I'm sure this was not a burglar." She paused. "I am almost certain it was my daughter. And *that* is why I don't want the police involved."

"It wasn't a rug too big for a woman to carry?"

She shook her head. "A three-by-five-foot antique Kerman."

I winced. "For three thousand dollars—?"

Her smile was dim. "You obviously don't have your uncle's knowledge of rugs. I was offered more than I care to mention for it only two months ago. My daughter is—adopted. She has been in trouble before. I have *almost* given up on her. We had a squabble the day my husband and I went down to visit friends in Rancho Santa Fe. When we came home the rug was gone and so was she."

I wondered if it was her daughter she wanted back or the rug. I decided that would be a cynical question to ask.

"We have an elaborate alarm system," she went on, "with a well-hidden turnoff in the house. It couldn't have been burglars." She stared bleakly past me. "She knows how much I love that rug. I feel that it was simply a vindictive act on her part. It has been a—troubled relationship."

"How old is she?" I asked.

"Seventeen."

"Does she know who her real parents are?"

"No. And neither do we. Why?"

"I thought she might have gone back to them. How about her friends?"

"We've talked with all of her friends that we know. There are a number of them we have never met." A pause. "And I am sure would not want to."

"Your daughter's—acceptable friends might know of others," I suggested.

"Possibly," she admitted. "I'll give you a list of those we know well."

She told me her daughter's name was Janice and made out a list of her friends while I filled in the contract. She gave me a check, her unlisted phone number, and a picture of her daughter.

When she left, I went to the window and saw her climb into a sleek black Jaguar below. My hunch had been sound; this was the town that attracted the carriage trade.

I went downstairs to thank Vartan and tell him our next lunch would be on me at a restaurant of his choice.

"I look forward to it," he said. "She's quite a woman, isn't she?"

"That she is. Was she ever more than a customer to you?"

"We had a brief but meaningful relationship," he said coolly, "at a time when she was between husbands. But then she started talking marriage." He sighed.

"Uncle Vartan," I asked, "haven't you *ever* regretted the fact that you have no children to carry on your name?"

"Never," he said, and smiled. "You are all I need."

Two elderly female customers came in then and I went out with my list of names. It was a little after three o'clock; some of the kids should be home from school.

There were five names on the list, two girls and three boys, all students at Beverly Hills High. Only one of the girls was home. She had seen Janice at school on Friday, she told me, but not since. But that didn't mean she hadn't been at school Monday and Tuesday.

"She's not in any of my classes," she explained.

I showed her the list. "Could you tell me if any of these students are in any of her classes?"

"Not for sure. But Howard might be in her art appreciation class. They're both kind of—you know—"

"Artistic?" I asked.

"I suppose. You know—that weird stuff—"

"Avant-garde, abstract, cubist?"

She shrugged. "I guess, whatever *that* means. Janice and I were never really close."

From the one-story stone house of Miss Youknow, I drove to the two-story Colonial home of Howard Retzenbaum.

He was a tall thin youth with horn-rimmed glasses. He was wearing faded jeans and a light gray T-shirt with a darker gray reproduction of Pablo Picasso's *Woman's Head* emblazoned on his narrow chest.

Janice, he told me, had been in class on Friday, but not Monday or yesterday. "Has something happened to her?"

"I hope not. Do you know of any friends she has who don't go to your school?"

Only one, he told me, a boy named Leslie she had introduced him to several weeks ago. He had forgotten his last name. He tapped his forehead. "I remember she told me he works at some Italian restaurant in town. He's a busboy there."

"La Famiglia?"

"No, no. That one on Santa Monica Boulevard."

"La Dolce Vita?"

He nodded. "That's the place. Would you tell her to phone me if you find her?"

I promised him I would and thanked him. The other two boys were not at home; they had baseball practice after school. I drove to La Dolce Vita.

They serve no luncheon trade. The manager was not in. The assistant manager looked at me suspiciously when I asked if a boy named Leslie worked there.

"Does he have a last name?"

"I'm sure he has. Most people do. But I don't happen to know it."

"Are you a police officer?"

I shook my head. "I am a licensed and bonded private investigator. My Uncle Vartan told me that Leslie is an employee here."

"Would that be Vartan Apoyan?"

"It would be and it is." I handed him my card.

He read it and smiled. "That's different. Leslie's last name is Denton. He's a student at UCLA and works from seven o'clock until closing." He gave me Leslie's phone number and address, and asked, "Is Pierre an Armenian name?"

"Quite often," I informed him coldly, and left without thanking him.

The address was in Westwood and it was now almost five o'clock. I had no desire to buck the going-home traffic in this city of wheels. I drove to the office to call Leslie.

He answered the phone. I told him I was a friend of Howard Retzenbaum's and we were worried about Janice. I explained that she hadn't been in school on Monday or Tuesday and her parents didn't know where she was.

"Are you also a friend of her parents?" he asked.

"No way!"

She had come to his place Friday afternoon, he told me, when her parents had left for Rancho Santa Fe. She had stayed over the weekend. But when he had come home from school on Tuesday she was gone.

"She didn't leave a note or anything?"

"No."

"She didn't, by chance, bring a three-foot-by-five-foot Kerman rug with her, did she?"

"Hell no! Why?"

"According to a police officer I know in Beverly Hills, her parents think she stole it from the house. Did she come in a car?"

"No. A taxi. What in hell is going on? Are those creepy parents of hers trying to frame her?"

"Not if I can help it. Did she leave your place anytime during the weekend?"

"She did not. If you find her, will you let me know?"

I promised him I would.

I phoned Mrs. Whitney Bishop and asked her if Janice had been in the house Friday when they left for Rancho Santa Fe.

"No. She left several hours before that. My husband didn't get home from the office until five o'clock."

"Were there any servants in the house when you left?"

"We have no live-in servants, Mr. Apoyan."

"In that case," I said, "I think it's time for you to call the police and file a missing persons report. Janice was in Westwood from Friday afternoon until some time on Tuesday."

"Westwood? Was she with that Leslie Denton person?"

"She was. Do you know him?"

"Janice brought him to the house several times. Let me assure you, Mr. Apoyan, that he is a doubtful source of information. You know, of course, that he's gay."

That sounded like a non sequitur to me. I didn't point it out. I thought of telling her to go to hell. But a more reasonable (and mercenary) thought overruled it; rich bigots should pay for their bigotry.

"You want me to continue, then?" I asked.

"I certainly do. Have you considered the possibility that one of Leslie Denton's friends might have used her key and Janice told him where the turnoff switch is located?"

I hadn't thought of that.

"I thought of that," I explained, "but if that happened, I doubt if we could prove it. I don't want to waste your money, Mrs. Bishop."

"Don't you worry about that," she said. "You find my rug!"

Not her daughter; her rug. First things first. "I'll get right on it," I assured her.

I was warming some lahmajoons Sarkis's wife had given me last Sunday when I heard my office door open. I went out.

It was Cheryl, my current love, back from San Francisco, where she had gone to visit her mother.

"Welcome home!" I said. "How did you know I moved?"

"Adele told me. Are those lahmajoons I smell?"

I nodded. She came over to kiss me. She looked around the office, went through the open doorway, and inspected the apartment.

When she came back, she said, "And now we have this. Now we won't have to worry if your roommates are home, or mine. Do you think I should move in?"

"We'll see. What's in the brown bag?"

"Potato salad, a jar of big black olives, and two avocados."

"Welcome home again. You can make the coffee."

Over our meal I told her about my day, my lucky opening day in this high-priced town. I mentioned no names, only places.

It sounded like a classic British locked-room mystery, she thought and said. She is an addict of the genre.

"Except for the guy in Westwood," I pointed out. "Maybe one of his friends stole the rug."

Westwood was where she shared an apartment with two friends. "Does he have a name?" she asked.

I explained to her that that would be privileged information.

"I was planning to stay the night," she said, "until now."

"His name is Leslie Denton."

"Les Denton?" She shook her head. "Not in a zillion years! He is integrity incarnate."

"You're thinking of your idol, Len Deighton," I said.

"I am not! Les took the same night-school class that I did in restaurant management. We got to be very good friends. He works as a busboy at La Dolce Vita."

"I know. Were you vertical or horizontal friends?"

"Don't be vulgar, Petroff. Les is not heterosexual."

"Aren't you glad I am?"

"Not at the moment."

"Let's have some more wine," I suggested.

At nine o'clock she went down to her car to get her luggage. When she came back, she asked, "Are you tired?"

"Nope."

"Neither am I," she said. "Let's go to bed."

I was deep in a dream involving my high school sweetheart when the phone rang in my office. My bedside clock informed me that it was seven o'clock. The voice on the phone informed me that I was a lying bastard.

"Who is speaking, please?" I asked.

"Les Denton. Mr. Randisi at the restaurant gave me your phone number. You told me you were a friend of Howard Retzenbaum's. Mr. Randisi told me you were a stinking private eye. You're working for the Bishops, aren't you?"

"Leslie," I said calmly, "I have a very good friend of yours who is here in the office right now. She will assure you that I am not a lying bastard and do not stink. I have to be devious at times. It is a requisite of my trade."

"What's her name?"

"Cheryl Pushkin. Hold the line. I'll put her on."

Cheryl was sitting up in bed. I told her Denton wanted to talk to her.

"Why? Who told him I was here?"

"I did. He wants a character reference."

"What?"

"Go!" I said. "And don't hang up when you're finished. I want to talk with him."

I was half dressed when she came back to tell me she had calmed him down and he would talk to me now.

I told him it was true that I was working for Mrs. Bishop. I added that getting her rug back was a minor concern to me; finding her daughter was my major concern and should be his, too. I told him I would be grateful for any help he could give me on this chivalrous quest.

"I shouldn't have gone off half-cocked," he admitted. "I have some friends who know Janice. I'll ask around."

"Thank you."

Cheryl was in the shower when I hung up. I started the coffee and went down the steps to pick up the *Times* at my front door.

A few minutes after I came back, she was in her robe, studying the contents of my fridge. "Only two eggs in here," she said, "and two strips of bacon."

"There are some frozen waffles in the freezer compartment."

"You can have those. I'll have bacon and eggs." I didn't argue.

"You were moaning just before the phone rang," she said. "You were moaning, 'Norah, Norah.' Who is Norah?"

"A dog I had when I was a kid. She was killed by a car."

She turned to stare at me doubtfully, but made no comment. Both her parents are Russian, a suspicious breed. Her father lived in San Diego, her mother in San Francisco, what they had called a trial separation. I suspected it was messing-around time in both cities.

She had decided in the night, she told me, to reside in Westwood for a while. I had the feeling she doubted my fidelity. She had suggested at one time that I could be a younger clone of Uncle Vartan.

She left and I sat. I had promised Mrs. Bishop that I would "get right on it." Where would I start? The three kids I had not questioned yesterday were now in school. And there was very little likelihood that they would have any useful information on the present whereabouts of Janice Bishop. Leslie Denton was my last best hope.

I took the *Times* and a cup of coffee out to the office and sat at my desk. Terrible Tony Tuscani, I read in the sports page, had out-pointed Mike (the Hammer) Mulligan in a ten-round windup last night in Las Vegas. The writer thought Tony was a cinch to cop the middleweight crown. In my fifth amateur fight I had kayoed Tony halfway through the third round. Was I in the wrong trade?

And then the thought came to me that an antique Kerman was not the level of stolen merchandise one would take to an ordinary fence. A burglar sophisticated enough to outfox a complicated alarm system should certainly know that. He would need to find a buyer who knew about Oriental rugs.

Uncle Vartan was on the phone when I went down. When he had finished talking I voiced the thought I'd had upstairs.

"It makes sense," he agreed. "So?"

"I thought, being in the trade, you might know of one."

"I do," he said. "Ismet Bey. He has a small shop in Santa Monica. He deals mostly in imitation Orientals and badly worn antiques. I have reason to know he has occasionally bought stolen rugs."

"Why don't you phone him," I suggested, "and tell him you have a customer who is looking for a three-by-five Kerman?"

His face stiffened. "You are asking *me* to talk to a Turk?"

I said lamely, "I didn't know he was a Turk."

"You know now," he said stiffly. "If you decide to phone him, use a different last name."

I looked him up in the phone book and called. A woman answered. I asked for Ismet. She told me he was not in at the moment and might not be in until this afternoon. She identified herself as his wife and asked if she could be of help.

"I certainly hope so," I said. "My wife and I have been scouring the town for an antique Kerman. We have been unsuccessful so far. Is it possible you have one?"

"We haven't," she said. "But I am surprised to learn you haven't found one. There must be a number of stores that have at least one in stock. The better stores, I mean, of course."

An honest woman married to a crooked Turk. I said, "Not a three-by-five. We want it for the front hall."

"That might be more difficult," she said. "But Mr.—"

"Stein," I said. "Peter Stein."

"Mr. Stein," she continued, "my husband has quite often found hard-to-find rugs. Do you live in Santa Monica?"

"In Beverly Hills." I gave her my phone number. "If I'm not here, please leave a message on my answering machine."

"We will. I'll tell my husband as soon as he gets here. If you should find what you're looking for in the meantime—"

"I'll let you know immediately," I assured her.

I temporarily changed the name on my answering machine from Pierre Apoyan Investigative Service to a simple Peter. Both odars and kinsmen would recognize me by that name.

Back to sitting and waiting. I felt slightly guilty about sitting around when Mrs. Bishop was paying me by the hour. But only slightly. Mrs. Whitney Bishop would never make my favorite-persons list.

Uncle Vartan was born long after the Turkish massacre of his people. But he knew the brutal history of that time as surely as the young Jews know the history of the Holocaust—from the survivors.

I read the rest of the news that interested me in the *Times* and drank another cup of coffee. I was staring down at the street below around noon when my door opened.

It was Cheryl. She must have been coming up as I was looking down. She had driven in for a sale at I. Magnin, she told me. "And as long as I was in the neighborhood—"

"You dropped in on your favorite person," I finished for her. "What's in the bag, something from Magnin's?"

"In a brown paper bag? Lox and bagels, my friend, and cream cheese. I noticed how low your larder was this morning. Did Les Denton phone you?"

I shook my head.

"I bumped into him in front of the UCLA library this morning," she said, "and gave him the old third degree. He swore to me that he and Janice were alone over the weekend, so she couldn't have given her house key to *anybody*. I was right, wasn't I?"

"I guess you were, Miss Marple. Tea or coffee?"

"Tea for me. I can't stay long. Robinson's is also having a sale."

"How exciting! Your mama must have given you a big fat check again when you were up in San Francisco."

"Don't be sarcastic! I stopped in downstairs and asked your uncle if you'd ever had a dog named Norah."

"And he confirmed it."

"Not quite. He said he thought you had but he wasn't sure. Of course, he probably can't even remember half the women he's— he's courted."

"Enough!" I said. "Lay off!"

"I'm sorry. Jealousy! That's adolescent, isn't it? It's vulgar and possessive."

"I guess."

"You're not very talkative today, are you?"

"Cheryl, there is a young girl out there somewhere who has run away from home. That, to me, is much more important than a sale at Robinson's or whether I ever had a dog named Norah. This is a dangerous town for seventeen-year-old runaways."

"You're right." She sighed. "How trivial can I get?"

"We all have our hang-ups," I said. "I love you just the way you are."

"And I you, Petroff. Do you think Janice is in some kind of danger? Why would she leave Les's place without even leaving him a note?"

"*That* I don't know. And it scares me."

"You don't think she's—" She didn't finish.

"Dead? I have no way of knowing."

Five minutes after she left, I learned that Janice had still been alive yesterday. Les Denton phoned to tell me that a friend of his had seen her on the Santa Monica beach with an older man, but had not talked with her. According to the friend, the man she was with was tall and thin and frail, practically a skeleton.

"Thanks," I said.

"It's not the first time she's run away," he told me. "And there's a pattern to it."

"What kind of pattern?"

"Well, I could be reading more into it than there is. But I noticed that it was usually when her mother was out of town. Mrs. Bishop is quite a gadabout."

"Are you suggesting child molestation?"

"Only suggesting, Mr. Apoyan. I could be wrong."

And possibly right. "Thanks again," I said.

A troubled relationship is what Mrs. Bishop had called it. Did she know whereof she spoke? Mothers are often the last to know.

Ismet Bey phoned half an hour later to tell me he had located a three-by-five Kerman owned by a local dealer and had brought it to his shop. Could I drop in this afternoon?

I told him I could and would.

And now what? How much did I know about antique Kermans? Uncle Vartan would remember the rug he had sold, but he sure as hell wouldn't walk into the shop of Ismet Bey.

Maybe Mrs. Bishop? She could pose as my wife. I phoned her unlisted number. A woman answered, probably a servant. Mrs. Bishop, she told me, was shopping and wouldn't be home until six o'clock.

I did know a few things about rugs. I had worked for Uncle Vartan on Saturdays and during vacations when I was at UCLA.

I took the photograph of Janice with me and drove out to Santa Monica. Bey's store, like the building Vartan and I shared, was a converted house on Pico Boulevard, old and sagging. I parked in the three-car graveled parking lot next to his panel truck.

The interior was dim and musty. Mrs. Bey was not in sight. The fat rump of a broad, short, and bald man greeted me as I came in. He was bending over, piling some small rugs on the floor.

He rose and turned to face me. He had an olive complexion, big brown eyes, and the oily smile of a used-car salesman. "Mr. Stein?" he asked.

I nodded.

"This way, please," he said, and led me to the rear of the store. The rug was on a display rack, a pale tan creation, sadly thin and about as tightly woven as a fisherman's net.

"Mr. Bey," I said, "that is not a Kerman."

"Really? What is it, then?"

"It looks like an Ispahan to me, a cheap Ispahan."

He continued to smile. "It was only a test."

"I'm not following you. A test for what?"

He shrugged. "There have been some rumors around town. Some rumors about a very rare and expensive three-by-five Kerman that has been stolen. I thought you may have heard them."

What a cutie. "I haven't heard them," I said. And added, "But, of course, I don't have your contacts."

"I'm sure you don't. Maybe you should have. How much did you plan to spend on this rug you want, Mr. Stein?"

"Not as much as the rug you described would cost me. But I have a rich friend who might be interested. He is not quite as—as ethical as I try to be."

"Perhaps that is why he is rich. All I can offer now is the hope that this rug will find its way to me. Could I have the name of your friend?"

I shook my head. "If the rug finds its way to you, phone me. I'll have him come here. I don't want to be involved."

"You won't need to be," he assured me. "And I'll see that you are recompensed. You were right about this rug. It is an Ispahan. If you have some friends who are not rich, I hope you will mention my name to them."

That would be the day. "I will," I said.

I drove to Arden from there, and the boss was in his office. I told him about my dialogue with Bey and suggested they keep an eye on his place. I pointed out that they could make some brownie points with the Santa Monica Police Department.

"Thank you, loyal ex-employee. We'll do that."

"In return, you might make some copies of this photograph and pass them out among the boys. She is a runaway girl who was last seen here on your beach."

"You've got a case already?"

"With my reputation, why not?"

"Is there some connection between the missing girl and the rug?"

"That, as you are well aware, would be privileged information."

"Dear God," he said, "the kid's turned honest! Wait here."

He went out to the copier and came back about five minutes later. He handed me the photo and a check for the two days I had worked for him last week and wished me well. The nice thing about the last is that I knew he meant it.

From there to the beach. I sat in the shade near the refreshment stand with the forlorn hope that the skeleton man and the runaway girl might come this way again.

Two hours, one ice cream cone, and two Cokes later, I drove back to Beverly Hills. Uncle Vartan was alone in the shop. I went in and related to him my dialogue with Ismet Bey.

"That tawdry Turk," he said, "that bush-leaguer! He doesn't cater to that class of trade. He's dreaming a pipe dream."

"How much do you think that rug would bring today?" I asked.

"Pierre, I do not want to discuss that rug. As I told you before, that was a sad day, maybe the saddest day of my life."

Saddest to him could be translated into English as least lucrative. A chauffeured Rolls-Royce pulled up in front of the shop and an elegantly dressed couple headed for his doorway. I held the door open for them and went up my stairs to sit again.

I typed it all down in chronological order, the history of my first case in my own office, from the time Mrs. Whitney Bishop had walked in to my uncle's refusal to talk about the Kerman.

There had to be a pattern in there somewhere to a discerning eye. Either my eye was not discerning or there was no pattern.

Cheryl had called it right; my larder was low. I heated a package of frozen peas and ate them with two baloney sandwiches and the cream cheese left over from lunch.

There was, as usual, nothing worth watching on the tube. I

went back to read again the magic of the man my father had introduced me to when I was in my formative years, the sadly funny short stories of William Saroyan.

Where would I go tomorrow? What avenues of investigation were still unexplored? Unless the unlikely happened, a call from Ismet Bey, all I had left was a probably fruitless repeat of yesterday's surveillance of the Santa Monica beach.

I went to bed at nine o'clock, but couldn't sleep. I got up, poured three ounces of Tennessee whiskey into a tumbler, added a cube of ice, and sat and sipped. It was eleven o'clock before I was tired enough to sleep.

I drank what was left of the milk in the morning and decided to have breakfast in Santa Monica. I didn't take my swimming trunks; the day was not that warm.

Scrambled eggs and pork sausages, orange juice, toast, and coffee at Barney's Breakfast Bar fortified me for the gray day ahead.

Only the hardy were populating the beach. The others would come out if the overcast went away. I sat again on the bench next to the refreshment stand and reread Ralph Ellison's *Invisible Man*. It had seemed appropriate reading for the occasion.

I had been doing a lot of sitting on this case. I could understand now why my boss at Arden had piles.

Ten o'clock passed. So did eleven. About fifteen minutes after that a tall, thin figure appeared in the murky air at the far end of the beach. It was a man and he was heading this way.

Closer and clearer he came. He was wearing khaki trousers, a red-and-tan-checked flannel shirt, and a red nylon windbreaker. He nodded and smiled as he passed me. He bought a Coke at the stand and sat down at the other end of the bench.

I laid down my book.

"Ralph Ellison?" he said. "I had no idea he was still in print."

He was thin, he was haggard, and his eyes were dull. But skeleton had been too harsh a word. "He probably isn't," I said. "This is an old Signet paperback reprint. My father gave it to me when I was still in high school."

"I see. We picked a bad day for sun, didn't we?"

"That's not why I'm here," I told him. "I'm looking for a girl, a runaway girl. Do you come here often?"

He nodded. "Quite often."

I handed him the photograph of Janice. "Have you ever seen her here?"

He took a pair of wire-rimmed glasses from his shirt pocket and put them on to study the picture. "Oh, yes," he said. "Was it yesterday? No—Wednesday." He took a deep breath. "There are so many of them who come here. I talked with her. She told me she had come down from Oxnard and didn't have the fare to go home. I bought her a malt and a hot dog. She told me the fare to Oxnard was eight dollars and some cents. I've forgotten the exact amount. Anyway, I gave her a ten-dollar bill and made her promise that she would use it for the fare home."

"Do you do that often?"

"Not often enough. When I can afford it."

"She's not from Oxnard," I told him. "She's from Beverly Hills."

He stared at me. "She couldn't be! She was wearing a pair of patched jeans and a cheap, flimsy T-shirt."

"She's from Beverly Hills," I repeated. "Her parents are rich."

He smiled. "That little liar! She conned me. And what a sweet young thing she was."

"I hope 'was' isn't the definitive word," I said.

He closed his eyes and took another deep breath. He opened them and stared out at the sea.

I handed him my card. "If you see her again, would you phone me?"

"Of course. My name is Gerald Hopkins. I live at the Uphan Hotel. It's a—a place for what are currently called senior citizens."

"I know the place," I told him. "Let's hold our thumbs."

"Dear God, yes!" he said.

From there I drove to the store of the tawdry Turk. He was not there but his wife was, a short, thin, and dark-skinned woman. I told her my name.

She nodded. "Ismet told me you were here yesterday." Her

smile was sad. "That man and his dreams! What cock-and-bull story did he tell you?"

"Some of it made sense. He tried to sell me an Ispahan."

"He didn't tell *me* that!"

"He also told me about some rumors he heard."

"Oh, yes! Rumors he has. Customers is what we need. Tell me, Mr. Stein, how can a man get so fat on rumors?"

"He's probably married to a good cook."

"*That* he is. Take my advice, and a grain of salt, when you listen to the rumors of my husband, Mr. Stein. He is a dreamer. It is the reason I married him. I, too, in my youth, was a dreamer. It is why we came to America many years ago."

Send these, the homeless, tempest-tost to me. I lift my lamp beside the golden door . . .

I smiled at her. "Keep the faith!" I went out.

My next stop was the bank, where I deposited the checks from Mrs. Bishop and Arden and cashed a check for two hundred dollars.

From there to Vons in Santa Monica, where I stocked up on groceries, meat, and booze. Grocery markups in Beverly Hills, my mother had warned me, were absurd. Only the vulgar rich could afford them.

Mrs. Bey might believe that all the rumors her husband heard were bogus. But the rumor he had voiced to me was too close to the truth to qualify as bogus. It was logical to assume that there were shenanigans he indulged in in the practice of his trade that he would not reveal to her. To a man of his ilk the golden door meant gold, and he was still looking for the door.

I put the groceries away when I got home and went out to check the answering machine. Zilch. I typed the happenings of the morning into the record. Nothing had changed; no pattern showed.

There was a remote chance that Bey might learn where the rug was now. That was what I was being paid to find. But, as I had told Les Denton, the girl was my major concern.

It wasn't likely that she was staying at the home of any of

her classmates. Their parents certainly would have phoned Mrs. Bishop by now if she hadn't phoned them.

Which reminded me that I had something to report. I phoned the Bishop house and the lady was home. I told her Janice had been seen on the Santa Monica beach on Wednesday and that a man there had told me this morning that he had talked with her. She had lied to him, telling him that she lived in Oxnard.

"She's very adept at lying. Did you learn anything else?"

"Well, there was a rug dealer in Santa Monica who told me he had heard rumors about a three-by-five Kerman that had been stolen. I have no idea where he heard them."

"There could be a number of sources. My husband has been asking several dealers we know if they have seen it. And, of course, many of my friends know about the loss."

"Isn't it possible they might inform the police?"

"Not if they want to remain my friends. And the dealers, too, have been warned. If Janice has been seen on the Santa Monica beach, the rug could also be in the area. I think that is where you should concentrate your search."

It was warm and the weatherman had promised us sunshine for tomorrow. Cheryl and I could spend a day on the beach at Mrs. Bishop's expense.

"I agree with you completely," I said.

I phoned her apartment and Cheryl was there. I asked her if she'd like to spend a day on the beach with me tomorrow.

"I'd love it!"

I told her about the groceries I had bought and asked if she'd like to come and I'd cook a dinner for us tonight.

"Petroff, I can't! We're going to the symphony concert at the pavilion tonight."

"Who is *we?*"

"My roommates and I. Who else? Would you like to interrogate one of them?"

"Of course not! Save the program for me so I can see what I missed."

"I sure as hell will, you suspicious bastard. What time tomorrow?"

"Around ten."

"I'll be waiting."

I made myself a martini before dinner and then grilled a big T-bone steak and had it with frozen creamed asparagus and shoe-string potatoes (heated, natch) and finished it off with lemon sherbet and coffee.

I had left *Invisible Man* in the car. I reread my favorite novel, *The Great Gatsby*, after dinner, along with a few ounces of brandy.

And then to my lonely bed. All the characters I had met since Wednesday afternoon kept running through my mind. All the chasing I had done had netted me nothing of substance. Credit investigations were so much cleaner and easier. But, like my Uncle Vartan, I had never felt comfortable working under a boss.

Cheryl was waiting outside her apartment building next morning when I pulled up a little after ten. She climbed into the car and handed me a program.

"Put it away," I said. "I was only kidding last night."

"Like hell you were!" She put it in the glove compartment. "And how was your evening?"

"Lonely. I talked with the man Denton's friend saw with Janice on the beach. She told him she had come down from Oxnard. He gave her the bus fare to go back."

"To Oxnard? Why would anybody want to go back to *Oxnard*?"

"She claimed she lived there. Don't ask me why."

"Maybe the man lied."

"Why would he?"

"Either he lied or she lied. It's fifty-fifty, isn't it?"

"Cheryl, he had no reason to lie. He told me the whole story and he has helped other kids to go home again. He gave me his name and address. Mrs. Bishop told me yesterday afternoon that Janice was—she called her an adept liar."

"And she is a creep, according to Les. Maybe Janice had reason to lie to the old bag."

"A creep she is. A bag she ain't. Tell me, what are you wearing under that simple but undoubtedly expensive charcoal denim dress?"

"My swimsuit, of course. Don't get horny. It's too early in the day for that."

It was, unfortunately, a great day for the beach; the place was jammed. They flood in from the San Fernando Valley and Hollywood and Culver City and greater Los Angeles on the warm days. Very few of them come from Beverly Hills. Most of those people have their own private swimming pools. Maybe all of them.

We laughed and splashed and swam and built a sand castle, back to the days of our adolescence. We forgot for a while the missing Janice Bishop and the antique Kerman.

After the fun part we walked from end to end on the beach, scanning the crowd, earning my pay, hoping to find the girl.

No luck.

Cheryl said, "I'll make you that dinner tonight, if you want me to."

"I want you to."

"We may as well go right to your place," she said. "You can drop me off at the apartment tomorrow when you go to the weekly meeting of the clan. It won't be out of your way."

"Sound thinking," I agreed.

What she made for us was a soufflé, an entree soufflé, not a dessert soufflé. But it was light enough to rest easily on top of the garbage we had consumed at the beach.

The garbage on the tube, we both agreed, would demean our day. We went to bed early.

The overcast was back in the morning, almost a fog. We ate a hearty breakfast to replace the energy we had lost in the night.

I dropped her off at her apartment a little after one o'clock, and was the first to arrive at my parents' house. Adele was the second. She had brought her friend with her, Salvatore Martino, known in the trade as Ronnie Egan.

It was possible, I reasoned, that I could be as wrong about

WILLIAM CAMPBELL GAULT // 253

him as Mrs. Whitney Bishop had been about Leslie Denton. I suggested to him that we take a couple of beers out to the patio while my mother and Adele fussed around in the kitchen.

We yacked about this and that, mostly sports, and then he said, "I saw three of your amateur fights and both your pro fights. How come you quit after that?"

"If you saw my pro fights, you should understand why."

"Jesus, man, you were *way* overmatched! You were jobbed. I'll bet Sam made a bundle on both of those fights."

Sam Batisto had been my manager. I said, "I'm not following you. You mean you think Sam is a crook?"

He nodded. "And a double-crossing sleazeball. Hell, he's got Mafia cousins. He'd sell out his mother if the price was right."

That son of a bitch . . .

"Well, what the hell," he went on, "maybe the bastard did you a favor. That's a nasty, ugly game, and people are beginning to realize it. Have you noticed how many big bouts are staged in Vegas?"

"I've noticed." I changed the subject. "How did you make out with the commercial?"

"Great! My agent worked Adele into it. And the producer promised both of us more work. We're going to make it, Adele and I. But we can't get married until we do. You understand that, don't you?"

"Very well," I assured him. "Welcome to the clan."

My mother had gone Armenian this Sunday, chicken and pilaf. One of Sarkis's boys hadn't been able to attend; Salvatore took his place at the poker session.

That was a red-letter day! Salvatore was the big winner. And for the first time in history Mom was the big loser. I would like to say she took it graciously, but she didn't. We are a competitive clan.

"Nice guy," I said, when Adele and he had left.

She sniffed. "When he marries Adele, *then* he might be a nice guy."

"He told me they're going to get married as soon as they can afford to."

"We'll see," she said. "He could be another Vartan."

The day had stayed misty; the traffic on Sunset Boulevard was slow. I dawdled along, thinking back on the past few days, trying to find the key to the puzzle of the missing girl and the stolen Kerman. The key was the key; who had the key to the house and why had only the rug been stolen?

One thing was certain, the burglar knew the value of antique Oriental rugs. But how would he know that particular rug was in the home of Whitney Bishop?

It was a restless night, filled with dreams I don't remember now. I tossed and turned and went to the toilet twice. A little after six o'clock I realized sleep was out of the question. I put the coffee on to perc and went down the steps to pick up the morning *Times*.

The story was on page one. Whitney Bishop, founder and senior partner of the brokerage firm of Bishop, Hope, and Nystrom, had been found dead in a deserted Brentwood service station. A local realtor had discovered the body when he had brought a potential buyer to the station on Sunday morning. Bishop had been stabbed to death. A loaded but unfired .32 caliber revolver had been found near the body.

According to his wife, Bishop had been nervous and irritable on Friday night. His secretary told the police that he had received a phone call on Friday afternoon and appeared agitated. On Saturday night, he had told his wife he was going to a board meeting at the Beverly Hills Country Club. When he hadn't come home by midnight, Mrs. Bishop had phoned the club. The club was closed; receiving no answer there, she had phoned the police.

When questioned about the revolver, she had stated that she remembered he had once owned a small-caliber pistol but she was almost sure it had been lost or stolen years ago.

A murdered husband. . . . And there was no mention in the piece about a missing daughter or a stolen rug. Considering how many of her friends knew about both, that was bound to come out.

When it did, I could be in deep trouble for withholding information about the rug and the girl. But so could she for the same reason. And spreading those stories to the media could alert and scare off any seasoned burglar who had been looking forward to a buy-back deal. That was the slim hope I tried to hang on to.

I put the record of my involvement in the case under the mattress in my bedroom. I showered and shaved and put on my most conservative suit after breakfast and sat in my office chair, waiting for the police to arrive.

They didn't.

I thought back to all the people I had questioned in the past week. And then I realized there was one I hadn't.

I went down the stairs and asked Uncle Vartan if he had heard the sad news.

He nodded and yawned. He had heard it on the tube last night, he told me. I had the feeling that he would not mourn the death of Whitney Bishop.

"You told me you went with Mrs. Bishop when she was between husbands. Who was her first?"

"A man named Duane Pressville, a former customer of mine."

"Do you have his address?"

"Not anymore. It has been years since I've seen him. What is this all about, Pierre?"

"I was thinking that it was possible he still had the key to the house they shared and would know where the alarm turnoff switch was hidden."

He stared at me. "And you think he stole the rug? That's crazy, Pierre! He was a very sharp buyer but completely honest." He paused. "And now you are thinking that he might be a murderer?"

"The murder and the rug might not be connected," I pointed out. "Tell me, is he the man who bought the Kerman from you?"

"Yes," he said irritably. "And that's enough of this nonsense! I have work to do this morning, Pierre."

"Sorry," I said, and went up the stairs to look up Duane Pressville in the phone book. There were several Pressvilles in the book but only one Duane. His address was 332 Adonis Court.

I knew the street, a short dead-ender that led off San Vicente Boulevard. Into the Camaro, back on the hunt.

Adonis Court was an ancient neighborhood of small houses. It had resisted the influx of demolitions that had invaded the area when land prices soared. These were the older residents who had no serious economic pressures that would force them to sell out.

332 was a small frame house with a shingled roof and a small low porch in front of the door.

I went up to the porch and turned the old-fashioned crank that rang the bell inside the house.

The man who opened the door was tall and thin and haggard, the same man who had called himself Gerald Hopkins on the beach.

He smiled. "Mr. Apoyan! What brings you to my door?"

"I'm looking for a rug," I said. "An antique Kerman."

He frowned. "Did Victoria send you here?"

"Who is Victoria?"

"My former wife. What vindictive crusade is she on now? No matter what she might have told you, I bought that rug with my own money. It was *my* rug, until the divorce settlement."

"Why," I asked, "did you lie to me on the beach?"

He looked at me and past me. He sighed and said, "Come in."

The door opened directly into the living room. It was a room about fourteen feet wide and eighteen feet long. It was almost completely covered by a dark red Oriental rug. It looked like a Bokhara to me.

The furniture was mostly dark mahogany, brightly polished, upholstered in well-worn velour.

"Sit down," he said.

I sat in an armchair, he on the sofa.

"Have you ever heard of Maksoud of Kashan?" he asked.

"I think so. Wasn't he a famous Oriental rug weaver?"

He nodded. "The finest in all of Persia, now called Iran. But in his entire career, with all the associates he had working under him, he wove his name into only two of his rugs. One of them is in the British Museum. The other is the small Kerman I bought from your uncle. I remember now—you worked in his store on Saturdays, didn't you?"

I nodded.

"You weren't in the store that day this—this *peddler* brought in the Kerman. It was filthy! But far from being worn out. My eyes must be sharper than your uncle's. I saw the signature in the corner. I made the mistake of overplaying my hand; I offered him a thousand dollars for it, much more than it appeared to be worth. That must have made him suspicious. We dickered. When I finally offered him three thousand dollars, he sold it to me."

"And I suppose he has resented you ever since that day."

He shrugged. "Probably. To tell you the truth, after he learned about the history of the rug I was ashamed to go back to the store."

"To tell the truth once again," I said, "where is your daughter? Where is Janice?"

"She is well and safe and far from here. She is back with her real parents, the parents who were too poor to keep her when she was born. I finally located them."

"You wouldn't want to tell me their name?"

"Not you, or anybody else. Not with the legal clout Victoria can afford. Do you want Janice to go back to that woman she complained to when her third father tried to molest her, that woman who called her a liar? I did some research on Bishop, too. He was fired by a Chicago brokerage firm for churning. He had one charge of child molestation dropped for insufficient evidence there. So he came out here and married money and started his own firm."

"And was stabbed to death Saturday night not far from here."

"I heard that on the radio this morning." His smile was cynical. "Are you going to the funeral?"

I shook my head. "According to the morning paper he must have been carrying a gun. But he didn't fire it."

"The news report on this morning's radio station explained that," he told me. "The safety catch was on."

"I didn't hear it. What do you think that Kerman would bring today?"

"Fifty thousand, a hundred thousand, whatever the buyer would pay." He studied me. "Are you suggesting that the murder and the rug are connected?"

"You know I am. My theory is that Bishop got the call from the burglar on Friday and decided not to buy the rug, but to shoot the burglar."

"An interesting theory. Is there more to it?"

"Yes. The burglar then stabbed him—and found another buyer. Bishop might have reason other than penuriousness. He might have known the burglar knew his history."

He said wearily, "You're zeroing in, aren't you? You're beginning to sound like a detective."

"I am. A private investigator. I just opened my own office over Uncle Vartan's store."

"You should have told me that when you came."

"You must have guessed that I was an investigator when we met on the beach. Why else would you have lied?"

He didn't answer.

"If Janice's real parents are still poor," I said, "fifty or a hundred thousand dollars should help to alleviate it."

He nodded. "If the burglar has found the right buyer. It should certainly help to send her to a first-rate college. And now I'm getting tired. It's time for my nap. I have leukemia, Pierre. My doctor has told me he doesn't know how many days I have before I sleep the big sleep. I know what you are thinking, and it could be true. I'm sure you are honor bound to take what I have told you to the police. I promise I will bear you no malice if you do. But you had better hurry."

"There is no need to hurry," I said. "Thank you for your cooperation, Mr. Pressville."

"And thank you for your courtesy," he said. "Give my regards to Vartan."

I didn't give his regards to Uncle Vartan. I didn't even tell him I had talked with his former customer. I had some thinking to do.

For three days I thought and wondered when the police would call. They never came. Mrs. Bishop sent me a check for the balance of my investigation along with an acerbic note that informed me she would certainly tell her many friends how unsuccessful I had been in searching for both her rug and her daughter.

I had no need to continue thinking on the fourth day. Duane Pressville was found dead in his house on Adonis Court by a concerned neighbor. I burned the records of that maiden quest.

PART IV

MODERN CLASSICS

CRIMSON SHADOW

BY WALTER MOSLEY

Watts

(Originally published in 1995)

1

"What you doin' there, boy?"

It was six a.m. Socrates Fortlow had come out to the alley to see what was wrong with Billy. He hadn't heard him crow that morning and was worried about his old friend.

The sun was just coming up. The alley was almost pretty with the trash and broken asphalt covered in half-light. Discarded wine bottles shone like murky emeralds in the sludge. In the dawn shadows Socrates didn't even notice the boy until he moved. He was standing in front of a small cardboard box, across the alley—next to Billy's wire fence.

"What bidness is it to you, old man?" the boy answered. He couldn't have been more than twelve but he had that hard convict stare.

Socrates knew convicts, knew them inside and out.

"I asked you a question, boy. Ain't yo' momma told you t'be civil?"

"Shit!" The boy turned away, ready to leave. He wore baggy jeans with a blooming blue T-shirt over his bony arms and chest. His hair was cut close to the scalp.

The boy bent down to pick up the box.

"What they call you?" Socrates asked the skinny butt stuck up in the air.

"What's it to you?"

Socrates pushed open the wooden fence and leapt. If the boy hadn't had his back turned he would have been able to dodge the stiff lunge. As it was he heard something and moved quickly to the side.

Quickly. But not quickly enough.

Socrates grabbed the skinny arms with his big hands—the rock breakers, as Joe Benz used to call them.

"Ow! Shit!"

Socrates shook the boy until the serrated steak knife, which had appeared from nowhere, fell from his hand.

The old brown rooster was dead in the box. His head slashed so badly that half of the beak was gone.

"Let me loose, man." The boy kicked, but Socrates held him at arm's length.

"Don't make me hurt you, boy," he warned. He let go of one arm and said, "Pick up that box. Pick it up!" When the boy obeyed, Socrates pulled him by the arm—dragged him through the gate, past the tomato plants and string bean vines, into the two rooms where he'd stayed since they'd let him out of prison.

The kitchen was only big enough for a man and a half. The floor was pitted linoleum; maroon where it had kept its color, gray where it had worn through. There was a card table for dining and a fold-up plastic chair for a seat. There was a sink with a hot plate on the drainboard and shelves that were once cabinets—before the doors were torn off.

The light fixture above the sink had a sixty-watt bulb burning in it. The room smelled of coffee. A newspaper was spread across the table.

Socrates shoved the boy into the chair, not gently.

"Sit'own!"

There was a mass of webbing next to the weak lightbulb. A red spider picked its way slowly through the strands.

"What's your name, boy?" Socrates asked again.

"Darryl."

There was a photograph of a painting tacked underneath the light. It was the image of a black woman in the doorway of a house. She wore a red dress and a red hat to protect her eyes from the sun. She had her arms crossed under her breasts and looked angry. Darryl stared at the painting while the spider danced above.

"Why you kill my friend, asshole?"

"What?" Darryl asked. There was fear in his voice.

"You heard me."

"I-I-I din't kill nobody." Darryl gulped and opened his eyes wider than seemed possible. "Who told you that?"

When Socrates didn't say anything, Darryl jumped up to run, but the man socked him in the chest, knocking the wind out of him, pushing him back down in the chair.

Socrates squatted down and scooped the rooster up out of the box. He held the limp old bird up in front of Darryl's face.

"Why you kill Billy, boy?"

"That's a bird." Darryl pointed. There was relief mixed with panic in his eyes.

"That's my friend."

"You crazy, old man. That's a bird. Bird cain't be nobody's friend." Darryl's words were still wild. Socrates knew the guilty look on his face.

He wondered at the boy and at the rooster that had gotten him out of his bed every day for the past eight years. A rage went through him and he crushed the rooster's neck in his fist.

"You crazy," Darryl said.

A large truck made its way down the alley just then. The heavy vibrations went through the small kitchen, making plates and tin-ware rattle loudly.

Socrates shoved the corpse into the boy's lap. "Get ovah there to the sink an' pluck it."

"Shit!"

"You don't have to do it . . ."

"You better believe I ain't gonna . . ."

". . . but I *will* kick holy shit outta you if you don't."

"Pluck what? What you mean, pluck it?"

"I mean go ovah t'that sink an' pull out the feathers. What you kill it for if you ain't gonna pluck it?"

"I'as gonna sell it."

"Sell it?"

"Yeah," Darryl said. "Sell it to some old lady wanna make some chicken."

2

Darryl plucked the chicken bare. He wanted to stop halfway but Socrates kept pointing out where he had missed and pushed him back toward the sink. Darryl used a razor-sharp knife that Socrates gave him to cut off the feet and battered head. He slit open the old rooster's belly and set aside the liver, heart, and gizzard.

"Rinse out all the blood. All of it," Socrates told his captive. "Man could get sick on blood."

While Darryl worked, under the older man's supervision, Socrates made Minute rice and then green beans seasoned with lard and black pepper. He prepared them in succession, one after the other on the single hot plate. Then he sautéed the giblets, with green onions from the garden, in bacon fat that he kept in a can over the sink. He mixed the giblets in with the rice.

When the chicken was ready he took tomatoes, basil, and garlic from the garden and put them all in a big pot on the hot plate.

"Billy was a tough old bird," Socrates said. "He gonna have to cook for a while."

"When you gonna let me go, man?"

"Where you got to go?"

"Home."

"Okay. Okay, fine. Billy could cook for a hour more. Let's go over your house. Where's that at?"

"What you mean, man? You ain't goin' t'my house."

"I sure am too," Socrates said, but he wasn't angry anymore. "You come over here an' murder my friend an' I got to tell somebody responsible."

Darryl didn't have any answer to that. He'd spent over an hour working in the kitchen, afraid even to speak to his captor. He was afraid mostly of those big hands. He had never felt anything as strong as those hands. Even with the chicken knife he was afraid.

"I'm hungry. When we gonna eat?" Darryl asked. "I mean I hope you plan t'eat this here after all this cookin'."

"Naw, man," Socrates said. "I thought we could go out an' sell it t'some ole lady like t'eat chicken."

"Huh?" Darryl said.

The kitchen was filling up with the aroma of chicken and sauce. Darryl's stomach growled loudly.

"You hungry?" Socrates asked him.

"Yeah."

"That's good. That's good."

"Shit. Ain't good 'less I get sumpin' t'eat."

"Boy should be hungry. Yeah. Boys is always hungry. That's how they get to be men."

"What the fuck you mean, man? You just crazy. That's all."

"If you know you hungry then you know you need sumpin'. Sumpin' missin' an' hungry tell you what it is."

"That's some kinda friend to you too?" Darryl sneered. "Hungry yo' friend?"

Socrates smiled then. His broad black face shone with delight. He wasn't a very old man, somewhere in his fifties. His teeth were all his own and healthy, though darkly stained. The top of his head was completely bald; tufts of wiry white hovered behind his ears.

"Hungry, horny, hello, and how come. They all my friends, my best friends."

Darryl sniffed the air and his stomach growled again.

"Uh-huh," Socrates hummed. "That's right. They all my friends. All of 'em. You got to have good friends you wanna make it through the penitentiary."

"You up in jail?" Darryl asked.

"Yup."

"My old man's up in jail," Darryl said. "Least he was. He died though."

"Oh. Sorry t'hear it, li'l brother. I'm sorry."

"What you in jail for?"

Socrates didn't seem to hear the question. He was looking at the picture of the painting above the sink. The right side of the scene was an open field of yellow grasses under a light blue sky. The windows of the house were shuttered and dark but the sun shone hard on the woman in red.

"You still hungry?" Socrates asked.

Darryl's stomach growled again and Socrates laughed.

3

Socrates made Darryl sit in the chair while he turned over the trash can for his seat. He read the paper for half an hour or more while the rooster simmered on the hot plate. Darryl knew to keep quiet. When it was done, Socrates served the meal on three plates—one for each dish. The man and boy shoveled down dirty rice, green beans, and tough rooster like they were starving men; eating off the same plates, neither one uttered a word. The only drink they had was water—their glasses were mayonnaise jars. Their breathing was loud and slobbery. Hands moved in syncopation; tearing and scooping.

Anyone witnessing the orgy would have said that they hailed from the same land; prayed to the same gods.

When the plates were clean they sat back bringing hands across bellies. They both sighed and shook their heads.

"That was some good shit," Darryl said. "Mm!"

"Bet you didn't know you could cook, huh?" Socrates asked.

"Shit no!" the boy said.

"Keep your mouth clean, li'l brother. You keep it clean an' then they know you mean business when you say sumpin' strong."

Darryl was about to say something but decided against it. He looked over at the door, and then back at Socrates.

"Could I go now?" he asked, a boy talking to his elder at last.

"Not yet."

"How come?" There was an edge of fear in the boy's voice. Socrates remembered many times reveling in the fear he brought to young men in their cells. Back then he enjoyed the company of fear.

"Not till I hear it. You cain't go till then."

"Hear what?"

"You know what. So don't be playin' stupid. Don't be playin' stupid an' you just et my friend."

Darryl made to push himself up but abandoned that idea when he saw those hands rise from the table.

"You should be afraid, Darryl," Socrates said, reading the boy's eyes. "I kilt men with these hands. Choked an' broke 'em. I could crush yo' head wit' one hand." Socrates held out his left palm.

"I ain't afraid'a you," Darryl said.

"Yes you are. I know you are 'cause you ain't no fool. You seen some bad things out there but I'm the worst. I'm the worst you ever seen."

Darryl looked at the door again.

"Ain't nobody gonna come save you, li'l brother. Ain't nobody gonna come. If you wanna make it outta here then you better give me what I want."

Socrates knew just when the tears would come. He had seen it a hundred times. In prison it made him want to laugh; but now he was sad. He wanted to reach out to the blubbering child and tell him that it was okay; that everything was all right. But it wasn't all right, might not ever be.

"Stop cryin' now, son. Stop cryin' an' tell me about it."

"'Bout what?" Darryl said, his words vibrating like a hummingbird's wings.

"'Bout who you killed, that's what."

"I ain't killed nobody," Darryl said in a monotone.

"Yes you did. Either that or you saw sumpin'. I heard it in your deny when you didn't know I was talkin' 'bout Billy. I know when a man is guilty, Darryl. I know that down in my soul."

Darryl looked away and set his mouth shut.

"I ain't a cop, li'l brother. I ain't gonna turn you in. But you kilt my friend out there an' we just et him down. I owe t'Billy an' to you too. So tell me about it. You tell me an' then you could go."

They stared at each other for a long time. Socrates grinned to put the boy at ease but he didn't look benevolent. He looked hungry.

Darryl felt like the meal.

4

He didn't want to say it but he didn't feel bad either. Why should he feel bad? It wasn't even his idea. Wasn't anybody's plan. It was just him and Jamal and Norris out in the oil fields above Baldwin Hills. Sometimes dudes went there with their old ladies. And if you were fast enough you could see some pussy and then get away with their pants.

They also said that the army was once up there and that there were old bullets and even hand grenades just lying around to be found.

But then this retarded boy showed up. He said he was with his brother but that his brother left him and now he wanted to be friends with Darryl and his boys.

"At first we was just playin'," Darryl told Socrates. "You know—pushin' 'im an' stuff."

But when he kept on following them—when he squealed every time they saw somebody—they hit him and pushed him down. Norris even threw a rock at his head. But the retard kept on coming. He was running after them and crying that they had hurt him. He cried louder and louder. And when they hit him, to shut him up, he yelled so loud that it made them scared right inside their chests.

"You know I always practice with my knife," Darryl said. "You know you got to be able to get it out quick if somebody on you."

Socrates nodded. He still practiced himself.

"I'ont know how it got in my hand. I swear I didn't mean t'cut 'im."

"You kill 'im?" Socrates asked.

Darryl couldn't talk but he opened his mouth and nodded.

They all swore never to tell anybody. They would kill the one who told about it—they swore on blood and went home.

"Anybody find 'im?" Socrates asked.

"I'ont know."

The red spider danced while the woman in red kept her arms folded and stared her disapproval of all men—especially those two men. Darryl had to go to the bathroom. He had the runs after that big meal—and, Socrates thought, from telling his tale.

When he came out he looked ashy, his lips were ashen.

He slumped back in Socrates' cheap chair—drowsy but not tired. He was sick and forlorn.

For a long time they just sat there. The minutes went by but there was no clock to measure them. Socrates learned how to do without a timepiece in prison.

He counted the time while Darryl sat hopelessly by.

5

"What you gonna do, li'l brother?"

"What?"

"How you gonna make it right?"

"Make what right? He dead. I cain't raise him back here."

When Socrates stared at the boy there was no telling what he thought. But what he was thinking didn't matter. Darryl looked away and back again. He shifted in his chair. Licked his dry lips.

"What?" he asked at last.

"You murdered a poor boy couldn't stand up to you. You killed your little brother an' he wasn't no threat; an' he didn't have no money that you couldn't take wit'out killin' 'im. You did wrong, Darryl. You did wrong."

"How the fuck you know?" Darryl yelled. He would have said more but Socrates raised his hand, not in violence but to point out the truth to his dinner guest.

Darryl went quiet and listened.

"I ain't your warden, li'l brother. I ain't gonna show you to no jail. I'm just talkin' to ya—one black man to another one. If you don't hear me there ain't nuthin' I could do."

"So I could go now?"

"Yeah, you could go. I ain't yo' warden. I just ask you to tell me how you didn't do wrong. Tell me how a healthy boy ain't wrong when he kills his black brother who sick."

Darryl stared at Socrates, at his eyes now—not his hands.

"You ain't gonna do nuthin'?"

"Boy is dead now. Rooster's dead too. We cain't change that. But you got to figure out where you stand."

"I ain't goin' t'no fuckin' jail if that's what you mean."

Socrates smiled. "Shoo'. I don't blame you for that. Jail ain't gonna help a damn thing. Better shoot yo'self than go to jail."

"I ain't gonna shoot myself neither. Uh-uh."

"If you learn you wrong then maybe you get to be a man."

"What's that s'posed t'mean?"

"Ain't nobody here, Darryl. Just you'n me. I'm sayin' that I think you was wrong for killin' that boy. I know you killed'im. I know you couldn't help it. But you was wrong anyway. An' if that's the truth, an' if you could say it, then maybe you'll learn sumpin'. Maybe you'll laugh in the morning sometimes again."

Darryl stared at the red spider. She was still now. He didn't say anything, didn't move at all.

"We all got to be our own judge, li'l brother. 'Cause if you don't know when you wrong then yo' life ain't worf a damn."

Darryl waited as long as he could. And then he asked, "I could go?"

"You done et Billy. So I guess that much is through."

"So it ain't wrong that I killed'im 'cause I et him?"

"It's still wrong. It's always gonna be wrong. But you know more now. You ain't gonna kill no more chickens," Socrates said. Then he grunted out a harsh laugh. "At least not around here."

Darryl stood up. He watched Socrates to see what he'd do.

"Yo' momma cook at home, Darryl?"

"Sometimes. Not too much."

"You come over here anytime an' I teach ya how t'cook. We eat pretty good too."

"Uh-huh," Darryl answered. He took a step away from his chair.

Socrates stayed seated on his trash can.

Darryl made it all the way to the door. He grabbed the wire handle that took the place of a long-ago knob.

"What they put you in jail for?" Darryl asked.

"I killed a man an' raped his woman."

"White man?"

"No."

"Well . . . bye."

"See ya, li'l brother."

"I'm sorry . . . 'bout yo' chicken."

"Billy wasn't none'a mine. He belonged to a old lady 'cross the alley."

"Well . . . bye."

"Darryl."

"Yeah."

"If you get inta trouble you could come here. It don't matter what it is—you could come here to me."

6

Socrates stared at the door a long time after the boy was gone; for hours. The night came on and the cool desert air of Los Angeles came in under the door and through the cracks in his small shack of an apartment.

A cricket was calling out for love from somewhere in the wall.

Socrates looked at the woman, sun shining on her head. Her red sun hat threw a hot crimson shadow across her face. There was no respite for her but she still stood defiant. He tried to remember what Theresa looked like but it had been too long now. All he had left was the picture of a painting—and that wasn't even her. All he had left from her were the words she never said. *You are dead to me, Socrates. Dead as that poor boy and that poor girl you killed.*

He wondered if Darryl would ever come back.

He hoped so.

Socrates went through the doorless doorway into his other room. He lay down on the couch and just before he was asleep he thought of how he'd wake up alone. The rooster was hoarse in his old age, his crow no more than a whisper.

But at least that motherfucker tried.

RIKA

BY JERVEY TERVALON

Baldwin Hills

(Originally published in 1994)

L ook at this. Wondered how many people would show up considering the kind of fool you were but you've got a crowd to bury you. I can't join them, you know. See how beautiful that casket is and the flowers. Picked them out didn't I. Because you knew what happened was going to happen and you didn't want some low-rent funeral. You wanted to look good going down. I have taste. I took care of it. You just didn't think that I'd be the one. It's fine down here at the foot of Forest Lawn. I don't need to join the crowd. I know what everything looks like; the yellow and white roses and tulips, the gold and pearl casket. Not your colors as much as mine. You were always too much into purple. Couldn't leave the gaudy behind. I know your mother's crying, Ollie's cursing me out. I know your associate's looking my way, checking the car out, trying to see if it's really me. Wonder what he thinks. I'm not a fool. I can come back anytime—you're not going anywhere.

It's night now. Sitting in the car above the lights. Bet you wonder how I make it. How you used to talk to me, "Can't do a damn thing for yourself cept spend money." But it's not like that. I know what I'm doing. Look at the roaches walking by. The jungle is buzzing tonight. Roaches after crumbs. I'm tired of watching, see what you've done to me. They look just like me. Noses open, sprung. Looking for a blast. Drive further up the hill, not like I'm living down in the jungle or anything. I might not be staying on the Westside but Baldwin Hills isn't the projects.

Oh yes, my uncle has a beeper for a reason. He's an architect, blueprints cover the kitchen table. See, they have a marble foyer with a coat rack. Now, if I can sneak to the bedroom everything will be right with the world. The TV's on in the living room. Sounds like *Wheel of Fortune*.

"She's back."

It's my uncle's voice.

"Rika, could you come here?"

Oh no.

"What?"

Gotta get to the third door on the left. Lock myself in, wait them out. Here they come. Uncle Jack, gray-haired but quick, pushes me aside and blocks the way. Must have been playing tennis at Dorsey, still in his sweat-stained whites. Mother looks shocked as usual. My fat auntie leads us into the living room, nice view of the Hollywood Hills but the setting sun is still too bright. I need my shades.

"You left again," Uncle Jack says.

"You can't leave," my mother says. Her eyes, red and desperate.

"Where did you go?" my aunt asks.

I don't say anything. I smile.

"Jesus! She's high again."

Mother stands and runs to the other side of the room and starts crying. I start for the bedroom but my uncle is forcing me down into a bean bag. I make a big slosh as I land. He's so mad he's sputtering.

"Do you know what you're doing to your mother, us? We are trying to help you. And you go out in your robe and slippers wearing a rag on your head like you're some kind of cheap hooker on Normandie."

I don't look at him. Instead I look at my slippers. What's wrong with my slippers? They're clean.

"We took you and your mother in because she needs help. We're going to give her that help. If we can't help you here we're going to have to commit you. But you're going to get help."

276 // Los Angeles Noir 2

He keeps saying give, get and going. Maybe I should get going.

"Don't you have something to say?"

I shake my head.

"Where did you go, to the jungle to buy crack?"

"I did not!" I say but a scream comes out. Everybody jumps. I try to struggle out of the bean bag but I tumble over. My mother rushes over, grabbing me, holding on like I'm going to run.

"Baby, baby, were you with that boy? You weren't with him, were you?"

With him? Wow, I thought she knew.

"I saw him but I wasn't with him."

They're looking at me, all in my face.

"I thought you promised me you wouldn't see him after all he's done to you," Mother says, tears rolling down her face. She cries even better than before.

"I wasn't with him. I saw him . . . from a distance."

"I bet he's the one who gave it to her," Jack says, positively irate.

Auntie throws her hands up and goes for the phone. "I'm calling. There's no way we can handle this. This girl needs professional help."

Mother pulls me out of the bean bag, with one hand, just yanks me up.

"See, she's making the phone call. We can't handle this. We can't watch you twenty-four hours a day."

Funny, they keep saying the same things.

"Why are you laughing?"

"Me?"

Jack grabs me by the arm and drags me to the room I was trying to get to in the first place. He pushes me in, Mother watching.

"You're not going anywhere."

Mother comes in and gives me a hug. She's wearing Chanel. "We love you. You've got to try . . ."

I wait for her to complete the sentence. Fill in the blank. To get ahold of myself. To control myself. Not hurt myself.

"Jesus. She's laughing again. She's not listening to anything."

"I'm listening!" Another scream.

Mother almost jumps off the bed. Uncle Jack shakes his head and leaves.

"You really are sick," Mother says, whispering like she doesn't want me to hear.

"I'm okay."

"You need so much help."

"You should get a cut like mine. It's very summery."

Mother draws back. Pulls my hand from her hair. She should get it dyed too, I don't care for all of that gray. Now she's holding on to me crying again. Softly, so Uncle Jack can't hear. He's so full of himself.

"Rika. You got to promise me not to see that Doug again."

"Mother, I thought you knew. Doug's no longer with us."

"What?" she says, her blue eyes streaked with red.

"He's gone to his reward."

"He's dead?"

"Yes, Mother. They buried him today."

"And you went to the funeral in a bathrobe?"

"I didn't get out of the car. It was okay."

"Are you sure . . . ?"

Mother's so happy. She doesn't want to believe me.

"Yes, I'm very sure."

"Why didn't you tell us? It explains so much."

"I thought I did."

"Oh, baby. I really didn't know."

Again, she wraps her arms around me and cries, tears drip onto my cheeks. It's embarrassing.

"Mother, you should go and get some rest. I'll be fine."

She looks at me, what's the word? Forlorn, forlornly. I've made her so sad.

"I am tired."

She kisses me and heads for the door.

"If you need me . . ."

I nod. She tries so hard. I hear Uncle Jack at the door locking me in. I hope nobody's smoking in bed! What's on the tube? I turn it on and turn down the sound. Who needs the words and lie back. What time is it? Eight-thirty. Much too early to go to bed. But I am tired too.

What I don't understand is how I feel. Suddenly everything changes. I don't feel good at all. Comes in waves, my good humor washing away like sand castles. Isn't that it. That nothing lasts, nothing keeps, specially a buzz. I'm not like you, though. You're the kind of man that would make his woman sit in a car; yes, it was a Benz but so what, and for how long? Once, I sat in that leather-lined pimpmobile for four hot hours, getting out only once to use the bathroom. Knocked on the door of that run-down house and there you were, with your associates, four or five very dumb-looking future felons watching a basketball game in a smoky living room. Then it was only the smoke of the best Ses but soon we would all be smoking the roach powder. You actually looked pissed as though I had no reason at all for interrupting the festivities, even if I did have to go in the worst way. You looked at me like I was the stupidest, the ugliest bitch in the world but you failed to notice the way your associates were ogling me. You saw me like everyone first saw me, a fine, high-yella bitch, who looked like a model with good hair and green eyes. Wasn't I a trophy? I had to be stuck up, I had the look of someone who had to be stuck up. And you had to have it. You had to train me because I needed to be turned into a obedient bitch, and because I have certain problems I went along with the program. But you didn't know then, that because you made me sit and fetch and wait on hot leather seats for master to bring me a bone, that I wouldn't forget, that the bitch would bite that bone.

Let me turn out the light, turn off that TV, this room looks like an ugly motel, cottage cheese ceiling, hot green, oversized couch—where did they get this stuff? Better in the dark, cooler.

It didn't start that way. You came into the Speak Easy like you were going to yank some girl off the dance floor and take her to the car and do a Ted Bundy on her. I'm sure you thought you were the most dangerous player there, bigger, younger, better looking.

But baby, baby, nobody was fooled. The girls there knew, knew you had the wrong zip code, even if you have a fat wallet. Too, too wet for a girl who wanted a legitimate money man, that's why you didn't get much play. You were in the wrong neighborhood. I saw you coming but you know, right then, you were just the thing for me, what I was looking for. I really hate to be bored. More than anything, more than getting slapped by a man who doesn't know he'd prefer a boy or driven up the coast and left to find my way home. See, all of that wasn't fun, but baby, I wasn't bored and I got their numbers, paid them back in kind. So when I saw you, a young buck-wild businessman, I just knew you were the ticket to go places I've been and wanted to get back to.

"Are you with somebody?" is the first thing you said to me leaning back in your chair to show your thousand-dollar suit to its best advantage.

"No," I said. And gave you a wet-lipped smile and, Douglas baby, you were sprung. I could have had it then, twisted you into the most vicious knots I could have imagined but I wanted to see, see how far we were going to go. Just how bad it was going to be.

Somebody's at the door. Probably Mother, wondering if I'm okay, or Uncle Jack wondering if I managed to slip out again. They think because it's deadlocked I'm securely tucked away. Too stupid. Soon enough and I'll be making like a roach and bug on out of here.

Oh, how nice. I slept. At least three hours of beauty rest. See, with you we never had time for sleeping; either we were chasing the rock or fucking or fighting. But now, since you've gone on to your reward, I actually find time to rest. That's why I look better, that haggardness is gone. Sleep is truly a wonderful thing. What's it like to be dead? Do you see me? Do you see me when I smoke your money and you're not there to share the happiness, the bliss? Do you see me getting on my knees and giving a high school boy the best blowjob of his life for a couple rocks? Not that I have to do it, I still have quite a stash, but baby, I'm not being simply frugal, though frugality is to be admired, really, the kick is imagining you spinning in your ten-thousand-dollar coffin. How sweet!

I should go. I'm not getting any happier. Sooner or later I'm going to have to get back to it. The job of feeling good about myself, going on a mission to shake my money maker. It's distasteful. Compared to the creeps I have to deal with now that you're gone, you were the perfect gentleman. Even though you were inclined to punch and slap and burn, you did it with conviction, that's the kind of lover you were, resentful, mistrustful and destructive, but we shared those qualities. But Douglas, to these young men, a woman is less than a dog, less than a shrimp plate at Sizzler. They have no idea what relationship is all about. It's like a woman doesn't exist other than for a fuck or to cut. Too simple for my tastes. But I have a taste for the burning white smoke, rolling into my lungs to restore my good humor for five good minutes, smoke it all, my five-O limit. I can exert self-control, something you never managed to do. See, I smoke so I won't be sour, I prefer anything to being sour. Remember when we smoked fifteen hundred worth, and you started choking, really, turning code blue? What was I supposed to do? Call 911? But that's not me, no. You laid there on your back gasping, vomiting, looking like you had bought it. I knelt by your side, saying, "I told you nobody can smoke that much." Sure, it was after the fact, but did you listen? I don't know what happened because I had to leave, couldn't sit there and watch you expire. Just like I can't lie here and reminisce about the good old times. One has to live in the present.

What's a deadlock if you have the key? There I go being ironic, but you never understood irony so you don't get the joke. Outside my dark room the hallway is brightly lit, and in the kitchen, near the living room, is my Uncle Jack, dead asleep. I guess he thought he could find out how I do it, make such quick exits. The front door opens without a creak and I slip out. Oh, the sweet fresh air, how I love it. Slip into the auto, take it out of gear and coast downhill. Yes. And the land quickly changes. From the upper-middle-class split-level ranches down to the jungle apartment complexes. Not stopping, no, not for a stop sign, I'm on a mission. I got a surprise for the fat man. How unusual, no one is lurking in front of the Kona apartments, but the yellow light is on. Where are they, the police? It would be stupid to just rush out and plunge headlong into trouble. But what the hey. Yes, the door is unlocked. Inside, I don't see anyone waiting to do something nasty to me. Are things askew or am I getting more and more paranoid? Guess I'll mosey up and see with my own God-given eyes the situation. The hard steel door hurts my knuckles but I knock sharply anyway. Someone walks to the door, must be looking through the spy hole at me. I put my eye to the cold metal of the door. "Fuck" is said and I hear the door unlock even through the noise of the TV. It swings open and there he is, Alton, Mister Tub O'Lard.

"Hey, it's Miss It. She's back."

He grabs me by the arm and leads me into the little nut hole of a living room, nowhere to sit but a nasty couch.

"You got money, or is it gonna be the usual?"

I nod.

"What's that mean?"

I shrug.

He opens his ham-sized arms wide and gestures for me to see the almost empty room.

"We closing up shop. Too hot round here. Police be sweating a brother twenty-four-seven."

He comes over, perspiring like he's drunk, and opens my robe.

"Ooh, that bra is cute but you don't need to be wearing one flat as you is."

I smile sweetly, as he pulls my bra aside and takes hold of my nipple and rubs it clumsily. Thinking of what the next few minutes will bring, I smile even more sweetly.

"Aw, baby, you should take better care of yourself. Bet you slipped out the house with them curlers in your hair, wearing them silly slippers, to get a blast. You know, ya still pretty, you oughta slow down."

Oh, how nice, fat boy is giving me the just-say-no line while he's leading me into the bedroom. I guess we're going to be doing it on the mattress. Doesn't look very sanitary.

"What's it gonna be? Do it like I like, two rocks, like you like it, just one."

He pulls my robe up, forces me stomach down onto that piss-stained mattress. Down come my panties. I hope you're watching. I hope you see what he's going to do to me. He's grabbing my hips, trying to put it inside my ass, but I wiggle making him slip, hoping he'll just do it the normal way. He pushes me away, and I roll to the wall.

"You know how I like it. You don't give it to me I'm gonna take it."

It's gonna get ugly. Is it time for the surprise? He turns me over and grabs my hips again, and yanks my curlers.

"Don't you have oil?"

"Naw. I like the friction."

See, he's forcing my hand down again, trying to push it in. It won't go. I won't let it. Pull the cute little .22 auto out the robe pocket and point it at his big stomach. He stops crawling across the nasty mattress to me. Actually, he's backing up, smiling like a big fat Cheshire cat.

"Baby, baby, what you need? I must be scaring you. I got it in the other room, everything you need. Rocked and ready to go."

I smile. How sweet, he's begging just like a dog. I might be a crazy bitch but he's a begging dog.

"Pull up your pants."

"Baby," he says whining pitifully, he really thinks I'm going to shoot him.

"Kneel," I say, he does. We're both the same height now.

"Were you going to hit me?"

"Hit you? Baby, it ain't like that. You didn't hear me right."

"Didn't hear you about what?"

With my left hand, I pull up my panties, the gun feels light in my right. Wonder if it's loaded. I think I loaded it but now . . . oh well. We both kneel there awhile, him looking at the gun then my eyes. I know he's going to go for it. He stands up, big belly aquivering.

"Fuck you. You ain't gonna shoot me."

He comes toward me, then launches himself like a big, fat

blanket into the air. His big hams stretched out for me. I squeeze the trigger three times. Three sharp cracks and he's flying in reverse, rolling to the wall, all bug-eyed, trying to scramble to his feet. He can't, must have broken a bone in his leg. But he's not bleeding badly. Look, he's covering his big bald head, must be afraid I'm going to crack it like a big brown egg.

"It's in the kitchen. Take it. You don't gotta shoot me."

"Baby, isn't that for me to decide?"

"Sure, whatever." His big eyes are tugging at me. Pleading for me to let him live. I bet he has a wife and a child at home or a old mother he has to support.

I leave the fat boy and go into the kitchen. Talk about dirty dishes, all kinds of filth. There's what I need on the table, still in the pan. Empty the cake into a plastic bag, and take my leave. In the living room I see Mr. Tub O'Lard's gun, it's a big one, something to have, so I put it in my other pocket and go to the door. Shit, it's deadlocked. He's got the key. Back in the bedroom, he's out, slumped against the wall.

"I need the key."

Oh shit. He's out. He can't be dead. I don't touch the deceased. And he's bleeding. I hate the sight of blood. Ugh, must I push him over?

"I got it. Kaiser card's in the wallet."

Oh, he's not dead. Just delirious. Pants are too tight though. How I'm supposed to get the keys?

"I need the keys," I say sweetly.

"Key? Oh yeah, the keys." He reaches around into his back pocket, must be painful the way he's flinching, but like the good boy he is, he comes up with them and tries a toss but they roll out of his hand onto the brown carpet that's quickly turning red.

"Thanks," I say and cut for the door. Must be nervous because I fumble with the keys, takes what seems like hours to get the door unlocked. Can't be too hasty. Peek before you leap. The hallway is empty, but they're watching, waiting to see who comes running out. Police are probably on their way. I crack the door open. One light for the whole hallway. Point Tub's big gun. Have to use two hands to point this big thing. Smooth, that's what you said. How to pull the trigger. *Boom! Boom!* Plaster flies everywhere. The light still shines. Damn gun just about broke my wrist. *Boom! Boom! Boom!* There she blows and I'm in the dark. Drop the gun outside and run. The two lowlifes watching from across the street scatter when they see me coming but I bet they'll sneak over and find Fat Boy's gun before the police get here. It's worth a dozen rocks.

"They're shooting in there!" I yell. Sometimes it's good to state the obvious. I get to my car, throw myself in and burn rubber up the hill. In the rearview mirror I see the red and blue strobes snaking onto Hillcrest. Good, Don Diablo. Who named these streets? I hit the garage opener and pull the car in. See, Douglas, it's not hard to get what you want if you know what you want and you're willing to work for it. Now if I wanted to die, all I would have to do is leave this car running and close the garage door and inhale. Sure, this Lincoln would have shit-stained seats but that wouldn't be my problem. But I don't have a problem, at least not right now. I've got cake in my pocket. Crack off a piece, a nice-sized chunk, and fit it into the pipe and fire it up. The red flame turns blue and I can see myself in the rearview mirror. My eyes, pupils are wide as plates, couple of full-lunged hits, though, shrinks them to the size of pinpoints. The buzz-expand-run-run-run till the soft spot hums. Is that it? I try another and another and another till every part of me hums. How much do I have to smoke till I get enough? I don't know but we'll find out.

I don't sleep, just close my eyes, but when I open them again, I see the pipe in my stiff fingers. Still lots of night left. I much prefer the night. Maybe that's what I am, a vampire. Sucking smoke instead of blood. I really have to stop this, Douglas. There's no future in it. And though you couldn't see life without the pipe, even you should be able to appreciate my position. I'm carrying your child. You wouldn't want "it, the unknown" for your firstborn? Well, it wouldn't truly be your firstborn, but those poor, drug-addled tramps that carried your seed don't count. I count. Because I'm the queen of your desire, or is it the bitch of your desire. Anyway, let's be honest. I'm going to smoke that baby to hell.

* * *

"Get up. You're going!"

Oh, it's morning. I'm in bed and here's Uncle Jack and the rest of his merry crew. He just yanks me up and marches me through the house to the car. And doesn't Mother look disappointed. She slides in next to me, Uncle Jack takes the wheel, and my butterball of an aunt gets into the backseat. I guess it's time to go to where they put people like me. To the funny farm where life is gay all the time. The garage door swings open and we pull out into the bright light of day. Mother is crying again as usual, but she wants to say something, gagging on the words.

"How could you? We trusted you."

"It's too bright. I need sunglasses."

"We aren't stopping so you can run off. You know where you're going."

They're really going to do it this time.

"We found the drugs. A whole pocket full. How much did it cost? How'd you get the money?"

"I got it for free."

"She got it for free, hah. What did you sell?" Uncle Jack says. Mother is crying buckets. What a callous thing to say in front of her.

"I certainly did not sell anything that you're implying. I got it for free. I have ways."

"My God, she needs help," Uncle Jack says.

And here's the hospital.

"Emma, you park the car. I'm walking this young lady in."

Uncle Jack slams the brakes, stopping us right behind an ambulance, slides out from behind the wheel and pulls me along, my robe comes open but he doesn't wait. It's like being on a roller coaster the way he's pulling, jerking me one way and then the other.

"What's the rush?" I say, digging in my heels.

He looks at me, his brown face wonderfully twisted in a perfect sneer.

"How could you bring that shit into my house."

"But Uncle Jack, it's so expensive. I couldn't just leave it outside."

His hand flashes up and smashes me across the face. I spin out of his grip and run for the sliding doors. But he has me, carries me, squirming mightily to the nurse's station.

"We've made arrangements for this young lady."

He's in great shape. I'm twisting around like my dog used to do, twirling against his chest, but his grip doesn't break. The robe opens all the way, my pink panties are for the world to see. The nurse looks embarrassed for him. Mother and Aunt Emma walk into the lobby and see me wrapped in Uncle Jack's arms, ass out, the robe all about my shoulders like a straitjacket, and are even more embarrassed. The nurse gets it together. I'm too tired to keep up the fight so I watch as the forms are presented and signed. And everyone looks relieved to be getting the paperwork out of the way.

"Wait a minute! They can't commit me. I didn't sign anything."

The nurse barely looks at me, instead she shuffles papers. "You're not being committed. This is a drug treatment program. They've placed you in our care. The doctor will be out shortly to explain to you how our program works."

I nod enthusiastically. "That sounds great. I can't wait!" I shout and the nurse flinches.

Oh, since the papers have been signed, two big men in white suits appear, and they have a wheelchair I suppose they want me to sit in. I wonder if I could make it to the sliding glass double doors. Wild on the streets once again. But don't I need this. Don't I need to find out why I'm the way I am. Don't I need to dry out for the baby's sake, don't I, Douglas? Isn't this all a pathetic cry for help? Yes, I guess it is. I'm one sick bitch. It's bright and sunny here in this lobby, with fine, sturdy, modern furniture in soothing pastels. It might be time for a change. The doctor, balding and thin, comes up. He's wearing running shoes. He extends his hand. I extend mine. I shove hard against his chin and knock him into Uncle Jack and it's off to the races.

"Rika" is an excerpt from the novel Understand This *(University of California Press, 2000).*

LUCÍA

BY YXTA MAYA MURRAY

Echo Park

(Originally published in 1997)

L oca friend, you're all messed up, Girl. What we gonna do?
When a woman can't walk it's like she ain't the same kind
of woman. You ever seen a girl's legs when they're all broke
like that? Star Girl, she used to be my pretty chola. She was mean
as a shark and she was strong enough to twist and hook a fish as
big as me. But I knew she was mine.

"I'm out of it, I ain't grouping no more," Star Girl kept saying
now, and she had that dead light in her eyes. Almost like the sheep
do after they figure things out. No, I didn't want her different. I
wanted my old Girl back.

But I saw what that C-4 did. She showed me after I brought
her home from the hospital, and she was quiet and dumb the
whole ride home cause of all them pills. I wheeled her into her
bedroom so she can get some rest and I helped drag her up. Before
she got shot we'd got her all set up special in her own place and
she had this princess-pink bed from the Lobo money, a superfancy
four-poster. It didn't look so pretty now, though. You can't climb
under the covers if you don't got your legs working right.

When I lifted up her shirt she looked down, and her face
didn't tight up with hurt or curl with shame. Nothing. "It ain't
bad, chica, you gonna heal right up," I kept saying, making like it's
true. I turned the lamp on her naked skin and touched her light
like I was her mama. Star Girl had this round thick scar on her
back, a twisted tree-stump–looking cut. There's white shiny skin
lines like roots spreading out from where the doctors dug the bullet out. She was broke, all right. Her hands loose in her lap, like

she can't hold on. And I'd seen before how her legs looked smaller because she can't use them no more, they was only hanging down from that silver wheelchair.

She shook her head again. "I'm out of it for good."

"You're out of it when I say so," I tell her, trying to sound tough as nails. Like I'm still her jefa and she's got to listen. But she don't. She only turned her head to the window and rubbed her dry mouth. It's all over, ésa, is what she's saying to me. Can't bring back the dead. Well don't I know it. She's looking outside at the blue-black night and what I see is her red eyes and them white cracked lips. There's dusk colors washing down over her face that ain't never gonna be the same.

It reminds me of something bad, that's right. Something I can't forget even if I close my eyes tight. No, I don't have *no* shame, but it don't matter. I can't ever shut my eyes tight enough to black it all out.

So I opened them up real wide. I wouldn't look away. Gonna get them for *you*, Girl, I thought to myself. You ain't never known something better than a crazy angry woman, and when I saw her busted up, staring out by the window and the night's coming down dark over her, something in me went SNAP. You've been here before, something tells me. So get loca mad before that monster eats you up.

I started dreaming about that C-4 shooter all night long. His blank face was teasing me and when I wake up, I almost feel his steel-chain hands grip down on my throat. My teeth are chattering like I'm freezing. I can't even think about the business no more. The only thing in my head is how my Girl's all broke up.

"You go and kill him, right, Beto?" I asked him. When I got back from seeing Star I wrapped my arms around his neck, trying to kiss his lips and cheeks like the sweetest, nicest sheep he's ever seen. I made like he's the prince and cried on him just like a girl so he feels sorry. "You're gonna make him hurt, eh? Can you do it for me, baby?" I cooed, kissing his hands, his fingers. Acting like a geisha, but I didn't care a stitch. Inside I was feeling wild and mean and it took all my strength not to bash him on the head. You just DO IT, I wanted to scream in his ear, and my hands was itching and burning from wanting to scratch at his face till he finds me that C-4 killer.

But I couldn't. He was the boss of the Lobos now after that rumbla. It didn't matter that it was Chico who came to *me*, these days Beto was maddogging his ass down the street and all the vatos was watching him. He wasn't weak yet, like Manny got. The man was still full of fire, and it was gonna burn me bad if I didn't work him right. "Stop your whining, ésa. Keep it down," he'd started saying, waving at me with his hand when I'm telling him something. So I had to be more careful since he thinks he's Mr. Bad. Fine, we'll play it that way, I'm thinking. I'll sheep you so hard you'll walk weak-kneed all day. So Beto did what I want and that slick boy thought he was doing me favors. "Help me out, right?" I asked him again, and then smiled sweet. Yah, I'm thinking inside. You do for me. Tell your fools to drive on down to Edgeware and bring me home a dead man.

"All right, linda," he said, looking down at me and getting that big-daddy face on. He puts his hands under my shirt where it's warm and closes his eyes. "I'll show that vato where I'm from."

I should of known not to waste my breath. Beto got his homies running around asking questions and trying to get somebody from the eastside to rat out, but that didn't do me one bit of good. "Eh, ése, you know about the C-4 that tagged a Lobo sheep? You tell me, vato, our little secret." We didn't get no names. Whoever tagged my Girl was hiding out where I couldn't find him.

I got my hopes up when Beto sent these locos Montalvo and Rudy to Edgeware on a first-class mission to get me some answers about who shot my Girl. I sat up all night by my phone waiting to hear something, watching the wallpaper and the carpet and listening to some cricket chirp outside my window. I knew my bad time's gonna end once I get that call. But you don't send warriors on a job like that. Montalvo and Rudy was two baby-faced hot-blooded Oaxaca brothers who wore these red shirts and flashed their Lobos sets on the street looking for fights like blockheads so they could make a tough name for themselves in la clika. Instead of asking around cool and careful, they ran down to the Avenida de Asesinos, this dirty alley where the yellow dogs deal their powder. Them two started screaming RIFA and shooting crazy as soon as they see C-4 vatos giving them bad eyes. It's no good to me. Montalvo got hit with one in the shoulder and came home showing off his emergency-room war wound like he was a hero, and Rudy was maddogging around cause he got so close to the Avenida. But they didn't find out who that C-4 was.

"You got me a name, right?" I ask them after. I drove on over to where they lived, this cheapie flophouse on Savanna Street full of homeboys sleeping on the floor, flojos snoring on the couches, three tangled in a bed. There's white paint peeling back from the shutters and these busted windows pieced with electric tape. It was a grouper crash, the place where the vatos go when their mamas yell them out of the house. I walked up and banged on their door early in the morning and didn't even blink when Montalvo answers it and I see how one of his arms is wrapped up with bandages, a pink stain seeping through. "I *know* you got me a name, son."

"Sorry, ésa," Montalvo says to me. He's wearing this bag-lady–looking T-shirt and boxers and I can see all the red on his skin from the Avenida. But under them scrapes he's giving me icicle eyes to show he don't care one way or another. "Couldn't get nothing," he said, then shrugs.

I knew I was in trouble when he looks at me like that, forgetting who I am. That I'm la primera. Something crawls into my belly then, sitting there cold and making me feel weak and seasick. "You didn't find nothing because you don't want to," is what I say, knowing he thinks I'm just this crazy chavala who's trying to get payback for a sorry crippled sheep. Montalvo don't care I got Beto's ear, one woman's the same as the next to him. The neighborhood's quiet with everybody still sleeping and I'm trying to make my voice mean and low, but instead it grows bigger, bending up and stretching like a howl. "You don't *want to*," I tried to say again but then I hear I'm only screaming sounds at him, *crying* sounds, filling up the streets and the sidewalks and the trees with my sad noise.

Those was some black bad days. I'd look in the mirror sometimes and see this white-faced llorona, with skinny bones sticking out her face and big shiny eyes, like I'm sick. I remind myself how I used to be swinging around here telling locos what to do, not looking like some old ghost. You've gotta be that strong chica, I'd whisper to myself, staring at what I see. You didn't come this far to crack your head up. It don't matter Star Girl can't walk none, it don't hurt you, does it? Sit tight, woman, I'd say, and try to smile. But all my talking didn't make the bruja in the mirror run off, she just showed me her sharp bad wolf teeth.

A chica like me, she ain't meant to be crazy. I don't got time to be weak. I remember when I was a niña, tough as iron even then. Not the baby bandido hiding under the bed. I remember the one watching the world with her smart head and checking out what goes which way. There's the busboys and slick suits walking in my mami's house, there's me standing out in the hall listening. And even when Manny was beating me down, I kept my nose above water. Remember to breathe, that's what I do best. Breathe and keep living. So I didn't know why I was going all loose now. It seemed like I couldn't keep myself together no matter how hard I tried.

The only thing that made me feel strong was playing payback big. And I did it till it hurt.

"You all right, Lucía?" Chique asked me after I screamed crazy at Montalvo. I hadn't been right in the head for a while there, shivering and talking to myself, hiding out in my house. I knew she was checking up on me. "What's up, girl?" she said, standing over by the refri in her shiny black boots and mall-girl clothes and staring at my face like she sees something crazy there, like she sees my llorona. But she ain't stupid. She didn't try and touch me light on the arm, or tell me things are okay. She knew me good enough by then.

Back when Star Girl was walking, Chique knew she was always my second. I didn't hide that I loved Star special. I'd give her the lookout jobs and made her the main picker, the big dealer. But Chique was my right hand now. She was the one doing the lookouts and keeping her ear to the ground for me just like Star Girl used to. Girl didn't even wanna see me no more. Every day she's not walking she just got harder and meaner, but not like before. This was the hard you get when you lose something. She'd told me that she didn't want nothing more to do with la clika. "I paid enough, you see that," she'd said, turning her head up at me from her chair so I see that pale mouth, her stringy hair. She didn't even wanna get the C-4 who banged her. "It ain't gonna make me walk now, is it?" She wheeled herself around her place, her squeaky-sounding chair moving over the carpet. I thought, Give Girl time, give her time. We're gonna patch things up right.

Chique fit herself right into that empty space. She snugged herself by my side after the rumbla and acted like she'd always been my main gangster. And being a big head these days suited Chique good, I could tell that, turning my eyes from my wall and seeing her stand in my kitchen door waiting to hear what I've got to say. She just wanted to crawl up on top same as any other gangbanger, and with Star Girl gone she'd got this new shine in her eye. She'd permed her hair out curly and started wearing this butter-soft black leather jacket, a skin-tight skirt. Her skin glowed out like warm satin, and even though she was still pig-slop fat she was wearing it better, shifting her heavy ass back and forth down the street so you'd turn and look. The woman was even making sexy eyes at some of the vatos and acting tough with the sheep. She still had her head on straight, though. That girl could tell there was something up with me.

But she didn't have to worry about me too hard. I'm a woman who's always gonna keep standing strong. After all them days looking crazy at myself in the mirror, staring at my walls and my floors, I'd made up my mind. I already knew how I was gonna get my C-4. And having that plan set into me pushed up my bones, it put a shield in my hands. I was almost feeling good and scrappy again now that I knew what I was gonna do.

"So. Lucía. You all right?" Chique said again. She was staring at me patient.

"Just fine, ésa," I told her, flashing out a grin. "You go on and get me some Garfield babies and I'll be doing even better."

It all comes down to Garfield, that's where we fought our war. Garfield's full of mainly westside Parker kids cause it's on our side of the line but some of your C-4 babies go there too. Just walk around and look through the chain-link fence sometime. You'll see them little niños from both sides playing recess ball and laughing on the playground, stomping the flat black asphalt and screaming down from the bars like little monkeys. They're too young yet to know they can't be friends, but I'm changing that. All over the school walls there's Lobo and C-4 tags now, these big black and yellow sets tangled together and warring out over who's the main clika. It used to be that Garfield's nothing but a money bag for me, I'd look through the fence and only see curious-cat junior high schoolers with a little pocket change. Now Garfield looked lots different. I knew if I got them greenhorns to go with the Lobos, we'd get so big nobody could hide from me. Not even that blank-faced C-4 boy.

If you wanna take over a place, you've got to piss all over it. And the first thing we did is fuck with Chico's head by crossing out all the C-4 tags and get a graffiti war started. Warming up. It was too easy, almost. We got the finest taggers here in the Lobos.

In the clikas, you got your warriors and you got your taggers. Taggers are usually third-raters cause they're the little bow-legged stubby locos that can't fight good. They got spray cans instead of pistols and go on their midnight tagging missions like they're ninjas. A Lobo tagger will paint our set up on the buildings, on the storefronts, on the stop signs, so that everybody knows who we are. You've seen it. ECHO PARK! in thick black blocky letters ten feet high blasting on down from the freeway signs. Our taggers have got their names painted proud all over town, and that's their black zebra stripes crossing out the lemon yellow C-4 tags on the walls. Around here, crossing out a homeboy's set is serious business. If a gangster walks by and sees your big old black line drawn through his name, he's gonna start hunting for you. He has to do something or else he loses face. Getting crossed out means somebody's slamming on your manhood. And rebels think that if they don't got their respect, they don't got nothing else either.

Well, that never used to matter to me none. That was all scratching and crowing, a waste of my time. "See how many tags I got, homes?" the tagger vatos would say to each other, and there'd be red and black and blue all over their hands. "I got me twenty-three last night, ése. I'm doing firme, you know what I'm saying." Stupid roosters. What did I care about that? The only thing that matters to me is money and my ladies. But I can play these boy games if I need to. The rules are real simple. You got to tag your territory or else it ain't really yours.

"Go out to Garfield and cross out all the C-4 you can see, eh?" Beto told the vatos, with me standing behind him quiet. Now that Hoyo was dead—there's this big RIP HOYO tag up by the 101—the main Lobo taggers was Tiko and Dreamer. Tiko, he knew how to butcher streets ugly by running down the sidewalk with his thumb on the spray-gun trigger. Dreamer, though, he's the best tagger in L.A. The number-one paint boy. A short dude, with this jailbird buzz cut and a slow buffalo walk, but he had these mile-a-minute hands. He was so fast with his can that even the cops knew his name. He'd tagged every big wall between here and Edgeware three times already.

Those two tagger boys started crossing out C-4 sets regular. They'd do it at night, dressing in black jeans and sweater, black cotton cap on to cover up. Dreamer would lead, and him and Tiko would sneak on down to Garfield quiet and careful with their black backpack full of cans, scope out all the C-4 sets, and then cross them out with a long black line and write up LOBOS after. They sprayed the whole school as black and red as a ladybug, and after a couple nights of missions there wasn't an inch of yellow anywhere in sight.

We had some bad rumblas then. The taggers was dog-fighting bloody over walls and right-hand vatos from both sides was circling Garfield, not even doing coke deals now but trying to jump in the junior high babies. "Hey, ése, you come over here a minute?" Gangsters would run on down after school's over and all the niños was walking home dressed in their sweaters and white scuffy sneakers. "You with us now, hear it?" the vatos would say, slapping them around a little. Most of them little boys would try and tough it out, but sometimes they'd be crying and looking around scared with their mouths hanging open. It didn't matter. Either way they swore they'd go with whatever clika was beating them.

Even I started to get some grouping done. About a month after Star Girl got shot, me and Chique went down to Garfield with Beto's boys looking for a couple of fresh-meat chicas to rough. Now that Girl was gone it was just the two of us, and I wanted a whole crowd of cholas under my feet. I wouldn't set my sights on just one or two. I'd get myself a dozen, twenty, and they'd all be scrappy and mean-hearted. Not at first, mind you. I wouldn't expect nothing of them pigeon-toes at first except some bawling and thumb sucking. But after I got through with them they'd be as tough as leather.

"Hey, *cholita*, pretty girl, you come right on over here, wanna talk to you," Chique was calling out to the sixth graders, watching out for a good one. My old homegirl Chique, she was the best jumper I ever saw. She cornered this little thing with a swingy ponytail who was walking home, later we called her Conejo because she was a round-faced bunnyrabbit-looking girl, her nose and eyes getting all pink. "Yah, I'm talking to *you*, ésa," Chique hissed at her, getting in her way on the sidewalk and then reaching down and grabbing her skinny arm. "You're a Lobo now, ain't you?"

"No, I ain't nothing," I heard Conejo tell Chique, making up this street voice, but she knew it wasn't no use.

I was standing right there in front of them and giving Chique my proud eyes, but in my head I saw how it was when I jumped in Star Girl. How we'd been warm and laughing there on the cold grass after, looking at the sky and feeling like familia.

"Yah, chica, you is," I heard Chique saying now, her breath coming up fast.

I looked off, over where a couple Lobos was messing with the little Garfield boys. They was the same as us, crowding and pushing and buzzing around like hornets. I could make out Rudy and Montalvo twisting around some scrubby-headed niño and Beto laughing at them on the side. Chevy was standing around with his hand in his pocket and hooting, "Chavala!" Even Dreamer was there, with his black shades on and arms crossed in front like a big head now that he'd done all them tough tagging jobs. And far out, outside them, there was my old tired man. He was peeking his head over the vatos and then sloping back and watching them quiet same as me. Oh yah, that's good, I'm thinking. I see you, Manny. Loser boy. And looking at him then, it seemed like so long since everything. Wacha me, right? I got what I wanted. Here's me jumping in a chola and there's him, way gone.

I'd heard that Manny was crawling around here already, that he'd started walking the junkie streets just a few months after the rumbla even though he'd got hurt so bad. I have to say he'd healed up pretty quick, cause he looked almost as strong as he used to even though you could still see how his shoulder was bent in and hunched some from Beto's knife. It almost made me sorry to see him outside, cause I know how cold that life is. He's got this sheepdog face on like he wants to help out with the Lobo jumping, but the vatos was turning their eyes from him and butting up their shoulders so he can't squeeze on in the circle. The homeboy looked poor too. He was wearing this raggedy old shirt and black wool cap pulled down to his eyes. I heard he was sometimes crashing at Chevy's and making his ends by doing little stickups at liquor stores, pushing his guns in them bodega ladies' faces the same as any old third-rater's gonna do. I knew he was hoping like hell to get back on in with la clika, that's why he's standing over there like a scarecrow. But it couldn't happen. Once you've been a jefe, that's it. You get a stink on you.

"Why don't you just head your ass on home, ése?" I screamed at him over the sound of Chique banging Conejo around, and the little one's crying now. "Go on back to your mama!"

I don't know if he heard me. Maybe he turned his eyes over

my way to see me standing over my cholas and watching him hard. Maybe he don't wanna see me cause he knows he's just a beggar-looking Mexican wearing hobo clothes now. All I'm thinking is, Things sure are different, son, and I almost get softhearted there remembering how he used to be. But it don't last. When I'm listening to them jumping sounds I start seeing that same picture again, there's Star Girl on the grass, smiling up at me with the fog of her breath twining up in the night air with mine. And then there's that woman sitting in her chair, and I see again how the dark sky's coming. Yah, things are different now, I think on over to him again, but colder.

I turned back to look at Chique doing her work. "Beat her good if you have to," I tell her. "Cause this little chola ain't going nowhere."

The Lobos grew bigger and spilled over with all of that new junior high blood. Soon we had almost double the number of vatos scamming the streets and fighting any C-4 they lay eyes on. Beto was strutting around with his bluffy big talk and his hitman swagger, but instead of a fedora he'd wear a Stetson. "You *know* you chose good," he'd say, making a muscle and then trying to give me his weak-mouthed French kiss. Well baby, either way it don't matter, I'd think on back to him. You could be anybody. You're worse than anybody. With me too busy dreaming on the C-4's blank face and with Beto playing king, the Lobo business had shrunk up and almost died. Now that Manny was gone Mario wasn't coming by no more, and the locals had heard we'd run out of supplies. But so what. I'll deal with that thing later, I told myself. I still had my own job to finish.

I'd got together a whole posse of chicas by then. I called them my Fire Girls. Hey, you're on fire now, girl, I'd tell them after they got jumped in and they'd look over at me with their wet eyes and scuffed-up faces then try and give me a smile. We got that Conejo, she was a big crybaby at first, a second-generation Sunday school chavala chewing on her nails and running home, but she warmed up quick enough once I showed her how good gangbanging can be. After that we snatched Payasa. I named her that cause she's clown funny with some big curly Bozo hair. And then Sleepy, this heavy-lidded cholita, and Linda and Thumper, these two sisters from Jalisco. Thumper banged her leg on the chair when she's happy and Linda didn't want no new clika name, so we let her stay the way she was. That was us, the Fire Girls. They was only twelve and thirteen years old but you want them young ones cause they can be the meanest. You just gotta kick that girlie out of them. It ain't so hard, once you scratch their dresses off and give them baggies and lipstick and taks, they take to it real nice.

A woman's clika does it different than the men. And not how you'd think, neither. I don't got no pink-dress lunch club, there ain't no softies in my gang. After we jump in a chica, she acts as wicked as a snake. She'll take on a vato if we tell her to, smack him right over the head with a lead pipe if that's what I want. No, a woman gang's different than a man's cause women need more love. The locos swing around Echo Park thinking they don't need nothing. They've got their clika brothers, right, but a man can just stand alone if he's got to. My girls, they're looking at me for something they don't got at home. Their daddies are whoring around and Mama's crying in the closet or wiping up the kitchen sink and *gritando* ugly if their niña misses a confession. Everybody's looking at the brother like he's the man of the house and who cares about little sister? Well, I do, I tell them. I'm gonna care for you good, girl, you'll be special here. You should see them open up, a woman's gonna bloom like a cut rose in water if you talk to her special. And once you hook a chica like that, she'll throw down worse than any man you'll ever know. They can be some vicious kick-ass bitches if you work them right.

That's why just after we'd jump them in by beating them down on the street and calling out, Take it bitch, I'd change from a wolf to a kitten so fast that all their hurt and scared would crumple right into my hands. "We're your familia now, ésa," I'd tell my little girls, touching them soft on their shoulder like I'm their mama. "And you ain't never gonna be a sheep, all right? Now you're acting like you got some *respeto*. Don't forget it. I take care of my own, you hear that."

I'd say all the right words that they wanted to hear and then they'd look up at me with their flashlight faces, those sunny smiles, but I didn't feel their heat. I was saying the same things I told Star Girl and Chique all that time ago, but now I was talking through a cold wind. No matter how hard I tried I couldn't get that feeling like before, like when I was just a little loca myself, jumped in and brand new under them stars.

But you do what you do. Me and Chique got them started off picking pockets on the downtown streets at six o'clock when all the businessmen are walking home fast and hungry for dinner. Conejo and Linda would bump the gabachos and Sleepy and Thumper would dig down and snatch the wallets then come running back home to me flashing dollar bills. I even got my own big head meetings going, with Chique standing right by my side and my Fire Girls bringing me the money then sitting down in my living room. Hushed, watching me. They was listening to everything I'd say, lined up in a row and looking like sparrows waiting on a wire. "Do it like *this*, ésas," I'd tell them, showing them how to flick open a zipper on Chique. It almost made me feel like my old self, cause I could tell I hadn't lost my touch.

But the main job I had for my girls was for them to keep their eyes wide, their ears open. They was my lookouts. I had them scooting around the westside and even the sidelines of Edgeware and Crosby, watching out and listening hard for anything I might wanna hear. "Check out for the C-4, eh?" I told them. "You keep quiet and you'll hear some loco bragging sooner or later." Those girls was perfect spies cause they get dark in the shadows, go green around grass. They're invisible to men. If a chica stands around quiet long enough, a man just forgets her. He'll let forty cats out of their bags before he turns around and sees her watching him, her ears as big as jugs.

Well. Maybe. Even though I had them chicas, it still took me months before I got my payback. That C-4 hid out from me so tricky that even with my girls poking around after him night and day all I got was ghost stories, nothing I could sink my teeth into.

"Hear he's some C-4 big head, way up top," Thumper told me,

hooking her thumbs in her pockets and poking her beak out at me. Or there's Linda, kicking the sidewalk with her sneaker and not looking me in my eye. "Lupe told me he was some C-4 vatito who moved away, jefa. Back to Arizona or something."

No, it took me months. My babies was coming back home with rumors and empty hands, and that blank-face C-4 was just teasing me with a sawtooth smile. I was dreaming about him every night then, his shadow creeping over the park, the sounds of the shot ringing, the feel of that cold wet grass over and over and the yells and screams of the rumbla while I'm racing away with wings on my feet. And Star Girl with her white cheeks out on the bench, her dry mouth like a pale flower and her eyes staring out the window. It almost got me shook up again, cause things wasn't fixing fast like I needed. Chasing that vato made my blood thin and my eyes cloud over, and that llorona started fighting me down harder than before. She'd raise up in me bigger and blacker and grin out from the mirror on late nights when I couldn't sleep good. I wanted that C-4 boy so bad I could taste it bitter on my tongue.

So when my Fire Girls told me they can't find nothing, when they'd scrape their shoes on the street and mumble into their hands, it got real hard to stay still. It got almost more than this chica could take. I'd pull out my pack and light up a Marlboro nice and slow, breathing in that black smoke deep to keep my hands from shaking the same as two leaves, to keep them from reaching out at my girls like biting snakes. Watch it, woman, I tell myself inside. Keep it cool.

"I don't wanna hear that," I'd say, slitting my eyes at them, my voice getting dark like the dusk before a bad fight. "You *find* him, eh? You go on out there and find out who my man is."

But a woman don't die from waiting. I've looked enough at the viejas around here to learn a lesson or two about long life. You've got to sit down on your ass sometimes and let the devil wander your way. And that's when you catch him. When he ain't looking.

I got my payback in the chilly autumn after a long hot summer of Lobos and Bomber rumblas. The enemies was busy hoofing up and down their turf and naming their streets, and the drivebys got random and cold blooded, even worse than before. The locals started hiding in their houses behind window bars and double-bolt locks, so the streets emptied and the air cleared of most everything except for the sounds of racing cars and shootouts and the once-in-a-while crying of a siren. Beto was getting himself a vato loco name even down in East L.A. from all the craziness, and I was grouping big too. Me and Chique and my Fire Girls jumped in five new fresh babies that winter, and they kept me rolling in pickpocket money and gossip news. Still. It seemed like my C-4 was gonna get the better of me, the better of my Star Girl. The Lobos and my cholas never stopped crawling around the Park and trying to sniff him out, but for a while there it looked like he'd hid out too good for even this mean perra.

I never forgot him for one day, though. I let all that fire-and-brimstone feeling sink down deep inside of me, so I'm swimming in it. I was looking up at the sky from the bottom of a lake, through all this black water. And it got so that I could see that llorona in the mirror and not feel scared no more, even if she jumps out and tears me with them wicked teeth. Well, chingado. I'm the one biting bloody now.

It was a cold California Saturday, the kind when there ain't no rain or no clouds but the air's sharp blades sticking you when you're outside, that they saw what I could do. Don't you mess with me or my own, I showed them. Cause you won't wanna pay my price. I can hurt you in the soft little place you didn't even know you had.

I remember every minute like it was yesterday. It's a late foggy morning and I'm trying to cool out by kicking my feet up on my table and rolling Marlboro smoke rings off my tongue like Dolores Del Rio. I'm all alone just the way I like it. I don't got to make nice to no jefe or landlord over chicas. I had a spell to sit there thinking my own thoughts. It was peaceful almost, a cigarette in my fingers and time on my hands, listening to the leaves rustle outside my window and the far-off holler of morning TV, but it don't last. I'm not dreaming there ten minutes when I get jangled by these vatos who start screaming down the street.

Hey man! I hear them outside. Órale! some loco yells, and it sounds like he's real close by. Their noise makes me sit up straight and bend my ear so I can hear better. Chique rushes me then, banging down my door with her two fists like the war's coming. "This better be good," I say when I open up, and she's standing there looking *chistosa*, her permed hair funky twisted from the wind and her big red lips yelling at me how we got to go down to Garfield *now*, that she found out my shooter man.

"Some Lobos got his baby brother Mauricio down at the school, Lucía," Chique tells me. I feel her hot breath on my skin and even though it's so cold her face is sweaty, but then I can't feel or see nothing. What she say? Baby brother. Baby brother, I keep thinking it over in my head. I know that name. I used to know it.

"All right, ésa, check it," she says, and it's like she's trying not to jump out her own skin. "Montalvo caught this little C-4 tagger crossing out Lobo sets at Garfield and when he gets to beating on him, the baby starts going on how the Lobos better watch it cause he's Chico's brother, and how Chico will kill all of us, that kind of shit. 'He'll kill you and your women,' he says. Like that one he took out at the rumbla. The one he shot in the back.

It takes me a minute, but then it hits me solid in the chest. The vato that started the whole thing finished it too. "We're gonna talk straight up, Lucía. I hear there ain't no other Lobo who's got it together." That's what he told me through the crack in my door and I felt full of spice and flame when he said them words. Then he's fighting Manny at the rumbla and after Beto takes over you couldn't see nothing but arms and legs bending and the blur of faces. There was the sounds of guns popping and the pounding of the Bombers running up by the benches and so I'd raced off, leaving my Star Girl to try and kill the loco that took out her Ghost man, her with them weak hands she had and she couldn't hold the gun right, but Chico don't show her no mercy. He just walks up while her back's turned and puts a clip right in her spine.

"How you hear this?" I ask Chique, filling out that C-4 blank face in my head. Halfie fuck. Greaser rubia hair like a girl, pinkie skin that can't take no sun. You're a strung-out white boy can't do your fights fair, eh? Can't walk away like a man. Got to go and bang on my chola cause you can't hold tight. Old Chico. That's the vato I've been dreaming about, and I know him too good. I knew you when, boy. When you was nothing. "How you hear?" I say again, but mostly so I hear my own voice out loud. I'm standing there in my doorway but it feels like my heart ain't even beating.

"Girl, you're gonna be the *last* Lobo to find out," Chique says, pulling my arm and making me get in my car. "I guess there was some homeboys around and word's spreading in the neighborhood like wildfire."

When I got there, after screaming on over to the school like a dragracer and jamming on all the reds, I looked around to see what my battle was gonna be. I'd have to be careful, cause once a man goes down in this neighborhood it seems like everybody hears electric fast at the same time, and I knew the C-4s would be racing over here to help out their jefe's baby brother as soon as they got wind. "Good thing, eh?" I said to Chique when we set foot on asphalt, eyeballing the playground for any badasses. But I didn't see any Bomber locos yet. There's just a crowd of Lobos far off, standing in a circle and looking down. Montalvo, Rudy, Madball, Dreamer. I see some of them have red warrior bandannas sticking out their pockets like blood roses, but now they look as still and timid as schoolteachers. And there's some sheep on the sidelines, keeping their mouths shut but playing nervous with that fried hair of theirs. I even see Manny waiting on the outside as usual and wearing his loser hangdog face.

I can't make out what they've got there. I figure it's that Mauricio beat up bad on the ground cause they ain't kicking or laughing at nothing, only keeping their shaved heads bent. Watching. It's quiet as a cloud. There's still a little baby blue morning color in the sky so nobody's out yet, and you can't hear a peep coming from the vatos. Nothing was coming from baby brother neither.

More Lobos show when I start walking up to that little circle. Beto comes around, and I see Chevy and Wanda driving up. Rocky and Tiko and Popeye are coming through the gate behind me. Even Cecilia's racing on in and beelining for Manny. "It's gonna be hot, ésa," Chique's saying next to me, and my heart starts steamrolling cause I know I'm gonna get that C-4 back after all this time.

"What you homeboys up to, eh?" I say, my voice breezy. I'm making my way up there slow the same as a big head would instead of running and flapping my hands like a henpecking woman, and I'm still keeping a lookout for any sign of C-4. "What up?" I ask again but nobody's talking. I don't get one sign from them till I get real close and then Dreamer looks up at me, and he don't have no buffalo to him right then. He's wearing this face as ragged and thin as worn cotton, and from the pinch of his eyes I see how he's fighting down shame.

I push them open and see this red-colored beat-up kid bent up double on the ground like babies do in their mamas' bellies. His shirt's scraped off, his arm's twisted the wrong way, and there's that yellow tagging paint on his open hands, capping his fingers. I can't make out his face, but that vatito looked right, dark like I remembered, and he wasn't more than nine or ten even though his head's half buzzed clika style and he's got a Bomber tak scratched on his bony boy chest. He looked like Chico's. But he'd took it bad. From what I can see of his skin, already blue and purple in places, there's some stripe cuts bleeding down his ribs and slashing up his neck and face. I know them marks. He got them from getting kicked when he was already flat down. This puppyboy was whipped worse than any full-sized loco I'd ever seen except for old dead Ghost, but he still was breathing. I see his lips flutter up like they'd caught a breeze.

"This the baby brother?" I ask, and I see Manny standing behind them begging at me with his glassy eyes as big as mirrors, asking me can he have a piece.

Montalvo nods his head, looking at me careful but not like before when he was thinking I'm some bird-brained nobody screaming on his front steps. Now he's scared *he*'s the crazy Mexican cause he'd beat some empty-handed tagger baby near dead. "Yah, he was yelling something about Chico shooting off a sheep at the rumbla."

"What's that?" Beto'd caught up by then and the homeboys

stepped aside easy, but when he sees Chico's boy he shuts right down. He leans back on his heels and whistles low while the homies watched him careful to see what he's gonna do. But he didn't do nothing but keep standing there as dumb and fix-eyed as a cow, and they started coughing and twitching their heads around nervous.

"All right éses, looks like you done real good," I start saying, keeping that voice of mine nice and light.

I could tell they was getting weak on me there, that they was gonna curl up the same as that boy on the ground if I didn't make my move. But it don't surprise me none they can't take it. Like I said before, clikas used to have rules. We used to have some religion. Time was, the locos had to leave the pride-and-joy women and babies alone and keep the fighting to themselves. But not no more. Chico broke up my Girl and left her with that tree stump cutting her back open, the white shiny roots stretching down to her loose legs. My homeboys was staring at that C-4 baby like they don't wanna know what their own monster hands can do, but I can look it straight in the face any damn day then swallow it down and smile. Baby brother there with the eyes beat shut ain't gonna ruffle my feathers. He had it coming.

All of a sudden the light flickers and it looks like his eyes was gonna open, or that his mouth's twitching like a smile, and I think he's gonna sit right up and laugh at me the same as old Lazarus. But it wasn't nothing but a shadow falling on his bent-up self. It flashed in my head then how Manny and me used to be the same, rock sharp and strong all the way through down to the bones, I remembered that when Manny moved quick by me and I hear his breath close to my ear and he blocks the sun from the baby on the ground. Manny was switching his hands up like he was gonna do something, gonna grab hold of that boy and beat him worse to show me he could still sing for his supper, but when I turn and look at him I see he don't have his old hot stare or the same steel jaw sticking at me prideful. He's only some burn-out veterano now, with a skinny face and glassed-out carga eyes, wearing that wool cap pulled low and some ripped-up dumpster pants. He's not the same vato I used to know. With his mashed arm Manny couldn't give a good featherweight punch these days even to save his own skin.

"Yah, you vatos done a real nice job here, but we better scoot off, hear me?" I say, pushing Manny soft with my hand, and he gave easy, backing down like a hit dog, and Beto's vatos close around me again.

I know it for sure then. Nobody, nobody can tough it out like this chica can. I see past Manny how the sheep was looking over at me scandalous and making their tight mouths like I'm this empty-bellied bruja. Some even got muddy crocodile tears running down their faces from crying over the little C-4. Cecilia's staring at me wicked out of that dirt-colored face of hers, thinking I'm some baby-eating witch who's stealing up her brother. And my home-boys was circling me, their lips pulling sad like they're some viejas at a funeral.

"Órale. Looks like he's hurt bad," Beto says, bending down and poking the brother with his finger, but the thing down by my shoes wasn't moving an inch.

"Well fuck him then. Got it?" I start up, steel-tough sounding now and Beto gives me some cold-water eyes, the same as Manny got when he figured me out, but I don't care. They can see me all they like cause I can tell we're all gonna be standing around here like lazy brains when the C-4 bigs get here, and they're gonna give us an eye for an eye cause it looks like we killed one of their babies. "Let's GO, they're coming quick, you hear that?" I'm yelling at them now, that llorona bumping up in me big. It feels dark and windy when I watch them walk away from the brother in slow motion, dragging their heels even though this is for my Girl, this is our payback, leaving a half-dead C-4 baby twisted on the ground like my Star Girl on the grass waiting for la chota to bring her back to Kaiser. The Bombers can't just bang a Lobo woman and get off scot-free. This is the one thing that's gonna make us equal.

"Come ON," I say, hitting Beto hard in the arm so that he wakes up, and we scattered on out of there. I ran as fast as the vatos with the air cold on my cheeks, hearing the sheep crying behind me and leaving that busted brother with all the life bleeding out of him for Chico to find. I got this blast of heat that was singing through my arms and legs and making me feel like my old self again, knowing that soon he'd see his pride-and-joy C-4 baby and put his red wet face in his hands cause I hurt him so bad, the same as he hurt me.

I didn't care about nothing then when I was pounding my way back. I wasn't thinking about Chique or the Lobos or doing deals or even Star Girl with that dark sky over her face. I only felt cut loose and fire-hot inside, thinking how I'm the only one in this town who can do it. *Wáchale*, man! I felt that steering wheel tight in my hand and I was gunning my Maverick down the street, laughing loud as a banshee the whole way home cause I knew it. Check it on out. Nothing's keeping this chola down. I'm the only woman or man in this place, the only one in Echo Park, who can scratch on up to the top and stay there.

"Lucía" is an excerpt from the novel Locas *(Grove Press, 1997).*

TALL TALES FROM THE MEKONG DELTA

BY KATE BRAVERMAN

Bel Air

(Originally published in 1990)

I t was in the fifth month of her sobriety. It was after the hospital. It was after her divorce. It was autumn. She had even stopped smoking. She was wearing pink aerobic pants, a pink T-shirt with KAUAI written in lilac across the chest, and tennis shoes. She had just come from the gym. She was walking across a parking lot bordering a city park in West Hollywood. She was carrying cookies for the AA meeting. She was in charge of bringing the food for the meeting. He fell into step with her. He was short, fat, pale. He had bad teeth. His hair was dirty. Later, she would freeze his frame in her mind and study it. She would say he seemed frightened and defeated and trapped, "cagey" was the word she used to describe his eyes, how he measured and evaluated something in the air between them. The way he squinted through hazel eyes, it had nothing to do with the sunlight.

"I'm Lenny," he said, extending his hand. "What's your name?"

She told him. She was holding a bag with packages of cookies in it. After the meeting, she had an appointment with her psychiatrist, then a manicure. She kept walking.

"You a teacher? You look like a teacher," he said.

"I'm a writer," she told him. "I teach creative writing."

"You look like a teacher," Lenny said.

"I'm not just a teacher," she told him. She was annoyed.

"Okay. You're a writer. And you're bad. You're one of those bad girls from Beverly Hills. I've had my eye on you," Lenny said.

She didn't say anything. He was wearing blue jeans, a black leather jacket zipped to his throat, a long red wool scarf around his neck, and a Dodgers baseball cap. It was too hot a day for the leather jacket and scarf. She didn't find that detail significant. It caught her attention, she touched it briefly and then let it go. She looked but did not see. They were standing on a curb. The meeting was in a community room across the boulevard. She wasn't afraid yet.

"You do drugs? What do you do? Drink too much?" he asked.

"I'm a cocaine addict," she told him.

"Me too. Let's see your tracks. Show me your tracks." Lenny reached out for her arm.

"I don't have any now." She glanced at her arm. She extended her arm into the yellow air between them. The air was already becoming charged and disturbed. "They're gone."

"I see them," Lenny told her, inspecting her arm, turning it over, holding it in the sunlight. He touched the part of her arm behind her elbow where the vein rose. "They're beautiful."

"But there's nothing there," she said.

"Yeah, there is. There always is if you know how to look," Lenny told her. "How many people by the door? How many steps?"

He was talking about the door across the boulevard. His back was turned. She didn't know.

"Four steps," Lenny said. "Nine people. Four women. One odd man. I look. I see."

She was counting the people on the steps in front of the meeting. She didn't say anything.

"Let's get a coffee later. That's what you do, right? You can't get a drink? You go out for coffee?" Lenny was studying her face.

"I don't think so," she said.

"You don't think so? Come on. I'll buy you coffee. You can explain AA to me. You like that Italian shit? That French shit? The little cups?" Lenny was staring at her.

"No, thank you. I'm sorry," she said. He was short and fat and sweating. He looked like he was laughing at her with his eyes.

"You're sorry. I'll show you sorry. Listen. I know what you

want. You're one of those smart-ass teachers from Beverly Hills," Lenny said.

"Right," she said. She didn't know why she bothered talking to him.

"You want to get in over your head. You want to see what's on the other side. I'll show you. I'll take you there. It'll be the ride of your life," Lenny said.

"Goodbye," she answered.

Lenny was at her noon meeting the next day. She saw him immediately as she walked through the door. She wondered how he knew that she would be there. As she approached her usual chair, she saw a bouquet of long-stemmed pink roses.

"You look beautiful," Lenny said. "You knew I'd be here. That's why you put that crap on your face. You didn't have that paint on yesterday. Don't do that. You don't need that. Those whores from Beverly Hills need it. Not you. You're a teacher. I like that. Sit down." He picked the roses up. "Sit next to me. You glad to see me?"

"I don't think so." She sat down. Lenny handed the roses to her. She put them on the floor.

"Yeah. You're glad to see me. You were hoping I'd be here. And here I am. You want me to chase you? I'll chase you. Then I'll catch you. Then I'll show you what being in over your head means." Lenny was smiling.

She turned away. When the meeting was over, she stood up quickly and began moving, even before the prayer was finished. "I have to go," she said softly, over her shoulder. She felt she had to apologize. She felt she had to be careful.

"You don't have to go," Lenny said. He caught up with her on the steps. "Yeah. Don't look surprised. Lenny's fast, real fast. And you're lying. Don't ever lie to me. You think I'm stupid? Yeah, you think Lenny's stupid. You think you can get away from me? You can't get away. You got an hour. You don't pick that kid up from the dance school until four. Come on. I'll buy you coffee."

"What are you talking about?" She stopped. Her breath felt

sharp and fierce. It was a warm November. The air felt like glass.

"I know all about you. I know your routine. I been watching you for two weeks. Ever since I got to town. I saw you my first day. You think I'd ask you out on a date and not know your routine?" Lenny stared at her.

She felt her eyes widen. She started to say something but she changed her mind.

"You live at the top of the hill, off of Doheny. You pick up that kid, what's her name, Annie something? You pick her up and take her to dance school. You get coffee next door. Table by the window. You read the paper. Then you go home. Just the two of you. And that Mex cleaning lady. Maria. That her name? Maria? They're all called Maria. And the gardener Friday afternoons. That's it." Lenny lit a cigarette.

"You've been following me?" She was stunned. Her mouth opened.

"Recon," Lenny said.

"I beg your pardon?"

"In Nam. We called it recon. Fly over, get a lay of the land. Or stand behind some trees. Count the personnel. People look but they don't see. I'll tell you about it. Get coffee. You got an hour. Want to hear about Vietnam? I got stories. Choppers? I like choppers. You can take your time, aim. You can hit anything, even dogs. Some days we'd go out just aiming at dogs. Or the black market? Want to hear about that? Profiteering in smack? You're a writer, right? You like stories. I got some tall tales from the Mekong Delta for you, sweetheart. Knock your socks off. Come on." He reached out and touched her arm. "Later you can have your own war stories. I can be one of your tall tales. I can be the tallest."

The sun was strong. The world was washed with white. The day seemed somehow clarified. He was wearing a leather jacket and shaking. It occurred to her that he was sick.

"Excuse me. I must go," she said. "If you follow me, I shall have someone call the police."

"Okay. Okay. Calm down," Lenny was saying behind her. "I'll save you a seat tomorrow, okay?"

She didn't reply. She sat in her car. It was strange how blue the sky seemed, etched with the blue of radium or narcotics. Or China blue, perhaps. Was that a color? The blue of the China Sea? The blue of Vietnam. When he talked about Asia, she could imagine that blue, luminescent with ancient fever, with promises and bridges broken, with the harvest lost in blue flame. Always there were barbarians, shooting the children and dogs.

She locked her car and began driving. It occurred to her, suddenly, that the Chinese took poets as concubines. Their poets slept with warlords. They wrote with gold ink. They ate orchids and smoked opium. They were consecrated by nuance, by birds and silk and the ritual birthdays of gods and nothing changed for a thousand years. And afternoon was absinthe yellow and almond, burnt orange and chrysanthemum. And in the abstract sky, a litany of kites.

She felt herself look for him as she walked into the meeting the next day at noon. The meeting was in the basement of a church. Lenny was standing near the coffeepot with his back to the wall. He was holding two cups of coffee as if he was expecting her. He handed one to her.

"I got seats," he said. He motioned for her to follow. She followed. He pointed to a chair. She sat in it. An older woman was standing at the podium, telling the story of her life. Lenny was wearing a white warm-up suit with a green neon stripe down the sides of the pants and the arms of the jacket. He was wearing a baseball cap. His face seemed younger and tanner than she had remembered.

"Like how I look? I look like a lawyer on his way to tennis, right? I even got a tan. Fit right in. Chameleon Lenny. The best, too." He lit a cigarette. He held the pack out to her.

She shook her head, no. She was staring at the cigarette in his mouth, in his fingers. She could lean her head closer, part her lips, take just one puff.

"I got something to show you," Lenny said.

The meeting was over. They were walking up the stairs from

the basement of the church. The sun was strong. She blinked in the light. It was the yellow of a hot autumn, a yellow that seemed amplified and redeemed. She glanced at her watch.

"Don't do that," Lenny said. He was touching the small of her back with his hand. He was helping her walk.

"What?"

"Looking at that fucking watch all the time. Take it off," Lenny said.

"My watch?" She was looking at her wrist as if she had never seen it before.

"Give it here, come on." Lenny put his hand out. He motioned with his fingers. She placed her watch in the palm of his hand.

"That's a good girl," Lenny was saying. "You don't need it. You don't have to know what time it is. You're with me. Don't you get it? You're hungry, I feed you. You're tired, I find a hotel. You're in a structured environment now. You're protected. I protect you. It doesn't matter what time it is." He put her watch in his pocket. "Forget it. I'll buy you a new one. A better one. That was junk. I was embarrassed for you to wear junk like that. Want a Rolex?"

"You can't afford a Rolex," she said. She felt intelligent. She looked into his face.

"I got a drawerful," Lenny told her. "I got all the colors. Red. Black. Gold."

"Where?" She studied his face. They were walking on a side street in Hollywood. The air was a pale blue, bleeding into the horizon, taking the sky.

"In the bank," Lenny said. "In the safety deposit with everything else. All the cash that isn't buried." Lenny smiled.

"What else?" She put her hands on her hips.

"Let's go for a ride," Lenny said.

They were standing at the curb. They were two blocks from the church. A motorcycle was parked there. Lenny took out a key.

"Get on," he said.

"I don't want to get on a motorcycle." She was afraid.

"Yes, you do," Lenny told her. "Sit down on it. Wrap your arms around me. Just lean into me. Nothing else. You'll like it. You'll be surprised. It's a beautiful day. It looks like Hong Kong today. Want to go to the beach? Want lunch? I know a place in Malibu. You like seafood? Crab? Scampi? Watch the waves?" Lenny was doing something to the motorcycle. He looked at her face.

"No," she said.

"How about Italian? I got a place near the Marina. Owner owes for ten kilos. We'll get a good table. You like linguini?" Lenny sat down on the motorcycle.

She shook her head, no.

"Okay. You're not hungry. You're skinny. You should eat. Come on. We'll go around the block. Get on. Once around the block and I'll bring you back to the church." Lenny reached out his hand through the warm white air.

She looked at his hand and how the air seemed blue near his fingers. It's simply a blue glaze, she was thinking. In Malibu, in Hilo, in the China Sea, forms of blue, confusion and remorse, a dancing dress, a daughter with a mouth precisely your own and it's done, all of it.

Somewhere it was carnival night in the blue wash of a village on the China Sea. On the river, boats passed with low-slung antique masts sliding silently to the blue of the ocean, to the inverted delta where the horizon concluded itself in a rapture of orchid and pewter. That's what she was thinking when she took his hand.

She did not see him for a week. She changed her meeting schedule. She went to women's meetings in the Pacific Palisades and the Valley. She went to meetings she had never been to before. She trembled when she thought about him.

She stopped her car at a red light. It occurred to her that it was an early-afternoon autumn in her thirty-eighth year. Then she found herself driving to the community center. The meeting was over. There was no one left on the street. Just one man, sitting alone on the front steps, smoking. Lenny looked up at her and smiled.

"I was expecting you," Lenny said. "I told you. You can't get away from me."

She could feel his eyes on her face, the way when she lived with a painter, she had learned to feel lamplight on her skin. When she had learned to perceive light as an entity. She began to cry.

"Don't cry," Lenny said, his voice soft. "I can't stand you crying. Let's make up. I'll buy you dinner."

"I can't." She didn't look at him.

"Yeah. You can. I'll take you someplace good. Spago? You like those little pizzas with the duck and shit? Lobster? You want the Palm? Then Rangoon Racket Club? Yeah. Don't look surprised. I know the places. I made deals in all those places. What did you think?" He was lighting a cigarette and she could feel his eyes on her skin.

She didn't say anything. They were walking across a parking lot. The autumn made everything ache. Later, it would be worse. At dusk, with the subtle irritation of lamps.

"Yeah. I know what you think. You think Lenny looks like he just crawled out from a rock. This is a disguise. Blue jeans, sneakers. I fit right in. I got a gang of angry Colombians on my ass. Forget it." Lenny stared at her. "You got a boyfriend?"

"What's it to you?"

"What's it to me? That's sharp. I want to date you. I probably want to marry you. You got a boyfriend, I got to hurt him." Lenny smiled.

"I can't believe you said that." She put her hands on her hips.

"You got a boyfriend? I'm going to cut off his arm and beat him with it. Here. Look at this." He was bending over and removing something from his sock. He held it in the palm of his hand.

"Know what this is?" Lenny asked.

She shook her head, no.

"It's a knife, sweetheart," Lenny said.

She could see that now, even before he opened it. A push-button knife. Lenny was reaching behind to his back. He was pulling out something from behind his belt, under his shirt. It was another knife.

"Want to see the guns?"

She felt dizzy. They were standing near her car. It was early in December. The Santa Anas had been blowing. She felt that it had been exceptionally warm for months.

"Don't get in the car," Lenny said. "I can't take it when you leave. Stay near me. Just let me breathe the same air as you. I love you."

"You don't even know me," she said.

"But you know me. You been dreaming me. I'm your ticket to the other side, remember?" Lenny had put his knives away. "Want to hear some more Nam stories? How we ran smack into Hono-lulu? You'll like this. You like the dope stories. You want to get loaded?"

She shook her head, no.

"You kidding me? You don't want to get high?" Lenny smiled.

"I like being sober," she said.

"Sure," Lenny said. "Let me know when that changes. One phone call. I got the best dope in the world."

They were standing in front of her car. The street beyond the parking lot seemed estranged, the air was tarnished. She hadn't thought about drugs in months. Lenny was handing her some-thing, thin circles of metal. She looked down at her hand. Two dimes seemed to glare in her palm.

"For when you change your mind," Lenny said. He was still smiling.

They were sitting on the grass of a public park after a meeting. Lenny was wearing Bermuda shorts and a green T-shirt that said CANCÚN. They were sitting in a corner of the park with a stucco wall behind them.

"It's our anniversary," Lenny told her. "We been in love four weeks."

"I've lost track of time," she said. She didn't have a watch anymore. The air felt humid, green, stalled. It was December in West Hollywood. She was thinking that the palms were livid with green death. They could be the palms of Vietnam.

"I want to fuck you," Lenny said. "Let's go to your house."

She shook her head, no. She turned away from him. She began to stand up.

"Okay. Okay. You got the kid. I understand that. Let's go to a hotel. You want the Beverly Wilshire? I can't go to the Beverly Hills Hotel. I got a problem there. What about the Four Seasons? You want to fuck in the Four Seasons?"

"You need to get an AIDS test," she said.

"Why?" Lenny looked amused.

"Because you're a heroin addict. Because you've been in jail," she began.

"Who told you that?" Lenny sat up.

"You told me," she said. "Terminal Island. Chino. Folsom? Is it true?"

"Uh-huh," Lenny said. He lit a cigarette. "Five years in Folsom. Consecutive. Sixty months. I topped out."

She stared at him. She thought how easy it would be, to reach and take a cigarette. Just one, once.

"Means I finished my whole sentence. No time off for good behavior. Lenny did the whole sixty." He smiled. "I don't need an AIDS test."

"You're a heroin addict. You shoot cocaine. You're crazy. Who knows what you do or who you do it with." She was beginning to be afraid.

"You think I'd give you a disease?" Lenny looked hurt.

Silence. She was looking at Lenny's legs, how white the exposed skin was. She was thinking that he brought his sick body to her, that he was bloated, enormous with pathology and bad history, with jails and demented resentments.

"Listen. You got nothing to worry about. I don't need a fucking AIDS test. Listen to me. Are you hearing me? You get that disease, I take care of you. I take you to Bangkok. I keep a place there, on the river. Best smack in the world. Fifty cents. I keep you loaded. You'll never suffer. You start hurting, I'll take you out. I'll kill you myself. With my own hands. I promise," Lenny said.

Silence. She was thinking that he must be drawn to her vast emptiness, could he sense that she was aching and hot and always listening? There is always a garish carnival across the boulevard. We are born, we eat and sleep, conspire and mourn, a birth, a betrayal, an excursion to the harbor, and it's done. All of it, done.

"Come here." Lenny extended his arm. "Come here. You're like a child. Don't be afraid. I want to give you something."

She moved her body closer to his. There are blue enormities, she was thinking, horizons and boulevards. Somewhere, there are blue rocks and they burn.

"Close your eyes," Lenny said. "Open your mouth."

She closed her eyes. She opened her mouth. There was something pressing against her lip. Perhaps it was a flower.

"Close your mouth and breathe," Lenny said.

It was a cigarette. She felt the smoke in her lungs. It had been six months since she smoked. Her hand began to tremble.

"There," Lenny was saying. "You need to smoke. I can tell. It's okay. You can't give up everything at once. Here. Share it. Give me a hit."

They smoked quietly. They passed the cigarette back and forth. She was thinking that she was like a sacked capital. Nothing worked in her plazas. The palm trees were on fire. The air was smoky and blue. No one seemed to notice.

"Sit on my lap. Come on. Sit down. Closer. On my lap," Lenny was saying. "Good. Yeah. Good. I'm not going to bite you. I love you. Want to get married? Want to have a baby? Closer. Let me kiss you. You don't do anything. Let me do it. Now your arms. Yeah. Around my neck. Tighter. Tighter. You worried? You got nothing to worry about. You get sick, I keep you whacked on smack. Then I kill you. So why are you worried? Closer. Yeah. Want to hear about R and R in Bangkok? Want to hear about what you get for a hundred bucks on the river? You'll like this. Lean right up against me. Yeah. Close your eyes."

"Look. It's hot. You want to swim. You like that? Swimming? You know how to swim?" Lenny looked at her. "Yeah? Let's go. I got a place in Bel Air."

"You have a place in Bel Air?" she asked. It was after the meeting. It was the week before Christmas. It was early afternoon.

"Guy I used to know. I did a little work for him. I introduced him to his wife. He owes me some money. He gave me the keys." Lenny reached in his pocket. He was wearing a white-and-yellow warm-up suit. He produced a key ring. It hung in the hot air between them. "It's got everything there. Food. Booze. Dope. Pool. Tennis court. Computer games. You like that? Pac Man?"

She didn't say anything. She felt she couldn't move. She lit a cigarette. She was buying two packages at a time again. She would be buying cartons soon.

"Look. We'll go for a drive. I'll tell you some more war stories. Come on. I got a nice car today. I got a brand-new red Ferrari. Want to see it? Just take a look. One look. It's at the curb. Give me your hand." Lenny reached out for her hand.

She could remember being a child. It was a child's game in a child's afternoon, before time or distance were factors. When you were told you couldn't move or couldn't see. And for those moments you are paralyzed or blind. You freeze in place. You don't move. You feel that you have been there for years. It does not occur to you that you can move. It does not occur to you that you can break the rules. The world is a collection of absolutes and spells. You know words have a power. You are entranced. The world is a soft blue.

"There. See. I'm not crazy. A red Ferrari. A hundred forty grand. Get in. We'll go around the block. Sit down. Nice interior, huh? Nice stereo. But I got no fucking tapes. Go to the record store with me? You pick out the tapes, okay? Then we'll go to Bel Air. Swim a little. Watch the sunset. Listen to some music. Want to dance? I love to dance. You can't get a disease doing that, right?" Lenny was holding the car door open for her.

She sat down. The ground seemed enormous. It seemed to leap up at her face.

"Yeah. I'm a good driver. Lean back. Relax. I used to drive for a living," Lenny told her.

"What did you drive? A bus?" She smiled.

"A bus? That's sharp. You're one of those sharp little Jewish girls from Beverly Hills with a cocaine problem. Yeah. I know what you're about. All of you. I drove some cars on a few jobs. Couple of jewelry stores, a few banks. Now I fly," Lenny said.

Lenny turned the car onto Sunset Boulevard. In the gardens of the houses behind the gates, everything was in bloom. Patches of color slid past so fast she thought they might be hallucinations. Azaleas and camellias and hibiscus. The green seemed sullen and half asleep. Or perhaps it was opiated, dazed, exhausted from pleasure.

"You fly?" she repeated.

"Planes. You like planes? I'll take you up. I got a plane. Company plane," Lenny told her. "It's in Arizona."

"You're a pilot?" She put out her cigarette and immediately lit another.

"I fly planes for money. Want to fly? I'm going next week. Every second Tuesday. Want to come?" Lenny looked at her.

"Maybe," she said. They had turned on a street north of Sunset. They were winding up a hill. The street was narrow. The bougainvillea was a kind of net near her face. The air smelled of petals and heat.

"Yeah. You'll come with me. I'll show you what I do. I fly over a stretch of desert looks like the moon. There's a small manufacturing business down there. Camouflaged. You'd never see it. I drop some boxes off. I pick some boxes up. Three hours' work. Fifteen grand," Lenny said. "Know what I'm talking about?"

"No."

"Yeah. You don't want to know anything about this. Distribution," Lenny said. "That's federal."

"You do that twice a month?" she asked. They were above Sunset Boulevard. The bougainvillea was a magenta web. There were sounds of birds and insects. They were winding through pine trees. "That's 30,000 dollars a month."

"That's nothing. The real money's the Bogotá run," Lenny said. "Mountains leap up out of the ground, out of nowhere. The Bogotá run drove me crazy. Took me a month to come down. Then the Colombians got mad. You know what I'm talking about?"

"No."

"That's good. You don't want to know anything about the Colombians," Lenny said again.

She was thinking about the Colombians and Bogotá and the town where Lenny said he had a house, Medellín. She was thinking they would have called her *gitana,* with her long black hair and bare feet. She could have fanned herself with handfuls of hundred-dollar bills like a green river. She could have borne sons for men crossing borders, searching for the definitive run, the one you don't return from. She would dance in bars in the permanently hot nights. They would say she was intoxicated with grief and dead husbands. Sadness made her dance. When she thought about this, she laughed.

The driveway seemed sudden and steep. They were approaching a walled villa. Lenny pushed numbers on a console. The gate opened.

He parked the red Ferrari. He opened the car door for her. She followed him up a flight of stone steps. The house looked like a Spanish fortress.

A large Christmas wreath with pinecones and a red ribbon hung on the door. The door was unlocked. The floor was tile. They were walking on an Oriental silk carpet, past a piano, a fireplace, a bar. There were ceiling-high glass cabinets in which Chinese artifacts were displayed, vases and bowls and carvings. They were walking through a library, then a room with a huge television, stereo equipment, a pool table. She followed him out a side door.

The pool was built on the edge of the hill. The city below seemed like a sketch for a village, something not quite formed beneath the greenery. Pink and yellow roses had been planted around two sides of the pool. There were beds of azaleas with ferns between them and red camellias, yellow lilies, white daisies, and birds-of-paradise.

"Time to swim," Lenny said.

She was standing near the pool, motionless. "We don't have suits," she said.

"Don't tell nobody, okay?" Lenny was pulling his shirt over his head. He stared at her, a cigarette in his mouth. "It's private. It's walled. Just a cliff out here. And Bernie and Phyllis aren't coming back. Come on. Take off your clothes. What are you? Scared? You're like a child. Come here. I'll help you. Daddy'll help you. Just stand near me. Here. See? Over your head. Over baby's head. Did that hurt? What's that? One of those goddamn French jobs with the hooks in front? You do it. What are you looking at? I put on a few pounds. Okay? I'm a little out of shape. I need some weights. I got to buy some weights. What are you? Skinny? You're so skinny. You one of those vomiters? I'm not going to bite. Come here. Reach down. Take off my necklace. Unlock the chain. Yeah. Good. Now we swim."

The water felt strange and icy. It was nothing like she expected. There were shadows on the far side of the pool. The shadows were hideous. There was nothing ambiguous about them. The water beneath the shadows looked remote and troubled and green. It looked contaminated. The more she swam, the more the infected blue particles clustered on her skin. There would be no way to remove them.

"I have to leave," she said.

The sun was going down. It was an unusual sunset for Los Angeles, red and protracted. Clouds formed islands in the red sky. The sprinklers came on. The air smelled damp and green like a forest. There were pine trees beyond the rose garden. She thought of the smell of camp at nightfall, when she was a child.

"What are you? Crazy? You kidding me? I want to take you out," Lenny said. He got out of the pool. He wrapped a towel around his waist. Then he wrapped a towel around her shoulders. "Don't just stand there. Dry off. Come on. You'll get sick. Dry yourself."

He lit a cigarette for her. "You want to get dressed up, right? I know you skinny broads from Beverly Hills. You want to get dressed up. Look. Let me show you something. You'll like it. I know. Come on." He put out his hand for her. She took it.

They were walking up a marble stairway to the bedroom. The

bedroom windows opened onto a tile balcony. There were sunken tubs in the bathroom. Everything was black marble. The faucets were gold. There were gold chandeliers hanging above them. Every wall had mirrors bordered by bulbs and gold. Lenny was standing in front of a closet.

"Pick something out. Go on. Walk in. Pink. You like pink? No. You like it darker. Yeah. Keep walking. Closet big as a tennis court. They got no taste, right? Looks like Vegas, right? You like red? No. Black. That's you. Here. Black silk." Lenny came out of the closet. He was holding an evening gown. "This your size? All you skinny broads wear the same size."

Lenny handed the dress to her. He stretched out on the bed. "Yeah. Let go of the towel. That's right. Only slower."

He was watching her. He lit a cigarette. His towel had come apart. He was holding something near his lap. It was a jewelry box.

"After you put that crap on your face, the paint, the lipstick, we'll pick out a little something nice for you. Phyllis won't need it. She's not coming back. Yeah." Lenny laughed. "Bernie and Phyllis are entertaining the Colombians by now. Give those boys from the jungle something to chew on. Don't look like that. You like diamonds? I know you like diamonds."

Lenny was stretched out on the bed. The bed belonged to Bernie and Phyllis but they weren't coming back. Lenny was holding a diamond necklace out to her. She wanted it more than she could remember wanting anything.

"I'll put it on you. Come here. Sit down. I won't touch you. Not unless you ask me. I can see you're all dressed up. Just sit near me. I'll do the clasp for you," Lenny offered.

She sat down. She could feel the stones around her throat, cool, individual, like the essence of something that lives in the night. Or something more ancient, part of the fabric of the night itself.

"Now you kiss me. Come on. You want to. I can tell. Kiss me. Know what this costs?" Lenny touched the necklace at her throat with his fingertips. He studied the stones. He left his fingers on her throat. "Sixty, seventy grand maybe. You can kiss me now."

She turned her face toward him. She opened her lips. Outside, the Santa Ana winds were startling, howling as if from a mouth. The air smelled of scorched lemons and oranges, of something delirious and intoxicated. When she closed her eyes, everything was blue.

She didn't see him at her noon meeting the next day or the day after. She thought, Well, that's it. She wasn't sorry. She got a manicure. She went to her psychiatrist. She began taking a steam bath after her aerobics class at the gym. She went Christmas shopping. She bought her daughter a white rabbit coat trimmed with blue fox. She was spending too much money. She didn't care.

It was Christmas Eve when the doorbell rang. There were carols on the radio. She was wearing a silk robe and smoking. She told Maria that she could answer the door.

"You promised never to come here." She was angry. "You promised to respect my life. To recognize my discrete borders."

"Discrete borders?" Lenny repeated. "I'm in serious trouble. Look at me. Can't you see there's something wrong? You look but you don't see."

There was nothing unusual about him. He was wearing blue jeans and a black leather jacket. He was carrying an overnight bag. She could see the motorcycle near the curb. Maybe the Colombians had the red Ferrari. Maybe they were chewing on that now. She didn't ask him in.

"This is it," Lenny was saying. He brushed past her and walked into the living room. He was talking quickly. He was telling her what had happened in the desert, what the Colombians had done. She felt like she was being electrocuted, that her hair was standing on end. It occurred to her that it was a sensation so singular that she might come to enjoy it. There were small blue wounded sounds in the room now. She wondered if they were coming from her.

"I disappear in about five minutes." Lenny looked at her. "You coming?"

She thought about it. "I can't come, no," she said finally. "I have a child."

"We take her," Lenny offered.

She shook her head, no. The room was going dark at the edges, she noticed. Like a field of blue asters, perhaps. Or ice when the sun strikes it. And how curious the blue becomes when clouds cross the sun, when the blue becomes broken, tawdry.

"I had plans for you. I was going to introduce you to some people. I should of met you fifteen years ago. I could have retired. Get me some ice," Lenny said. "Let's have a drink."

"We're in AA. Are you crazy?" She was annoyed.

"I need a drink. I need a fix. I need an automatic weapon. I need a plane," he said. He looked past her to the den. Maria was watching television and wrapping Christmas presents.

"You need a drink, too," Lenny said. "Don't even think about it. The phone. You're an accessory after the fact. You can go to jail. What about your kid then?"

They were standing in her living room. There was a noble pine tree near the fireplace. There were wrapped boxes beneath the branches. Maria asked in Spanish if she needed anything. She said not at the moment. Two glasses with ice, that was all.

"Have a drink," Lenny said. "You can always go back to the meetings. They take you back. They don't mind. I do it all the time. All over the world. I been doing it for ten years."

"I didn't know that," she said. It was almost impossible to talk. It occurred to her that her sanity was becoming intermittent, like a sudden stretch of intact road in an abandoned region. Or radio music, blatant after months of static.

"Give me the bottle. I'll pour you one. Don't look like that. You look like you're going down for the count. Here." Lenny handed the glass to her. She could smell the vodka. "Open your mouth, goddamn it."

She opened her mouth. She took a sip. Then she lit a cigarette.

"Wash the glass when I leave," Lenny said. "They can't prove shit. You don't know me. You were never anywhere. Nothing happened. You listening? You don't look like you're listening. You look like you're on tilt. Come on, baby. Listen to Daddy. That's good. Take another sip."

She took another sip. Lenny was standing near the door. "You're getting off easy, you know that? I ran out of time. I had plans for you," he was saying.

He was opening the door. "Some ride, huh? Did Daddy do like he said? Get you to the other side? You catch a glimpse? See what's there? I think you're starting to see. Can't say Lenny lied to you, right?"

She took another sip. "Right," she agreed. When this glass was finished she would pour another. When the bottle was empty, she would buy another.

Lenny closed the door. The night stayed outside. She was surprised. She opened her mouth but no sound came out. Instead, blue things flew in, pieces of glass or tin, or necklaces of blue diamonds, perhaps. The air was the blue of a pool when there are shadows, when clouds cross the turquoise surface, when you suspect something contagious is leaking, something camouflaged and disrupted. There is only this infected blue enormity elongating defiantly. The blue that knows you and where you live and it's never going to forget.

Editor's Acknowledgments

In pulling together the table of contents for this anthology, I read hundreds of short stories that steeped me in the richness, diversity, breadth, and depth of classic short fiction about Los Angeles. In addition to my own research, I avidly sought out opinions from others.

So thanks to everyone who recommended authors or stories for me to read. I truly appreciate your enthusiastic suggestions, even if your favorite didn't make it into this volume.

A tip of the fedora to Steven Cooper for John Fante, Tom Nolan for Ross Macdonald, Margaret Millar, and Leigh Brackett, Francis M. Nevins and Jim Pascoe for Cornell Woolrich, Judith Freeman for Raymond Chandler, Bill Pronzini for Erle Stanley Gardner, Kenny Turan for Paul Cain, Rodger Jacobs for Charles Bukowski, Robert Bloch, and Richard Matheson, Naomi Hirahara and Greg Robinson for Hisaye Yamamoto, Michael Nava for Joseph Hansen and for his own brilliant short story "Street People," which unfortunately proved too long for this collection. Thanks also to Gary Phillips and Emory Holmes II for ongoing discussions but especially for Donald Goines, Wanda Coleman, Iceberg Slim, and Budd Schulberg's collection *From the Ashes, Voices of Watts*, Richard Yarborough for answering my questions about *Players Magazine* (I still think that would make a good thesis for someone), Paula Woods for Roland S. Jefferson, and thanks to Stephen Sohn, Daniel A. Olivas, Susan Baker Sotelo, and Sarah Cortez.

And lastly, thanks to the hard-working librarians at the Glendale and Los Angeles public libraries who helped me track down some of the more obscure and out-of-print titles. They are the true private eyes of the literary world.

ABOUT THE CONTRIBUTORS

LEIGH BRACKETT (1915–1978) was born in Los Angeles. Although best known for her fantasy and science fiction, she also wrote mystery novels and Hollywood screenplays. Her first novel, *No Good from a Corpse*, published in 1944, was a hard-boiled mystery in the tradition of Raymond Chandler and led to her cowriting the scripts for *The Big Sleep* and *The Long Goodbye* (both based on Chandler novels). Shortly before her death, she wrote the screenplay (with additional revisions made by Lawrence Kasdan and Geroge Lucas) for *The Empire Strikes Back*, which won a Hugo Award in 1981.

KATE BRAVERMAN is the author of *Lithium for Medea, Palm Latitudes*, and two other novels that define the sordid pseudo-tropics of Los Angeles. She is also a poet and essayist, but is best known for her short stories, described as the "gold standard" for contemporary female fiction. All the rumors are true.

JAMES M. CAIN (1892–1977) was born in Annapolis, Maryland, and served in World War I. After a stint as the managing editor at the *New Yorker*, he moved to Hollywood in the 1930s. His first novel, *The Postman Always Rings Twice*, a crime-fiction classic, was said by Albert Camus to have inspired him to write *The Stranger*, and has been adapted into several films. *Double Indemnity* and *Mildred Pierce* are among his other classic novels that inspired classic films. In 1970, the Mystery Writers of America named Cain a Grand Master.

PAUL CAIN (1902–1966) is the pseudonym of George Carol Sims, who authored a series of hard-boiled detective novelettes for the pulp magazine *Black Mask* beginning in 1932. The son of a police detective, Cain was born in Des Moines, Iowa, and moved to Southern California in 1918. He eventually scripted nine films for major studios under the pen name Peter Ruric, including *The Black Cat* in 1934. His increasing problems with alcoholism killed off his pulp career by 1936, and his Hollywood career ended in 1944. Sims spent much of the late 1940s and '50s in Europe. He attempted a Hollywood comeback in 1959, but found his reputation kept studio doors closed to him. Cain contracted cancer and died in a cheap apartment in Hollywood in the summer of 1966.

RAYMOND CHANDLER (1888–1959) was born in Chicago and spent much of his youth in England. After returning to the United States, he settled in Los Angeles, which would become the setting for his short stories and novels. At the age of forty-four, after being fired from his job as vice president at an oil syndicate for excessive drinking and womanizing, Chandler began his writing career, publishing stories in the pulp magazine *Black Mask* before moving on to novels. He is best known for his tough but honest private detective Philip Marlowe, who appears in all seven of his novels, including *The Big Sleep* (1939), *Farewell, My Lovely* (1940), and *The Long Goodbye* (1953). Along with Dashiell Hammett and James M. Cain, he is regarded as one of the founders of the hard-boiled crime-fiction genre. Chandler also wrote critically acclaimed screenplays, most notably *Double Indemnity*, *The Blue Dahlia* (winner of an Edgar Award), and *Strangers on a Train*. After the death of his wife, Cissy Pascal, he fell into a deep depression, and his drinking grew heavier. He died in La Jolla, California, of pneumonia either caused or aggravated by his heavy drinking.

JAMES ELLROY was born in Los Angeles in 1948. His L.A. Quartet novels—*The Black Dahlia*, *The Big Nowhere*, *L.A. Confidential*, and *White Jazz*—were international best sellers. His novel *American Tabloid* was a *Time* magazine Best Fiction Book of 1995; his memoir, *My Dark Places*, was a *Time* Best Book of the Year and a *New York Times* Notable Book for 1996. His novel *The Cold Six Thousand* was a *New York Times* Notable Book and a *Los Angeles Times* Best Book for 2001. Ellroy lives in Los Angeles.

WILLIAM CAMPBELL GAULT (1910–1995) was born in Milwaukee and began his career as a sports and mystery writer in the mid-1930s, publishing short stories in *McClure Newspaper Syndicate* and many pulp magazines. He wrote under his own name as well as the pseudonyms Roney Scott and Will Duke. Gault wrote two crime-fiction series, including one that featured Brock "The Rock" Callahan, an ex–L.A. Rams lineman turned South California PI, and another that featured Los Angeles–based Italian PI Joe Puma. He won an Edgar Award for his first crime-fiction novel, *Don't Cry for Me*, in 1952, a Shamus Award in 1982 for *The Cana Diversion* (featuring Joe Puma), and a Life Achievement Award from the Private Eye Writers of America.

DENISE HAMILTON writes the Eve Diamond series and is editor of *Los Angeles Noir*, an anthology of new writing that spent two months on the best-seller lists, won the Edgar Award for Best Short Story, and won the Southern California Independent Booksellers' award for Best Mystery of the Year. Her latest novel, *Los Angeles Times* best seller *The Last Embrace*, has been compared to James Ellroy and Raymond Chandler. For more information, visit www.denisehamilton.com.

JOSEPH HANSEN (1923–2004) wrote nearly forty books under a number of pseudonyms and in a variety of genres. He is best known for his Dave Brandstetter mystery novels about a tough but decent insurance investigator who is also unapologetically gay. The first novel in the series, *Fadeout*, was published in 1970 a year after the Stonewall Inn riots in New York, with the final book *A Country of Old Men* (1991) appearing twenty-one years later and winning him a Lambda Literary Award. He won the 1992 Lifetime Achievement Award from the Private Eye Writers of America and continued to write throughout his life, publishing the mystery story collection *Bohannon's Women* (2002) and the Nathan Reed novel *The Cutbank Path* (2002) as his health deteriorated. An openly gay man, he had an unconventional but happy home life, living for over fifty years with his lesbian wife, the artist Jane Bancroft, and their transgendered child, Daniel. Hansen died from heart failure at his California home in 2004. A new Brandstetter omnibus, containing all ten mysteries, was published in 2007.

CHESTER HIMES (1909–1984) was born in Jefferson City, Missouri. After being arrested and found guilty of armed robbery in 1929, he began writing fiction in prison, and his early short stories were published in national magazines such as *Esquire*. Upon his release in 1936, Himes joined the Federal Writers' Project and became friendly with the poet Langston Hughes. He spent the 1940s in Los Angeles, working as a screenwriter and publishing two novels, *If He Hollers Let Him Go* and *Lonely Crusade*. His brief career as a screenwriter for Warner Brothers ended due to racial prejudice, and he eventually moved to Paris, France, where he joined a group of black writers and artists that included James Baldwin, Richard Wright, and Ollie Harrington. There, he concentrated on writing a series of books about two Harlem detectives, Coffin Ed Johnson and Grave Digger Jones, including *The Real Cool Killers, All*

Shot Up, and *Cotton Comes to Harlem*. In the 1970s, he published two volumes of autobiography, *The Quality of Hurt* and *My Life of Absurdity*. He died in Moraira, Spain, from Parkinson's disease.

NAOMI HIRAHARA, born and raised in Southern California, won an Edgar Award for her third mystery in the Mas Arai series, *Snakeskin Shamisen*. She writes crime fiction and also novels for younger readers; her short story "Number 19" was published in the original *Los Angeles Noir*. She contributes a mystery serial for an English-language weekly in Japan and regularly leads writing workshops. Her fourth Mas Arai mystery, *Blood Hina*, is being published in 2010. For more information, visit www.naomihirahara.com.

ROSS MACDONALD (1915–1983) is the pseudonym of the American-Canadian crime-fiction writer Kenneth Millar. He is best known for his highly acclaimed series of eighteen hard-boiled novels set in Southern California featuring private detective Lew Archer. The series includes the best sellers *The Goodbye Look*, *The Underground Man*, and *Sleeping Beauty*, and concluded with *The Blue Hammer* in 1976. In 1938, he married writer Margaret Millar. Several of his books were adapted into film, two of them starring Paul Newman as Lew Archer. In 1973, the Mystery Writers of America named him a Grand Master.

MARGARET MILLAR (1915–1994) was born in Kitchener, Ontario, and moved to the United States after marrying Kenneth Millar (better known under the pen name Ross Macdonald) in 1938. They resided for decades in the city of Santa Barbara, which was often utilized as a locale in her later novels, under the pseudonyms of San Felice or Santa Felicia. Her book *Beast in View* won the Best Novel of the Year Award from the Mystery Writers of America, and in 1983 the MWA named her a Grand Master.

WALTER MOSLEY is one of the most versatile and admired writers in America today. He is the author of more than twenty-nine critically acclaimed books, including the major best-selling mystery series featuring Easy Rawlins. His work has been translated into twenty-one languages and includes literary fiction, science fiction, political monographs, and a young adult novel. His short fiction has been widely published, and his nonfiction has appeared in the *New York Times Magazine* and the *Na-*

tion, among other publications. Mosley is currently working on a new mystery series set in New York City, about a private investigator named Leonid McGill. The first of the series, *The Long Fall*, was published in March 2009. He is the winner of numerous awards, including an O. Henry Award, a Grammy, and PEN America's Lifetime Achievement Award. He lives in New York City.

YXTA MAYA MURRAY is the author of six novels, including the forthcoming *The Good Girl's Guide to Getting Kidnapped* and *The Conquest*, winner of a 1999 Whiting Writers' Award. She is a professor at Loyola Law School and lives in Los Angeles.

JERVEY TERVALON lives in Altadena, California, with his two daughters. He teaches creative writing at the University of Southern California and is currently revising the manuscript of *Hope Found Chauncey*, a sequel of sorts to his best-selling novel *Understand This*. His essay "The Slow Death of a Chocolate City," originally written for the *LA Weekly*, won a Los Angeles Press Club Award in 2008.

Also available from the Akashic Books Noir Series

LOS ANGELES NOIR
edited by Denise Hamilton
360 pages, trade paperback original, $15.95
*A *Los Angeles Times* best seller and winner of an Edgar Award.

Brand-new stories by: Michael Connelly, Janet Fitch, Susan Straight, Patt Morrison, Robert Ferrigno, Gary Phillips, Naomi Hirahara, Jim Pascoe, Diana Wagman, Héctor Tobar, Emory Holmes II, and others.

"Akashic is making an argument about the universality of noir; it's sort of flattering, really, and *Los Angeles Noir,* arriving at last, is a kaleidoscopic collection filled with the ethos of noir pioneers Raymond Chandler and James M. Cain."
—*Los Angeles Times Book Review*

ORANGE COUNTY NOIR
edited by Gary Phillips
312 pages, trade paperback original, $15.95

Brand-new stories by: Susan Straight, Robert S. Levinson, Rob Roberge, Nathan Walpow, Barbara DeMarco-Barrett, Dan Duling, Mary Castillo, Lawrence Maddox, Dick Lochte, Robert Ward, Gary Phillips, Gordon McAlpine, Martin J. Smith, and Patricia McFall.

Orange County, California, brings to mind the endless summer of sand and surf, McMansion housing tracts, a conservative stronghold, massive shopping centers where Pilates classes are run like boot camp and real-estate values are discussed at your weekly colonic, and ice-cream parlors on Main Street, U.S.A., exist side-by-side with pho shops and taquerías. *Orange County Noir* takes you for a hardboiled tour behind the Orange Curtain where nobody is who they seem to be.

D.C. NOIR 2: THE CLASSICS
edited by George Pelecanos
326 pages, trade paperback original, $15.95

Classic stories by: Langston Hughes, Edward P. Jones, Marita Golden, Paul Laurence Dunbar, Julian Mayfield, Elizabeth Hand, Richard Wright, James Grady, Ward Just, Rhozier "Roach" Brown, and others.

"Dark as many of these stories are, there's light in them yet, and it's the layering of the two that helps the collection to dazzle."
—*Washington Post Book World*